P.O.W.

The craters were now alive with the black figures moving forward. He counted at least fifty of them as he was hurriedly taken back toward Russian lines, stumbling dizzily over heavily cratered ground littered with the rotting corpses of what had been the American airborne. But for all the horror, the thing that struck David most was the catlike grace with which the black-suited Russian commandos moved, up and over the deep craters to remove the airborne's dog tags.

It was only after they took his own dog tags that he realized why he hadn't been killed on the spot. A very fit, no-nonsense, English-speaking Russian NCO ordered them to remove their uniforms. Walking behind him was a private, his arms festooned with wire coat hangers, one for every prisoner, and a small plastic garbage bag for personal effects. A fellow prisoner, a British private, reached across to David, brushing a sprig of sticky pine from his sleeve. "Don't want 'em all messy, do we?"

David looked puzzled.

"When they cut your froat," said the cockney. "Makes a mess of the uniform."

Also by Ian Slater

FIRESPILL
SEA GOLD
AIR GLOW RED
ORWELL: THE ROAD TO AIRSTRIP ONE
STORM
DEEP CHILL
FORBIDDEN ZONE*
WORLD WAR III*

Published by Fawcett Books

RAGE OF
BATTLE

Ian Slater

FAWCETT CREST • NEW YORK

A Fawcett Crest Book
Published by Ballantine Books
Copyright © 1990 by Bunyip Enterprises, Inc.

Library of Congress Catalog Card Number: 90-93291

ISBN 0-449-21988-7

Manufactured in the United States of America

First Edition: January 1991

For Marian, Serrena, and Blair

ACKNOWLEDGMENTS

I would like to thank Professors Peter Petro and Charles Slonecker who are colleagues and friends of mine at the University of British Columbia. Most of all I am indebted to my wife, Marian, whose patience, typing and editorial skills continue to give me invaluable support in my work.

There are no guarantees that a Stalinist will not succeed Gorbachev.

—Andrei Sakharov

CHAPTER ONE

FROM THE REDDED-OUT control room beneath the USS *Roosevelt*'s sail, Capt. Robert Brentwood reached the forward torpedo room in under ten seconds. Stepping into the compartment, he saw Evans, previously one of the quietest and best-behaved seamen aboard the sub, backed into a corner near the number one torpedo tube, slashing the air with a long, thin screwdriver, screaming, "Fucking snakes! Get 'em away—get 'em away!"

The bosun and another crewman, an electrician first-class, were moving in on Evans, the bosun trying to shush him. "For Christ's sake! They'll hear you in Moscow!"

"Where's the hospital corpsman?" Robert Brentwood asked quietly.

"In sick bay," the bosun told him. "Down with the flu. What I reckon, Evans has probably—"

Brentwood knew there was only one thing to do but felt queasy even as he gave the order. "Get a syringe here fast. Valium—twenty milligrams."

"Yes, sir," the bosun answered, and was gone.

The electrician was so alarmed by Evans's fit and screaming that he didn't notice the fine beads of sweat breaking out on Brentwood's forehead as he'd given the order for the hypodermic. It was a secret fear, one shared only by Robert Brentwood's two younger brothers and sister, Lana, a navy nurse. He hadn't even told Rosemary Spence, his fiancée back in England. For the quietly competent graduate of Annapolis, top of his class and commander of the most awesome weapons launcher in history, a confession to Rosemary or to his crew that the very thought of a hypodermic made him weak at the knees would have been nothing less than an

1

abject humiliation. Whenever he had to have a blood test, he'd always looked away, out the window, at a painting, a piece of fly dirt on the wall—anything to avoid the sight of the cold steel puncturing taut skin, sliding into the vein. But now, with the hospital corpsman out of it with the virulent influenza that had been rampant in the United Kingdom and which Brentwood believed might have temporarily unhinged Evans, it would be up to him as captain to remember his officer training in subcutaneous and intramuscular injections, to push the needle into the wild-eyed sailor who was still yelling, the long, thin screwdriver keeping Brentwood and the electrician at bay. The problem would be to talk Evans down, to get him calm or preoccupied enough to give him the shot.

"What's all the racket?" the corpsman asked the bosun groggily, his eyes all but closed in the grip of fever.

"Evans!" explained the bosun. "Off his fucking head. Wake up the dead, let alone the Russians. Where's the Valium?"

"Diazepam," the corpsman corrected him, full of self-importance despite his malaise. "How much did you say?"

"Ah—twenty ccs."

"Who you want to kill?" drawled the corpsman, shuffling toward the locked drug cabinet. "Evans or the whole fucking crew?"

"What?"

"Twenty milligrams, you mean. Not ccs."

"Give me the fucking vial—and a syringe."

When the bosun reentered the torpedo room, there was a strong chemical smell. Everything in the "rigged for red" glow seemed pink. Evans was on the deck—the foam from a carbon dioxide extinguisher Brentwood had used so they could get near him stained with blood from a bad gash on the left side of Evans's head. The bosun almost slipped, the deck slicked with foam. "What the—" he began.

"Quickly!" ordered Brentwood. "Give me the syringe." He wished to God his sister, Lana, were here. Slippery from the foam, Evans's arm kept eluding Brentwood's grip. "Goddamn it!" It was the first time the bosun had heard the skipper use any kind of profanity since he'd taken command of the *Roosevelt* two years before. Brentwood lowered Evans's arm and stepped over him to his right side.

"Pull down his pants," Brentwood ordered. Gritting his teeth, Brentwood plunged the hypodermic into the torpedo man's buttocks and pushed the plunger in, surprised by the resistance, looking away, focusing on the stainless steel prop of one of the thirty-five-hundred-pound Mk-48 torpedoes until he felt the plunger wouldn't depress any farther.

"All right," he said, his breathing short and hard as if he'd just sprinted a hundred yards. "Get him to sick bay. Restraining straps. One of you stay with him."

"What happens when he wakes up, sir?" asked the electrician. "He's gonna start up again."

Brentwood handed the emptied hypodermic to the bosun. "Tell the corpsman—if he's well enough—to keep Evans heavily sedated until further notice. If the corpsman's not up to it—come and tell me."

"What you think's wrong with him?" asked the electrician, looking apprehensively from Brentwood to the bosun.

"Darned if I know," said the bosun.

"Bosun," ordered Brentwood, "you'd better get a stretcher. Watch yourself on this deck. I'll send someone down to dry it off."

The hospital corpsman said he thought it must be the DTs— "Delirium tremens."

"Bullshit!" said the bosun. "He doesn't even smell of booze. Anyway, we left Holy Loch over twenty hours ago—"

"Worst time," said the corpsman in a tone calculated to impress the electrician, who'd helped carry Evans on the stretcher. The corpsman tried to stifle a racking cough with one hand, giving the restraining straps for the stretcher to the bosun with the other. "Secret boozer maybe," he continued. "So long as they get their daily dose, they're okay. Miss one, and brother—they see snakes, elephants, you name it."

"The sub's dry," said the bosun impatiently.

"Right," said the corpsman, "and I'm Scarlett O'Hara. Engine room solvents, cough medicine—" The corpsman stopped. "Man, they'll drink anything."

"Uh-huh," said the bosun, recalling the corpsman's smart-ass crack about twenty ccs instead of twenty milligrams. The bosun tapped the antiroll-secured drug cabinet above the corpsman's head. "Better check *your* supplies, *Doctor*. I'll bet tits for bits you've got some water in your alcohol jars.

You being in sick bay yourself is probably what stopped him getting his daily shot of booze. *If* you're right."

"Well," responded the corpsman, weighing the possibility of having to explain any alcohol missing from the sick bay. "Maybe he has the flu."

"Right," said the bosun, "and I'm Scarlett O'Hara."

"Scarlett," said the electrician, "will you marry me?"

"Piss off," said the bosun, "and get back to the fucking torpedo room. After the racket Evans made, it's a fucking wonder if their whole fucking Northern Fleet didn't hear."

As well as being profane, the bosun was quite wrong. The Northern Fleet hadn't heard them. But with the sound waves from Evans's commotion racing out through the underwater world at four times the speed of sound in the air, a Russian cruiser, on silent station—her orders to find and kill the *Roosevelt—had* heard them, her sonar now locked on to the American sub.

CHAPTER TWO

LIKE HIS CREW, Ivan Stasky, captain of the Russian cruiser *Admiral Yumashev*, had never paid much attention to politics—to the fact that the honeymoon between Moscow and Washington, and Gorbachev's Nobel Prize for peace, were long past, that the American government had been as naive about what would happen after Gorbachev as it had been about Deng's "Open Door" policy in China—until the door slammed shut, Tiananmen Square awash in blood.

The *Yumashev* and her crew were nothing more and nothing less than instruments of Soviet national policy. One of the Soviets' ten seventy-six-hundred-ton Kresta II–class cruisers, under the command of Capt. Ivan Stasky, her sole job was to hunt and kill American submarines that were escorting the critical NATO resupply convoys from Halifax and other North American East Coast ports to beleaguered Europe.

Three months into the war and four hundred miles south of the GIN (Greenland-Iceland-Norway) Gap, the ice shelf enveloping her in dense autumn fog, the *Yumashev* had been devoting all her talents to stalking the *Roosevelt*, for this sub, an "up-gunned" Sea Wolf class II, which was reported to have departed Holy Loch on Scotland's west coast twenty-four hours before, was much more than a protector of NATO convoys. As one of the Americans' 360-foot-long, 17,000-ton dual-role Hunter/Killer/ICBM subs, the *Roosevelt* was capable of acting not only as a fast hunter/killer of other subs, but as a defensive retaliatory launch platform for the six eight-warhead-apiece Trident II missiles stowed aft of its twenty-five-foot sail.

Happily for Ivan Stasky and his crew aboard the *Yumashev*, a Soviet rocket attack two days earlier had destroyed the Loch's degaussing, or magnetic signature erasure, station. This meant that *Yumashev*'s computer, able to identify the sub through its "noise signature" as being that of the *Roosevelt*, could, by drawing on its memory bank of enemy captain profiles, also tell the cruiser's captain that his counterpart aboard the U.S. sub was either a Robert Brentwood, age forty-three, a graduate of Annapolis, or a Harold Brenner, forty-four, also from Annapolis, the prestigious naval academy. The fact that there were two captains involved was due to the American nuclear submarines being so self-sufficient in food, reactor fuel, and in producing so much fresh water a day that they had to pump out the excess, that the sub needed two crews, gold and blue. Because of such self-sufficiency, it was the men, not the sub, who needed to be rested after a totally submerged forty-five- to seventy-day war patrol.

This time, however, several hours after the *Roosevelt* had left Scotland's Holy Loch, the *Yumashev*'s communication center was to find out who was skippering the *Roosevelt* on this cruise by listening to the flippant chitchat of a Glasgow rock station. One of its disc jockeys, a longtime Soviet operative, informed the *Yumashev*, by working an LFL—letter for letter—code into his nonstop patter, that it was the blue crew which had been seen reporting to Holy Loch. And so it was that Ivan Stasky knew Capt. Robert Brentwood was his opponent.

The *Yumashev's* first mate, reading the printout's description of Brentwood—six feet, brown eyes, brown hair—made a joke about the blue eyes, how the American captain would soon be singing the blues. Stasky took no notice. For many Russian commanders, the computer profiles of their American counterparts—the information about them assiduously gathered in the Gorbachev era, when Americans and Russians had actually invited one another to attend maneuvers—could sometimes help a Soviet captain formulate tactics. Stasky, however, a tough, stocky Azeri from Kirovabad in Azerbaijan, believed the profiles were, in the main, a waste of rubles. *"Akademiki"*—"high-tech boys," he would say, watching the computer spewing out the information about the adversaries he'd never seen. "Playing games in Moscow," he'd charge, considering the money could have been better spent giving aid to his native, non-Russian, republic of Azerbaijan. Had it not been for the war, Stasky believed, the never-ending and increasing dissent of minority groups in the USSR such as the Armenians and the Azerbaijanis would have posed a far greater danger to Moscow than the Americans.

On occasion, however, he had to admit, albeit grudgingly, the psychological profiles of enemy captains *did* pay off—the most important information being whether the American captain, like an ice hockey coach, was offensively or defensively minded. This was especially helpful given the dual-role capacity of the up-gunned Sea Wolf.

In addition to its speed—over forty knots—and its silence, Stasky knew that the Sea Wolf had an unmatched ability to "mow the lawn"—that is, its wide side-scan sonar was able to simultaneously and in great detail search both sides of the deep oceanic canyons that plummeted either side of the seven-thousand-foot-high mid-Atlantic ridge.

It was a question of who heard whom first, neither Americans nor Russians wanting to use "active radar," preferring instead to run "passive," *listening* for the other sub, instead of sending out echo-creating pulses which could give away your own position. And Stasky knew that even if a Sea Wolf hadn't found out *exactly* where you were, any one of its twenty-eight-mile-range Mk-48 homing torpedoes set loose could run a search pattern around you and then home in.

Even if a surface vessel like the *Yumashev* could cut engines enough to reduce its noise signature to a faint murmur in the sound channel, as it had done on silent station listening for the *Roosevelt*, it was not safe. For while this might deny any approaching torpedo an exact fix on the surface vessel, a torpedo exploding anywhere nearby would implode the hulls of most ships, except perhaps the double-titanium alloy of the Soviet Alfa boats. And if the Americans' torpedoes didn't get you, they could use any of five forward tubes to launch one of the cruise missiles they carried. These were able to hit either surface ships, submarines, or land targets fifteen hundred miles away with a CEP, or circular error of probability, of only plus or minus three hundred feet! In addition, any one of its forty-eight independently targeted reentry nuclear warheads was capable of melting Moscow into oblivion, the sub's total firepower over three thousand times greater than the Hiroshima A-bomb.

Even so, *Yumashev*'s captain knew that for all the Sea Wolf's awesome power, making it the primary target of the Russian navy, the American sub was only as good as its captain and crew. Besides, *Yumashev* had already sunk two Allied submarines, one a British Oberon-class diesel-electric, the other a Trafalgar—a seventy-five-hundred-ton British nuclear-powered ballistic missile sub. When Stasky had used his helicopter-borne "dunking" sonar mike to pick up the movement of the enemy submarines, then launched his ASROCS—airborne antisubmarine rockets—he had been struck once again by the paradox of the hunt. Whereas the obsessive silence of the subs was their greatest weapon, it was a singular one, for the moment they fired, their silence was gone, the advantage immediately shifted to the surface ship and its deadly array of ASW weapons. Sometimes the sub didn't have to fire at all in order for your sonar to detect it. If you had your helicopter out, and its dunking sonar picked up the enemy sub's noise signature, you simply dumped a homing depth charge or two to finish it off.

"What I want to know, Ilya," the *Yumashev*'s captain asked his first officer, "is whether or not the *Roosevelt* is heading out for convoy escort duty—or is it hunting like we are?"

"It left Holy Loch alone, Captain."

"Yes, but with forty to forty-five knots submerged, it could now be on the flank of a convoy. That would put it in a defensive mode, and that changes our mode of attack.''

"We haven't received any information from Glasgow on a convoy forming,'' answered the lieutenant.

"I'm not talking about a convoy leaving Scotland,'' said Stasky, "with nothing but empty holds. I mean a convoy *approaching* the U.K. even as we speak—loaded to the gills for NATO resupply. The American sub could be coming out to take over escort duty at the halfway mark.''

"But the British navy have responsibility for this side of the Atlantic, Captain.''

"Yes,'' said Stasky, "but the British have only eight . . .'' he remembered the Trafalgar he'd sunk ''. . . seven nuclear submarines, Comrade. They can't do it alone. They need American help.''

Stasky requested a printout of *Roosevelt*'s total complement—officers and crew. KGB's First Directorate had assigned agents in Britain and the United States to follow family members of some of the U.S. submarine crews. Whenever one of the family went to a post office, the KGB agent, usually a woman, waited patiently behind the person in line. Chatty and friendly, the agent would "accidentally" bump the family member, apologizing profusely, quickly retrieve the dropped mail, and in the process deftly affix a quick-stick microdot chip transmitter to the targeted envelope. The transmitter could then hopefully be traced through "fleet mail.'' The failure rate was high, as most of the time the microdot chip would become mangled by the post office or its shape otherwise ruptured along the way. But occasionally the concerted effort paid off. The key to the KGB's success was their ability to keep track of the highly sophisticated "Japanese'' microdot tracer sets via KRYSAT, the intelligence satellite named after Vladimir Kryuchkov, who had been personally appointed and ordered by Gorbachev in 1988 to launch the biggest KGB espionage operation since World War II to secure as many military and industrial secrets from the West as possible.

On several occasions KRYSAT was able to keep an ELLOK, or electronic lock, on one of the microdot transmitters, allowing it to be traced all the way to a fleet area. Once in the area proper, the weak transmitter signal, on the same frequency as a thousand other pieces of electronic equipment in the area, was drowned in a sea of much stronger frequencies, so that the *exact* position of the American sub that the targeted crew member was on was not known. But the general area of the battle group, to which sub armament resupply vessels were attached, narrowed the search area considerably. This made up for the fact, which Stasky and every other Soviet captain was aware of, that the Russian Tupolev reconnaissance aircraft, NATO designation "Bear," with its thirty-six-foot-wide rotodome, though good enough for general maritime patrols up to seven thousand miles away, was not much help in hunting for enemy subs. The Bear's four Kuznetsov turboprop engines were capable of only 540 miles per hour, its armament in the otherwise impressive remotely controlled dorsal and ventral twin twenty-three-millimeter gun barbettes no match against the dazzling virtuosity of the American F-15s.

Unfortunately for Stasky, while the general fleet area of the *Roosevelt*, like that of the two subs he'd already sunk, had sometimes been known to him, courtesy of the First Directorate's dogged electronic surveillance, the American sub had always acted as a lone wolf. He would have to find her by himself.

To this end Stasky gave orders for the *Yumashev*'s "Hormone" helicopter to be launched, and reemphasized the need for full battle readiness to the 108 men manning the 54 torpedo/depth charge tubes that festooned the cruiser's sleek flanks. As the cruiser increased speed, both men and launchers were splattered by spray as the elegant curve of the long, gray ship's bow bucked and sliced its way through mounting seas. Next, after checking the SATNAV, satellite navigation, printout—something he could not always rely on during severe solar flare activity—the Russian captain ordered his chief engineer to be ready at a moment's notice to *"ekhat' polnym khodom"*—"pull out all the stops." Bringing the sub chaser to its maximum speed of fifty-nine knots would give Stasky an advantage of fifteen knots over the American.

Binoculars slung about his neck, Stasky moved out to the windward side of the flying bridge, the sudden rush of cold sea air at once invigorating and numbing. He looked down at the foredeck of his long, gray ship as it knifed through a heavy swell and knew he was ready, confident of his command, his crew, and the ship's impressive armament. At the same time, he was too old a captain not to realize that in addition to speed and ASW weaponry—which the technical experts ashore referred to rather grandly as the "determining elements"—what you needed was *udacha*—"a bit of luck."

As the cruiser raced eastward, hoping to close the gap between herself and her American quarry, Stasky found himself trying to imagine what the enemy captain, Brentwood, and his crew were like. Was there *anything* in the profile printouts that he could pick up on, turn to his advantage? Despite all the mumbo-jumbo and psycho-babble of some of the printouts, which had gotten worse during the "liberalism" of Gorbachev's time, Stasky had to admit that sometimes a submarine had been found out and sunk because of a small inattention to detail by just one member of its crew. He recalled the Soviets' loss of a state-of-the-art Alfa-class HUK sub because a disgruntled crewman on garbage disposal detail had failed to make sure the compacted bale of trash had been properly weighted and bound. Loose foil from the frozen food wrappers bobbing up to the surface, though invisible to the naked eye, especially in fog, had nevertheless been picked up by a U.S. satellite's infrared eye.

Going back inside the bridge, Stasky ordered the officer of the deck to give him a printout of all the *Roosevelt* crew member "summaries" on file. Glasgow had reported, for example, that Robert Brentwood was engaged—to a schoolteacher in Surrey. But this information, garnered from the London *Times* announcements column, didn't strike the Russian captain as in any way significant. That is, until his first officer pointed out, half-jokingly, that at least Brentwood's insurance rates would fall. When Stasky asked what he meant, the officer explained that on one of the prewar *programma voennogo obmena*—"military exchange programs"—he'd been on in America, he had discovered that in the United States and other capitalist countries, when a man is married or has children, his insurance rates fall because the insurance companies' statistics showed that with increased responsibility for a wife and/or children, a man tended to be much more cautious, to drive more carefully, *bol'she oboronitez'no*—"more defensively."

Stasky nodded thoughtfully, looking down at Brentwood's printout again. More defensive! It was the *samy kray*—"the edge"—that might make all the difference, especially if the *Roosevelt* was heading out for convoy patrol. Such escort duty was an added incentive for a sub captain not to fire the first shot, not to do anything that might betray his position.

To play defensively rather than offensively. Oh, certainly it might account for only a fraction of a second, but in a fraction of a second—another man's hesitation—Stasky knew he could fire everything he had.

CHAPTER THREE

Oxshott, Surrey

"YES?" ASKED ROSEMARY Spence, indicating the student at the back of her Shakespeare class, the boy's eyeglasses opaque discs in the artificial light.

"Well, miss, it seems as if Lear only makes sense when he's crazy. I mean, when he's sane, he doesn't make any sense at all."

Normally Rosemary Spence would have pressed the student on why he thought that about Lear—was it his own or had he lifted it from Orwell's essay, "Lear, Tolstoy and the Fool"? But this afternoon her heart wasn't in it, her attention waning as she worried about Robert.

On the night before he'd left Oxshott on his way back to Scotland, there had been antiaircraft missile fire all along England's southeast coast—the Soviet air forces pounding the ports, all but destroying a convoy of forty ships that had made the long and dangerous three-thousand-mile voyage from Newfoundland only to come under the fierce bombardment of over five squadrons of Soviet fighter/bombers as the weary convoy approached the Southampton loran station. As the stalks of searchlights clustered like enormous celery sticks, separated, and closed again, trying to hold their Soviet targets, the explosions of iron bombs shattering the docksides of southern England, and the yellow tails and scream of air-to-air and ground-to-air rockets ripping the night sky asunder, she and Robert had made love. And now she held the memory close, it helping her get through the daily anxiety of wondering where he was, whether he was safe. She also tried to escape from the worry by burying herself in her work. But teaching Shakespeare always brought her back to the multitudinous calamities that befall even the most innocent, let alone those at war. To make matters worse, every day more and more countries were being drawn into the maelstrom—all the experts proven disastrously wrong as the war leaders, fearing a nuclear holocaust, held back from pushing the button, unleashing instead a conventional, albeit high-tech, war that was now three months old and showed no signs of letup as country after country, fearful of being caught alone in the storm, threw in its lot with either the NATO alliance or the Soviet armies.

The bell rang at 3:30 for the end of class, but no one could leave the shelter because a salvo of intermediate-range rockets launched from Hamburg batteries had penetrated the AA screen along the Channel, and the "all clear" had not yet sounded. Most of the students used the time to start their homework, but the new boy, Wilkins, who had guffawed at the other boy's comment on Lear and who was also the manic class clown, began his repertoire of rude noises. It took all Rosemary's effort to check him, a task that not only a week before she had felt herself more than equal to. Now she simply wished a bomb would fall on him.

Her anxiety about Robert, about everything, had grown much worse after their engagement had been officially announced a few days before he left. Till then, she had never believed herself to be superstitious, but now that their plan to marry was officially proclaimed, she found herself performing small ceremonies of obeisance to some higher order—God, whomever, whatever—as apprehensive, she realized, as those students she'd seen exhibiting obsessive behavior whenever exams were in the offing, their ceremonies of repetition insurance against malevolent forces.

While she and Robert had been together, she hardly knew the war existed, but with him gone to sea, and people congratulating her on the engagement, she suddenly felt more vulnerable, as if both of them, having publicly declared their love, were tempting fate. Then again, she wasn't sure it was that at all which had driven her into her present and, for her, strange mood of melancholy. Perhaps, she thought, it had more to do with the death of her younger brother, William. After the convoy he was in had been attacked by acoustically detonated mines in the mid-Atlantic, William had been taken to Newfoundland, where the Brentwood connection had first been made with Robert's sister, Lana, and where, despite an initial healthy prognosis, William died from complications.

"Complications." In Rosemary's lexicon, it was simply another word for the inexplicable. Her parents and her sister, Georgina, now a student at LSE, had all been so hopeful that young William would come home. The suddenness of his death had affected them in markedly different ways, but it colored everything they did. For Rosemary, the tragic passages of Shakespeare she had to teach offered no catharsis but rather intensified her awareness of the arbitrariness of one's life, the dark hand of chance made at once more tangible and terrible during Robert Brentwood's first visit. He had brought them William's few trinkets, ID tags, the wristwatch their father had given him, together with a long, touching letter from Lana Brentwood, William's nurse. It was a letter so devoid of maudlin sentiment yet so uninhibitedly personal, so typical of Americans, Robert excepted, that the Spence family felt that Lana Brentwood had known William as well as any of them. It was Shakespeare again, Rosemary thought, for had it not been for the man-made Tempest that had destroyed most of the convoy on which William had sailed, she would probably not have met Robert Brentwood. A stranger who, with two weeks leave while the submarine he commanded was rearmed and her hull repainted in Holy Loch, had taken it upon himself—in a moment of boredom more than anything else, as he later confessed to Rosemary— to personally deliver Lana's letter and William's few remaining effects.

He had meant to stay only overnight, caught out by the disrupted train schedule, but had stayed in Surrey with the Spences for the remainder of his leave. Rosemary's father had been taken aback by the rapidity of the romance, but her mother, who Rosemary knew would voice any parental objection if any were to be made, had surprised everyone by instantly accepting the situation. Though grief-stricken by her son's death, Anne Spence encouraged them both, taking it upon herself, in another act that took her husband, Richard, and two daughters by surprise, to make all the arrangements for the wedding, which would take place during

Robert's next leave. It was, in fact, Anne Spence's salvation.
There was so much to do, so much initiative called for to
overcome the scarcities of wartime rationing—a lack of everything from sugar for a wedding cake to paper—that the
attention she had to give to all the details for the wedding
filled her hours and kept a nervous breakdown at bay.

Richard retired now and then to his study, with the little
available brandy he could afford, to calm himself after seeing
what she was doing to their savings account. At one point he
had seriously considered writing a letter to the local manager
of Barclay's Bank, in Oxshott, to cancel their credit card. But
as fall ended, the NATO forces still reeling from the juggernaut and sheer brute strength of the Soviet forces, Richard
Spence let his wife spend. It was quite possible that within a
year or two they would all be dead. Besides, after William's
death, nothing was the same anymore. Even Rosemary,
whom Richard had thought the steadiest and most sensible
of them all, had confided to him that she, too, felt adrift; all
her own beliefs—her once steady vision of the universe, of
cause and effect—no longer held. For her the mere thought
that she and Robert—that all of them—were no more than
flotsam on the wild sea of the world was terrifying. Her once
powerful sense of optimism seemed to have been swept away
forever. She was lost, and only in Robert's arms had she felt
safe. She wondered whether she'd agreed to marry him too
hastily, more from the fear of a loveless world than the hope
of a loving one.

The "all clear" began its wail, as mournful as the earlier
air raid warning had been, and as she waited for the students
to file out of the shelter, she thought again of how easily she
and her class—the entire school, for that matter—could become entombed at any time. It would take only one of the
high-explosive iron bombs—as deadly to a shelter as a depth
charge to a submarine. She said a prayer—but was anyone
listening?

She heard a tearing noise—and laughter. Wilkins, his eyes
bright with mischief, was making farting sounds. She was
sure that if the school received a direct hit, everyone would
die save Wilkins. What she couldn't stand was his stupid,
bovine optimism. She doubted he even knew where most
of Europe was, let alone the fact that, except for western
France and Spain, it had been all but overrun by the Soviet

armies. At the beginning of the war, before Wilkins had shown up, she had encouraged her pupils to keep an up-to-date situation map on the shelter wall. But as the enemy armies smashed through NATO's central front around Fulda Gap and to the south along the Danube while simultaneously wheeling with thousands more tanks across the North German Plain to Hamburg and Bremen on the way to secure the NATO ports, the students had finally given up on the map.

To make it even more discouraging, the media coverage of the battles was confusing. Unlike the two previous world wars, when newspapers could broadly indicate the ebb and flow of battle, now the battles within the larger battlefields were impossible to follow at times. In the course of a morning, a NATO counterattack with A-10 Thunderbolts—the tank-killing American aircraft—seemed to have the better of it. Then, by midafternoon, the dust was so thick that friend and foe were indistinguishable in satellite photos. In one place it was a raging war of movement. In other zones, with combatants more quickly exhausted in the strain of high-tech combat than in previous, conventional wars, whole companies, especially those of NATO, were reported digging in, either in an effort to catch their breath in the frenzy of retreat or to play for time against the attacking echelons. Here, parts of the crooked front crisscrossed with barbed concertina wire resembled the moonscapes of World War I, which the experts had predicted could never happen, as beleaguered NATO troops anxiously waited for urgently needed refit for their savaged armored divisions and infantry reinforcements, which, despite being mobile, had to renegotiate overextended supply lines under constant air attack.

And amid all this, Wilkins. Rosemary tried to imagine the parents of such a boy, but she knew that one was inevitably wrong. Some of the most disruptive in class had iron discipline at home, and at the other extreme, well, some of the parents were really worse than the students. She thought his card had said his mother was an accountant in Leatherhead, his father something to do with insurance.

Going up in the lift from the shelter, one of the girls squealed and jumped as if stung. Everyone laughed afresh except the girl, face red as beet root. Wilkins was grinning, his callow expression infuriating Rosemary. "Wilkins!"

"Yes? Me, miss?"

"Was that you?"

"*Me*, miss?"

"Saturday morning for *you*. Three hours."

He was still grinning. She had to stop herself from making it four hours. And when she got home, Georgina, who had come down for the weekend from LSE, was all-knowing, at dinner full as usual of sociological theory, claiming that such a boy was "society's fault." The boy's acting up, she told Rosemary, was "quite clearly a cry for attention."

"Well, he'll get it," Rosemary replied tartly. "I've given him a Saturday morning."

"You see?" responded Georgina, pausing as she reached over a textbook opened ostentatiously to the left of the bread rolls. Georgina's new habit of reading at the table was, Rosemary had no doubt, another of her younger sister's defiances of bourgeois manners. Besides, reading while you were eating was something Rosemary had never mastered. For the moment their father was either keeping out of it behind his newspaper or simply wasn't paying attention.

"See what?" demanded Rosemary, glaring across at Georgina. "What on earth are you talking about?"

"This boy Wilkins," replied Georgina, breaking a stale ration roll, buttering it with nonchalant grace. "I think he wants you all to himself."

"Don't be absurd, Georgina. He's a recalcitrant yobbo."

"I mean," said Georgina, astonishing Rosemary with her ability to have broken the roll without a fall of crumbs onto the pressed white linen tablecloth, "he probably has a *thing* for you."

Rosemary's face turned beet red. She glanced at their father, but he was hidden behind the *Daily Telegraph*. Anne Spence, who'd just entered the dining room from the kitchen as the exchange between her daughters was heating up, looked wearily down at her younger daughter. "Don't be ridiculous, Georgina. Rosemary's old enough to be his mother."

"Exactly," countered Georgina knowingly.

A rush of exasperation came from behind the *Telegraph*, Richard Spence lowering the newspaper, breaking its back, folding the broadsheet to a quarter its size. "That fool Knowlton's at it again!"

"Who?" asked Georgina. Her father peered over his reading glasses, unsure of whether she knew or not. "Knowlton—Guy Knowlton. That idiot professor who keeps taking out ridiculous advertisements.''

"Oh," said Georgina, "the man who wants to collect all our hair dryers to save energy.''

"Yes. That's him.''

"He sounds like a harmless enough eccentric to me, Father.''

"That's not the point, Georgina. I was telling your mother—you were here, weren't you, Rosemary?''

"Yes, Daddy.''

"Here we are, desperately short of all kinds of things, paper not being the least of them, and yet they persist in allowing this, this madman to waste space in—''

"It's a free country, Daddy," said Rosemary, tired of his constant harping about the dotty professor. For Richard Spence, Dr. Guy Knowlton, the author of a text on archaeology, continued to represent all that was self-indulgent and wasteful in a country that was fighting for its life and yet in which old fools like Knowlton were allowed to squander valuable resources.

"Do you really think so?" asked Georgina, looking at Rosemary.

Rosemary lifted the teapot lid, seeing it pointless to try to squeeze any more out of the exhausted tea leaves. "Think what?''

"That it's a free country," continued Georgina, taking the last of the milk for her tea.

Anne Spence pointedly left the room.

"Don't upset her like that," said Richard. "You know how quarrels upset her.''

"It's not a quarrel, Daddy," replied Georgina. "I'm merely stating a fact. Just because we're at war doesn't mean we can't question whether we're really living in a free—''

"Georgina!''

In the strained silence that followed her father's rebuke, Georgina returned to her book and Rosemary could hear the steady, heavy ticking of the grandfather clock in the living room, recalling that the last time she had been so aware of its presence was after she and Robert had made love, when—ironically—at the height of the Soviet rocket attack, she had felt so safe in his arms.

Georgina finished the bread roll and, licking her fingers,

ran them around the bread-and-butter plate to gather up the remaining crumbs.

"My God, Georgina," exclaimed Richard. "Is that what they teach you up there—?"

"It's very proletarian, Daddy," said Rosemary. "Didn't you know?"

Georgina poured herself more tea as if squeezing the pot. "This is a bit weak, isn't it?"

"We have to use the leaves over again," said Rosemary. "Rationing. Or don't you have that in London?"

"I don't know why you're so shirty, Rose," retorted Georgina.

"She's worried," said her father.

"We all are," said Georgina. "This wretched war has mucked everything up. It's the same old story. Big capital against—"

"Not at the table," said Richard.

"I would have thought," put in Rosemary, "that the war suited you very nicely. Liberating women from the bourgeois apron strings. Kitchen to factory. Manpower shortage and all."

Georgina's cup stopped in midair and she replaced it on the saucer without having sipped the tea. "Why didn't I think of that? Rosey—that's quite brilliant."

"Thank you," said Rosemary. "I'm glad we poor country folk occasionally think of—"

"Still," cut in Georgina, "I bet I'm right about Willie."

"Who?" asked Richard, looking up from his newspaper. He had thought she said, "William."

"That boy—Williams."

"Wilkins," Rosemary corrected her.

"He's got the hots for you, Rosey."

Richard Spence's paper shot away from him. "What a vulgar expression. Insulting people, is it? Is that what you're learning up there?"

"Oh really, Daddy. It's just an expression—"

"Yes, and I don't care for it."

There was another long, strained silence.

"Well," said Georgina finally, "and how about this Robert Brentwood? Bit sudden, Rosey, you sly fox. When do I get to meet him?"

"Excuse me," said Rosemary, pushing her chair back from the table, brushing her lips quickly with the napkin.

"I only wanted to—" began Georgina. Richard Spence folded the newspaper neatly, ran his hand down the crease, and taking his reading glasses off, rubbed his eyes. "I thought you had grown out of it, Georgina."

"Out of what?"

"Don't be obtuse. Your willful aggressiveness. You're not happy until you push people to the edge. God knows where you get it from." He looked hard at her. "Why do you do it?"

Georgina said nothing, holding her teacup like a communicant's chalice, staring ahead.

"Is it because," Richard said, "you think we don't—care for you?"

"*Care?*" said Georgina, her tone defensively hostile as she turned on him. "You can't even say the word, can you?"

"Your mother and I have never made *any* distinction—"

"The word's *love*, Daddy. Or was that just for William?"

"You astound me."

"Really?"

"What, pray, is that supposed to mean?"

"I've always known it, of course," she said bitterly, putting the cup down hard.

"Known what?"

"Oh, for Heaven's sake, Father," she said, vigorously folding and refolding her napkin on the table. "Rosey's always had your heart."

"Do you think—"

"I *know*," cut in Georgina. "Ever since we were children. I'm not being churlish about it. It's merely an observation anyone could—"

"I've always cared for you. Your mother and—"

"If," said Georgina slowly, a tension clearly crackling in her voice, "you say *cared* once more, I'll scream!"

The phone was ringing, and as Richard Spence got up to answer it, Georgina avoided his distracted gaze, her eyes brimming with tears. She heard her father only vaguely, yet despite her hurt, could tell that something was terribly wrong.

"I'll tell her," she could hear him say. "Yes. Yes. Thank you for calling." He put down the receiver slowly and, turning, called for Rosemary.

"She's gone out," said Georgina, holding her teacup in both hands, elbows on the table, something Richard Spence could not abide.

"Where?" he asked her.

"I've no idea," said Georgina.

Richard Spence went to the hall and opened the closet, taking out his mackintosh and gum boots. "If your mother asks, tell her I've gone looking for her."

"What's wrong?"

Her father scooped the keys from the hall stand, put on his deerstalker, and was gone.

CHAPTER FOUR

ABOARD THE *ROOSEVELT*, submariner Evans had been silenced. Forever. Yet even in death he seemed to be screaming, his face an agony frozen in time, the cheek beneath his left eye swollen so that the eye was little more than a slit, the left side of his face appearing longer than his right, his mouth agape, right eye open and staring. His whole expression was one of terror, paralyzed before the second of impact. The bosun who had aided Robert Brentwood in giving the seaman the shot of Valium to quieten him down was trying to make sure the hospital corpsman had given him the correct dosage. Maybe the corpsman, unwell himself at the time, had somehow given him a larger dose than he meant to give him. But the corpsman shook his head, his tone adamant.

"No way, José. I didn't give you an overdose. Don't pin it on me. Here—" He turned away, trying to abort a sneeze—unsuccessfully. He took down the sick bay clipboard, tapping the day's entry with his Vicks inhaler. "There it is, Chief. Twenty milligrams. You signed for it."

"Then what the hell—" began the bosun, the corpsman using the inhaler to dismiss the bosun's question.

"Who knows? Could've had a stroke. Heart attack. Combination of factors."

"Skipper thinks he killed him."

Despite his fever, the corpsman, though looking across at the bosun with rheumy eyes, still managed an air of a professional clinician. "Natural psychological reaction. Skipper's not used to doing it."

"Yeah, well, anybody kick off after you've given them a shot?"

"No." The corpsman stared at him, then shifted his gaze to Evans, pulling back the sheet by the government-issue tag. "By the look of him—I'd say he died of fright. Pink elephants. Sure as hell didn't die of a cold."

"What the hell you mean?"

"Delirium tremens. Like I told you before. That's where pink elephants come from."

"Stop jerking me around."

"Listen," said the corpsman, sticking the Vicks inhaler into his nostril, one finger flattening the other nostril as he took a deep breath, "I'm telling you, Chief. Alcoholics who're forced dry see more than pink elephants."

The bosun remembered Evans screaming about snakes. Maybe the corpsman was right. "But I thought the Valium was supposed to calm him. Take the edge off?"

"Not enough," said the corpsman. "Once you've flipped out, normal dose doesn't do much for you. I could've told the old man that."

"Why the hell didn't you?"

"I wasn't asked."

"Shit, you weren't there. Back here sittin' on your ass."

"Listen, man, I was pushing a one oh five."

"What?"

"Temperature. Fever—or hadn't you noticed?" With that, the corpsman took a thermometer from its sheath, glanced at it, shook the mercury column down before slipping it under his tongue. " 'Sides, I thought it best to keep away from everyone. It's one mother of a virus."

The corpsman, thermometer sticking out like a small cigarette from his mouth, looked down at his watch.

"Then," said the bosun, pulling the sheet back over Evans's face before they took him to a forward food freezer, "what the hell did kill Evans?"

The bosun has his thumb on the intercom button and asked someone to come up and help him with the corpse. Looking at Evans, still puzzled, he told the hospital corpsman, "You know, they say that flu in 1918 killed more guys than the war did.'' He thought the hospital corpsman was going to bite the thermometer clean in half.

The bosun had merely meant it to take a little wind out of the corpsman's sails, but later, when he entered the *Roosevelt*'s redded-out control room, which smelled like an auto showroom, unlike the disinfected sick bay, he saw the officer of the deck, First Mate Peter Zeldman, standing forward of Brentwood, directly behind the planesman's console, and asked him if any of the crew on watch had gone off sick, reported a fever. But he didn't get his answer, the sonar operator cutting in, ''We have an unclassified surface vessel— five thousand yards. Closing.''

''Signature check?'' Zeldman asked Sonar, conscious of Brentwood moving over from the periscope island, watching the ''shattered ring'' pulse on the pale green screen.

''No known signature,'' replied Sonar, moving his head closer to the console, working the constant compromise between volume and tone needed to discriminate one noise from another in what nearly everyone but a sailor assumed to be a quiet domain. In reality the sea was a never-ending ''frying pan'' of energy, a night jungle of noise, countless billions of shrimp, microscopic organisms, clicking and sizzling amid the eerie haunting trumpets of the giant mammals in constant search for food.

''Could it be using baffles?'' put in Brentwood.

''Signature pattern congruent with full hull, sir.'' He meant that there was no sign of the kind of blistering effect on the outer ring of the echo pulse that might indicate symmetrical baffles.

''Put it on the PA,'' Zeldman ordered Sonar. ''Squelch button.'' The next second all the crewmen in the control room could hear the muted engine sounds of the unknown surface vessel. Zeldman was ambivalent about the procedure. Sometimes he thought it only made everyone more edgy, but he'd been told by Brentwood how putting incoming noise on the PA, provided it wasn't loud enough to send out its own pulse reverberating through the hull, could sometimes help the sonar operator. Those enlisted men who had been sailors in civilian life could not only help identify the vessel type but sometimes even luck out on its probable nationality. This could save a captain or his executive officer from ordering a preemptive launch of a torpedo or Tomahawk cruise missile, which, while it would almost certainly take out the oncoming vessel, would also end the submarine's greatest weapon, its silence, revealing its exact location.

The UCV speed was now showing twenty knots on the digital readout—too fast for most noncombat vessels. But Brentwood knew that in trying to maintain the U.S. Navy's "rollover" strategy—rolling over all obstacles, including Russian sub packs, in order to get vital resupply to NATO and Europe—the United States had made up for lost time with an industrial miracle that even dwarfed previous Japanese achievements. The industrial "miracle," spurred on by uncertainty about the level of Japan's commitment to the war effort, beyond her helping to ferry American troops across to Korea, was that the U.S. East Coast shipyards and those in San Diego were producing "prefab thirty-thousand-ton merchantmen," called "Leggo ships" by the submarine crews, at the rate of one every seven days. It wasn't as fast as the one Liberty ship every four days achieved by the American Kaiser Shipyards in World War II, but for a computer age, it was impressive, the Leggo ships stronger because of the laser spot welding, and faster.

Brentwood put it to Zeldman and the RO that it was quite possible the noise they were hearing was that of a Leggo. With the merchantmen rolling off the slipways at more than three a week, there was no way, he pointed out, that *Roosevelt*'s computer could have all Leggo noise signatures in its memory. Each time the subs returned from patrol, they were routinely issued the top secret taped signatures of the thirty-five Leggos built in the yards during the patrol. Besides, the moment the merchantmen were completed, they were pressed into service, without the normal time set aside for sea trials during which the noise signatures of ships were normally taped and refined to register any changes made by the yardbirds.

"Could be one of ours," conceded Zeldman, watching Brentwood's expression, trying to anticipate which course of action he would take.

"Forty-three hundred and closing," came Sonar's coolly modulated tone. The ship was coming right for them. In just over seven minutes it would be directly over the *Roosevelt*, now lying still, on listening mode only.

Brentwood ordered everything closed down except the "coffee grinder," the reactor at the very heart of the sub that not only powered the Sea Wolf but which would take hours to fire up. Zeldman was worried that Brentwood was placing too much faith in the anechoic paint layer on the hull, which absorbed sonar pulses from another source, thus minimizing, sometimes eliminating, echo ping and so denying a hunter any "noise scent" at all.

Suddenly, with each man silent, rigid, as if welded to his post, the submarine seemed to shrink inside. It was true that for the men who had experienced life in the old diesel-electric subs and for one or two who had served, when very young, in the last boats of World War II, the Sea Wolf was infinitely more spacious. Curtained for privacy, individual bunks in nine-man dormitories, good-sized lockers beneath, rack space large enough to hang a full dress uniform, a sound-proofed audio booth and video room for two movies a week, the modern Sea Wolf was a limousine compared to a standard sedan. Still, for most of the crew, who didn't know the old pigboats, who hadn't experienced what it was like at the end of your watch to have to roll into the sweat-soaked bunk of your replacement, and, except for the cook and the oiler, to be allowed only one three-minute shower a week, the *Roosevelt* was still crowded. Every now and then even a fully trained crewman would crack from what was euphemistically called DCS—developed claustrophobia syndrome.

As he listened to the heavy, gut-punching throb of the approaching vessel, it occurred to the hospital corpsman that perhaps Evans hadn't had the DTs after all. Maybe he'd cracked under the strain of such claustrophobia. No matter how much bigger the *Roosevelt* was, compared to the old pigboats, it was still a submarine, with every available space jammed with equipment, including lead shot which could be jettisoned to accommodate new equipment so as not to alter the sub's buoyancy. The corpsman knew that by any landlubber's reckoning, the sub was still a long, steel coffin, and every man aboard knew that below her "crush" depth of three thousand feet, the enormous pressure driving her toward the bottom at over a hundred miles an hour, the sub would implode—flattened like a beer can beneath a boot.

"Two thousand and closing," reported Sonar, his voice not so steady now, and hoarse, the sound of the UCV's props increasing, having changed from a deep, rhythmic pulse to a churning noise that now seemed to be coming at them from every direction.

"Torpedoes ready?" asked Brentwood.

"Ready, sir," confirmed Zeldman.

Brentwood glanced up at the fathometer. They were in shallower water. It made him more vulnerable to shock waves from any explosion.

"Set forward one and two for SI. Stern five and six for SI," ordered Brentwood, quietly and distinctly, his command heard clearly in both forward and aft torpedo rooms, the fish being set for SI, or sensor impact, the unknown surface vessel now so close that the trailing wires which normally ran back from the torpedoes to the sub need not be used—the close proximity of the oncoming ship in effect a point-blank target for the twenty-eight-mile Mark-48s.

"Fifteen hundred. Closing," came Sonar's voice. "Speed increasing to twenty-seven knots. Most likely a cruiser, Captain. Friendly or not, I can't tell."

The choice for Brentwood was clear and stark. Under the authority of chief of naval operations, he could risk attacking any UCV if the UCV had not been identified by signature. In the cruel equation of war, the risk of sinking a "friendly" did not come near to the cost of losing a Sea Wolf, with its capacity as "platform of last resort" to take out a minimum of twenty-four major Soviet cities and/or ICBM "farms" from over two and a half thousand miles away. Yet Brentwood knew that even if the ship wasn't using a chopper-dangled sonar mike because of the vicinity of its mother ship's noise, if he fired, the UCV's on-board sonar would instantly have his precise position. He could then expect to be dumped on by a cluster of "screamers," as the U.S. sailors called the Soviet RBU—*Raketnaya Bombometnaya Ustanovka*—antisubmarine rockets. Fired in paired sequence from twelve-barrel horseshoe-configuration launchers, the five-foot-long, forty-two-pound warheads would rip the *Roosevelt* apart. The later models, being fitted by the Soviets with World War II–type Stuka dive-bomb whistles, were given the name "screamers," and their noise, traveling much faster underwater than in air, struck deep into the collective psyche of all NATO submariners.

"Thirteen hundred yards and closing."

The signature computer was still running, maddeningly indecisive, flashing orange bars across its green screen, indicating possible "enemy" match-ups with a plus or minus ten percent error in noise signatures. But only if the orange stripes went to kit-kats, solid brown stripes, would it mean an enemy vessel for sure—light blue bars representing possible "friendlies," solid blue for confirmed.

"One thousand and closing. Still stripe orange."

Zeldman said nothing, jaw clenched, his reflection staring back at him in the computer's screen, guessing that if Brentwood had decided to risk the *Roosevelt's* silence, he would have fired already. Instead it seemed he was gambling that the surface vessel—a cruiser, by the multiple echoes coming in via *Roosevelt's* towed sensor array—was now having its active sonar blanketed in the shallower water by the thrashing of its own props. If so, the cruiser might pass over them, waiting for a clearer echo.

But on the *Yumashev*, Captain Stasky could still pick up enough echo from the submarine's bulk. If it was the American sub from Holy Loch, he knew that the whooshing sound of one of its 280-mile-range Tomahawk missiles, capable of being fired from the torpedo tube eighty feet beneath the surface, would alert not only the *Yumashev* but every Soviet Hunter/Killer south of the Greenland-Iceland-Norway Gap.

Also knowing the primary mission of the Sea Wolfs was to wait, to keep the United States' last weapons platform intact should the Soviet ICBMs be unleashed, and that *Roosevelt's* captain was engaged to be married, Stasky believed that it was all the more likely that the American somewhere beneath the *Yumashev* had deliberately held his fire. The American might also be confused by the new refit baffles welded on the *Yumashev* at the Tallinn Yards. Whatever the reason, the fact was that the American had held his fire, and Stasky believed that despite the *chrezmerny zvuk machiny*— "override clutter"—the *Yumashev* was getting from its own sonar echoes in the shallower water, the sub that his cruiser had picked up earlier must be in the near vicinity.

"Gotontes! Vesti ogon gruppoy RBU!"—"Roll drums! Fire RBU! All clusters!"

"Drums rolling," confirmed the first mate, who then flipped up the Perspex protector, pushing the fire button for both twelve-barrel rocket launchers on either side of the stern helicopter hangar and the other two twelve-barrel launchers in the foc's'le. From the starboard wing, the cruiser's third mate and a midshipman, collars buffeted by the cold wind, watched the oil-drum-sized depth charges plopping unceremoniously over the stern, quickly disappearing in the ship's boiling wake, the scream of the first salvo of antisub rockets filling the air, along with the thudding noise from gray bunches of mallet-shaped depth charges fired high in a scatter pattern, leaping into the air like grotesque quail.

The officer of the deck, already having started the clock, was counting, "One, two, three—" the drums timed to go off at greater depths than the RBUs. Stasky saw the first blip on the screen, the sonar alarm bipping frantically like a smoke detector. *"Torpeda v nashem napravlenii! Napravo!"*—"Homing torpedoes! Hard right!"

The *Yumashev* heeled to starboard, discharging a cascade of *khlam*—"chaff," aluminum strips and wafers designed to addle American torpedo sensors. As the RBU rockets were influence-fused, for magnetic signature, the *Yumashev's* skipper knew the chaff might prematurely trigger them, but the old-fashioned drum charges set only for depth might still do the trick, though with the Americans' titanium-reinforced hull, a drum charge would have to strike the hull itself to implode the sub.

"Dive—two thousand!" ordered Brentwood. It meant approaching crush point, but the stern planesman to his left didn't hesitate and there was the surge of water pouring into the tanks. During the "hard," steep-angled dive, Brentwood braced himself against the girth rail that ran around the raised periscope island as to his right the bow planesman watched depth gauge and trim as the *Roosevelt*, already having fired four Mk-48s, sank like a stone, nose first.

Six . . . seven . . . eight seconds, and aboard the *Yumashev*, Stasky knew something had gone wrong. The sea astern, off his port quarter, should be erupting in towering greenish-white mushrooms streaked with black oil from the sub's ruptured hydraulic systems. Instead the *Yumashev's* captain looked out on a sea that was exploding only here and there. He estimated that less than twenty percent of the RBUs and depth charges were detonating.

"Bozhe moy, Mendev!"—"My God, Mendev!" he said, turning to his first mate. *"Chto zhe tut takogo?"*—"What's wrong?"

* * *

On *Roosevelt*, the depth gauge's needle was passing the two-thousand-feet mark and quivering. There was a hiss, then a jet of water—thinner than a needle. Coming in at over a thousand psi, it created a stinging aerosol, a "car wash" mist in the control room, temporarily blinding the planesman and the chief petty officer watching the ballast tank monitors. In six seconds the *Roosevelt* had reached twenty-one hundred feet. There was a dull thump, then another, the sound punching Brentwood so hard in the stomach, he could tell the depth charge was even closer than the sound indicated. The sub leveled out at twenty-three fifty, its pressure hull starting to groan. Three minutes passed and nothing. Then another explosion so close that it threw him back against the periscope rail, the *Roosevelt* shuddering so violently it blurred the red-eyed squares of the monitors, more jets of water shooting into the control room, creating an even denser aerosol.

"Up angle!" shouted Zeldman.

In the forward torpedo room, rivets began popping, one ricocheting about the titanium casing until it lodged in a crewman's brain, splattering the pinkish-gray mass over the bulkhead, another smashing a Perspex fire button protector, sending off a torpedo. The torpedo was not yet armed, but its impact inside the tube was like that of a bullet in a closed barrel, its flame-burst concussing several crewmen in the torpedo room. The fire in the tube quickly died through lack of oxygen, but not before the meticulously tooled lining of the tube had been badly scoured. The first torpedo that *Roosevelt* had fired from the forward section and the two fired from the stern had gone haywire, heading into the fallen "chaff," but these torpedoes' premature explosion sent shrapnel whistling high into the air, inadvertently clearing a path for the lone stern-fired Mark-48 that was still running. It glanced the *Yumashev*'s starboard bow beneath the waterline—not enough to sink her, but the shock wave of methane and carbon dioxide from the explosive gases was enough to buckle the cruiser's outer plating, imploding it with an elliptical gash twelve feet long and three feet wide.

The Russians were quick to the pumps, however, and with watertight compartments sealed, the cruiser was able to limp away at five knots, her two twin Goblet antiaircraft missiles, which could also be used in an antiship role, intact as well as her Kamov-26 over-the-horizon missile-targeting helicopter. The Kamov was already airborne, its contra-rotating rotors catching afternoon sunlight, its bug-eyed face, remarkably like that of a blowfly, hovering off the ship's port quarter, its chin-mounted Bulge-B surface-search radar already scanning the horizon for any NATO ships that might be diverted to the area by the British commander of the western approaches. The helicopter's radar and its height allowed it to pick up hostile targets well beyond the seventy-nautical-mile limit of the *Yumashev*'s head net-C air search radar.

The Allied ships the *Yumashev* expected didn't materialize, most of them within steaming distance committed to the vital convoy duty farther south, where the Gulf Stream curves into the North Atlantic drift. But Allied aircraft did come, the Russian sub chaser detected by another sub chaser, a Dassault-Breguet Atlantic-2 patrol aircraft, which, too slow, low on fuel, and not equipped to attack the seven-thousand-ton cruiser, relayed the information to St. Mawgan, the USAF communication center in Cornwall.

Within five minutes, south of St. Mawgan, in the lush and windswept countryside, the orange jet of flame from a Sepecat Jaguar could be seen as the aircraft taxied out of its hardened "splashed-greens" camouflaged shelter onto a short stretch of highway, the blacktop marked off by detour signs. The plane's high wing would enable it to take off from half the tarmac length usually used in its close support and reconnaissance role. Normally a light-strike aircraft kept for coastal defenses and photographic overflights of the battle-fields across the Channel, the Franco-British jet had been scrambled because RAF fighter squadrons were in the process of intercepting large incoming Soviet formations over the North Sea. The Jaguar, its dark green-gray shape fleetingly veiled in fog, began its short run, the two eight-thousand-pound Adour turbofans, on afterburner, thrust into the mottled sky over England's Land's End, taking it to Mach 1.1 in less than a minute. The pilot, Roger Fernshaw, kept the plane low, where its small wing and fly-by-wire touch controls enabled the Jaguar to skim over the ruffled, cobalt-colored sea without emitting telltale radar signals, its FIN digital inertial navigation and weapon aiming system going through its paces, Fernshaw checking his HUD or head-up display and the Ferranti laser range and marked-target seeker. The late sun glinted momentarily off the metallic sea as Fernshaw punched in the coordinates for the *Yumashev*'s last reported position as relayed via St. Mawgan by the Dassault-Breguet patrol aircraft.

He saw a fleeting shadow below him, began evasive action, then realized it was the shadow of the external fuel pod needed to give the Jaguar an extended range of twenty-one hundred miles as it streaked west sou'west, armed on all five hard points, including two fifteen-hundred-pound Exocet missiles.

Inside the *Roosevelt*, everything was shaking violently, as if in an earthquake, both the deep rumble and high-pitched screeching of her bent prop reverberating throughout. Suddenly the sub jerked hard right, sending Brentwood and Zeldman crashing into the scope island, Brentwood striking his head on the girth rail.

A crewman grabbed for one of his sneakers floating in the ankle-deep pool now sloshing between the control room's sill and the forward electronics room.

"What the hell—" Brentwood began, but now the noise had suddenly decreased, the chief engineer apparently having dropped the sub's speed to five knots on his own initiative as the sub leveled out fifty feet above her crush depth. Yet Brentwood knew that despite the reduction in the noise level and the fact that most of the leaks had been sealed, his sub was in serious trouble. The noise was still a problem, a giveaway to an enemy sub anywhere within fifty miles or so. And now a bank of square red eyes, circuit monitors, grew bright, the control room's light dimming with the drop in current.

In the gloomy light the sound of the sloshing water created an ominous overtone amid the crunching noise of the prop's warp and, above, the rhythmic pulse of the pumps. He gave the order to reduce speed still further, but the vibration unexpectedly grew worse and for a second *all* monitors faded.

"Fucking great!" someone said.

"Hold your tongue!" snapped Brentwood. "Mr. Zeldman!"

"Sir?"

"Shut down the prop."

"Yes, sir."

For a moment all was quiet, the sub in neutral buoyancy, no longer diving or rising. Then they could hear a choking, gurgling noise, the only sound above the rapid purr of the pumps that were sucking up the water, transferring it to number one ballast tank. Brentwood ordered the other tank vented to keep the sub in neutral trim and listened to the damage reports coming in. Someone had thrown up and the stench was overpowering, telling Brentwood that the air-conditioning was out of action. In an effort to get the crew's full attention back on their job, he chewed out a forward torpedo room bosun for not responding earlier but was chagrined to discover the bosun had already done so—that what he was now receiving was a follow-up report.

"You were out for a bit, sir," explained Zeldman. Brentwood apologized to the bosun over the intercom, then turned to Zeldman.

"Where's the Russian?"

"Three miles off, sir, and limping. Looked like we banged him up pretty—"

"Damn it! Give me a bearing."

"Yes, sir. Zero three seven, sir."

"Very well." He called the reactor room. "You all right back there, Chief?"

"Yes, sir."

"Stern room?" asked Brentwood.

"Man missing, sir."

"Who?"

"We're not sure, Captain. We had a 'Rover' working the watch overlap."

"Well, find out."

"Yes, sir."

"Probably in the can," said Zeldman, risking a note of levity after the tension of the Russian attack. The sonar operator gave a forced laugh.

Brentwood saw the square red eyes of the circuit monitors lighting up—full power restored. He shook his head. It was an infuriating dilemma, enough to elicit a record three "damns" from him in as many seconds. Here was the pride of the U.S. Navy, America's vessel of last resort, with power to burn, its reactor-driven steam turbines back to generating enough power to light a city of over a hundred thousand. But to what effect? With a damaged prop, the sub, even if it used its auxiliary diesel hookup or, failing that, the "bring it home" capability of the smaller "dolphin dick"—the emergency screw slotted in the stern ballast—could only make a maximum of three to five knots. It meant that for combat purposes, self-defense included, the *Roosevelt* was virtually dead in the water—a sick whale in a sea full of sharks. On top of this, Zeldman informed him that the hydraulic line for the sail's starboard diving plane was losing pressure—a possible perforation. It couldn't be repaired; they'd have to go to manual override, a slow business at the best of times.

Another report came in from the forward torpedo room. Using a chain pulley to recradle one of the three-and-a-half-thousand-pound Mark-48 torpedoes which had shaken loose in the pitch darkness that had followed the final salvo of RBU rockets, the torpedo crew found the missing seaman, an electrician's mate. They were unable to identify him for five minutes or so, his dog tags embedded in the bloody mash that had been his head.

Brentwood issued orders for the emergency prop to be extended from its ballast sheath and engaged. Its fanlike whir was quiet enough, picked up by the sub's implant hull mikes, the TACTAS, or towed array, mikes having been knocked out by two of the Russian drum charges. Brentwood tapped on the NAVCOMP keys, the computer screen's warm amber readout informing him that at its maximum speed of five knots, it would take *Roosevelt* twelve days at least, through enemy-sub-infested waters, to reach Land's End at the southwestern tip of England. If they turned about and headed south against the stream, to Newfoundland, it would take them much longer. Either way, they would be in constant danger of being discovered through the noise of the emergency prop. If this happened, the *Roosevelt* would have only five knots against a Hunter/Killer's forty.

Brentwood ordered the emergency prop resheathed. They would wait for the next scheduled rendezvous with the TACAMO—take charge and move out—aircraft due in seventy-three hours time. He would take her up, out of the sea noise, give a signal requesting emergency assistance, then go down and wait rather than move and risk "noise shorts"—any noise from inside the sub that could resonate loudly enough from the hull to give away its presence. But Robert Brentwood knew that the waiting was by far the hardest thing for a submariner to do.

"Don't sweat it," the quartermaster told one of the fire control technicians in the forward compartment. "With the freshwater converter and our freezers, we've got enough food and fresh water down here to last us a year. Hell, we convert so much fresh water, we have to dump half of it.'' It was meant to be a reassuring thought until an electrician's mate pointed out that by now the noise of their engagement with the cruiser must have been picked up by both sides' ocean-bottom arrays scattered at various points throughout the North Atlantic. Further reducing their chance for a pickup tow by a fast navy tug to one of the big sub tender/floating docks was the gale warning from the last TACAMO contact. On top of that, there was the problem of whether the TACAMO aircraft would arrive on schedule, if at all, given the increasing Russian air cover of Soviet Hunter/Killer packs which had broken out south of the Greenland-Iceland Gap and the Iceland-Faroes Gap.

Brentwood knew the only other choice he had was to take the sub to the surface just minutes *before* the next scheduled TACAMO contact and risk "pop-up, pop-down"—putting up the vertical VHF (very high frequency) aerial with which *Roosevelt* could send a high-intensity "burst" message more quickly than from the slower "fishline" trailing VLF aerial. He would expose the HF aerial for no more than thirty seconds, then retract and submerge. Even so, the danger was that any penetration of the sea's surface could be picked up by Soviet satellite—not so much by the protrusion of the aerial itself but rather from discoloration or "ruffle" caused by the warm water envelope around the sub entering the surface temperature zone. Nothing could be done to prevent this warm envelope, the result of pumps having to continually cool the "coffeepot" or nuclear reactor, from rising to the surface with the sub. Brentwood knew that a Soviet satellite spotting the TD, or temperate differential, "patch" would give the Soviet Hunter/Killers the *Roosevelt*'s *exact* position rather than that reported by the Russian surface vessel that had attacked him. He could keep the *Roosevelt* deep to eliminate the thermal patching, but this would make him unable to use the VHF to ask for help. Any way he moved, it was risky.

In the meantime he decided to take her up halfway toward VLF depth, where any thermal patching would not be as recognizable via satellite and could be interpreted as local upwelling from one of the millions of oceanic springs venting from the sea floor.

In the quiet, redded-out control room the bulkhead was now beaded in flamingo-colored droplets of condensation.

He called for the chief electrician's mate in charge of the stern torpedo room and also for the next shift's sonar operator.

"Chief, I want you to get a MOSS. Here—" Brentwood showed him the drawing of the mobile submarine simulator. "Here, I've drawn a sketch of what I want you—"

"Sir!"

It was the hospital corpsman, looking worried. "We're going to have to deal with Evans. . . ."

For a second Brentwood thought Evans must be alive after all—awakening from a deep coma that they'd mistaken for death. Lord knows it had happened before. In the old days, navy regulations held that before placing a body in a canvas shroud, a stitch of catgut had to be made, passing the needle through the skin fold between the nose and lips—one of the most sensitive areas—to make sure the man was really dead. Dealing with Evans's corpse was the last thing Brentwood wanted to think about, but he knew the corpsman was correct. Modern-day regulations made it mandatory that a body which may be harboring infectious disease must be frozen as soon as possible and while "in this condition must be dispatched" no matter what the state of sea.

"Very well," Brentwood answered. "Ten minutes. Flag party astern." But he wanted no part of it. All he knew for certain was that Evans had died shortly after he'd given him the shot of diazepam. Worst of all, quietening him had done no good—the Russian ship having zeroed in on the *Roosevelt* anyway. Evans's death had achieved nothing but cast a pall of pessimism about the boat. *Roosevelt* was the world's most modern vessel, but a death aboard was as bad an omen to its crew as it had been for the sailors of Vasco de Gama and Columbus. For many aboard the sub who did not have the religious faith of their seagoing forebears, it was worse. Not a warning but a prophecy.

For Brentwood, Evans's death wasn't the first he'd witnessed at sea, but it was the first in his command, the first he was directly responsible for. During the Russians' attack, he'd forgotten about it, but now it returned with the corpsman and he felt it start to gnaw at him like an old childhood shame—a terrible thing said to one's parents, an act of deliberate cruelty to a family pet—like something one conceals for years now rising up from a hidden deep. It was not Evans's death alone that began eating away at Robert Brentwood but the sudden and totally unexpected loss of control he'd seen in the man—the putrid stench of the seaman's body the unmistakable sign of a body having lost all self-control. Brentwood was determined he would put it out of his mind, but as with so many things hidden under great pressure, the childhood fear of losing control wormed its way back to consciousness. Brentwood kept talking about the MOSS. To dwell on death, his father had told him, was a surefire way to self-pity, and then you didn't belong on a sub, you belonged on a couch. Couches, said the admiral, were places for people to escape from facing things head-on—the way some men went to sea to get away from their wives.

For a second Robert Brentwood thought of his brother Ray, captain of a guided missile frigate, who had been horribly burned after a swarm of North Korean missile boats had attacked his ship, the USS *Blaine*, off South Korea. Ray, it was said by some, had lost control, giving the order to abandon ship when it was still salvageable. Others said he hadn't given any such order—that one of the ship's mates had mistaken a hand signal from Ray in the inferno that engulfed the *Blaine*'s bridge movements after impact. Whatever had happened, Ray no longer had a command. And only now, three months and eight operations later, did the tightly polished skin, grafted from thigh and buttocks, even begin to make his face look anywhere near human.

As the chief electrician's mate and the next watch's sonar operator turned and walked away with his sketch, Robert Brentwood got tough with himself. He didn't agree with his father about a lot of things, including his view of psychiatrists, but he knew his father was right about the captain of a ship. He, Robert Jackson Brentwood, was supposed to be one of the navy's best and brightest, commander of the most powerful warship in history and his country's last line of defense. If he couldn't handle it, he should hand it over to Zeldman right now. It was time to bury Evans.

"Excuse me," he said briskly as he passed the electrician's mate and the sonar operator, who were also headed for the stern section with the sketch of the MOSS. Without turning to them, Brentwood ordered, "Don't wait until we finish with Evans. Get started on that right away."

"Be a bit crowded, sir."

"I know, but it can't be helped. They're still mopping up the forward torpedo room. I want it done in ten hours, well before the next scheduled TACAMO station."

The mate frowned, the red glow accentuating his baldness as his hand swept from eyebrows to the back of his head. "Sir, I don't know if we—I mean, we'll have to use a torch and—"

"Ten hours!" said Brentwood.

Sonar turned to the mate. "He's a hard bastard. Doesn't give a shit about Evans."

"Yeah, well," said the chief. "Nothing we can do for Evans now, is there?"

"The skipper needn't have given him that shot."

"Old man's call, Sonar."

"That's what I mean."

"Come on," said the chief. "Can't do the fucker by ourselves." For a moment Sonar thought the chief meant Evans. When they got to the machine shop and showed him the sketch, the machinist shook his head, pointing at the skipper's arrowed instructions with an oil rag. "No way, Chiefie. Not in ten hours."

"Why?" asked the chief, surprising Sonar.

"That shank," said the machinist, "is titanium-reinforced. Isn't a fucking wiener."

"What's the matter? I thought you were Mr. fucking 'Can-Do,' " said the mate.

"Can-Do," a big, gangly man from West Virginia, fixed Sonar in his stare. "What do you think?"

Sonar made a face bordering on neutrality. One of the ROs came over, asking where the captain was.

"Aft torpedo room, I guess," answered the Virginian.

The RO, who came from Utah and had only been aboard for one other patrol, was already known as "Mr. Clean" because of his pink baby-face complexion, despite him being in his early forties. He didn't like Can-Do's tone and bawled out the Virginian for wearing "booties," the yellow rubber shoe covers worn by men as they entered the reactor room so as to prevent transporting any radioactive dust throughout the sub. "Take those back to the reactor room," said the RO.

"Sorry, sir, I forgot," said Can-Do, giving the RO an "up yours" sign as the officer walked out into the ruby sheen of the passageway.

"Crack in the coffeepot," said Can-Do, reaching down for the yellow booties. "That's why he's so goddamned testy."

"Bullshit!" said the electrician's mate. "If the reactor had a fissure in it, we'd have a bright patch on our chest." Sonar craned his neck, looking down for any color change in his dosimeter.

"I don't mean the outer casing," continued Can-Do. "The inner wall."

"Christ—it's the strongest thing on the boat," said the mate.

"You telling me it's impossible?" asked Can-Do.

"Un-fucking likely," said the mate. "Anyway, keep it to yourself. You'll frighten young Sonar here."

Sonar was keeping right out of it, giving all his attention to the skipper's diagram, knowing he'd have to test it when Can-Do was finished—if he was finished in time.

As it turned out, the Virginian was wrong—there wasn't a fissure in the reactor, the officer was upset because he'd just heard Evans was about to be deep-sixed. The RO was a "mustang," a man who'd come up through the ranks, and he identified more than most officers with the enlisted men. He was also a practicing Mormon, and though he hadn't known Evans personally, he offered to help the burial party.

"Shroud has to be weighted heavily at this depth," Brentwood told him. "Don't want anything floating topside giving us away. Those Russians probably got a new noise signature from us after those depth charges. No good helping them to pinpoint our—"

"I'll look after it, sir," said the RO.

"Very well."

The officer thought Brentwood could have shown a little more sensitivity about Evans rather than simply treating the corpse as a nuisance to get rid of. It didn't jibe with what he'd heard about the skipper, who, among *Roosevelt*'s crew, was affectionately known as "Bing." Something to do with Bing Crosby was it?—maybe the skipper sang in the shower or something. But apparently the nickname had nothing to do with his love of old-fashioned music, "Bing" deriving more from his old-fashioned nature. Rumor had it that, knowledgeable as he was about the world of the submarine, he was, despite his engagement to some Englishwoman, extraordinarily naive when it came to the opposite sex. Mr. Clean had never discovered precisely why the crew was convinced of this, other than it had something to do with what the English called a "trollop," a woman of easy virtue, approaching him at some party in Scotland, and Brentwood, ever so polite, trying to gracefully decline her advances, whereupon the woman started screaming at him, calling him a straitlaced "old bastard"—a "Bing Crosby." Had the revered crooner from the 1940s held rigid views about premarital sex? Anyway, the RO didn't care whether the skipper was considered unpracticed in matters of sex. Maybe, in a world of AIDS, he was merely being careful. All the RO wanted to know was how good a sub captain the forty-three-year-old skipper was. Maybe his apparent lack of sensitivity as far as Evans was concerned might in fact be his preoccupation with the array of hard choices that confronted him if *Roosevelt* was to have any hope of survival. He saw the hospital corpsman walking down the passageway with what looked like two plastic garbage bags except for the glistening of the zippers on the body bags. Two of the men wounded in the depth charge attack had died.

Aboard the *Yumashev*, Captain Stasky was breaking radio silence. He knew that, slowed down as he was and with his general position probably known because of the explosions of the few depth charges that *had* worked, there wasn't much chance of the enemy not knowing where he was. But even if this were not so, Stasky knew it was his duty, regardless of his own safety and that of his crew, to inform Northern Fleet headquarters immediately that more than half the depth charges he'd dropped had been duds.

It was not merely for the sake of the safety of the other ships in the Baltic, Mediterranean, and Pacific Fleets, however, that Stasky ordered the coded message be sent without delay—but because of his own status as commander of a cruiser bearing the coveted white-backed red star with four black circles, the highest antisubmarine warfare efficiency rating awarded by the fleet commander. His own career was at stake.

Aboard the USS *Roosevelt*, six men crammed in around the torpedoes, their caps off as Robert Brentwood began the service, the men's faces showing the strain of the *Yumashev*'s depth attack on them, lines of tension etched deeply in their faces in the red battle light, several of the men gripping their blue baseball-style caps. Only the reactor room officer appeared calm, a serenity about him that Brentwood found more disconcerting than helpful, especially when, as captain, he was trying to present the coolest demeanor he could while reciting the age-old prayer for those killed at sea. At such moments, Brentwood, though he was the one speaking, often felt outside himself, more an observer, he thought, than a participant in the proceedings.

As he closed the prayer book, Brentwood nodded to the torpedoman's mate. The mate palmed the clearing control for tubes seven and eight. There was a dull thud, a gush of water like a toilet flushing, then a hiss of compressed air as the shrouds were shot out, the mate immediately venting the tubes, readying them to receive Mark-48 torpedoes. There were tears in Brentwood's eyes. He turned away and cleared his throat, then turned to the small clump of men before he left for the eighty-two-yard walk back to control. "Thank you for being here."

There was an awkward murmured response, one of the men, a yeoman, watching intently as Brentwood stepped over the sill of the watertight door, past the reactor room, heading into "Sherwood Forest," where the six Trident C missiles stood, their silos dwarfing their human controllers.

"Thanks for being here?" said the yeoman. "Where the hell else would we be? On Coney Island?" He glanced across at a young quartermaster to get his reaction. The quartermaster gave a noncommittal shrug. He was enjoying the show.

"He meant thanks for coming, you asshole," chimed in an off-duty planesman.

"I fucking know that," said the yeoman.

"Then what are you bitching about?"

The yeoman didn't know specifically, only that Brentwood's tears disturbed him. Perhaps Brentwood reminded him too much of his old man, a typewriter salesman, who'd always cut an imposing figure most of the time. A no-nonsense, strong type—a heap of quiet self-confidence—before computers. Too old to change, and sometimes he'd start thanking you for doing the simplest thing when it was your job. Got all weepy and scared the hell out of you—whole world seemed it would come apart and just swallow you up. It meant he was against the ropes about something—couldn't handle it himself anymore.

"Little things are important," the yeoman answered the planesman obliquely. With his old man, it hadn't been anything spectacular at first—nothing you'd really notice. Just a few drinks to begin with. Then a few pills to "calm my nerves." Then he couldn't get up mornings. Pretty soon he was incapable of making any important decision. "See your mom" became the cry. The yeoman told the planesman the scuttlebutt from the hospital corpsman was that Captain "Bing" had been white as a toilet, hand shaking, as he'd given Evans the shot. What the yeoman didn't tell the planesman was that his father had been scared shitless of needles too. And so was he. That's what was wrong—pretty soon his old man had started freaking him out too. The planesman dismissed the scuttlebutt. "Aw, shit—corpsmen always like to make things bigger than they are. Makes 'em feel important. Hell, I know plenty of guys who don't like getting shots. Go weak at the knees. So what? What do you want? Joe Montana?"

"Fucking right," said the yeoman.

"Then, buddy," put in a torpedoman, "you're on the wrong friggin' boat."

"That's what I'm thinkin'."

"Well—what are you planning to do about it?" the planesman said. "Swim?"

"Nothing you can do, is there?" replied the yeoman.

"For Christ's sake, you're making a big thing out of squat all."

"Listen, man. It's the little things that count. Right? Isn't that how they weed everyone out at the school? Guy panics for a second in the dive tank and he's out."

"Balls!" said the torpedoman. "Don't know anyone who liked being in the tank."

"Yeah—but you didn't show it, right?" pressed the yeoman.

"Hey," said the torpedoman. "I'd rather the guy running this boat show a little compassion than have some hard-ass Quigg."

"Who's Quigg?" asked the yeoman.

The torpedoman looked across at the planesman disbelievingly. "He doesn't know who Quigg was."

"So?" said the yeoman. "You gonna tell me?"

"You don't have to worry," cut in the planesman. "Bing'll get us out of this. He'll get us home."

"Yeah," added the torpedoman. "We'll be in Faslane before you know it." Faslane was the village for Holy Loch.

· "At five knots," said the yeoman, "it'll take a fucking year."

"Not to worry, yeo, we've got enough food to—"

"Fuck! You told us that before. We're crawlin' along like some fucking turtle and you're worried about goddamned chow. You can't eat yourself out of a HUK pack. Their goddamned Alfas are faster than we are."

The planesman slapped on his submariner's cap and, without another word, left the torpedo room, making his way forward, the torpedoman following.

"Time he had furlough," said the planesman, half-jokingly. "He's more goddamned worried than the old man."

"Not surprised," said a voice behind them. The planesman saw it was a two-striper, the young quartermaster, who'd been draped against the torpedo, his neat dark beard matching the dark, short-sleeved uniform that distinguished him from the rest of the *Roosevelt*'s crew. He'd been so quiet, they'd almost forgotten he was there.

"What do you mean?" the torpedoman asked.

"He had a girl in Glasgow," explained the quartermaster. "Killed in one of the rocket attacks."

"Better keep an eye on him then," said the planesman.

"Who?" said the quartermaster. "Me?"

"You seem to know all about him."

"Hell, I hardly know him."

It was one of the problems on the big pigboats—on any large vessel. Even though the seventy-day assignments meant they were together on the sub for forty days straight, with twenty-five days tied up alongside Holy Loch, some of the ship's company, working eight hours on, twelve off, never met. Often all there was to know about a man apart from his technical qualification was whatever the scuttlebutt happened to pass on, and that was notoriously unreliable. "Hell," said the quartermaster, "I don't even know myself." The other two laughed. They thought it was a joke.

"Come on," said the torpedoman. "I've got to report to the chief up in the machine room. Bing's got him working on some special rig."

"What kind of rig?" inquired the planesman.

"I don't know. All I do know is the old man wants it ready before the next TACAMO rendezvous."

"There'll be no rendezvous," said the planesman. "Any

of our E-6As come this way, the Russians'll blow 'em out of the sky.''

"I think maybe the old man knows that," said the quartermaster.

"Then how we going to confirm our position?" argued the planesman. "Either way, we'll have to go up with an aerial."

"If the TACAMO comes, we can use the floater," proffered the quartermaster. He meant the floating low-frequency wire.

"Still have to go up a ways," said the planesman. "Takes too friggin' long for data transmission. Russkies'll be waiting for that. We need a burst message—a lot of data—quickly. Tell us where the fuck we are and what's going on up there. For my money, that means sticking our UHF out of the water."

"That's no friggin' good," said the torpedoman. "They could spot that on SATCON. Our warm wave'd be too close to the surface anyway. They'd pick us up on the satellite's infrared."

"Satellite can't cover the whole ocean," said the quartermaster.

"They don't have to with us doin' three and a half knots," put in the planesman.

"Shit!" said the quartermaster. "I thought that yeo was a rain face."

"Ah—" said the torpedoman, "what the hell? We're probably worrying about nothin'—right?"

No one answered.

Walking into his cabin, Robert Brentwood drew the green curtains shut, tossed his cap onto its hook, and stood for a minute studying the map of the North Atlantic taped to the bulkhead above the safe. Three things worried him. First, the navigation computer was malfunctioning as a result of the last depth charge, so that unless he had a clear sky for a star fix, it was imperative the TACAMO aircraft make its rendezvous to give them their exact position. Even as the sub rose via slow and quiet release of ballast, feeling its way toward the surface to wait for the TACAMO, it was already drifting off position. Second, once *Roosevelt* began to move under power of the "switchblade" prop now sheathed in the forward ballast tank, the resistance caused by the towed array, normally of no consequence when the sub was at full speed, would decrease its five knots to three. He was bothered, too, by a seemingly unimportant incident—the fact that the hospital corpsman had interrupted him about Evans when he was giving his instructions about the MOSS to the electronics mate and sonar operator. It wasn't the corpsman's cutting into the conversation that bothered Robert Brentwood, but the anxiety behind it. That could spread faster than the flu that had killed Evans. Or had it? And could the orders he had given the mate and Sonar be carried out before the scheduled TACAMO rendezvous?

He depressed the intercom button for "Control" and told Zeldman to wake him two hours before the ETA of the TACAMO aircraft.

"Will do," came Zeldman's breezy reply. Before he lay down on the bunk, Brentwood took off his rubber sneakers, the reason for them—no noise shorts—bringing back Evans's terrified face. He tried to think of something else, but it wasn't easy. Civilians, he mused, always thought you got used to seeing death. Maybe you did on the battlefield. Maybe his youngest David, who had fought in Korea shortly after the beginning of the war, was used to it. And Ray—well, no one could hope to know what Ray thought anymore. The photos of David and Ray were on his desk in the antiroll gimbals mounting, as were those of his mom and dad and Lana. Lana was really the loner in the family, but he felt closer to her than any of them. Maybe it was because she was the second oldest of the four. What had happened to her since the spate she'd gotten into in Halifax? What had happened to all of them? It would be months before he would know—if he ever did—his ship crippled somewhere west of the mid-Atlantic ridge, and Soviet Hunter/Killers breaking out through the Greenland-Iceland-Norway Gap. If he was a betting man, he thought he would sit this one out. But fate had thrown the dice and he had no choice.

He lay back and pulled out Rosemary's picture from his shirt pocket. He had had it laminated with plastic in London. It was crazy, he knew, but if he went down forever—if he was to die in the *Roosevelt*—the thought of her photo eaten away by the salt, devoured by some shark or other blood-crazed denizen, bothered him. If anyone else saw it, they would just assume he'd laminated it for normal wear and tear. True, too. He kissed her, popped the photo in his pocket, and reached up for his Walkman earphones. They were cold and he held them in his hands to warm them. A dank, sour smell assailed his nostrils. He sat up, peeled off a sock, and sniffed—"Holy"—took the other one off, and, balling them, prepared to pop them in the laundry hamper at the foot of the bunk. The first one was a perfect basket. The next shot was to be the winning goal in sudden death overtime. Seattle and the Celtics, eighty-four apiece. It missed. An omen?

Don't be damn silly, he told himself, and plugged in the earphones. Rewinding the tape, he heard the high screech—like a torpedo closing. He stopped it, pushed "play," and lay back. There were a lot of "ifs" hanging about, but one certainty he'd been taught at Annapolis was that when you're the commanding officer, "there is no possibility of assist." You had to be alert, and that meant you had to get sleep. "Remember Montgomery," one of his instructors had been fond of saying. "Delegate authority until you're needed." You simply had to wait. He closed his eyes and listened to the timbre of Johnny Cash and "Sunday Morning Coming Down." Problem was, would they finish the MOSS in time for the TACAMO rendezvous? He was wide awake.

CHAPTER FIVE

AS A SQUALLY rain swept down from the North Sea over Surrey and Oxshott heath, Richard Spence, in search of Rosemary, pulled up the collar of his mackintosh and, be-rating himself for not having brought an umbrella, made his way uneasily along the sodden, slippery path, having to stop every fifty yards or so to wipe the condensation from his bifocals. In the fading light the shapes of the trees in the distance momentarily took on the shape of people, of what he wanted to see rather than what was there. Yet despite the foul weather, the pelting of the rain and the wind roaring through the big oaks, Spencé found the ferocity of the storm strangely comforting. Compared to the quieter but tension-filled atmosphere of his house, the often bristling animosity between Rosemary and Georgina and the silent, but pain-filled, determination of his wife trying her best to cope with the death of their son, the vicissitudes of nature seemed to him, if not more manageable, then the least of his worries. He felt bad for feeling like this, realizing that for the men at sea, like Rosemary's Robert and those on NATO's lifeblood convoys en route from Canada and the United States, the Arctic-bred storms would be met with less equanimity. But at least nature didn't come with a net of complexes woven about it; *its* moods were direct and unequivocal. With his daughters—who knew? Georgina's smile could mean the very opposite of her intent, Rosemary's bad temper with Georgina the very antithesis of her normal disposition.

He saw a figure on the path about a hundred yards away coming toward him, but whether or not it was Rosemary, he couldn't be sure. From the walk, it seemed to be a woman, all right, but she was wearing a scarf about her head, the wind taking the cloth to a sharp point like one of the sleek bicycle race helmets that had been so popular following the Tour de France in July. The Tour de France—he wondered if he or the world would ever see one again.

Whoever it was had her head bent down against the rain, facial features hidden by the collar of a dark coat, dark brown like Rosemary's or black, he couldn't tell through the smear of the rain on his bifocals, the sweeping curtains of rain increasing in their intensity. He heard a dog barking some-where nearby, but how close it was, whether it was anywhere near the figure, he couldn't tell, his hearing these days not what it used to be, the main reason they had rejected him even for the army's administrative reserve, relegating him instead to the home guard *auxiliary*. Not even the proper home guard, he thought wryly. In a way, it was worse than being rejected outright—a kind of waiting list of old crocks. Yet inside he felt the same as when he was fifty, and at times stood staring at the mirror in the morning, finding it difficult, except for the few streaks of gray in his hair, to believe he was in his late sixties—that the reflection looking back was him. Sometimes he felt like two different people.

It *was* Rosemary approaching, hands thrust deep in her

brown jacket pocket, scarf whipping hard in the wind like the defiant flag of a surrounded army, reminding Richard of the trapped British Army of the Rhine, which, with the Americans' Ninth Corps, was still reeling, trying to catch its breath in the Dortmund-Bielefeld pocket.

"Daddy—what are you—?"

"That boy Williams—" he said, his face scrunching under the impact of freezing rain.

"Wilkins," she said.

"He's tried to kill himself."

Her head shot up, rain-streaked cheeks making it impossible to see whether she'd been crying after the row back at the house.

"But—" she began, and stopped, realizing it must have something to do with her. Or did it? Perhaps the school had wanted to notify her because she was the boy's teacher.

"Rose—" Now Richard Spence faltered, throat constricting, the sound of his voice swallowed by the frenzied sound of the wind in the big, dark oaks. Instead of finishing what he had intended to say, he put his hand on his daughter's arm, turned her toward home, and began anew, his voice rising through the howl of the storm. "He left some kind of note apparently. The headmaster said the boy wants to have a word with you." Richard stumbled and had to stop again to wipe his glasses. "I didn't get any more details," he lied. "We were rather flustered, I'm afraid, and Mother was worried about you being out in this."

"Why on earth would he—" began Rosemary, but her words either trailed off or were inaudible to her father as they passed through a new onslaught of rain. She was already beginning to feel responsible for Wilkins, just as her father knew she would.

"I think . . ." said Richard, his eyes fixed on a branch bending dangerously. "C'mon!" he shouted, indicating the branch. "That's near breaking point." As they passed through the thick copse of alder before crossing the road, Rosemary felt his grip tighten on her arm. "I think the headmaster would like a chat."

She pulled her coat higher against the storm's rage, the wind's rushing now like an angry sea, and for a moment she was assailed by fear for Robert, and the realization that the real reason behind her row with Georgina was her growing conviction that she was pregnant. Suddenly she felt guilty about everything, about what she now judged to be her unwarranted retorts to Georgina—she should have dealt with it with grace. She felt guilty about giving Wilkins a Saturday morning and for what she knew was an unreasonable anger toward the boy, wishing, for a dark second, that he had finished the job—her Shakespeare class would be much easier to teach.

As they emerged from the wooded area onto the grassy knoll, she was thinking how Shakespeare wasn't necessarily a civilizing influence. What he did was to tear the wrappings of civility aside.

"You must understand," Richard was saying, "the boy was—I should say *is* . . ." She didn't get the rest of it and had to ask him to repeat it. "Clearly," said Spence, "the boy's very disturbed, and I don't want you blaming yourself."

Oh my God, thought Rosemary. It *is* something to do with me. He must have written something in the suicide note saying she'd driven him to it. She didn't feel she could face Georgina.

When they reached the house, she saw Georgina at the window as they started up the crazy stone path. Richard saw her, too, as she left the window to open the front door.

"Now," Richard cautioned Rosemary, "don't you two start, for goodness' sake."

Georgina was the picture of sisterly concern. It was genuine—which made Rosemary feel worse. If she was pregnant—the thought of telling her parents mortified her. Besides, with a world at war, she wasn't sure anyone should have a child. But then, she didn't see how she could ever bring herself to—

"Rose!" It was her mother, holding one hand over the phone, looking frightened from the kitchen. "A Mrs. Wilkins wants to talk with you. She sounds terribly upset."

"Oh Lord—" said Georgina sympathetically. "Tell her she's not here, Mother."

"Well I *am* here, aren't I?" snapped Rosemary, instantly regretting her riposte. And then something else flew into her consciousness, like a bat suddenly exploding out of a deep, dark cave in a storm. It was the realization that Georgina's beauty would unquestionably overwhelm Robert. Americans, she knew, were obsessed about large breasts, and Georgina was far better endowed than she. Like a Jersey cow.

"Hello," she said, unknotting the head scarf as she took the phone. "Mrs. Wilkins—"

Georgina saw her sister pale.

CHAPTER SIX

IN LENINGRAD'S IMMACULATE and cream-colored Nakhimov Secondary Naval Academy, whence he could smell the cold freshness of the harbor and see the historic cruiser *Aurora* tied up nearby, Admiral Brodsky watched the ruffles of wind racing over the surface of the Neva River, a burst of sunlight changing it from slate gray to Prussian blue. As chief liaison officer between the Northern Fleet, based in Severomorsk just north of Murmansk on the Kola Peninsula, and the Baltic Fleet, Brodsky seized any opportunity to visit the city, its czarist beauty so stunning that he had long ago decided that upon his retirement in another three years, he and his wife would move here when the Soviet forces were victorious.

Sitting by the second-story window facing the Neva, Brodsky had taken a break from signing the latest authorizations for merit-earned transfer for able-bodied soldiers and sailors who, after distinguishing themselves at the front, had been recommended for entry into the elite Fleet Air Arm.

One such applicant was Sergei Marchenko, a tank battalion commander whose leadership in the surprise, and massive, Soviet breakthrough at the Fulda Gap on NATO's central front had earned him high marks, as did his later performance when the "river of Soviet T-90s," as the Western press had called it, split into two, one stream heading south toward Munich to link up with the armored spearheads rumbling west from Czechoslovakia along the fertile Danube Valley, the other stream wheeling to the right of Fulda, racing toward Germany's Northern Plain. Here the Soviet divisions had smashed through to Schleswig-Holstein, capturing the vital NATO ports of Bremen, Hamburg, and Antwerp, and were presently closing the pincers about the trapped British Army of the Rhine and elements of the U.S., German, and Dutch armies. To Brodsky's displeasure, Sergei Marchenko's name had been submitted to Brodsky by his father, Kiril Marchenko, a senior advisor to the Politburo, and there was no doubt that on the surface the applicant clearly deserved the chance to join the air arm. But Brodsky had refused. There had been the problem of a slight deficiency in the vision of his left eye. Despite the fact that he wore corrective contact lenses, which had obviously been more than adequate for duty in the tanks corps, the Fleet Air Arm demanded twenty-twenty vision. Kiril Marchenko had appealed the decision, using Politburo letterhead, brusquely pointing out that if Adolf Galland, Nazi Germany's top air ace, could fly with only one eye, surely the Fleet Air Arm could accept a man with two!

Brodsky refused. Now Marchenko's father had written Brodsky again, a little more contrite, saying that the operation to correct his condition was available in Moscow's famous *vertyashcheesya kreslo*—"revolving chair"—clinic, recognized before the war, even by the Americans, as one of the best in the world.

Brodsky moved away from the window and returned to his desk. He paused, gold Parker in hand, his aide, a captain, entering the office impatiently but stopping abruptly when he saw the pen wavering above the authorization form. Kiril Marchenko was a powerful man, twice denied. Then again, the captain knew the admiral was right not to sign anything without ruminating on it. You could end up as latrine inspector in Mongolia, signing things in too much of a hurry; a general, or rather ex-general, whom both of them knew had lost his dacha in the forest of Nikolina Gora outside Moscow because he'd hastily signed requisitions for three large American freezers and four hundred pairs of imported British shoes for a unit that didn't exist.

When Brodsky did sign the authorization, he added a rider that, as per regulations, his permission for Sergei's transfer to Fleet Air Arm school was conditional upon written confirmation from the eye clinic that not only had the operation been performed, but it was *satisfactory*.

Brodsky wrote slowly, as if, the captain mused, he were creating a work of art for the Leningrad Museum.

The admiral sat back, admiring his work and recapping the pen. "No more transfer requests, I hope. Someone has to get NATO dirt in their contacts."

The captain smiled dutifully, though he didn't get the connection. Nor did he care; the message just decoded from the *Yumashev* was alarming. No more than 20 percent of depth charges—RBU rockets and drum charges alike—had detonated during an attack on what was believed to be a U.S. nuclear submarine.

"What class?" asked Brodsky.

"Sea Wolf Two, I think, Admiral. We're not positive, but time/speed calculations make it possible it is an American submarine out of Holy Loch."

Brodsky pressed him on this, for while the *Yumashev* was important, the location of forty-eight independently targeted reentry warheads was infinitely more pressing.

The aide unrolled the chart of the North Atlantic. "We've dispatched three Hunter/Killers to the area," he assured Brodsky.

"In two hours it can be a hundred miles away in either direction," said Brodsky, waving his arm, the weak afternoon sun reflecting off his sleeve's four gold rings.

"The *Yumashev* thinks it inflicted damage on the sub, Admiral. There was a dramatic change in the sub's noise signature following the attack."

The admiral grumbled, grateful for small mercies. If the *Yumashev* was correct, this information would at least narrow the search area. "Have we aerial reconnaissance on this?"

"A long-range Badger with fighter cover, sir. The only plane available at the moment. Later today we might be able to request—"

"No—we can't wait," said the admiral, putting out his hand for the *Yumashev*'s message. "If they think it *is* a Sea Wolf, I don't want any time wasted. Order in-flight refueling for the fighters."

"Yes, sir." The captain had already done this, knowing he could always rescind the order if the admiral hadn't agreed.

Brodsky's heavily lined face beneath the thick, black hair that belied his age became a scowl as he read the message, jaw clenched. "Where were—?"

The aide handed him a sheet of the buff-colored top secret forms listing all RBU antisubmarine warfare rockets and drum charges as a batch originating from one of the armament factories in Tallinn, the Estonian capital.

Brodsky was sitting back as if to get away from the information, shaking his head. He blamed Gorbachev, as so many other senior officers had. *Glasnost* and *perestroika* were responsible. Gorbachev had given the upstarts in the Baltic states economic independence when any fool could have told him this would soon amount to de facto political independence and give encouragement to the Baltic resistance groups, especially those in Estonia.

"Find them," the admiral ordered, handing the captain back the papers.

The captain was pleased. Estonians had always considered themselves a cut above everyone else. It came from being too close to the capitalist nations, which exported disorder along with their technology to the USSR's Baltic states. Time the Balts were taught a lesson.

"How many other ships are affected?" asked Brodsky.

"We don't know yet, Admiral. At least another cruiser and a squadron of destroyers out of Tallinn and Riga."

Brodsky looked out at the Neva; now it looked as cold as he felt.

"Bystro!"—"Quickly!" he instructed the captain. "We must root out this nest of Jews immediately."

Whenever there was trouble, it was always "nests of Jews" with Brodsky. Of Jewish extraction himself, the admiral considered it necessary to be harder on such "rebellious elements" than any other Russian would have been.

Five minutes later, the captain handed Brodsky the order for military intelligence assist. Brodsky intended to keep the KGB out of the investigation if he could; the GRU—*Glavnoye Razvedyvatelnoye Upravlenie*—the main intelligence directorate of the Soviet general staff—was more like family and would give him more control. He signed the order immediately. "Get to it at once!" he told the aide again. "This could be a disaster." He paused. "For us as well as those other ships."

The captain knew he meant both of them.

"I'll see to it right away, Admiral."

"And keep me posted on that Sea Wolf." He paused. "It has to be destroyed."

Within the half hour a coded "for your eyes only" five-group number-for-letter transmission was being relayed to Baltic Fleet headquarters at Baltiysk, near the Lithuanian port of Kaliningrad, which was also the headquarters for the Baltic Fleet's intelligence unit, which reported directly to the GRU.

CHAPTER SEVEN

IT WAS 5:03 A.M. on the graveyard—midnight-to-dawn—shift in La Jolla's Veterans' Administration Medical Center, where two nurses on the burn ward were trying to decide whether the information phoned in from New York by Capt. Ray Brentwood's father should be communicated to his son, who was on their ward. The older nurse, in her midforties, busy checking the medication trays, was for withholding the news until later in the day, after the daily assessments, including that of Ray Brentwood, had been made by the doctors on their rounds. The young nurse, on the other hand, not long out of college, argued that bad news should be communicated as soon as possible to a patient. "Quicker they know, the sooner they'll have to confront it. And overcome it," she said confidently, but the older woman, who had worked as a nurse's aide long before she'd become qualified as a fully trained nurse, regarded the younger woman's approach as typical of the college-trained nurses. They were all full of confrontation, "tell it like it is," encounter groups—mistaking forthrightness for professionalism. After many years on the job, the older nurse had come to believe that sometimes you had to keep the truth at bay, for a while anyhow—a lie if necessary. With all the daunting confidence of youth, the younger nurse stood her ground. "Sorry, I still think we should tell him. Be up-front about everything."

"Oh?" said the older nurse. "Then why'd you tell him he looked 'just great' the other day?"

The younger nurse thought for a moment. "I didn't."

"You did, honey. I heard you say it. You told him that the last plastic surgery was a 'terrific improvement.' I can't see any improvement at all."

"Well—that's—that's a subjective thing, I guess."

"Exactly."

"I still don't think you should keep something about his family from him. He'll probably get official notification from the Pentagon that his kid brother's missing anyway."

"Not for a week or so. Believe me. Washington doesn't move that fast."

"All right, you tell me—what's he going to think when he finds out we knew all along?"

"We don't have to tell him we knew."

"C'mon, Sue, by then he'll have read about it in the papers."

"About what?"

"You know—hand me that temperature chart, will you?—about how bad things are in Europe. About this Dortmund pocket or whatever they call it."

"Honey—there's nearly a million of our boys fighting over there. Ray Brentwood won't know where his kid brother was—until the War Department tells him. Even then, they're pretty vague about the area. They usually give the country, that's all."

The young nurse was flicking over the temperature charts, entering the readings into the computer, and wondered aloud what Brentwood's sister would do in the circumstances.

"Honey, she's back of beyond up there in the Aleutians. We're *here* and we're the ones making the decision."

"Regulations say you should tell them," said the young nurse.

"Regulations tell you you should use your discretion. Best judgment. That's what I'm doing."

The young nurse paused at the computer for a second. "Did I really say that? That he looked better?"

"God's my witness."

"Well, I don't believe in God. I'll have to take your word for it." She paused. "I guess we can hold off for a while."

"I'll tell him," the other one volunteered.

The younger one returned to tapping the temperatures into

the computer files. "Sue—is that true about his sister? About when she was in Canada? Did she really—?"

"Gossip."

"No—I'm not judging her. I think she was right—if that's what she did it for."

"Doesn't matter what she did it for. And if you don't want to end up back of beyond like her—don't you ever do it. It's easy, I know. You feel sorry for them. Nothing wrong with that, but we're professionals."

"I thought professionals were supposed to care."

The other nurse said nothing.

The younger one pressed, "You do believe it, then?"

The older woman pulled over three medication trays, took a tongue depressor, and began counting off painkillers to put in the array of paper portion cups. "All I know is Lana Brentwood was Little Miss Shy Shoes. Pretty brunette, the original Miss America figure, not too tall, not too short—'just right,' like they say in the nursery rhymes. Then, who knows? She married some bigwig, went to China, came back, and left her husband—or he kicked her out. Tried to hide away from the front pages, then decided to be Florence Nightingale. Next thing there's this rumpus over the young Brit, Spencer."

"Spence."

"Whatever. Anyway, she was lucky she wasn't court-martialed."

The young nurse saw one of the call lights go on. For a moment she thought it was Ray Brentwood and was much relieved when she realized it was the patient in the next bed over. "You sure know a lot about her. Where'd you pick up all that juicy stuff? Sounds to me like you've got her file."

"Gossip—well, she was in all the papers—over the marriage breakup."

"What papers? I never read anything in the papers about it."

The older nurse was blushing. "I don't know. Maybe the *National Enquirer* or something. Look—you'd better hop on down and see what Jensen—" They heard a torrent of abuse erupting from five rooms down on the west wing.

When she entered the room, the young nurse saw Ray Brentwood was awake, reading. He looked hideous—the night-light reflecting off the tight skin, stretched like pink plastic, blotchy here and there with dead spots. The eyes, having escaped the burn, appeared strange, fixed and protruding like those of a fish, but she realized it wasn't that anything was wrong with the eyes so much as the rest of his face, especially the nose—so horribly disfigured, off center, and pushed to one side—so that the eyes looked grotesque in their normalcy. She avoided their stare as she checked the frame that had been built over Jensen's bed, Jensen's burns being on the lower part of his body and, like Brentwood's, caused by the extraordinarily high temperatures from a ship's aluminum superstructure. While the light weight gave the modern ships more speed, the aluminum alloys were unable to sustain high temperatures. In the case of Brentwood's ship, the guided missile frigate USS *Blaine*, the white-hot superstructure, collapsing under the stress, tumbled into the fire of other explosions below, taking men down with it into the inferno of the ship's twisted entrails.

Brentwood was making a terrible piglike snorting noise as he breathed in. The young nurse pitied his wife and wondered how a woman, even with the best will in the world, could ever make love to a man after something like that.

"For Christ's sake!" Jensen cried. "Gimme a shot!"

"I'm sorry, Mr. Jensen. It isn't time."

Jensen was sobbing, and she wanted to tell him to stop it. It couldn't be that bad, she told herself.

"You'll be fine," she told him, and knew she was lying. He would be lucky to survive, and if he did, it would be a torture. He no longer had any genitals, and had to be constantly catheterized.

Brentwood's breathing was getting heavier. She hated it, asking herself why on earth she'd become a nurse in the first place. It had been a terrible mistake. But then, when she had been writing her finals only months before, the world had been at peace, and nursing a guarantee of a job. Now everything had changed. It was another world, one in which death and suffering on such a scale had been unimaginable to the young. The types of wounds she was seeing in this hospital simply hadn't been covered. Even automobile accidents paled by comparison. She remembered some professor in college assuring them that nuclear weapons had made world war "obsolete." She wished the fool could have been on the ward with her now, hearing, *smelling*, the death that hung about the night wards, giving her the creeps, like some obscene voyeur whose presence, though invisible, was palpable in the dark corners of the room.

CHAPTER EIGHT

THE SHARP BLACK peaks and volcanic sores of the windswept islands that stretched in a scythelike arc for over three thousand miles between Alaska and Russia first appeared to the astronauts like the emerald spine of some enormous exotic sea creature. There was nothing exotic about them for Lana Brentwood. From the moment she landed at Dutch Harbor on the northeastern end of tomahawk-shaped Unalaska Island, she thought there must be no lonelier place on earth. No wonder they called it America's Siberia.

Beneath the enormous steel-gray clouds of cumulonimbus that constantly rolled in over Makushin Volcano toward the narrow neck of the harbor, Lana saw a white dot bursting out from the fibrous sky that was mixed with steam coming off the sulfurous fumaroles of Mount Vsevidof on Umnak Island to the west. With unerring grace, the dot swooped down over the polished black clumps of kelp that washed in from the cold Bering Sea immediately to the north and from the Pacific to the south. She pulled the string of her parka hood tight against the bone-aching chill of late October and, stepping to the side of the road that skirted the forlorn haven of Dutch Harbor, fixed her binoculars on the bird. It was a glaucous-winged gull.

Two months before, the woman whose beauty had once gained her offers to model in New York and delivered her to a disastrous marriage with the tall, lean, and eminently successful Jay La Roche couldn't have told the difference between a glaucous-winged gull and any other of the hundreds of species of birds. But two months ago she had been a nurse, quietly nursing her psyche back to health after the trauma of her having left Jay. He was one of the high-flying conglomerate stars and chairman of the La Roche pharmaceutical and cosmetic empire, and his job had necessitated frequent business trips abroad. At first she'd been allowed to accompany him on his globe-trotting hops, from New York to London, Shanghai to Paris, and London to Melbourne, and at first she had enjoyed them. But then it soon became clear to her that Jay was combining business with a seemingly endless string of one-night stands.

Lana looked back now with a mixture of incredulity and self-loathing at how hard she'd tried to "accommodate" him—as he urbanely put it to her, in tones that made her feel nothing less than a country hick in the fast social world where the mores of an admiral's daughter seemed quaintly, even ludicrously, out of place.

At first she'd blamed herself, for her naïveté, for what Jay repeatedly reminded her was her "lack of experience." And she had blamed her parents for not having prepared her. It had taken her more than a year to realize that no one but a masochist could have prepared her for Jay La Roche, for whom a ménage-à-trois, which Lana would not participate in, was viewed as the least kinky of sexual preferences. Then one night in his apartment in Shanghai, just after his mother, whom Lana liked, had flown home from staying with them, and the servants were on their night off, she was trapped. She had seen how his mother's visit had put enormous pressure on him. Instead of being able to spend his days and nights whoring—he was always very careful to have the boys as well as the girls examined by his bevy of highly paid physicians—he'd been forced to show himself at home in the evenings, his stable of sexual partners quarantined in the luxurious surroundings of the Jinjiang Hotel. He told Lana he wanted her. She asked him why he didn't go to the Jinjiang. "No," he'd replied. "First, I want you." Twisting her hand till she was on her knees, he told her, smiling, his gray eyes glistening, "You don't understand, do you?"

"No," she said. "I don't." When she wouldn't let him urinate on her, as part of his latest complex ritual, he tried what he screamed at her was the "slut stuff," beating her so badly, it had nearly killed her. She vowed it would never happen again, thinking that now there was more than infidelity as a reason for leaving him, she was finally free. That no court in the land would refuse a divorce. But Jay's money and influence, she discovered, could fix that, too. He told her he'd contest any divorce.

"Why?" she had cried, or rather mumbled, through her swollen lips, sobbing, "You hate me. I hate you."

"No you don't," he told her arrogantly. "No matter how much you think you hate me, I was the first, baby. That counts for something. Forever."

She managed a contemptuous smile, not normally part of her repartee, the taste of blood metallic in her mouth. "*You're* not the first."

"You lying bitch!" He had her by the throat, screaming that he'd kill her, but now she didn't care. It was too indescribably awful to go on.

"Who was it?" he demanded, shaking her, throwing her to the floor.

"I'm not telling you," she gasped.

"Was it that fucking pilot?" he shouted, shaking her so violently, her head felt like a rag doll's.

It was the bravest thing she'd ever said to him, and she believed later that the only reason he hadn't killed her was that he was making so much noise about it, screaming and smashing everything in sight, that one of the wealthier Chinese playing at mah-jong and losing badly in one of the other penthouse suites complained to the police.

By the time the Chinese police arrived—two men in a motorcycle and sidecar—Jay had the minister for trade on the line, and the two policeman left with a dozen cans of Coca-Cola each—eight days wages. Lana still had enough courage to be scornful. "You think you can buy off a divorce with Coke?"

"With *Coke*," he said, turning the pun back at her, "I could buy Jesus Christ!"

"You're sick."

He unzipped his fly and, pouring Scotch on it, walked toward her. "Listen, you little daddy's whore, I could buy your chicken-shit daddy, the admiral, if I wanted. Don't you push me. I could have a dozen Chinks up here in a flash— all testifying you'd sucked them off in Tiananmen Square. I can buy anything in this country, and don't you forget it." His voice rose as he kept coming toward her, waving the Scotch for effect. "I can buy anything in any fucking country. *Cunt*-tree. Get it?"

Lana had sat cowering from him, but now she merely looked away in her revulsion. He was mad. And she knew if she looked at him now, he *would* kill her. He pushed it into her face, slapping her with it. "You try to divorce me, pussy willow, and I'll drag so much shit in the papers that your mommy and daddy won't show their faces outside their little fucking house. Understand?"

She didn't answer.

"Understand?" he bellowed. "And your fucking brothers'll be the fucking joke from here to Peoria. Got it?"

She was terrified.

"I can't hear you," he taunted in a singsong voice.

"Yes," she said very quietly.

"All right, you bitch. Now open your mouth." She wouldn't.

"You want Daddy and Mommy in trouble? And how about you? You want to end up a friggin' monster like that brother of yours?"

Her gut turned. She knew he was right. He *could* buy anything. It was childish to imagine anything else. He had bought half of Shanghai, and party officials from the Bund to Beijing. They were all in his pocket.

"Hey!" He grabbed her hair, shaking her violently. "I *own* half the tabloids, sweetheart. And I can buy the rest just like that—" He tried to snap his fingers but failed. Against all caution, in spite of her terror, or perhaps because of it, she laughed.

He had his hands around her throat again, pushing the thumbs hard up into her. As she gasped for air, he jammed it into her mouth, thumping her head against the wall, screaming again how he could ruin her, her family, how he could do anything he wanted. She thought of Frank Shirer, the pilot who had taken her out in Washington before she'd ever met Jay La Roche. They'd made love, but it hadn't been good—her first time and painful beyond belief—but Shirer had been kind the moment he realized he was hurting her. She could see him now, the pale blue eyes, quick yet serene, the eyes of one of the navy's top guns, of a man who wouldn't blink at danger, she'd thought, but a man who was warm and loving. And funny. He'd put on the "nuclear" eye patch that he'd kept since his stint as one of the pilots of Air Force One. It had frightened her at the time, but now she clung to the memory of it, so different it was from the horror of Jay in her mouth. Frank Shirer, wherever he was, was as different from Jay La Roche's type as you could imagine.

Suddenly La Roche's whole body shuddered violently, smacking her head hard against the wall, and then, breathing laboriously, satiated, he stumbled back from her, turning, his back to the wall, sliding down, eyes closed. "I love you," he said.

The terrible thing was, she knew he meant it. She ran to the bathroom and vomited.

Early in the morning, his eyes bleary from drink, he staggered from the bedroom, picking up a spilled bottle of Scotch on the way. She could tell from the way he paused to pick it up rather than kicking it out of the way as he normally would have that he was entering his magnanimous "let's be reasonable" phase—his "must," as he called it, now expended.

Still half-drunk, standing unsteadily in the bathroom doorway, his shirt out, his reflection reeling, disappearing from view in the mirror, his body reeking of deodorant, sweat, and booze—so powerful, it seemed to engulf her—he told her, his tone of magnanimity as revolting to her as the sight of his spent body, "If you don't want to stay with me, okay. But—" he used the bottle as a pointer "—don't you ever try for a divorce. You're mine."

No matter how much she had rinsed and washed her face, she still felt dirty. "So you want a respectable front," she said bitterly, holding an ice pack to her jaw.

He nodded. "So? That's what we all want, isn't it? A front. You don't know who the hell *you* are."

Lana wanted to say something about his mother—of what she would think if she knew the real Jay La Roche—but instinctively she refrained. It was too dangerous. He was offering a deal. Best to take it while she could. "All right," she said. "But I'm going back to the States."

He walked slowly away from the door, stopped, and came back, bottle of Scotch still in hand. "Lana!"

She cringed, her flesh turning cold and clammy, with the sensation of something reptilian crawling over it. She knew what he was going to say. She could tell him not to say it, but to do that would only drag the whole thing out. It was easier to go along, let him play it out, then he'd leave her alone for a few days, if past performance was anything to go by—enough time to pack and make the arrangements. "What?" she asked sternly.

"Love you, babe."

It was a different man speaking, but she despised the supine, ingratiating tone as much as she hated the psychopath who'd attacked her like an animal.

"Hear me?" he pressed, his voice even, modulated—as forgiving as a father making up with a child after a bad day.

"I hear you," she said without turning around from the sink.

"Look at me, babe!"

She stared up at him, lost in the mystery of how it was that she had ever been attracted to him. But of course, then he had been someone else. He met her stare and did not avert his eyes from the burning hatred he saw in them.

How could she ever begin to explain to anyone about the disaster that had been her marriage? She had told no one, not even her friends among the nurses she'd worked with in Halifax before her exile to the Aleutians. And certainly not her parents. All they knew was that "things hadn't worked out." Certainly she had never gone into any of the sordid details with anyone, and only in her letters to her older brother, Robert, somewhere on duty in the North Atlantic, had she hinted at anything like the full horror of it all.

"Can't you work things out?" her father had asked. "Your mother and I—well, we've had our tiffs now and then. But you don't just get up and—"

"No!" she had told him. They couldn't work things out. And that was that. There was no one at Dutch Harbor she could talk to, no one in whom she could confide. There was the padre, of course, but she was only a nominal churchgoer and, at least for now, couldn't bring herself to resurrect the things she wished exorcised.

She began walking back to the base. At Dutch Harbor, the lights were twinkling brightly against the cold, blue twilight, and beyond, the cloud cover was lifting. The isolation and boredom of the place would have been more bearable if the weather were not so foul, so unpredictable. It wasn't unusual for rain and snow driven by gale-force winds to sweep down from the Arctic and then the next minute to see clouds rent by the sun.

Her job so far had been to assist in making an inventory of medical supplies throughout the Aleutian Chain, and had it not been for the Unalaska–Alaska flights, the boredom would have been overpowering. Keeping to herself, she had not made any really close friends either here or in Halifax, except William Spence, the young British sailor, when turmoil had enveloped her again. Or had it really? Was her life more the consequence of her own actions than she was willing to admit? Was she what her father so disparagingly called "one of the world's willing victims"? Was there something deep in her psyche that sought to purge itself by seeking out the worst as a form of punishment? Did she enjoy the "heroic" pain of the victim as an athlete takes secret pride in the pain of the effort? How else could she have possibly become embroiled with the young Englishman, a boy really, who was to die before his twentieth birthday? His loneliness, she had thought, was there for anyone to see, and surely it had only been fate that had put her on the ward aboard the hospital ship when the big Chinook choppers brought young Spence in, hands bloody stubs which had to be amputated following a savage Russian Hunter/Killer attack on the British and American convoy hundreds of miles north of Newfoundland.

When he was first transferred from the chopper to the hospital ship as one of the most seriously injured from HMS *Peregrine* and one of the first casualties of the Atlantic war, he was simply that—another casualty—and one who, despite the double amputation, was given a fair chance of survival because of his youth. Then the oil-caused pneumonia—which so often lay undetected in a man's lungs for several days before it was discovered, when it was too late—began racking Spence's body, depleting his strength so quickly that the earlier prognosis for recovery suddenly changed. In those last desperate days, thousands of miles from home, Lana knew it was not at all unusual for a patient, especially a young man, to transfer to her all the adoration he might have given the woman he would have loved, had he lived. Like so many before him, in war or not, the intensity of William Spence's feeling for his nurse could be understood only by those who, like him, had lain in the morning hours in that death watch between two and four—who had known the chilling fear that soon they would be no more and who wanted nothing more than a human touch, to reassure them there was hope when there was none.

When the morphine ceased to work, the pain so intolerable that it shamed his manhood and he wept like a child, she drew the sheet down below his waist, unpinned her hair, letting it fall down on him, lips closing about him, her tongue enveloping and drawing him into her own ecstasy until it was his—in the way she had learned from Jay in his gentler honeymoon incarnation period. Was it possible that out of Jay's evil came good? And for that she was banished to "Devil's Island," as Dutch Harbor was called by the Waves. She told herself she no longer cared. She had helped a young man confront death, given him pleasure before the ultimate obscenity claimed him, and no matter how sordid a thing they would make of it behind her back, she knew she had been right and that they would not break her on this island or any other.

As Lana turned around, heading back to the thirty-bed hospital, the blue light changed dramatically. Invading masses of bruised cumulonimbus cloud swept in from the western sea, where the warm Kuroshio Current and the Bering Sea collided to produce the towering thunderhead storm clouds. It was the unmistakable signal that the 124 islands strung along the 3,000-mile arc were about to be hit by yet another *millimaw*, the name given to the wind storms by the Aleuts who had lived on the sparsely vegetated and forlorn islands even before the *promyshlenniki*, the Russian fur traders who had settled the barren but sea-rich volcanic outcrops over two hundred years before.

Lana watched the seabirds driven landward by the approaching storm—yellow-tufted puffins, their bright white faces and rust-red beaks atop the black bodies irrepressibly happy-looking, and always bringing a smile to her no matter how depressed she felt. But even in the abundant bird life, from cormorants and fulmars to kittiwakes, she saw pain and battle. Where others reveled in the wildness of the place, she yearned for the quiet life—not boring but the kind of life she had experienced in Nova Scotia while based in Halifax, doing what now she felt she did best, looking after others, hoping not only to help them bear their pain but to escape from her own.

The truth on Unalaska, however, was that to date there had not been much work to do. The island's main function was twofold: to provide safe anchorage in Dutch Harbor for the U.S., Japanese, and Korean factory ships from the storms that plagued the nutrient-rich fishing ground off the Aleutian Trench, and more important, to serve as a depot between the handful of American bases. As depot, its primary responsibility was to Adak Island Naval Station and tiny Shemya Island, which few Americans had ever heard of and which, being the most western extension of the United States, possessed an air force station and was, as all the interceptor and transport pilots knew, the most heavily armed piece of real estate in the Western world. If ever the Russians moved against the United States' western flank, Shemya Island and Adak, the big submarine base 360 miles eastward, would be more strategically important than Midway Island over five hundred miles south had been in World War II. The island, which, like England in the Atlantic, was in effect a United States forward aircraft carrier to the Soviet Union, was not something Lana Brentwood had given much thought to, for one's own world had a way of dwarfing world conflicts that were supposed to dwarf one's own. Besides, neither she nor anyone else believed the Russians would be so foolish as to head eastward and try to use the island arc as a stepping stone to America's back door through the Alaskan and the Canadian West Coast.

The millimaw was moving in fast, and by the time Lana reached the hospital, snow flurries mixed with rain were swept in by the millimaw at over ninety miles an hour, the rain and snow striking the Quonset huts horizontally, the only place in the world, the transport pilots told Lana, where such a phenomenon occurred. All around she could hear the beginning of the ''Aleutian wail,'' which some bureaucrats in Washington, over four thousand miles away, thought was ''Aleutian whale'' but which was the peculiar beating and howling sound of the millimaw on the sheer basaltic cliffs and treeless slopes of the islands. She could see the double-glazed windows in the Quonset huts as square orange eyes staring out from the bleakness. Unlike the native Aleuts, some of whom still lived in their underground sod houses or *barabaras* and who eked out a living subsisting on reindeer and seafood, Lana knew she would never get used to the place. Were it not for the VCR and the big high-definition TV screen they had at the recreation center for the three thousand inhabitants of Dutch Harbor, she believed there would be many more cases of severe depression—to date, the most common complaint at the base hospital.

Some of the men, most of them pilots, had attempted to alleviate their boredom by trying to date her, but she had refused most. Despite the gentleness she'd experienced with William Spence, after her experience with Jay La Roche, she was still leery of men, especially when she discovered that the confidentiality of her naval file, which had spelled out the reason for her banishment, had been breached. They obviously thought she was an easy lay.

The only exception she had even thought of making was a pilot, Lieutenant Alen, who regularly flew the resupply route to the big antisubmarine base on Adak halfway along the chain and on to Shemya and Attu loran station over 420 miles farther west near the international date line between the United States and USSR. He had asked her if she had wanted to go along for a ride to see Attu. She'd said no, but he wasn't one to be deterred, and this night as she walked into the officers' club, she saw his boyish grin.

"Can I buy you a drink?" he asked, brushing the snow off her collar.

She felt awkward. "Yes," she said. "Hot chocolate. If that's all right."

"One hot chocolate coming up." Alen ignored the guffaws of several pilots farther down the bar. Handing her the steaming mug, he asked her if she'd changed her mind about a flight—this time to Adak.

"Not particularly," she answered, not wishing to be rude but having already seen as many of the forty-six active volcanoes in the chain as she intended.

"What's the matter? You haven't got a sense of history? Big battle there in forty-three. Banzai attack by the Japanese. Just kept coming against our boys."

"Now *they're* our boys," she said.

"Well, sort of—"

"Last I heard, they're supposed to be on our side," she answered.

"Support capability. Escorted our troop ships to Korea. But they're crafty. Tokyo hasn't actually declared war on the Soviets. Or China."

"If they're supporting us, aren't they on our side?"

"What I'm saying is, they haven't pulled out the stops. Not even with the North Koreans hitting a few of their west coast ports. Economically they're more powerful than most, but they need oil, raw materials. If that stops, Japan stops. They want to alienate as few countries as possible."

"Sounds like a bit of a high-wire act to me," said Lana.

"It is. Come on, come see Adak. Your brother's on a pig-boat, isn't he?"

She didn't know whether he meant Ray or Robert.

"Sub," he explained.

"Oh, yes. He is."

"Then it's your patriotic duty to see Adak. Cheer the boys up. Big sub base there."

"I was going to watch the new movie tonight."

Alen shook his head. "There isn't any."

"Lieutenant," replied Lana, "I heard it announced this morning. Some new Jane Fonda movie."

"It got lost."

She glanced across at him, shaking her head. "You guys. You never forget. She apologized, you know—to the Vietnam vets."

"No, she didn't. She said she was sorry if she upset any of them. She didn't apologize for *what* she said. Still Hanoi Jane."

"That was a long time ago, Lieutenant. Anyway, I heard Vietnam might come in on our side—if China goes up against us."

"No one knows what China'll do," said Alen. "They don't like the Russians any more than we do. Anyway, to hell with it. Let me take you to Adak." He lowered his voice and smiled. "Maybe we can stop along the way."

She hesitated. "I'm still married, Lieutenant."

"Why don't you use your married name?"

"Because I don't like it and it's none of your damned business." She realized for a second that she would never have talked like that before she'd known Jay. He'd taken some of her civility along with her innocence, and she hated him as much for that as for anything else. And she'd been taught not to hate anyone.

"Sorry," said the lieutenant. "You're right. It's none of my business what name you—"

She didn't want to say any more, but something bottled up inside her kept rising. "You think I'm an easy mark?"

Alen's eyes avoided hers, his gaze now shifting out, looking at the swirling snow. "Yeah, I *did*," he conceded. He looked back at her. "I was out of line." He walked away and opened the door, to a howl of protest from the bar, greeting the icy wind.

"Lieutenant?" she called.

He turned, shut the door, hand still on the handle, flecks of snow in his sheepskin collar. "Yes?"

"Maybe some other time," she said.

"Sure."

When he left the Quonset hut, Lana felt drained; a conversation like that with a man these days was harder on her than the hospital's night shift. She always thought she'd be able to handle it better after knowing Jay, but her confidence had been so badly shaken by him, it penetrated any brave front she presented.

Arriving on the ward, she was told the head nurse wanted to see her. A rush of apprehension took hold of her. The last time a head nurse, the "Matron" in Halifax, had wanted to see her, it had been the disciplinary hearing about Spence, followed by exile to the godforsaken islands. Lana already felt guilty as she made her way around the potholed blacktop of the quad to the head nurse's station on the first floor, snow melting the moment it landed on her cape, the thought that each snowflake in the world was different comforting her. To date, the head nurse at Dutch Harbor had given no sign that she was a dragon, like Matron, a prune-faced, portly woman who acted quickly to dampen high spirits the moment anyone looked like they might possibly be enjoying themselves, if such a thing was possible on the Aleutian bases. Still, Lana knew that all head nurses, by bent of their responsibilities, were usually sticklers for rules and regulations, and as she entered the Quonset hut, she was trying to think of which one she'd violated. The clock above the reception desk showed she was five minutes late for her shift.

"I'm sorry," she said, "but the snow—"

The head nurse waved her apology aside and gave her the notification from the Department of the Army that her kid brother David, a member of a rapid deployment force, was missing in action—"somewhere" on NATO's central front.

They all thought she took it very well. The truth was, however, that as much as Lana wanted to cry—crying for her having always acted as a tranquilizer—she couldn't, for the simple fact was that she and David weren't that close. At twenty-four, being the youngest of the family, David hadn't seen much of Lana, who, though she hadn't finished college because of Jay, was in her third year when he was still in high school. There was simply too big a gap between them, so much so that they hardly ever wrote to one another, the only news between them passed on by her mother and father in his letters home before he'd been wounded. Yet in other families, different ages didn't seem to make a difference. Why was it? she wondered. Was it because of her father, a kind enough man but of the old "when the going gets tough, the tough get going" school? The boys had always been dissuaded from wearing their emotions on their sleeve. Or had it to do with their expectations, the difference of what they each wanted in life so disparate, David in political science before he joined the marines, she in the jet set world of Jay La Roche. Perhaps the lack of communication on David's part had more to do with his disapproval of Jay La Roche. He had said nothing about her leaving La Roche—whether it was desertion or disapproval, she didn't know.

As she walked back from the head nurse's station and into the ward, she felt as if she were suddenly in a goldfish bowl. Everyone clearly knew about her brother missing—how did news travel so fast?—expecting the gung ho "I can take it" exterior. It was a strain accepting the condolences. She felt smothered by everyone's sympathy, wishing they would just go away. She wanted to be alone, away from the island, a chance simply to sit, think for herself.

She dialed the pilots' quarters.

"Lieutenant Alen please?"

She heard whistling at the other end of the line and ribald laughter. She almost hung up, but he was on the line. His voice reminded her a little of Frank Shirer. From the noises she could hear in the background, he was taking a ribbing about talking to her, but he was polite, clearly refusing to be suborned by the grunts of the macho pack in the background.

She paused for a few seconds. "I don't know your first name," she said with some amazement.

"That's all right. It's Rick."

"When are you scheduled to go to Adak?"

"In the morning. Oh five hundred."

"Kind of early."

"There'll be a break in the weather then—or so they say."

"Okay, but if I come along, I'll have to be back for the dog watch. You think that'll be a problem?"

"No problem at all. Ah—Lana?"

It was the first time he'd called her by her first name.

"Yes?"

"Sorry about your brother."

"Thanks."

When he got off the phone, Alen stiffened his right arm from the elbow up, slapping his left hand hard down on the bicep, driving the rigid forearm into the air. "In like flint!"

There was a chorus of encouragement: "Way to go!" and someone yelling, "Rick the dick!"

He grinned boyishly, and immediately felt ashamed.

"Better strap her down, Rick. Could be a rough ride."

Everyone wanted to be copilot, but the assignments hadn't changed—nor had the forecast for a break in the cloud cover around five in the morning.

"Gobble, gobble!" shouted a navigator.

That night Alen slept fitfully, but he didn't worry. Sometimes when he was bone-weary, against all common sense, he got so hard, it felt like steel. The only thing that worried him was that if she touched him, he mightn't be able to wait. The closer it got to the 0400 preflight call, the more relaxed and sleepy he became. When he did doze off, he was in a dream—the plane on automatic pilot, the commanding officer of Adak now bawling Alen out for his violation of orders—bringing a Wave on a "goddamned joyride" in the middle of a combat zone. And Alen with no pants on, telling the CO that Lana was merely fulfilling the requirements of her posting—putting in at least thirty hours as required by Waves for the purposes of ATF— air time familiarization—which the pilots called "air time fucking." Alen also pointed out Washington's rationale—that in the event of the Aleutians being attacked, the Waves would have to help the pilots ferry back the most seriously wounded to either Dutch Harbor or beyond to Anchorage in Alaska, and yet the only flight time most of them had was on the civilian flight from the lower forty-eight states.

At 0407 on the morning of October 17, Alen was feeling so thick from lack of sleep, it took three cups of coffee to pump him awake. The weather report was holding, though in the "caldron of storms," as the volcanic Aleutians were called, the projected rise in barometric pressure could very quickly disappear. When he got to the fogbound airstrip, the latest weather posting, only an hour old, still called for clearing. But Lana was nowhere in sight.

"Come on," said the copilot, "let's go."

Alen looked plain miserable as the AC-130 E Hercules' four turboprops sputtered to life, throwing off curls of exhaust into the pea-soup morning. He glanced anxiously at his watch. The most he could delay on preflight recheck was ten minutes. And the weather was getting worse.

"Goddamnit!" said Alen, looking past the copilot at the fog-shrouded runway. "C'mon, c'mon! What the hell's she doing?"

"Checking her diaphragm!" shouted the copilot.

CHAPTER NINE

COMING IN AT eight hundred miles an hour on the vector given him when he left Cornwall, the sea a wrinkled bluish slate racing backward beneath him, Roger Fernshaw altered trim, heard the Jaguar's target-lock-on tone, and fired one of his two Exocets.

The *Yumashev*'s radar saw the blip of the Jaguar's Exocet but lost it thereafter in sea clutter echo. Fernshaw, monitoring the head-up display, itself monitoring the side-scan and umbrella radar feed, glanced at the sky above—white cumulus and breaking. A Russian pilot's radar that, technically speaking, might pick him up wasn't Fernshaw's major concern, however, for he was flying so low, trained in the dangerous twisting and turning low-level runs through the glens of Scotland, that he was initially "on the deck," forty feet above the waves, where the Jaguar's image would hopefully be lost in the sea clutter blanketing any active radar signals beamed his way.

Firing the second missile fifteen seconds and forty miles after the first, Fernshaw was still safely beyond the Russian cruiser's best thirty-mile-range Goblet surface-to-air missiles. As he began his turn, doing visual as well as instrument checks, needing height to complete the maneuver, he momentarily took himself out of the clutter. He saw a wink of red against the cobalt-blue sea, most likely the first Goblet leaving the cruiser. For a moment he was struck by the perverse fact that if the twenty-foot-long Russian missile had been upgraded with boosters for a fifty- or even forty-five-mile range, he would be, as his American colleagues in Cornwall were fond of saying, "up Shit Creek without a paddle." The count for the Exocet missile was now down to thirty-one seconds, and while his radar lit up with Goblet and other AA ordnance opening up at him, the Exocet feed stayed live. At seven seconds Fernshaw saw an orange wink on the horizon blossom, then fade, and on his channel scanner he was picking up excited Russian chatter, presumably radio traffic emanating from the cruiser itself. He didn't see his second missile hit the cruiser, and scribbled "P/D" on his knee pad, indicating a "probable" or "dud." He also noted that the seven-second gap between the time the Exocet should have impacted the cruiser and the time it actually did suggested the Jaguar's ground crew should do a computer overhaul of the fire control system as soon as he returned.

The Exocet hit the *Yumashev* abaft the starboard beam and below the head-net C radar aerial, the second missile's explosion gulped by the inferno of the first, though striking farther back in the deck housing below the headlights' radar, which only minutes earlier had been tracking the incoming Jaguar. The damage to the cruiser's superstructure would have been much worse had the missiles been better spaced, for much of the second missile's impact was in an area already hit. Even so, the Exocet's explosion, on the waterline, well below the head-net aerial, effectively gutted the cruiser, sailors suddenly sucked out from what only moments before had been warm, watertight compartments, their bodies, like so much flotsam, pouring like stunned fish into the ice-cold Atlantic. Only a few of those in the water showed any signs of life as their comrades in the rescue squads threw out the tethered Malvinsky raft-drums, the halves of each container opening in the shape of an ugly mouth into tent rafts whose blossoming was like enormous orange flowers on the heaving surface of the sea.

Forty miles to the northeast, the two Soviet Sukhoi Flagon-Fs accompanying the long-range Badger dispatched by Admiral Brodsky had seen the blue line of the Jaguar's Exocet as it streaked at deck level toward the sub-chaser *Yumashev*, but the Sukhois did not leave the Badger. Although capable of a dual role, as a medium bomber and maritime reconnaissance aircraft, the Tupolev-16 Badger, with a maximum speed of 615 miles per hour, was ill suited to go it alone in any seek-and-destroy mission against the reported American Sea Wolf. It badly needed the "in-flight refueled" Sukhois to guard its flanks, and its captain knew that whether or not the two escorting Russian fighters would be called upon to fire their weapons would depend entirely on the pilot of the Jaguar. With the NATO fighter almost certainly approaching the end of its fuel-pod-extended radius of one thousand miles, the Badger's six-man crew were making wagers as to whether the Allied pilot would engage them in an effort to take out the Badger's twenty-thousand-pound load of sub-detecting air-launched sonobuoys, MAD-magnetic anomaly detection—gear, and its free-fall ordnance of air-launched depth charges and torpedoes.

For Pilot Officer Fernshaw, however, seeing three Russian aircraft on his radar screen, a decision about whether or not he would attack them was more difficult than they could imagine. The problem was the fighting in Europe. It was going badly for the Western Allies, the half million British, American, and German troops trapped in the Dortmund-Bielefeld pocket surrounded by a steel ring of six hundred T-90s pounding away at them with laser-guided 135-millimeter armor-piercing and high-explosive shells. In the air of sustained crisis in the Allied camp, the decisions being forced upon Whitehall for all British combatants as far down the chain as individual pilots like Fernshaw were often as confused as they were urgent. SACEUR—Supreme Allied Commander in Europe—headquarters, Brussels, was now reporting to England that if all available NATO air cover was not marshaled in defense of the Dortmund-Bielefeld pocket, then NATO's shriveling central front would cease to be and trip off full-scale collapse all along the German front from the North Sea to Switzerland.

Accordingly, in Whitehall, the minister of war, bearing what Washington called the "big picture" in mind, advised the headquarters of all United Kingdom air forces, in Wycombe, and Royal Navy Commander, Western Approaches, that if a pilot was confronted with the choice of running low on fuel in pressing an attack, thereby risking the loss of his aircraft, he was to exercise "discretion." What this meant to Fernshaw and others like him in the "Highways Department," as the STOL—short takeoff and landing—Jaguar arm was referred to, was that if Whitehall, the Admiralty, or the Royal Air Force didn't like the decision you made, you would be up another creek—and smartly at that. At the same time, the Admiralty was arguing, "wherever possible," attacks to protect the SSBN/SNs must be pressed home *"at all costs."* And Fernshaw knew their reasoning was sound, for if Germany was lost, France would fall, and with it the vitally needed ports for NATO, making resupply from America impossible. Then the SSBN/SNs and the relatively few Stealth bombers would be left as a mobile deterrent. On the other hand, a single Jaguar, its superb fly-by-wire avionics making it one of NATO's best ground-hugging, close-support fighters, could knock out ten times its number in tanks.

Normally Fernshaw, his plane entering thick stratus, wouldn't have found the decision a difficult one to make, but like so many of the other outnumbered Allied pilots called upon day after day, night after rain-sodden night, to rise from carrier England and stem the "surge" tactics of the Russian air forces, Fernshaw was exhausted. Fatigued from having lost twelve pounds in a week due to the wrenching G forces, he wasn't sure that the decision whether or not to engage the Badger and its outriders was a case of weighing military priorities or a plain old-fashioned matter of funk versus guts. He headed for cloud.

Both the Russian leader, front right of the Badger, and the second Sukhoi to the Badger's left rear and higher, covering his leader's *konus ranimosti*—"cone of vulnerability"— spotted the Jaguar climbing fast, forty-three miles ahead. The Russians' confidence with the two-to-one advantage was further boosted by the fact that their Sukhoi Flagon-Fs' speed—up to 2.5 Mach should they go as high as thirty-six thousand feet—was much faster than the Jaguar's 1.6 Mach. The sun was also behind them, and no matter how sophisticated the electronics of the Anglo-French plane's fire control and weapon-aiming computer were, the sun in your visor was still a distinct disadvantage. In the millisecond world of fighters so fast they could outstrip some of their missiles, direct sunlight, Polaroid visors notwithstanding, could produce *oslepitel 'nost'*—"glare-out"—on the dials.

The Jaguar was climbing hard and fast into high-piled

cumulus, the Russian leader glimpsing the Jaguar's round-chisel-shaped nose, telling him he was up against a state-of-the-art British-Ferranti weapon-aiming system. But he had no clue as to whether the British pilot was going for "high ground" in cloud cover to attack or to escape. The Russian pilot, knowing that radio silence had been broken earlier by the cruiser's transmission to Soviet Northern Fleet head-quarters, switched on, instructing his wingman, "Stay with Mother. I'll *sbiyu*—'knock off'—our friend in Heaven."

With the wingman acknowledging, the leader's Flagon, now approaching the same height as the Jaguar 40.1 miles away, hit the Turmansky afterburner. In straight vertical climb, the wings' flash in sunlight gave the fighter beauty as well as the aspect of pure power as it rocketed five thousand feet in less than ninety seconds, giving the Russian a ceiling of eleven thousand should the Jaguar be contemplating an attack after all. If the NATO fighter was carrying a second Exocet on one of its hard points, then the Badger and the two Sukhois would now be within range. Everyone, except pilots, the Russian pilot knew, thought electronic warfare had made modern aerial combat little more than a superfast computer game. The fact, however, was that there were so many variables, from sunlight and weight of ordnance to a bird looking like a fighter for a fraction of a second, that machines couldn't do it all.

Now the Jaguar, forty-six miles away, invisible in cloud but a clear blip on the Flagon's "Skip Spin" intercept long-range radar screen, was heading nor'nor'east—toward south-western England. But this could well be a feint.

Leveling out, the Russian pilot saw a faint orange ball in the cloud. He banked fast left, until he realized the orange ball and the others like it were decoy flares the Jaguar was jettisoning as protection from heat seekers. The Russian pushed the select button for one of his two air-to-air Amos "actives," flicked the cover, and fired, watching the missile streaking, at over a thousand meters a second, toward the Jaguar over thirty miles away, its radar-seeking head pro-gramed to ignore infrared signatures, going instead for the enemy's own radar pulse. Then the Russian pilot saw his own warning radar screen go to fuzz, the Jaguar obviously drop-ping chaff to jam the Amos's radar guidance. The Russian fired both of his heat-seeking AA-3s.

Fernshaw saw his warning lights flashing frantically and

heard the "Bogey" tone. His Jaguar perilously low on fuel, the Sukhoi engaging him with a three-hundred-miles-per-hour speed advantage, Fernshaw knew that unless he dropped his extra fuel pod to gain more speed, he would not escape. He released the external pod and shut off all radar, heading higher into cloud, noting his fuel consumption rapidly increasing in the thinner air, and the three Russian missiles closing.

Seeing the Jaguar's drop tank tumbling, reflecting like foil in the sun, the Russian leader shut off his active radar in case the British pilot had tried to be clever, going high to fire off a radar seeker of his own. The Russian banked sharply to his left, ordering his wingman to stay with the Badger and both of them to go as low as possible to evade the western approaches' long-range over-the-horizon radar. He then went to radio silence, leaving only his channel scanner turned on. Within a second his radio surged—the panic-stricken voice of the Badger's observer—and in a flash he knew what had happened. The Jaguar had outfoxed him, shutting off its radar, doubling back in the cloud rather than running, while he, the Russian, had been looking for the Jaguar up ahead.

Immediately the Russian went into a tight turn and dove, his nose starting to bleed profusely in the G force, the Badger already under attack, the Jaguar passing on its forward right side four miles away and firing its remaining Exocet at the big, droning maritime reconnaissance plane.

. With the extra speed afforded by the release of the fifteen-hundred-pound Exocet, the British fighter, its twenty-eight-foot six-inch wingspan six feet shorter than the Sukhoi's, was in its classic tight turn, coming in fast behind the second Sukhoi, whose pilot was now breaking right and, in an effort to beat the Jaguar at its own game, fired a cluster of six 120-pound Aphid passive heat seekers, which would ignore all radar signals, homing in only on exhaust. At eight hundred miles per hour, the Aphids were twice as fast as the oncoming Exocet, but their best mode of attack, because they were heat seekers, was rear entry. They needed to do a U-turn, but it was too tight.

They missed the Exocet, but two of them had now locked on to the exhaust of the Jaguar itself as the British fighter, completing a turn in a sound barrel of rolling thunder, passed behind the Badger, the tracer from the Badger's top turret ceasing for a split second as the Jaguar flashed past the airplane's three-story-high tail. The 23-millimeter cannon in the Badger's radar-guided rear turret, however, was still firing even as the Exocet slammed into the plane's starboard exhaust flange, the explosion blowing the plane in two, the tail assembly tumbling more slowly than the forward section, whose engines, or rather, the red-hot mass that had been the twin Mikulin turbojets, plummeted like a rock, the entire section upside down, cockpit intact as it slammed into the sea, disintegrating in spumes of steam and spray. Yet before it had gone down, the half-second burst from its radar control rear turret had strafed the Jaguar, the fighter's cockpit now whistling, the splintered Perspex and metal fragments from the demolished HUD screen disintegrating in the hail of the Badger's 23-millimeter cannon. The Jaguar was shuddering violently, yawing to the left. Fernshaw thought he must be hit but wasn't, his double-ply flying suit and visor protecting him from the peppering of the instrument panel's debris. But he couldn't see for several seconds. At first he thought it must be his visor scratched to a fog, but then he could smell electrical fire, realizing that the fog was smoke. He fought for control, but too many of the fly-by-wire microcircuits were blown. He felt the plane's nose drop suddenly, glanced at the altimeter but couldn't see it through the smoke, guessing it had been shot out anyway. Elbows tucked in, he took hold of the yellow and black zebra-striped hand grips. The bolt release fired. Icy air was roaring about his helmet. He prayed he was at least five hundred feet above the ocean. Smoke gone, he could now see he was at least a thousand feet above a sharply inclined slab of white-veined blue that was the sea.

He could spot only one of the Sukhois—a silver dot miles to the east. Then he thought he saw the second one, but it was only the hapless Hormone chopper several miles away hovering helplessly above the wreckage of the *Yumashev*, rescue harness extended, picking up survivors as Fernshaw struggled to crawl into the orange one-man tent raft.

CHAPTER TEN

HALF A WORLD away in Unalaska's Dutch Harbor, the woman in the jeep coming out of the mist toward the howl of Lieutenant Alen's Hercules was not the Wave Alen was expecting.

"Where's Lana?" he asked the Wave sergeant.

"Lieutenant Brentwood can't make it, sir."

"She sick?"

"No, sir. She's sorry, but Voice of America is doing a special report on the NATO front. She's hoping to pick up some more news about where her brother's division might be."

"Oh—" said Alen, trying not to show his disappointment. "Well—thanks for coming out and telling me." The Wave appeared not to hear him, or was she asking another question, one hand holding down her cap, the other cupped about her mouth against the howl of the Hercules' four props.

"So?" yelled the copilot to Alen. "What d'you say?" Alen was looking blankly at him. In his disappointment he hadn't been paying much attention to the Wave sergeant, and there was an awkward moment before he realized that she was asking if she could take the flight to Adak. Unconsciously Alen was letting his eye rove over her body. The Wave outfit was just about the sexiest uniform he'd seen on a woman—the snappy navy cap and the tunic that, whether or not the designer had intended it, had easily sailed through the sea changes of fashion, emphasizing the bust by trying to camouflage it.

"Sure," said Alen. "O'Sullivan, isn't it?"

"Reilley," she corrected him. "Sergeant Mary Reilley."

"It's Irish anyhow." Alen grinned. "Welcome aboard."

The tall, gangly engineer in his midtwenties from Texas whom they called "the Turk" for a reason no one could figure out was asked to make sure that Sergeant Reilley was strapped in tight. The two-hourly weather adjustment was for millimaws and more of the fog that one minute would obliterate the brutal majesty of the far-flung volcanic islands and the next be blown asunder by a millimaw, replaced by driving rain, snow, and hail all at once.

As the Hercules took off—all by instruments because of the fog—Alen banked quickly, taking the C-130 E, with twenty-one tons of food and electronic supplies for Adak, well away from the hidden and towering mass of Makushin Volcano. The sixty-seven-hundred-foot-high mountain rising immediately west of Dutch Harbor on the northern end of Unalaska was now visible only on his radar. Mary Reilly was asking the engineer on her helmet's flip mike whether or not it would be possible for them to "hop across" from Adak to Attu Island. She had been told a "horror story," she said, of how in World War II over fifteen thousand poorly equipped American soldiers, trained for desert warfare, had been sent in against a smaller but much better-trained and dug-in garrison of three thousand Japanese troops. Turk said he didn't know much about that war. "All I know, ma'am, is that the Japanese are our allies in this one."

Reilley, voice straining against the background noise of the Hercules, was asking him another question, but she kept forgetting to depress the talk button. She couldn't believe how much noise military planes made compared to civil aircraft. The Turk was just sitting there watching her lips move, which would have suited him nicely, but he didn't want to be rude and pointed again to the talk button.

"Oh, yes, sorry," said Reilley. "I heard they—I mean *we*—thought the Japanese would use the Aleutians as kind of—you know—stepping stones to the United States."

"They did," cut in Alen. "They attacked Dutch Harbor, middle of forty-two. Wanted to sucker our Pacific Fleet up here—what was left of it after Pearl Harbor. Course, they thought *we'd* use Attu and the other islands as stepping stones to *them*. You're in a very strategic area, Sergeant—"

"Call me Mary."

"Okeydoke, Mary."

"I'm surprised that the Russians haven't tried something up here," she said.

"They will," Alen answered. "When they're ready. Those sons of—" He paused.

"Bitches," she said.

"Yes, ma'am. Well, they've got their hands full right now."

"I dunno," countered the copilot. "What I hear is, they're doin' pretty good in Europe."

"Maybe so," said Alen, "but Ivan's tricky, man. They could still decide to go for it up here—try our back door. Sure as hell take the NATO heat off their western front."

"Russkies don't like two fronts," said the copilot. "That's what I heard."

"That's it," said Alen derisively. "Fight the last friggin' war. Sure way to lose this one."

"That where Lana's kid brother is?" asked Turk.

Christ, thought Alen, glancing over at the copilot. The Turk could always be depended on to open his mouth and screw everything up. Just when they were impressing big-chested Mary, Turk had to shift the conversation to another woman.

"Yeah," said Alen quickly, "he's somewhere over there."

"He's trapped in the Dortmund-Bielefeld pocket," said Mary.

"You sure know a lot about this war," said Turk ingratiatingly. Alen didn't mind—at least they were back talking about her.

"Not really," said Mary.

"Shit!" It was the copilot, his exclamation followed by a dull thump on the fuselage. Instinctively Mary pulled her head back. There was another. "Fuck—sorry, miss. Damn seabirds." Their dark blood and gizzards, splattered on the Hercules' windscreen, went into long, spidery, scarlet webs under the pressure of the head wind, the Hercules' air speed now at four hundred miles per hour. Despite the increasing turbulence, driving the birds into the aircraft, the big transport with its twenty-one tons of cargo and a maximum fuel load of thirty tons, loaded at Dutch Harbor to save refueling from Adak's precious store, was heavy enough to minimize the rough ride. Even so, the impact of the birds had given the Wave a bad fright, and Alen quickly and adroitly steered the conversation back to her knowledge of the war in Europe. Nothing like praise to calm the nerves.

"Heck," said Reilley bashfully. "I don't know that much

about it. It's just that Lana and I work the same shift and—
well, when she talks about her brothers, she keeps me up-
to-date, I guess—''

"How old is he?" asked Turk.

Oh, Christ! thought Alen. There he goes again.

"Oh," said the Wave, "David's in his early twenties, I
think. He's been around, though. He was in Korea first—
with Freeman."

Turk let out a low, respectful whistle.

"Well," interjected Alen impatiently, "if he's fought with
Freeman, he's a survivor. I wouldn't worry about him."

Mary Reilley was nonplussed by Alen's remark, a tone of
condescension in it, but for whom—David Brentwood? Because he, Alen, hadn't yet seen combat? Or was it disdain
for Freeman? Freeman was one of Mary Reilley's heroes in
a world where it was no longer fashionable to have heroes,
especially not military ones. To his troops, the general was
known as George C. Scott, for, like Patton, Freeman had
proved himself daring and, to many, insufferably brave. Convinced of his mission—to "drive back the Mongols," as he
put it, by which, his critics charged, the general meant anyone not born in either "the old British Empire" or "the new
American one"—Freeman had given America its first, and
so far only, good news in the war. As now, aboard the Hercules, whenever his name was mentioned, it evoked powerful emotions and left no middle ground. The media especially
was divided into those who hated to say anything good about
him and those who loved saying anything bad about him. But
on one point, as Mary Reilley pointed out, there was una-
nimity: he had turned things around in Korea.

"Yeah," agreed Turk. "We were damned near in the drink
over there."

Alen interjected that it was kind of "strange" for a nurse
to like a combat general, adding, "I heard Freeman was the
first general on our side to use women in combat. That
right?"

Mary said nothing. The lieutenant was starting to get on
her nerves, his comments less questions than taunts against
what he obviously thought were her "butch" sensibilities.
Hell, thought Mary, it wasn't her fault Lana couldn't make
it.

"That right?" pressed Alen. "Chopper One in the Pyongyang raid was flown by a 'skirt'?"

"You want to be in combat, miss?" asked Turk, looking puzzled.

"*I* don't want to be in combat, but heck, if you can do the job, what difference does it make whether you're—"

The next two thuds on the fuselage interrupted her. "But I mean if we're outnumbered by the Russians, and we are, then—"

The next instant she was flattened out, arms pinned hard back against the fuselage, her mouth gasping like a stunned fish. Turk was gone—out of the flapping, gaping hole where his monitor console had been—and there was a long, bluish light in front of her, fluttering like a silk scarf—a tongue of high-octane flame—and above it a roaring, then all about crashing sounds as the crated cargo shifted and came adrift, crashing through its webbing straps, the Hercules now in a spin, the suction tearing at her, ripping open her tunic, the icy blasts so powerful, she felt as if her nostrils were burning. Alen slumped in his seat, the copilot shouting, "Mayday! . . . Mayday! . . ."

Wreckage from the Hercules was found sliding up and down the swells about fifteen miles north of the smoking Okmok Caldera, a volcanic cone on the eastern end of Umnak Island 130 miles west of Dutch Harbor. In a feat of oceanographic skill unmatched since the Howard Hughes–CIA "Glomar Challenger" retrieval of a sunken Soviet Golf-class submarine in the 1960s, a U.S. Navy two-man submersible, flown in from Valdez over nine hundred miles away, located the black box from the Hercules.

As well as the hard disk recording of the chitchat between cockpit and the unauthorized Wave passenger, the USAF investigators flown in from Anchorage were able to agree that the transport had been operating under normal procedure. The radar, the black box showed, had been on, but the investigators noted that in the heavy fog, no doubt exacerbated by wind shear conditions from the approaching millimaw, an error could have been made by either Lieutenant Alen or his copilot in interpreting the blips occurring on the radar. Most of the blips recorded on the radar strip were confirmed by thumps faintly discernible on the sound disk; thus it appeared that whatever it was that had struck the Hercules, passing through the engineer's position, could have been mistaken for yet another seabird approaching—possibly a royal albatross. These big birds had a seven-foot wingspan and were easily capable of giving a very distinct blip on the plane's high-definition radar.

This explanation by the USAF investigators was accepted by the Dutch Harbor board of inquiry, particularly as meteorological reports from the small settlement of Nikolski on the western end of Umnak Island confirmed that quake tremors, registering 4.6 on the Richter scale, and intermittent volcanic activity from the seven-thousand-foot-high Mount Vsevidof on the western end of the island had been recorded. Volcanic activity in and about the Okmok Caldera, at the eastern end of the island, was suspected as boulder-sized rocks thrown up, even at subsonic speed, by either volcano could have easily doomed the aircraft. An act of God.

Even so, the commanding officer of Dutch Harbor was severely reprimanded for having allowed the unauthorized flight of Sgt. Mary Eileen Reilley, and the officer commanding the Wave detachment, Maj. Brenda Sharp, was named in the issuances of an upcoming naval inquiry as an "interested party." In navy parlance this meant that because Major Sharp had not signed a piece of paper, her career was effectively finished. For this, as well as for Sergeant Reilley's death, the major in her turn held Lana Brentwood directly responsible. The scuttlebutt—and now the gossip was much cruder and harsher than before—was that Brentwood had jerked off some Limey back East, had been sent to Siberia, and had now screwed up the Wave CO, and done in an NCO while she was at it. The advice given every new arrival to Dutch Harbor was "Stay away from Lana." She was unlucky.

The bodies from the Hercules were never found, no surprise to the fishermen who worked nets from Dutch Harbor to Amchitka or anywhere else around the seven-thousand-foot-deep Aleutian Trench. The Bering Sea was a protein soup, from the tiny plankton whose diurnal migrations cluttered your sonar to the big killer whales. If you were dead or couldn't move, you were feed—and quickly. In any event, Unalaska Coast Guard requested that any fishermen working the waters off the steaming black sands of Okmok Caldera should immediately report any debris they found. The coast guard was upbraided by SOWAC, the local Status of Women

Action Committee, for using the word "fishermen," and it issued the request for "fisherpersons" to assist.

As it turned out, one fisherman, Pete Bering—who was erroneously claimed by the locals to be a direct descendant of explorer Vitus Bering—and his crew were working the waters off Umnak but had been well off the southwestern tip of the island the day of the crash. As it might be a week before Bering had his boat's hold full of pollack and he could head back toward Dutch Harbor a hundred miles east of him, Bering radioed the coast guard to say that while he and his crew of three had heard a plane overhead, they'd been in heavy fog and so hadn't seen it go down.

CHAPTER ELEVEN

WHEN THE BROODING gray mountains of cumulus shifted above Unalaska, there were moments of stunning wild beauty—the United States' wind-riven bases in the Aleutians changing suddenly from fog-shrouded bleakness to a cold but clear sky, an expanse of Arctic turquoise that in a moment seemed to clear the mind of island fever. At nightfall the lights of Dutch Harbor would take on a sparkling quality in the pristine Arctic air, reminding Lana Brentwood of the summer nights as a child in the Sierra Nevada, of the days before the war when the whole family would go camping. The days had been hot and dry, the nights getting colder, just before Labor Day and the start of the new school year.

Those nights came back to her now as she went for her evening stroll on the road leading from the bluish cold of Dutch Harbor. She could smell the coming of winter in the air and instinctively pulled her Wave's parka about her, the Quallofil lining sighing as it collapsed, a sound that brought back memories of a favorite red down jacket her father had

given her. Things had been so predictable then, the sad end
of summer, the anxiety-veined anticipation of the new school
year, and a new jacket from her parents. Most kids took
jackets as standard fare, but her father wasn't an admiral
then, and on a captain's pay, with the three boys and her to
put through school, a new jacket was something to celebrate.
Later, when she married Jay La Roche, a mink coat was no
big deal, but now at least she didn't have to fear Jay anymore.
The world might be at war, but she wasn't—at least not with
him—and save for her brief encounter with the horror of
battle wounds she had seen when caring for young William
Spence aboard the hospital ship on the East Coast, the war
was a long way away from Unalaska.

She knew that with the western tip of the Aleutian chain
pointing toward Russia's Kamchatka Peninsula, her feeling of
isolation from the war was in fact very much an illusion. The
big Soviet missiles on Kamchatka pointing toward the United
States were countered by the United States' missiles on Shemya, which, despite its small size, was the most heavily armed
place on earth. Its missiles were only minutes from the Russian
mainland. Lana offered up a silent prayer to any power that
might exist that so long as the war remained CONHITECH—
in the jargon of the strategist, conventional high-tech war—a
war in where there might still be a chance that all would not
disintegrate, killing millions, suffocating the earth, reason
might yet prevail in the madness. She pulled the jacket more
tightly about her, the very chill of the thought of nuclear holocaust adding to the chill of the Arctic front.

If the war did go nuclear, then pray she'd go in the fireball
and not suffer the horrible, lingering death of radiation. The
thought of her hair falling out in clumps was more terrifying
to Lana than all the other horrible possibilities, like those
that had afflicted Ray, the burn on his face making him a
walking nightmare so that even his children could not find it
in them yet to look straight at him. According to the last
letter her mom had sent her, Ray's appearance was changed
again. Whether it was the eighth or ninth operation, Lana no
longer knew. And despite their mom's assertion that Ray was
looking "better and better," Lana saw no change in the photograph, an awful, polished plastic sheen instead of a face of
real skin that made it look like a tight mask, its stretched-
skinlike quality not diminished by the prints, which were not
glossy but matte-finished. Lana wondered whether her moth-

er's use of mattes instead of glossies was a deliberate attempt
to delude herself of the reality: that with all the magic of laser
and plastic surgery—and it was magic in what it could sometimes do—Ray would never look normal again. She was surprised that Beth and Ray were still together, with him a virtual
prisoner in La Jolla's Veterans' burn unit outside San Diego,
and Beth up in Seattle with the two children. For a moment
Lana was jealous—at least they were together in the way it
mattered. An old line from her favorite movie came to her,
and she could see Katharine Hepburn alone and lonely in
Venice and counseling a beautiful blonde who was complaining about her husband, "Don't knock it, cookie. Two's the
most beautiful number in the world." Well, it was if the other
one wasn't Jay La Roche.

Because she hadn't confided in anyone, especially her parents, she sometimes felt that her mother thought she expected
too much. But all she wanted was a marriage like Beth and
Ray's—not perfect by any means, but built on bedrock, not
on shifting sand. Or was it bedrock? Could it ever be? Perhaps Beth wasn't confiding in anyone either—keeping it bottled up inside and caged by pride. At least Beth would have
the children. Jay had wanted them, a son especially, but his
violence took care of that, too, and induced a miscarriage in
Lana. He'd got mad about that. As usual, that was her fault,
too, but—God forgive her—she had seen it then and saw it
now as a blessing, not to herself but for the child who would
have grown up with Jay—a nightmare that Beth, with all her
troubles, didn't have to contend with. Perhaps Jay would
change? No, she thought, he wouldn't.

The Humvee's horn startled her, and she stepped smartly
to the shoulder of the road and turned to see the driver.

"Lieutenant Brentwood?" It was a sergeant from Dutch
Harbor HQ. "You're wanted back at the base, ma'am. Commander Morin's request."

"Requested or ordered?" Lana asked, though she didn't
really care, her sharp tone merely one of fright.

"He didn't say, ma'am."

"It's all right, Sergeant," said Lana, moving around to the
passenger side. "I'm not going anywhere. Just out for my
daily constitutional."

"Yes, ma'am. Pretty soon you're gonna need more than
that anorak."

Jay La Roche still on her mind, Lana read more into the

sergeant's comment than he meant. They didn't call the Aleutian's "America's Siberia" for nothing—it felt like exile, the need for companionship, for women, ever greater than was usual for a military base. And for some, like Lana, who'd committed an infraction against the rules, the Aleutians posting was meant to be an exile, a punishment, and with your punishment came your file: "Severely reprimanded for conduct unbecoming an officer," in Lana's case. Would it have been unbecoming, she thought wryly, for a noncom nurse to have given young Spence the comfort of sexual release? There had been a lot of jokes in her wake about the "unbecoming" bit, but by now she was used to it. At least she'd developed an armor against the more vulgar suggestions and leers of men who had been given the choice of Unalaska or permanent latrine duty at Parris Island or Camp Lejeune. After what her brother David had gone through in marine boot camp at Parris Island, Lana could well understand why some chose the blustery isolation of the Aleutians. And now, David was God knew—

She turned on the driver. "Is it about my brother?"

The sergeant was pumping the brakes on a patch of black ice and shifting down so the truck roared. "What's that, ma'am?" he shouted.

"Colonel Morin—has he got news of my brother, David?"

"No idea, ma'am. All I was told was to come and get you."

She felt cold now in the pit of her stomach. What was so urgent that on this godforsaken island in this godforsaken chain, the base commander had sent out a Humvee for her? It was either David or Robert. Or was it their parents? Perhaps all of them. It couldn't possibly be—

"Ma'am?"

"Yes?"

"Can I ask you something off the record?"

She nodded—not sure whether she should have.

"You ever go out with enlisted men?" asked the sergeant.

"No."

"Just thought I'd ask."

"I—I'm sorry. I didn't mean for it to sound like that—it's not—I don't go out with anyone, Sergeant." Oh, Lord, she thought, now they'd say she was a lesbian. No they wouldn't—not after young Spence and her conduct "unbecoming an officer." Or maybe that wouldn't make any difference? From the men's point of view, up here, any woman would do. Even so, she hadn't meant to offend the sergeant. "I didn't mean to sound—"

"S'all right, ma'am. I understand."

No you don't, thought Lana. Now she was confused in her anxiety over why she'd been sent for. She desperately wanted reassurance, her old fears suddenly resurfacing; a feeling of vulnerability and fright combined overwhelmed her. She wished Shirer were here. What she wouldn't give for a man to hold her, to love her. Not sex, not to start with anyway. Just to be held. As she watched the light fading from Dutch Harbor, the hills around the base took on a chilling blue aura, at once beautiful, ethereal almost. And threatening.

"You wanted to see me, Commander?" asked Lana, trying to read in his face what it was all about before he spoke.

"Yes," answered Commander Morin. "Close the door, will you, Lieutenant." There was another man in the Quonset hut—a fisherman by the look of his rough white Cowichan knit sweater, its bald eagle wings in full span across the man's barrel-shaped chest. At first glance he gave the impression of being overweight, but Lana realized it was probably the oilskins covering his considerable frame that gave her the impression.

"Lieutenant Brentwood," said Morin, a small, stocky man, his height in marked contrast to the considerably bigger man, whom he introduced as "Mr. Bering," Bering's wild salt-and-pepper beard framing a time- and wind-ravaged face.

Bering reminded Lana of the prewar magazine *Alaska Men*—maybe it was still being published. In Alaska, men, outnumbering eligible females three to one—now five to one with the troops stationed there—had advertised in the magazine in the lower forty-eight states for prospective mates. Bering had a burly, honest look about him, clearly undaunted by the unfamiliar military surroundings, though it wasn't the kind of location she would expect to find him in. He looked born to the sea. Lana wondered why the man, in his late thirties, perhaps early forties, and fit-looking now that she saw him closer, wasn't in uniform until Morin introduced him as a "crabber." Shellfish meat from the Aleutians was now in ever-higher demand in Japan and the United States, with Japan's fleet of shellfish trawlers unable to break out north of Hokkaido Island into the fishing grounds of the vast

North Pacific because of the Soviet sub blockade that extended from Vladivostok to Kamchatka Peninsula. Without the American fish supply to Japan via Hawaii, and the long southern route around the sub packs, Japan would soon be in the same position as Britain had been when Hitler's U-boat blockade threatened to bring that country to its knees. All the Soviets had to do was delay the food supplies to Japan as effectively as they had interfered with the NATO reinforcements across the Atlantic—close the ring for another twelve weeks—and the equation of men and matériel would shift decidedly to the Soviets' favor. Then there would be no way out, except nuclear, and that was no way at all.

Morin was asking Lana how well she knew Captain Alen. She was sitting, feeling too bulky and hot in the overheated room, and asked for permission to remove her parka. Bering, who had taken a seat to the right of the commander's desk, sat with his arms draped nonchalantly about the back of the plastic molded chair, blue eyes unapologetically X-raying her newly revealed shape.

"I want you to understand, Lieutenant," began Commander Morin, shifting his gaze to Bering, "both of you, that this meeting is strictly off the record." It struck Lana then that Bering was really a regular naval officer—the unkempt beard and ruddy cheeks a front, along with the easy affability and apparently unconcerned air. But for what? Drugs on the base?

"Mr. Bering," explained Morin, "is a longtime resident of Unalaska."

"Oh—" said Lana, smiling. Waiting.

Morin looked down at a three-ring binder, paused for a moment. "How long did you know him, Lieutenant?"

Bering was making her feel undressed. "The pilot?" pressed Morin, irritated that he hadn't the effect on her that Bering obviously did. "The Hercules that crashed." Morin was looking up at her.

"Not long at all," said Lana.

"He'd invited you to fly to Adak with him. Is that correct?"

"Yes, sir."

"You didn't go?"

What was Morin on about? Lana wondered. It was a dumb question. Of course she didn't go—otherwise she'd be dead.

"Why was that? Records show you were off duty. You didn't report in sick, did you?"

"No, sir, but I'd just received a wire from the War Department about my brother the night before the flight. He'd been reported missing in action. On the morning I was to go with Lieutenant Alen, I picked up a VOA broadcast about the situation in Europe and I decided to stay and listen."

Morin nodded, his eyes back on the file, then up at her again. The sound of the electric clock on the wall behind him was a faint buzz, which Lana could now hear quite distinctly in the silence of the room.

"Yes," said Morin. "I'm sorry." He paused. "You ever see him drunk?"

Lana was nonplussed. "No—not that I—"

"I don't mean in duty," said the commander. "Socially?"

"No," replied Lana. "I hardly knew him. . . . He invited me up for the run to Adak, that's all."

"How about his copilot, then?"

"I didn't know him at all, Commander."

Morin was tapping a pencil on the desk, letting it slip through his fingers, reversing it, obviously in a quandary.

"I don't think," proffered Lana, "that he was the type to get drunk before a flight, sir, if that's what you're concerned about. Anyway, as far as I remember, the plane was hit by volcanic debris when Mount Vsevidof blew."

"Yes," said Morin, rolling the pencil back and forward between his hands. "That's what we thought. We did have a four point six on the Richter—but that's not unusual for this part of the world. Anyway, it doesn't usually accompany an eruption. Weather boys tell me they'd expect something around seven point one for the volcanoes to blow their tops." He paused, leveling the pencil at Bering. "This gentleman says he was in the area off Vsevidof that morning—how far out did you say?"

Lana liked Bering, so laid-back, his thumbs hooked in the pockets of his coveralls, legs outstretched as if he might be getting ready to take a nap. " 'Bout seven—ten miles," he told the commander. "Halfway between Mount Vsevidof and Okmok Caldera." He was smiling at Lana. "Next island west of us, miss. Caldera's the ash lip of the old volcano—still steams a lot. Adds to the fog. But I never heard the noise, you see—I mean the noise of anything being thrown up—volcanic rocks. They go through the air with a kind of hissing noise. Lava starts to cool as it flies through the air and when it hits the sea. Once you've heard it—you never forget.''

"But,'' cut in Morin, pressing into his left palm hard with the pencil's eraser and looking straight at Lana, "he thinks he heard—''

"*Know* I heard, Colonel,'' said Bering, though he was still watching Lana.

"All right,'' Morin corrected himself, "he *heard* another sound.''

"Well,'' said Bering, "like I said, I saw the flash first. Then a booming sound a few seconds later.''

"He thinks,'' said Morin, "that it was a missile.''

Now she told the commander she realized why he was so concerned—it looked as if one of their own aircraft in the fighter umbrella that constantly patrolled the Aleutian arc had accidentally shot down the Hercules, killing Alen, the copilot, engineer, and nurse Mary Reilley. The military called it "friendly fire,'' but you ended up just as dead.

"No,'' the commander corrected her. "I've done a thorough check of that possibility. No fighter cover over the area at that time.'' He glanced up at the map of the Aleutian arc, where he'd ringed the wild, grass-topped basalt group generally known as the Islands of Four Mountains, which thrust out of the sea three hundred miles west of Unalaska's Dutch Harbor.

"A Bogey?'' suggested Lana, surprised at her ready use of the preflight lingo she'd picked up at the base.

The commander shook his head. "Nothing on our radar. Nothing at all.''

"But,'' interjected Lana, "our radar at Shemya Island and Adak should have picked up anything coming our way. I mean—''

"Exactly,'' said Morin, mildly irritated that she knew enough to ask the question. "Shemya's phased radar and Adak Naval Station *should* have seen anything coming our way—at least half an hour warning. Even if they were flying at Mach 2.'' The commander paused. "Which is why the Russians would like to take those two stations out—reduce our warning time.''

"Then how,'' pressed Lana, "would a missile—''

"That's why I've asked you here,'' said Morin. "To check out Alen. If they'd goofed up, accidentally fired off a flare or whatever, it might have been what Mr. Bering believes—''

"It wasn't a flare, Colonel. I'd bet old *Sea Goose* on that." He smiled at Lana. "My trawler."

"Oh."

"It was going way too fast for a flare, Commander," continued Bering. "I've seen enough of those from Search and Rescue to know the difference." Without taking his hands out of his pockets, Bering indicated the map. "Looked to be coming *up* from the vicinity of Four Islands."

Now Lana realized precisely what it was that the commander was worried about. If a missile had been fired at the Hercules from a submarine, then it most likely had advance notice of the aircraft's destination and so its probable flight path. Lana was about to assure the commander that she certainly hadn't told anyone, but—"I—I did mention it to Nurse Reilley when I found out I couldn't go for the ride."

"The nurse who went instead of you?" asked Morin.

"Yes. She took my place. But she would hardly have had time to tell anyone—"

"I'm not saying she did," responded the commander. "But all it takes is for someone to send a millisecond burst signal to the sub. At least a dozen or so people on the base knew the plane was doing a supply run to Adak."

"But wouldn't we pick up a signal like that?" asked Lana.

"Yes, and I've checked all signals as well as fighter patrol times—and I've had the reports from Adak and Shemya cross-referenced on that day. Nothing. They don't show any sub intercept."

Lana thought he'd snap the pencil in half as he sought an explanation.

"I don't think you've got a security leak," said Bering. "Plane just happened to be there. Too much damn coincidence otherwise."

The pencil was still, Morin clearly relieved by Bering's implied conclusion—that no one in Morin's command was an agent, that it was simply coincidence, that the downing of the Hercules had occurred in Dutch Harbor's area of responsibility.

But the commander's satisfaction was short-lived as he reminded himself how the military was loath to believe in coincidence. It was too often a cover-up for incompetence. And God knew there were enough dissatisfied people posted to the Aleutians that he couldn't dismiss the possibility his command had a leak. In any event, it was a case of cover your ass, which meant checking out the Four Mountains as well as requesting a security sweep of any civilians on the island, many of them of Aleut-Russian heritage from the days when Dutch Harbor was used as the main base for Russian fur sealers. The Aleuts had been poorly treated during World War II, many interned in run-down fish canneries on the Alaskan mainland. It was quite possible the Russians had infiltrated at least a few of them. On the one hand, if he sent any of his men to do a search of the four small islands, it would raise the question of a possible spy or spies, and it wasn't a smart move careerwise to stir anything up if you couldn't deliver. On the other hand, if an aircraft could be brought down anywhere over the thousand-mile arc, America's back door was open.

Perhaps it had nothing to do with anyone on the island—perhaps a missile was fired from a sub. After all, in the Second World War Japanese subs—the big I boats—had shelled Oregon and California. But then, how could Morin explain how the noise of an enemy sub had gone undetected, given the extensive network of sonar arrays around the Aleutians? A sub story just wouldn't stand up. But if Bering was right, if a missile *had* been fired from one of the islands, it was unlikely that out of the ten types of Soviet air-to-surface missiles, they would use anything as big as an SS-19 with its range of forty-eight hundred miles. It was much more likely they would use something like the shorter-range, shoulder-mounted "Grails," which could have been fired low and fast enough to evade Dutch Harbor's radar 150 miles to the east. It would have taken only a few seconds from a base somewhere on the four small islands to bring down the big Hercules.

Morin asked Bering if, seeing he knew the island so well, he would be prepared to act as scout for a search-and-destroy mission to the Four Islands.

Bering thought about it and said he would—on one condition.

"Which is?" pressed the commander anxiously.

Bering replied that as an "independent fisherman," he didn't have the benefits of any group medical insurance, especially as he was separated from his wife, and that now his two teenagers were in "braces," the cost of dental treatment was keeping him broke.

"Leave it to me," said Morin. "From here on in, you're

covered. I'll get the paperwork done this afternoon. Don't worry about it.'' The commander's gaze shifted to Lana, then back to Bering. ''I'll organize a platoon and transport. But I want this whole operation kept under wraps.''

''Then we should use my trawler,'' put in Bering. ''If there is anyone on the islands up to no good, there's no point in advertising we're coming.''

''But you'll have to land somewhere. They'll see your trawler coming whether they suspect anything or not.''

''Not if I go in fog, they won't. And that's the forecast for the next week.''

''All right,'' said Morin, smiling appreciatively. ''Sounds good to me.''

''Okay,'' said Bering enthusiastically. ''Would you like to come along, Miss Brentwood?''

She blushed despite herself. Was he serious? ''I'll stay here with the commander.''

''Lucky commander,'' said Bering mischievously. Morin was decidedly embarrassed.

As she and Bering left the Quonset hut, the sky above them was studded with stars, but even now wisps of fog could be seen sneaking into the harbor, and for want of anything better to say, Lana noted the obvious. ''Think we've seen the end of the good weather for a while.''

''I'll be back,'' said Bering. ''I'd like to take you out when I get back. Okay with you?''

''Why—yes, I suppose—''

''Great.''

The next minute he was gone, into the night, heading back toward the docks of Dutch Harbor, his fisherman's wet-weather coat draped over his arm—like a helpless slave, Lana thought, and she felt a stirring in her.

''Heard the scuttlebutt?'' asked her roommate almost the moment she returned to barracks.

''What?'' asked Lana.

''They think there's some Commie missile base down on one of those islands. We're probably going to see some action around here shortly.''

Lana didn't know what shocked her most—news of the search-and-destroy mission having already leaked or that her roommate seemed so eager to see ''action''—which meant broken bodies for the Waves.

"After this gig," the girl told Lana, "in Civvy Street they'll be begging us to work in OR."

"If," said Lana, "there'll be any ORs left."

"Ah—we'll win, honey."

"Like we did in Vietnam," said Lana.

"You're a gloom cloud all of a sudden. Morin chew your ass out?"

"No."

"Cheer up then. Nobody's going to push the big button. They're not crazy, lady."

"If they're not crazy," said Lana, "they wouldn't have started a war in the first place."

"I don't know," said the bubbling roommate. "Sometimes there's no other way. Sometimes you have to fight."

What depressed Lana more was that her fellow Wave was right. Sometimes there was no other way. Either that or you simply walked away in defeat as she had with Jay.

Her roommate, running late for her shift, grabbed her cape. "You know anything about this Bering?"

"No," said Lana.

"Oh, come on, Lana. You were with him in Morin's office."

"Yes, but I mean I don't know anything about him. Some kind of—fisherman—I don't know."

"Some kind of fisherman . . . I'd like to go fishing with him. I'd like to get him under the sheets—in between them—or on top of them—and . . ."

"All right," said Lana.

Though he had just sunk the *Yumashev*, Robert Fernshaw's initial rush of victory as he ditched gave way to empathy for the hundreds of Russian sailors miles away who, like him, were at the mercy of the Atlantic. Now and then he could glimpse patches of them through the crazily tilting rectangle of his life raft's flap as the raft slid up and down the walls of ever-deepening troughs. The Exocet Fernshaw had fired had been so devastating that he knew many of the Russian crew wouldn't have had time to make for the life rafts. Caught for a moment atop a huge, sweeping swell, he saw the dot of the Russian chopper hovering over the stricken sailors, winching a dozen or so aboard and —it looked like—ferrying others from the oil-streaked water to the few lifeboats. But how far could the chopper go? Even on a full tank, the Hormone's range wasn't much more than four hundred miles.

Fernshaw stopped thinking about the Russians, any sympathy he may have had for them as fellow human beings being quickly dissipated by the reality of the war. It wasn't NATO's divisions that had breached the Fulda Gap and started the war. Anyway, they certainly weren't going to worry about him. He checked that his raft's SARS—salt-activated radio-to-satellite beacon—was working and was struck by the irony that if an Allied ship was over the horizon, it would probably see, via satellite relay photos, the scores of Russian sailors in the water first, and would miss him altogether if the beacon packed it in after the first few hours of full-power transmission.

The swells that had been mere scratches on a blue slate from the air were now growing alarmingly, the high, white cumulus bruising, and the ocean no longer deep blue but a relentless and endless gray. But perhaps, he told himself, the swells that seemed to have grown more precipitous in the last five minutes were not harbingers of worsening weather but merely appeared more ominous beneath the leaden sky. Then he saw the Hormone, its coaxial rotors a black blur, and for a moment or two Fernshaw was convinced he was about to die, his heart pounding, thinking of his wife and four-year-old boy, the cloying smell of the claustrophobic rubber raft closing in on him, making him nauseated.

All his training against G forces was of no avail in the heaving chaos of the sea, where one second he felt his whole body grow lighter as the raft swept up the side of a fifteen-foot swell before plummeting, his stomach churning, into the next trough. Not a religious man, Fernshaw nevertheless said a prayer for deliverance, and it was only when he glimpsed the Russian chopper suspended above him, a buoyancy bag inflated around each of its four wheels, a rescue cable and harness still dangling from its side door, that he dared hope fate was finally lending him a hand—that the old law of the sea of enemies helping one another when they were in peril might yet prevail. One of the Russians in the Hormone, immediately behind the copilot, was dimly visible through the salt-speckled Perspex of the chopper. On impulse, Fernshaw waved. The man waved back and the chopper rose.

In the chopper several of the *Yumashev*'s rescued crew

members made to cross the Hormone's cabin to look out, but the pilot, alarmed by their abruptly shifting the chopper's center of gravity, brusquely ordered them to *"Sadit'sya!"*— "Sit down!" A young cook, still shivering, ignored the order and remained standing, one hand on the cabin rail, the other clutching a rough woolen navy blanket about his shoulders, his wet hair and beard matted with oil sludge. As he watched the silvered barrel toppling from beneath the chopper, the bright orange raft slid bumpily down a swell's steep incline as the chopper banked.

The sea erupted seconds later, the depth charge's fuse set for *poverknostny kontakt*—"surface contact"—its shock wave visible, a huge ring shuddering and racing out from its epicenter, the tent-shaped raft miraculously still inflated but tumbling down the outside of a high, foaming column of water, as if caught in a mossy, green waterfall, the enemy pilot's body, limp and lifeless, hitting the water before the raft.

CHAPTER TWELVE

THE EXPLOSION, ITS range put at three miles by the *Roosevelt*'s sonar conversion computer, was heard aboard the sub as no more than a muffled cough, but it was loud enough to startle Robert Brentwood out of his light sleep, his photo of Rosemary sliding from his chest as his hand darted out to stop the Walkman from falling as he turned. Glancing up at the Control relay in his cabin, he saw the sub was maintaining the anticipated TACAMO rendezvous by crawling along at less than 3.5 knots on the emergency "bring it home" shaft against a crosscurrent. The current, surprisingly strong and not marked on the chart, was disconcertingly "mixed" in temperature and salinity.

As officer of the deck, Peter Zeldman lost no time in alerting everyone in Control to a possible inversion layer coming up. Soon every man aboard knew the sub might be approaching a "plume," a less dense area of water caused by either fresh or hot water springs from the earth's crust "streaming" through the colder, more dense sea around them. And everyone knew how many subs before them had suddenly plunged in a less dense column, hitting the bottom at over 130 miles an hour before tanks could be vented to regain neutral buoyancy.

The explosion, albeit muted in the distance, was at once an added strain and a possible relief for those in Control as it could mean that another Allied submarine was in the area, unknowingly taking the heat off them. On the other hand, as Zeldman pointed out to Brentwood, if it had been an enemy ASW aircraft or surface vessel searching for the *Roosevelt*, then the explosion some way off indicated that the sub's pursuers were way off course and had merely been attacking blind, looking for the sub around the last reported position of the *Yumashev*.

But whatever was going on about him, Robert Brentwood *was* certain of one thing—after his sinking the cruiser, the Russians would gather their forces, and he, like the convoys, could expect more determined and pervasive attacks en route to the haven of Scotland's Holy Loch, still over a thousand miles to the northeast. Brentwood also knew that now there was no way they could risk going up for a TACAMO rendezvous. They were on their own.

CHAPTER THIRTEEN

IN BALTIC FLEET headquarters at Baltiysk, near the Lithuanian port of Kaliningrad, a bad mood permeated the hallways, especially in the office of the Baltic Fleet's naval intelligence unit, which reported directly to the *Glavnoye Razvedyvatelnoye Upravienie*—the GRU, main intelligence directorate of the Soviet general staff. No one among the Estonian workers was cooperating, including those of Russian background. The large minority of Russians in Estonia, as well as native Estonians, had been approached to see if they had heard anything about who was sabotaging munitions in the factories in and around Tallinn, the Estonian capital. They said they had not.

The GRU general had no doubt they were lying, their silence taken by the GRU as yet another legacy of what was contemptuously referred to as Gorbachev's "glorious" reign. The Estonians had been permitted to pass laws forbidding Russian workers from voting unless they'd lived in Estonia for several years. The Estonian Russians had suddenly found themselves second-class citizens within the Soviet Union, and now they were in no mood to risk the wrath of the *Lesnye Bortsy za Svobodu*—"Forest Freedom Fighters" (the Estonian underground)—by helping military intelligence.

To make matters worse for the GRU, there had been an astonishing display of solidarity among workers of all backgrounds outside the Estonian capital as well. Not only were the shipyard and factory hands not saying anything, but Russian immigrant workers as far east as Kohtla-Järve, where most of them worked the oil shale deposits, were also proving to be uncooperative toward the GRU.

At first the GRU chief thought he could run the saboteurs to ground simply by tracing the serial numbers of the munitions that had been assigned to the *Yumashev*, most specifically the RBU rockets which had failed so miserably in the *Yumashev*'s attack upon the American submarine. But as his men fanned out amid the giant gantries of Tallinn's shipyards and to the various munitions assembly and distribution centers along the thousand miles of Baltic coastline, from Virborg in the northern sector of the Gulf of Finland east to Leningrad, then west again to Tallinn and Riga, and as far south as Kaliningrad in Lithuania, they made a troubling discovery—that many serial numbers had been duplicated, in some cases triplicated, in different ports and the same port. This was bad enough, but as they tried to narrow the problem down to what specific shift, what factory or yard, had installed the fuses, they found themselves in a quagmire of administrative chaos, one of the clock-in cards being signed "Miki Mouse," and responsibility for the mess being passed around like a game of musical chairs.

Back in Leningrad Naval Base, it wasn't a game Admiral Brodsky enjoyed playing. Below his office window, the Neva River looked leaden, the cloven sky morose, and in the autumn air he could smell the heavy mustiness of fallen leaves. An early winter predicted. This meant the Gulf of Finland could be iced over by Christmas, only five weeks off. Even with the few icebreakers he had available, Brodsky knew that early ice would spell disaster—resupply of the Baltic Fleet impossible. The thought of the fleet that had broken out into the Atlantic, after the joint Soviet forces' assault on the Denmark Straits and the NATO Danish base of Bornholm Island, being left without vital food and munitions, unable to press its attack against the U.S. submarines, was anathema to Brodsky.

"I cannot believe," Brodsky told his aide, "that in the more than fifty thousand shipyard and dockworkers we have for the Baltic Fleet, there is no one willing to talk."

"They were ready for us, Comrade Admiral," his aide explained. "They knew we'd discover the sabotage sooner or later. If I might make a suggestion . . ."

"Yes?"

"With due respect to our naval intelligence—we should hand this over from GRU to the MPO." He meant the *Morskaya Pogranichnaya Okhrama*, the maritime border troops of the KGB.

"What can their frigates and gunboats do that naval intelligence can't?"

"I wasn't thinking of that aspect, sir. I had their shore people in mind. Undercover, antiespionage division."

"Why would they know any more than our GRU?" asked the admiral, turning farther around in his chair.

"In 1949 British military intelligence, Department Six, were running an 'Operation Jungle' in the three Baltic states. KGB had it pinned from the very beginning."

Admiral Brodsky nodded, but it was only a dim memory. He was searching for a name. "That would have been Luki—"

"Lukasevics," put in his aide. "Yes, sir, his control was Carr. Well, Lukasevics single-handedly invented a partisan Baltic army, which MI6 was desperate to keep alive when the postwar was becoming the Cold War. Washington was just as desperate for information. Moscow center obliged. They had Lukasevics feeding Carr's MI6 disinformation, and Carr in turn fed the CIA. Carr kept recruiting and sending agents to the Baltic. Six networks in all. And we knew—that is, the KGB knew—who they were the moment they landed.''

The admiral shifted impatiently. "Where are you taking me, Captain?''

"Just this, sir. The KGB has kept a much closer watch on the Baltic than we have. Especially in Latvia and Estonia—most of all in Tallinn.''

"But eventually the British did find out," replied the admiral. "Their network's blown.''

"Blown, yes, Admiral, but networks don't simply close down. Some of those recruited by Lukasevics were genuine partisans. They didn't know they were being run by KGB. They reformed, waited for another chance—waiting for a Gorbachev—for anything to give them a chance. But Lukasevics waited also. He still had his informers and kept them in place within the new networks. They still believed he was London's man, you see.''

"You're telling me," said Brodsky, grimacing, massaging the swollen joints of his left hand, "we should turn the entire investigation over to KGB's maritime division?''

"Either that, Admiral, or they could let us have some of their files.''

Brodsky shook his head. He wasn't that naive about intelligence matters. "No, you were right the first time. If we must do it, Comrade, we will have to relinquish control of the investigation. As it is, they'll probably be surly that we left it so long. Further delay will only make matters worse. Perhaps I should put it in the form of a request? Let's see: 'To assist us in a case of national emergency'?'' He turned to the captain. "That should break the ice. It is also true. Though how their MPO troops can identify the source of the sabotage from the same serial numbers we have is beyond me.''

Sometimes Admiral Brodsky struck his aide as being bone-thick between the ears. A cautious naval tactician and plod-dingly able liaison officer between the Northern and Baltic Fleets, he did not possess the subtlety of mind necessary for intelligence work—nor the necessary toughness. Though a stern disciplinarian, he was nevertheless known to exhibit bourgeois sentimentality when it came to running personnel matters to ground, particularly in cases involving three-year conscripts who went AWOL early in their shipboard assignments. His detractors said he was weak on such matters because as a young conscript in the *michman*—"warrant officer"—program, he had fallen in love with one of the women conscripts, who, like most women between nineteen and forty at that time, were being trained as radio officers. She was an Estonian from Tallinn. Brodsky's parents had objected strongly, and it was said that only the urging of more sensible heads among his comrades had prevented Brodsky from going AWOL from his unit in MV Frunze, the Soviet Union's Annapolis, where he was in training as a surface vessel line officer.

The would-be marriage never happened, and a young man's passion became sublimated through the rigorous requirements of the Frunze academy and sea duty as a midshipman in the Baltic Fleet, where he'd learned the cold necessity of subjugating individual desires in duty to the state. In the Western navies, they called it setting your sights on your career, and women were supposed to follow, not impede.

Still, the gruff sixty-seven-year-old had never forgotten Malle Vesiland, the picture of her long, blond hair done up in a severe bun, as per regulations, making her twice as attractive to him, his youthful dreams of seeing it fall free in the flush of passion as fresh in his old man's heart as it had been a thousand years ago when they were young. Malle's features had blurred in the memory, and Brodsky had no doubt that she, like most women in the republics, would wear her age badly. But no matter; the unfulfilled dream he'd held as a young midshipman was as new in him now as the day he had first met her in Leningrad.

The closest they had got to the dream was to hold hands during their walks by the Neva until sunset touched the river with gold and to go to one of the small coffee shops by the river, where he would buy her a cup of real chocolate-flavored coffee, which she loved so much and which on occasion mysteriously found its way in from the West.

He regretted not having a picture of her, but in those days even the simplest and cheapest East German camera was beyond his means. Perhaps it was better not to have a photo, he sometimes thought—better to hold the ideal in the mind, where the ravages of time and the vicissitudes of war couldn't sully the dream.

He became aware of the captain standing beside him, placing the green form on his desk. "The authorization, Admiral."

As Brodsky unclipped his gold Parker pen, he pushed the smiling, happy image of Malle from his mind. For all he knew, she might be dead. But despite his effort to forget, he found himself remembering momentarily the color of her eyes, ice blue and yet nothing cold about them—rather something eternal—and her joyous smile, even for one of "them," the Russians, who had invaded and colonized the Baltic states on the heels of the Stalin-Hitler pact. It was one of the things he remembered best about her—that she didn't care about politics and took each person she met on his or her merits.

Brodsky read over the authorization, understanding that handing over the investigation to the MPO would effectively mean handing over any credit for the investigation to them as well.

Fifteen minutes later, the captain in charge of MPO's "Border troops Estonia" arrived at Brodsky's headquarters. Though he was dressed in full naval uniform, the gate guards immediately recognized him as MPO from his green shoulder boards and gave him a snappy salute. The colonel assured the admiral that MPO would get to the bottom of it.

Using the admiral's phone, without asking, the captain, Vladimir Malkov, a *kapitan pervogo ranga*—"naval captain first class"—in charge of MPO-Tallinn, in turn called the MPO's plainclothes section in Tallinn, which was responsible for protecting the borders against penetration by foreign agents and for preventing "unauthorized boat departure" by Soviet citizens.

Within a half hour Captain Malkov had a printout of all known informers and suspected counterrevolutionaries dating as far back as those involved in British intelligence's "Operation Jungle." The list of potential troublemakers in the Baltic states was long enough from the years of the Cold War, but after Gorbachev, there had been an exponential leap, the list quadrupling as the *zhdavshikh*—"wait and sees"—had become more militant and sure of themselves in their demands for autonomy from the Soviet Union. Given the urgency of the task, Malkov knew there was no possible way of working methodically through the list. Almost a thousand Russian sailors had been killed in the sinking of the *Yumashev*, and who knew how many more would die on other ships because they were firing dud, instead of live, ammunition? It called for drastic measures.

Just before dawn, twenty green-canvas-topped trucks, spewing smoky exhaust, rumbled into Tallinn's big Mustamäe apartment complex. The polluted yellowing concrete slabs of the ten-story apartment blocks were pricked here and there by dim lights as workers from the night shifts in the shipyards and factories arrived home, eager for breakfast after the grueling twelve-hour shifts. Other workers, many of them clerical, leaving the apartment block for work were stopped by the ring of MPO troops and asked for their work permit as well as their resident identification cards. After this, they were told to form four ranks stretching from the wide, grassy strips between the apartment buildings to the curbside, where the drivers of the yellow buses were told to keep going past the stops.

More MPO naval-uniformed troops fanned out quickly into the apartment buildings, stationing themselves by elevators and fire escape stairs, forbidding any movement from floor to floor as well as from the buildings themselves.

Malkov explained to his subordinates that he had chosen the Mustamäe because the "high density" was much more manageable from a military and psychological point of view than the sprawling shipyards. Even so, Malkov stressed that it was important that the inhabitants of the complex be unable to communicate among themselves within the apartments.

In apartment 703, in number one complex, closest to the road, a middle-aged and attractive grandmother, Malle Jaakson, her only concession to age a pair of glasses, looked down at more troops arriving. Her fifteen-year-old grandson, Edouard Jaakson, excited by the sight of the troops pouring out of the trucks around the buildings, asked, "Nana—what are they doing?"

When the youth turned and saw his grandmother's face, his boyish thrill gave way to a more mature realization—that the troops could only mean trouble.

He had grown up being taught about the Russians—their language, their history—but as well as the official syllabus, he had also heard the underground story of the "betrayal" of 1939 and the purges in 1941, after more than nine thousand teachers, intellectuals, journalists, and other "counterrevolutionaries" had been rounded up on the terrible night of June 13—family members literally torn from each other, dragged from city and farm alike to the railheads and then to the Soviet oblivion east of the Urals.

Then the Nazis had taken their share of the Stalin-Hitler Pact, with more than forty thousand Estonians forced to join the Wermacht. By the time the two totalitarians had finished their titanic war, a third of all Estonians were dead.

Now, seeing more trucks arriving, the fifteen-year-old was reminded of something else, passed down from generation to generation of Estonians—that as terrible as the Nazis had been, it was the KGB who had inspired the most fear, who had been the most barbaric.

For Malle Jaakson, clutching the boy tightly to her side, it was as if Estonia's nightmarish history had suddenly leapt from the past to terrify the children of those who had already suffered so abominably. Edouard's mother and father had not yet returned home from the shipyards. The first thing she must do was to warn them. She went to the phone to dial the Tallinn docks. She would keep calm, tell the floor foreman that it was urgent family business. A sudden illness.

The phone was dead. Perhaps, she thought, it was only their phone malfunctioning. Or cut off.

"Edouard, wait here. I'm going next door." She started to turn the handle.

"Vernut'sya v kvartiru!"—"Back in your apartment!" The soldier's voice made her jump in fright and she quickly obeyed.

Inside, she closed the door, leaning back on it, one hand beneath her throat as if she had trouble breathing.

"It's a conscript roundup," she told Edouard, her voice shaking.

"I won't leave you, Nana. I'll look after—"

"No, you must hide." She held him close to her again and could feel his heart beating—but he was still a boy, despite his bravery.

"I'll be all right," he tried to assure her. "I'm too young for the—"

"No one's too young for them," she said. "No one. You must—"

She heard a metallic tapping noise and guessed it must be the sound of the troops' metal-tipped boots as they ran into the building. She could see them disappearing into the various buildings of the complex like ants sucked up by some great anthill. Edouard broke from her tight embrace, looking down at her. "It's the heating vent, Nana. Somebody's tapping."

"What?"

"The heating vent."

"Yes," said Malle. How often her son had complained about a late party from the floor below, its sounds vibrating up the shaft. "Yes," Malle said hopefully. "Quickly—go and listen. I'll watch the door."

On all fours, Edouard put his ear close to the vent and waited. The tapping began again.

"Who is it?" he asked, careful not to give his own name first.

"Friida," came the tinny reply. "Friida Mägi. The apartment above you. Friida—you remember?"

"Yes, of course," replied Edouard, only now giving his name, recognizing her voice, though now it was little more than a hoarse whisper.

"They are arresting people."

"Who?" asked Malle, who had come in quickly from the kitchen, nervously casting one eye toward the door, its safety chain on.

"The KGB!" came the incredulous reply.

"No," said Malle. "*Who* are they arresting? What for?"

"God knows. But you must try—" There were echoes of loud knocking coming down the shaft. The warning voice ended abruptly, the heating vent clanging shut.

"Edouard—" began Malle in a panic, but not knowing what to tell him.

"Nana! The cover in the bedroom. The plumber's crawl space."

"Yes," she said hurriedly. "Good boy. Quickly, Edouard. Quickly!"

He turned, his excitement vanished now, her panic his. She saw it in his face and forced herself to calm down, steering him to the bathroom. "Go to the toilet first."

Suddenly he had a vision of him being hidden away for days, weeks, and became even more frightened so that for a

few seconds he just stood there over the toilet bowl, unable
to do anything.

"Hurry!" she urged.

As he flushed and hurried to his parents' bedroom, she
thrust a small jam jar of apple juice and a wedge of cheese
into his hands. He was crying.

They could hear the sound of heavy boots thumping along
the hallway. "Quickly!" she whispered, kissing him. In one
sweeping movement, surprising in its litheness for a woman
in her fifties, she snatched a small vase of dried flowers and
its crocheted doily from the main bedroom's low night table.
Next she took from it an ashtray full of coins, a comb, the
family Bible belonging to her daughter-in-law, and a pair of
whitish rubber earplugs sometimes used by her son at the
docks. In another second Edouard was stepping on the night
table, Malle steadying it on the bed, trying to push up at the
plumber's trap door. He couldn't reach it. Malle quickly
handed him one of her slippers. This gave Edouard the extra
reach to shift the trapdoor just enough for a hand hold. She
gave him a leg up and he was up inside, replacing the square
plasterboard tile.

The sound of boots outside ceased, but now the voices of
soldiers moving from door to door could be heard, and voices
coming up the heating vent from the apartment below, terrifyingly close so that to Malle, the very air seemed drenched
with the stench of fear.

She relaid the night table, careful not to make it too neat,
then suddenly saw the dusty imprints of the table's legs on
the bed cover where she had lifted it for Edouard to stand
on. She brushed it with her hand, but the dirt from one of
the legs was too ingrained. She stripped the bed of the cover,
threw it in the wicker laundry basket in the corner of the
bedroom, and rummaged frantically in the bottom drawer of
the wardrobe for the still-unused cover she'd given her
daughter-in-law as a wedding present: a colorful patchwork
quilt made by relatives of her father in America.

There was an argument going on next door. Malle felt
weak in the knees, exhausted. She brought the new cover up
over the pillows, smacking a crease beneath them, falling on
the bed, pushing herself back up. Next she walked back to
the kitchen and slumped down at the table, pushing back a
wisp of hair, still blond despite her years, and, her brain
racing, tried desperately to think what she should do next to

protect Edouard. Maybe they weren't after conscripts at all. Perhaps—

She saw two cups and two plates in the sink. She jumped up, washed one of each, and put them away. If they asked if anyone else lived in—no, they would *know* who lived in each apartment, but one dish and cup might convince them she was alone today. She chastised herself, told herself to calm down, get her story straight. She'd tell them Edouard had left for school. But it was too early. His bicycle—yes, his bicycle would have a flat and he'd had to leave early to walk to school. No, he could fix that. It had been stolen! But she'd have to give them its permit number, and when they checked downstairs in the racks and found it—

What about the Mustamäe's being surrounded? He would have been stopped had he tried to leave. No—no, her grandson was—she would use the Russian word for "conscientious"—*sovestlivy.* Her grandson was conscientious and had left for school earlier than usual. She would have to stick with that and not mention the bike. She repeated *"sovestlivy."* After that she wouldn't know what happened to him. Perhaps, she could suggest, he had become frightened, hearing police were at his parents' apartment. That would explain him not arriving at school. But then—

She stopped. She was galloping too far ahead, she told herself—one step at a time, Malle. She turned the radio on, put the kettle on to boil, and scrounged through the pile of newspapers in the kitchen corner, pulling out a copy of *Pravda*, hesitated, replaced it, and instead pulled down a worn Jaan Kross novel. Kross had been a proud Estonian, a nationalist—the Communist party newspaper would be too obvious a ploy to curry favor. People subscribed, but they didn't read it. No, proud but not obstructionist grandmother would be her best bet. She looked about the apartment again, her heart thumping so hard, she instinctively put her hand on her bosom to catch her breath. She rearranged the old photo of herself as a young conscript graduate-radio operator in the Baltic Fleet. In Russian uniform. That might help.

She sat down again, biting her lip, looking about the apartment once more, trying to imagine herself as a newcomer there, for any possible sign of Edouard hiding. She heard a police klaxon in the distance. The troops were still about the housing complex, and she could see several armored cars she'd missed before parked under the linden trees. Ideal camouflage, she thought—but what of her own camouflage against inquiries about Edouard? Looking beyond the complex, she could see the medieval spires of the old town piercing the peaceful autumn air. She could smell the odor of herring wafting up through the vent, and now she realized no one was talking next door. For a moment it was possible to believe that there was no war. Had they left? Had the neighbors been taken away? She waited. There was no sound.

Suddenly she rushed toward the master bedroom and looked up at the trapdoor, remembering she had given Edouard one of her slippers to push up the cover. There might be a smudge of dirt on the plaster cover. There was no sign of disturbance. As she lowered herself to the kitchen table again, the kettle began to whistle. It had the force of an informer screaming. So heavy was her relief that for a moment she felt drowsy. Seeing the needle spire of St. Olav's in the distance, steam rising in sharply defined clouds above the dome, Malle wished for a moment that, like her daughter-in-law, she could believe in God, in the Blessed Virgin. Her hands were trembling. Still she could hear no new noise in the building. Perhaps it wasn't a conscript raid after all and they had come looking for deserters or to arrest only one family. Pray it was someone else.

From somewhere below she could smell cabbage being cooked. It surprised her—not that someone was cooking vegetables so early but that the smell was so powerful. She had long thought her sense of smell was diminishing with age. Soon she became aware of noises all over the apartment—the hum of the small refrigerator and above it a high, almost inaudible whine that she did not recall having ever heard before. *"Tikho!"*—"Be still!" she whispered to herself, but she was praying for Edouard.

CHAPTER FOURTEEN

ROSEMARY'S GROWING ANXIETY about visiting young Wilkins increased as she entered the antiseptic and musty foyer of the school's old hospital. Resentful of young Wilkins yet obviously expected by the headmaster to be concerned as well as discreet, she had found the drive from Oxshott through the usually tranquil wooded countryside to be one of mounting tension. As if she didn't have enough to worry about with her exhausting day-to-day chores of teaching a coed class of adolescents, and her mother, who, not surprisingly, was given to bouts of blackest depression over young William's death. On top of this there was her own constant and growing anxiety about Robert, who had departed for Holy Loch in a rainstorm not unlike this.

Richard Spence, though fully occupied driving through the torrential rain on the winding, narrow road, was making reassuring fatherly noises about how the weather was bound to improve, seizing upon the weather as a metaphor for general improvement, even as the Audi was forced to slow more than usual around the curves because of the pelting rain. He swerved sharply to avoid a three-ton army lorry, the first of a long convoy en route to the south coast. "Reminds me of forty-four—D Day," he said, looking across at Rosemary.

"Hardly," said Rosemary in an uncharacteristically contentious tone. "You couldn't have been more than five."

"He would have been old enough," said Georgina from the backseat, having invited herself along for the ride, declaring she "adored" driving in bad weather. "Children remember more than you think. Freud—"

"Quite right, Georgina," said Richard. "I was six, to be

exact. But I remember it very well. Lorries from here to London.''

"Well, I daresay this isn't for D Day," said Rosemary. "It's more like Dunkirk." There was silence in the car. Rosemary was sure Georgina had merely come along to get a look at Wilkins—no doubt he'd be a wonderful conversation piece, another "bourgeois victim" for a seminar at LSE. Richard said nothing to counter her uncharacteristically bad-tempered retort about Dunkirk. Besides, her gloomy assessment, in his view, was probably an understatement of the true military situation. A military disaster seemed imminent. Even the most conservative papers, including the *Telegraph*, not usually given to hyperbole, were conceding that the Dortmund-Bielefeld pocket was on the verge of collapse despite what seemed to be a pause in the progress of the Soviet divisions. It was as if they were gathering their collective breath before launching the death blow to the already badly savaged British Army of the Rhine, the American Fifth Army, and the decimated remnants of the German armored and motorized divisions who had fought a tenacious but losing rearguard action following the Communist breakthrough at Fulda Gap.

In the strained silence of the car, the steady drumming of the rain began to make Richard sleepy. He turned the radio on to BBC4 and picked up part of the prime minister's speech. At first they thought it was coming direct from 10 Downing Street, but from the desk thumping and "hear, hears," it was obviously being reported directly from the House. There were angry questions about failure of intelligence services at home and abroad to predict the Communist breakthrough and the extent of Communist subversion in both NATO and the European Common Market long before the war had broken out. Against this, Labour Party backbenchers and Liberals were asking for assurances of individual rights—stating that they did not want to see the kind of "racialist-motivated internments" that had taken place in the dominions during the Second World War, most noticeably on the Canadian West Coast.

"Once again," the prime minister continued, "in the long but, I might add, often tenuous history of the democracies, democracy's fatal flaw in times of war is revealed by the opposition members' well-intentioned but, I daresay, militarily unsound concern." There was hooting, but the prime minister ignored it. "To be sure, our rights, precious to us, are the foundation stones upon which all our freedoms reside, but now—now it is high time for the honorable member to voice as much concern for national security as for individual rights. Far better—" There was more jeering in the background. "Far better we err on the side of national security than to lose the fight for our very survival—a survival without which individual freedoms cannot flourish—a survival which, if not secured in the face of the dark and titanic forces ranged against us, will plunge all Europe *and* the United States into a totalitarianism. A totalitarianism so bereft of all the good we have known, so dreadful in its every manifestation, that I submit we have no choice but to marshal all the strength we have, to suspend some of those rights we normally enjoy, to bury all differences we have within the European community—to forget all else but our duty to stand fast—to resist with every fiber in our being." There was a thundering of desks being pounded.

"Windbag," said Rosemary. "He's getting us ready for a new purge of habeas corpus."

"Really, Rose," objected Richard, wiping condensation from the windshield. "I hardly think 'purge' is the appropriate word—"

"I think it is," put in Georgina. "Rosey's quite right. The windbag's getting ready for another Dunkirk—only this time there'll be no miracle. The Russians won't hold back their tanks like Hitler did. He was too stupid to—"

"The Americans! The Americans!" cut in Richard Spence with some heat. "Do remember, you two, this time we've the Americans with us. This time they've been in it from the very beginning—"

"Americans! Really, Daddy." Georgina leaned forward from the backseat. "With all due respect to your Robert, Rosey, who I'm sure is very capable and—"

"Daddy!" Rosemary's tone was so imperious, he started in fright and almost lost control of the Audi as it turned sharply down the hill, past a copse of ancient oaks roaring in the tempest about them.

"For God's sake, Rosey!" began Richard. "What's the—"

"Stop the car! Please." She had her hand on the door handle. He pumped the brake, bringing the car to a standstill on the narrow shoulder of the road. Through the noise of wind and rain he thought he could hear another convoy approaching, alarmed at the prospect of the left-hand-drive American trucks bearing down on him, hugging the center line in the storm.

Rosemary had twisted herself around from the left front passenger's seat, hand clutching the diagonal seat strap, face flushed, bright with rage as she ordered Georgina out of the car.

"What?" said Georgina in astonishment.

"Go on!" yelled Rosemary. "Get out!"

Richard Spence reached over. "Rosey. Here—hang on, old girl."

"Get out!" screamed Rosemary. "You sod!"

"Rose!" said Richard, utter disbelief on his face. "What on earth—"

"Has gotten into me?" snapped Rosemary, turning on him. "*She* has! This—" She was sneering at her younger sister in a way the latter had never seen her do. "This inflated, left-sucking bitch. She's so consumed by her smart chitchat from LSE—her obligatory anti-Americanism. So caring, aren't you, Georgina? What was your ridiculous thesis on? London poor as victims of bourgeois values—or some such rubbish?" Rosemary turned back to her father. "Do you realize what your bourgeois money has got you, Father? A nineteen-thirties fellow traveler. She's so desperate to be 'in' with that brittle intellectual crowd up there, she'll even insult the man I chose to marry." Now she was turning on Georgina again. "Your type are all the same, Georgina. You love humanity but you hate people." The tears were rolling down Rosemary's cheeks. "Who are you to . . ." she yelled at Georgina, ". . . a man who might not come back . . . the only man I've ever—" She stopped, scrabbling in her purse for a tissue.

Richard Spence was so stunned by her outburst that all he could do was look aghast at his two daughters. He didn't know them.

"I'm sorry, Rosey," said Georgina quietly. "I—I shouldn't have said that about the Americans. I thought you of all people could face facts head on. I merely said we're being walloped, which we are. I didn't mean to cast aspersions—"

"Oh, spare me," said Rosemary, her face splotchy from crying, trying to unravel tissues from their tight, insufferable little balls, which weren't in her purse after all but hiding, as usual, in the very depths of her overcoat. "Do spare me the pained reason bit, Georgina. You and your precious 'facing facts.' It might work in most of the provinces, but not down here. I know you too well. When you want to be offensive—which is most of the time—you sheath your venom in 'facts.' You're a bundle of 'facts'!" Rosemary blew her nose hard.

Dimly Richard could see a figure running toward them from the direction of St. Anselm's gate, which he guessed must be still a few hundred yards off, hidden—an onslaught of yellowed maple leaves swirling about the figure approaching the car.

"Your facts," Rosemary kept on, "are Gradgrind facts. You're full of smart leftist theory while your country's fighting for its life. I suppose you think you're being all very . . . individualistic. You're a *child*. You parrot your Holy Trinity—thesis, antithesis, and synthesis—but you wouldn't know a decent human being if you saw one. If we lose this war, we'll be invaded and you'll get a chance to compare—see your rotten little theories in practice. I thought you would have seen enough after they tore down the Berlin Wall. Oh, it was all going to be sweetness and light—and look what's happened."

Georgina sat back, arms folded defiantly, her smile contemptuous. "Why, Rosemary, I always thought you were proud of your self-control."

"You *undo* me, Georgina."

"Obviously," retorted Georgina.

Undeterred, Rosemary shot back, "Tell me, why do you hate your country so much? Does that come with the government scholarship?"

"Don't be preposterous."

"Well, you do, don't you? You despise England."

"I don't know what you're—"

"No, Georgina. On second thought, I don't think you do."

The boy, a prefect, was tapping politely on Richard Spence's window. Richard wound the window down, but Rosemary was either oblivious to the fact or didn't care.

"Tell me, Georgina, do you love *anything*?"

Richard Spence was trying to listen to the boy, nodding politely, embarrassed beyond measure.

"Can you say you love your country, Georgina?"

Georgina was looking out the window now, watching the boy walking away.

"Well?" pressed Rosemary.

Suddenly Georgina turned on her sister. "Are you mad? You're raving!" Georgina looked at her father. "She's insane!"

"Do you, Georgina?" asked Rosemary, her voice quieter now. "Not England right or wrong or right or left. But England."

Georgina sat as far back in her seat as possible, finding Rosemary's attack of patriotism so sickly sentimental, she felt herself blushing with embarrassment. It was all so utterly ridiculous, yet she felt as if she was about to cry and kept looking outside the car, only slightly aware of it moving, the prefect running ahead and pointing to the left of the commissary—where to park.

"My God, I've never been so—" Richard began, but was unable to finish, so flustered, he forgot to depress the hand brake button and pulled the ratchet right through. "Damn!" He turned angrily to Rosemary. "I don't pretend to know what's going on between you and your sister. But if you're not up to it, I strongly suggest we turn around right this minute and—"

"I'm all right," said Rosemary evenly. "I'll talk to him." But she didn't move.

Richard glanced at Georgina in the rearview mirror. "I think perhaps you ought to stay with—"

"She can come in," said Rosemary. "I'm sure young Wilkins could do with some Marx. I imagine attempted suicide's another bourgeois tool to oppress the masses."

"Look here," said Richard firmly. Georgina sat still, refusing to move. He opened his door and pushed up the umbrella. "Are you coming, Georgina?" The rain was drumming on the umbrella, his brogues straddling a puddle.

As she got out of the car, Georgina, still visibly shaken by Rosemary's attack, forgot to lock the door. Rosemary was already shaking her umbrella, the headmaster, a small, stocky man in his late sixties, approaching her from the entrance hall.

"I think," Richard told Georgina as Rosemary walked ahead, "she's been under an awful lot of strain."

"She's terrified," said Georgina. "I think she's pregnant."

Richard Spence stopped abruptly.

"She's with child, Father, and the father is gone. Like our William has gone. And now this Williams—"

"*Wilkins*—" corrected Richard, though still in shock at what she had said, his umbrella still up, though they were inside. The prefect politely offered to take it for him.

"Er—what—oh, yes, yes, of course," said Richard. He felt utterly lost—the twentieth century and its sexual revolutions and all its other revolutions had passed him by in Surrey. It had taken him twenty years to use the word "period" instead of "that time" in front of his wife, Anne. Everything was falling down about him.

"Ms. Spence?"

It was the headmaster greeting Rosemary but in a second making it clear that her father and sister were not exactly welcome. How long, wondered Georgina—how long to wait until she *was* needed. If only Rosemary knew how much she wanted her love, how much she needed love. And here was Rosemary needed, called for.

The war was a bitter disappointment for Georgina. It had failed her utterly so far. With the entire planet in conflict, one was supposed to see the relativity of one's own unimportance—to lose oneself and ergo one's problems, one's loneliness absorbed by the larger struggle. In fact, Georgina discovered that one's problems were only exacerbated. From rationing to unquestioned patriotism, like Rosemary's, the commonality of everyone's shared experience only made one's unorthodox views more private, making one feel even more of an outsider from one's own family. Rosemary had touched a raw nerve, suggesting Georgina couldn't give herself to love, only to the love of an idea.

Now Georgina herself wondered if her flirtation with Marxism was, in reality, nothing more than an act of sublimation on her part, an avoidance of the real problem—that she was afraid of men. So long as her undergraduate enthusiasm had to wrestle with the pressing attack of hitherto totally alien ideas, she didn't have the time to wrestle, figuratively or otherwise, with sex, with her failure to find a man who would fit her ideal. Someone whose wit was matched by his sexual presence, at once alluring yet not chauvinist, considerate yet not effeminate. An "English and American literature" graduate, down from Oxford, had almost made the grade. In a rare moment, as unexpected as Rosemary's outburst, Georgina had let her passion override reason. But her tentative, nervous foreplay ceased when, flustered by not knowing some of the terms he was using, but clearly understanding his intent, she panicked, becoming all superior, demanding all but a declaration of her rights from him. To which he, not yet successful in getting her pants off, replied—and now the words rang in her ears—that what she needed was "a feminist with a big cock!"

"Well, you're neither!" she had shouted back, slamming the door. Despite her parting shot, which she harbored as one of her snappier ripostes to male chauvinist vulgarity, the adolescence of it all appalled her, only reminding her once again that age was no gauge of maturity. Look at Rosemary's outburst. But Rosemary was engaged. It had been the final blow. Rosemary, who had always been thought of as the one least likely to marry—lost to a world of Shakespeare's love sonnets, so shy she might have been permanently lost in the forest of Arden.

"Would you and Mr. Spence like to wait here?"

It was the headmaster, diplomatic but making it quite clear that only Rosemary had been requested to come and talk some sense into the boy.

When she entered the commissary room on the second floor, the first thing Rosemary saw was a lemon-colored screen. For what purpose, seeing there was no one else in the room, Rosemary didn't know. Inside the screen, his mother, a pretty, dark-haired woman, short, in her midforties perhaps, mumbled a greeting that expressed both gratitude and resentment, then left Rosemary alone to talk with the boy.

The boy Rosemary looked down on was not the callow youth of her Shakespeare class. Gone was the smart-alecky sneer of the sixth form clown. It might have been another boy altogether, for though he answered to the physical description the ambulance had given—a youth six feet in height, black curly hair, dark brown eyes—the eyes that were once full of rebellion and trouble were now doelike in their shame.

He had looked at Rosemary only once—the moment she had opened the door—but then had turned away. Rosemary almost wished for a return of his callow bonhomie of the past months; at least there had been some semblance of courage. Still standing by the bed, she was about to soften her rather formal stance and forced smile in order to ask him why he did it and whether or not she could be of help. But against this was her impulse to tell him off, to scold him for not being brave, whatever his problem was—pray God he wouldn't tell her—to tell him that other young men, like her brother, like her *dead* young brother, with God knew what fear all around them, had shown better mettle than he. But either tack seemed pompous and absurd. What did she know of the causes behind his attempted suicide—what did anyone know of anyone else's inner life anyway, the hidden and secret places, at once banal and terror-ridden, so often given in their public semblance to mistaking magnetic north for true? And what was true anyhow? Even the beginnings of such a concrete event as the war now seemed obscure. Even historians, if they survived, if anyone survived, would only do more to obscure it.

"Why did you want to see me?" she asked Wilkins. For a second, try as she might, she could not think of his Christian name, or, as Georgina would insist, his *first* name. He had only ever been Wilkins. G, she thought—Gerald?

He was still staring ahead, his eyes avoiding hers, his voice that of a whipped puppy. "I don't know, miss," he replied.

She didn't know what to say other than to tell him the headmaster gave her the impression he wanted to see her. He sneezed, and when he reached from under the sheet for a tissue, she saw his bandaged wrists. It surprised her. For some reason she had expected him to have tried it with pills—that was usually the way these days. Might well have been pills that caused it in the first place. Her anger with the boy was difficult for her to contain. She knew it unworthy of her, but here was this callow youth slashing his wrists for attention when young men like William had willingly suffered the slings and arrows of the worst fortune there was—yet was it their worst or their best? He looked a bit like William. She wondered how Robert's sister, Lana, had talked to William. Had she been so cold? Of course not, but then, William had fought bravely. Though even that, she didn't know for certain. It struck her with some force that she knew very little, in fact, about how William had been wounded and even less about the circumstances of his time aboard the hospital ship—only that Robert's sister had somehow given him the gift of love. God forgive me, thought Rosemary, but she wasn't up to God's love for Wilkins.

"I wanted to—" he began, then stopped.

"Yes—" she encouraged him.

"It's my father . . ."

"Yes?" Quickly Rosemary tried to recall the student record sheet. She remembered two parents were listed: father had something to do with marine insurance. Lloyds? No—St. Anselm's, though respectable enough, was a little *too* middle-middle-class for Lloyds.

Wilkins pulled another tissue from the box, wincing as he did so. Then another and another.

"Waste not, want not," she said, parroting one of the Department of Supply posters. Paper was especially scarce, England no longer having any timber for felling. Good Lord, she was as bad as that poor old Professor Whatsit, and his going on about not wasting electric current: hand in your hair dryers.

"What about him?" she asked Wilkins, then added, more gravely, "Your father, I mean?"

Though already lying practically flat in the bed, Wilkins pushed his head back farther against the bedstead, his feet sliding down under the sheet, eyes staring up at the ancient stone ceiling as if his spirit was willing but the body weak. Rosemary sat awkwardly, impatiently, and glanced at her watch, adjusted it like a bracelet, trying not to be rude. Besides, she wasn't going out anywhere that evening and had intended to sit up as late as possible in an effort not to think of her appointment with the family doctor in Oxshott in the morning. She was pretty sure she'd missed her period but couldn't remember *exactly* when her previous one had begun. Usually punctual about marking it in her diary, she had simply forgotten to note it the last time. Even so, it seemed that it certainly should have begun by now.

"I could come another time when you're feeling better, Graham?"

The name had suddenly come to her, once she realized she was in control of the situation.

"He's not my real dad, you see."

"Oh—I didn't realize. Is that—well, of course, I know these things do matter, but is it enough to—what I mean—" Georgina should be here after all, thought Rosemary. It was a job for the psychologists and Freudians or Jungians. Or Shakespeare. "I mean, does that upset you, that he isn't your real—natural—father?"

"No." He plucked another tissue and looked up at the ceiling again.

"Graham, I think you're probably very distressed now. Please don't misunderstand. If you'd like another—that is, I mean if you would like to talk something over with me, I'll be only too happy to come some other time. Just tell the headmaster—"

"I saw him, you see."

Rosemary's stomach turned. An extramarital affair. She didn't want to hear any sordid details. Was that why Wilkins hadn't wanted his mother there? "Graham, I'm your teacher. I think any family affair—any family matter is best discussed with the school chaplain. If you like, I'd be quite happy to call—"

The boy looked at her now. "Your old man's in the navy, isn't he?"

She utterly failed to see the relevance of the question but bristled at "old man." That was callow Wilkins. "No," she said, outwardly unfazed. "My father isn't in the navy."

"No. I mean your—boyfriend."

"Oh!" She still didn't like the familiarity, but now his question at least made more sense.

Wilkins was turning gingerly onto his right side, facing her, grimacing, trying not to put pressure on his right elbow. "I was wrong," he said. She noticed he was perspiring about the throat. "I mean I shouldn't have . . ." he continued. "I got drunk, miss, and I was—well, you know. Under a lot of stress. Exams and, well—you know—"

He was under stress! It was another modern disease—students under stress. What he needed was a good, swift kick in the backside.

"Sometimes when I get drunk I get, well—"

"A lot of people get depressed, Graham. Drink or not." She hesitated but then decided it was better she said it. "But they don't try to kill themselves. There's no answer in that."

"It was sherry." He said it as if that were explanation enough. Rosemary said nothing. Was this the answer? Hamlet had drunk sherry? She was sure now that either the boy was somewhat demented, probably as a result of the suicide attempt—either that or—

"Did you take anything else?" she asked him.

"Well, some tablets."

"What kind of tablets?"

"I don't know."

"Did you tell the doctor this?"

"He said they found the bottle. Hal—Hal something."

"You mean you just swallow any kind of tablets?"

He looked straight at her, his face suffused with anger. "What would you do," he charged, "if—"

"If what?" she cut in impatiently.

"Your old man's a spy."

Intuitively she looked about her. "Graham—what are you—" She caught her breath. Of course he understood how serious it was. "Then you should tell someone about it."

"I am." He was staring wildly at her. "I'm telling you." She heard voices nearby.

"*Me?* But you should tell the police—or—"

"My mum," he said. "I couldn't. It's—" He turned onto his back and slid down farther into the bed. All the color seemed to be draining from his face.

"Graham—this is a very serious accusation."

"You're telling me," he said, and in a hoarse voice, which had been caused by the stomach pump tube, he spoke to her and seemed older, wearier, than she. "I want you to tell them," he said.

She rose, holding her head with one hand, vaguely aware of clutching her purse with the other. "I—" She stopped, thinking at first the voices were next door, but then seeing it was near 7:00 P.M., she realized it was time for prep in the classrooms below. "Where is your father now?"

"Stepfather," he reminded her. "He's in Southampton today." A wicked, cynical grin—the kind she'd seen in class before—twisted the curve of his mouth. "Port comings and goings, you see."

Rosemary lowered her voice. "Graham—?"

"I've seen the brown envelopes," he said. "You know— OHMS—On His Majesty's Service. Nicked from some government offices, I expect. Makes it look all officiallike—if they were dropped and somebody picked them up accidentally. Full of cash. They're in a box at home. I know where he hides it all."

She was staring down at him, aghast at the enormity of what he was telling her. A man selling port schedules, tonnages, departures, of the NATO convoys to enemy agents. It was unthinkable that an Englishman—and now everything came into focus—the newspapers reporting, as much as they were able, the "in camera" trials of four spies caught in the past month. Some even said the surprise breaching of the Fulda Gap had been aided and abetted by well-organized and pervasive sabotage *behind* the NATO lines, the SPETSNAZ—Russian commandos, which the Americans called "special forces"—having been sold defense plans by East German spies who had come through to the West in the flood following the opening of the Berlin Wall.

"I thought," continued Wilkins, his throat so dry, he could barely talk, "that with your old man, miss—being in the navy and all and—well, I wanted to tell someone."

In turmoil but not wanting to panic the boy, she marshaled all the calm that was her teacher's stock in trade, not letting the class, the world, see inside. Unflappable Rosemary, in Georgina's absence, keeping the sheer terror of what such betrayal could mean to thousands of British and American seamen on the convoys bottled up inside her. She touched Wilkins gently on the shoulder. "I think it's pointless of me to say, 'Don't worry.' Of course, I know how you must feel. But, Graham, you mustn't mention this to anyone until I've talked to the authorities. Don't tell *anyone* until I've come back."

"You'll come tomorrow?" he asked. "Please?" He was like a child again.

"Yes, I'll come back tomorrow." Before she left, she asked him about his mother—about how it was possible that—

"Mum never asks where money comes from," Wilkins cut in. "She thinks I hate him anyway."

"Do you?"

He was reaching toward the mobile tray across the bed for the paper cup of water. Rosemary passed it to him.

"He's not my dad," he said. "Not really."

Rosemary looked back at him, her hand on the door. "Are you sure of what you've told me? That it's not simply your dislike of your—"

"He's not my father. I can show them the money. Everything. But you'll have to hurry, miss. He could be home by morning." Rosemary felt her stomach tightening again. "All right. I'll—I'll attend to it. Immediately. I promise. I'll come back tomorrow."

"Miss?"

"Yes?"

His eyes met hers in a look that was unmistakably sexual. She was shocked. And flattered.

By the time Rosemary rejoined Georgina, her father, and the headmaster, it was still raining, the wind continuing its mournful wail in the sodden oaks that surrounded the school. With the blackout curtains drawn, the school's lights seemed strangely dimmer and more depressing than usual. Graciously brushing the headmaster's apology aside, Rosemary told him she was glad he had called.

Their feet crunching on the wet gravel as they walked toward the Wolsley, she apologized to Georgina and her father for her "thoroughly foul mood."

"All right, Rose," said Richard. "We're all under stress these days, I'm afraid."

"Yes," said Rosemary. "We are."

Georgina said she didn't want to intrude, but did Rosemary think the Wilkins boy would try it again?

"I don't think so," said Rosemary. "It was—" She turned around in the darkness, the dim reflections of the slit headlights not enough to illuminate their faces, for which Rosemary was glad. It made her confession easier. "You were right, Georgina. I think he does have what I suppose you would call a 'crush' on me, though I blush to admit it."

"What?" asked Richard Spence. "At his age?"

"He's almost seventeen, Daddy," said Rosemary.

Richard mumbled his disapproval, but Rosemary barely heard him. She had far more to worry about than dealing with a schoolboy's infatuation.

In the backseat, so dark that the lights of the Audi's dash seemed far-off pinpricks of light, Georgina tried to imagine what had transpired in the boy's room. Slipping her shoes off, crossing one foot over the other, and stretching so that her stocking feet were pressing hard on the padded foot bar, she laid her head back on the soft imitation leather, reveling in its smell. Depressing the door lock, her left hand gripping the strap, she slipped her right hand beneath her black pleated skirt and, with the steady hum of the windshield wipers' rhythm in the background, closed her eyes in the darkness. Dreamily she heard Rosemary asking their father how late the Oxshott police station stayed open at night.

Robert Brentwood knew something the navy never mentioned to the public, not even to the enlisted submariners:

that the incidence of men going insane because of depth charge attack was the highest of any group in the armed services. The crack-up following depth charge attacks was not always a sudden madness, a single snapping of nerve, but more a gradual unraveling, like a tight ball of gut slowly but irrevocably undone, strung out, until its ability to spring back was permanently impaired. It made him grateful for, though puzzled by, the number of depth charges that the *Roosevelt*'s sensors had picked up splashing off the cruiser but which had failed to explode. Had the Russians' military passion for quantity overwhelming quality meant that much of their ordnance was highly unreliable? If so, Brentwood knew he should get the information to Washington as soon as possible.

But the *Roosevelt* could not send a message if it was sunk. He would have to get to Holy Loch. Or had there simply been a miscalculation in the setting of the fuses—which would testify to the efficacy of *Roosevelt*'s silent running confusing the cruiser's sonar?

CHAPTER FIFTEEN

ALTHOUGH HE WAS no longer in the navy, or even on the reserve list, Adm. John Brentwood, retired, felt that his job as one of the managing directors of the New York Port Authority inextricably linked him with two of his three sons and his daughter. The connection with his son Robert on the *Roosevelt* was obvious to anyone familiar with the U.S. Navy's "rollover" policy. This "sea lift" of men and matériel to reinforce Western Europe depended heavily on both the day-to-day administration of the U.S. home ports as well as on the protection afforded the convoys by submarines like the *Roosevelt*.

It was not a glamorous job at the Port Authority—not much media coverage. It was visual, all right, with the scores of ships passing through, but once you'd shot that, the real bureaucratic work of the Port Authority disappeared into overcrowded offices and banks of computers spewing out availability of loading cranes, tonnage, union liaison status boards, availability of docks, tide changes, and the other thousands of seagoing craft that had to be kept clear of the convoy-marshaling areas, where everything from condoms and microchips to yeast, sugar, and howitzer shells had to be crated, stored, counted, loaded, and transported as fast and efficiently as possible—while at the same time taking care to vary the departure times and convoy routes as much as possible to confuse any enemy sub packs lying in wait in the deep Atlantic trenches off the eastern seaboard.

It wasn't glamorous work for John Brentwood and his staff, their responsibilities disproportionate to the pay and the virtual lack of recognition. Yet for every dozen ships they managed to load and send off without a hitch, one mistake could make the news, and if the navy censor cut the story it would quickly get around the docks anyway, making the Port Authority a butt of more jokes about bureaucratic inefficiency.

One ship, the MV *Nagata*, a fifty-thousand-ton "Combo" or multipurpose oil/bulk cargo/container vessel, its bridge and stack in a stern housing and coowned by a Japanese-U.S. conglomerate, was a case in point. The ship left New York harbor as part of Convoy 24 on the night of October 2, bound for Antwerp. Thirty-two hours and 461 miles later, the *Nagata* was off New England. While maintaining radio transmission silence, she received word from ACLANT— Allied Command Atlantic—that Russian and East German divisions, thrusting west from Hanover and wheeling on Osnabrück, had driven a wedge between the westernmost perimeter of the Dortmund-Bielefeld pocket and the ports of Amsterdam, Rotterdam, and Antwerp. While the ports had not yet surrendered, it was believed this would only be a matter of time, so that now the convoys would have to head to Ostend seventy miles farther west on the Belgian coast, to Dunkirk twenty-seven miles farther south, just over the Belgian-French border, or to Calais, another thirty-odd miles southwest of Dunkirk.

By this time, the MV *Nagata* was no longer over the relatively shallow Georges Bank but had passed over the divide between the continental shelf and the continental slope, and was now over the continental rise. In two hours she had passed from water no more than five hundred feet deep to the nine-thousand-foot depths of Heezen Canyon. While their sudden passage from shallow to deep water beneath them was unknown to most of the crew, on the bridge the watch knew, their silence palpable as they waited anxiously to reach the more powerful current of the Gulf Stream. This would aid the thirty-ship convoy as it passed over the undersea mountains that lay before the Sohm Abyssal Plain, where the greatest danger was a submarine that could be lying undetected for weeks, even since before the war started, sonar pulses from any convoy escort vessel looking for subs scattered by the natural obstruction of the undersea mountains.

Before joining Convoy 24, the *Nagata* had hauled electronics and assorted containerized cargo from Japan to the United States. But on this trip it was carrying replacement nine-thousand-pound-thrust GE-100 turbofan engines and other spare parts for the close-support A-10 Thunderbolt antitank aircraft, together with a million rounds of thirty-millimeter ammunition for the Thunderbolts' multibarrel Gau cannon. In addition, its cargo consisted of five hundred MK-84 electro-optically guided bombs, and, in several "dry-maintained" holds, bulk goods and foodstuffs, from condoms and toilet paper to bread mix, flour, yeast, sugar, and freeze-dried combat rations.

As well as dispersing such cargo throughout the entire convoy so that if one ship was hit, the entire stock of any one item would not be lost, great care had been taken by John Brentwood and his staff with the loading of the bombs and ammunition on each ship. Wherever possible, the 6.06-by-12.19-meter containers of bombs and ammunition had been placed either side of the *Nagata*'s center line, the containers' sides almost flush with her gunwales. Some low-flash-point bunker C oil, as well as highly flammable jet fuel, was being carried in wing tanks and tanks at both ends of the segmented cargo space. Oil tanks nearest the stern were well insulated by cofferdams, or double-watertight bulkheads, against the possibility of fire spreading from engine and pump rooms.

The *Nagata*'s problems began as Convoy 24 began encountering increasingly rough seas off Newfoundland. A small fissure had developed at the bottom of the *Nagata*'s five and six bulk cargo tanks on the starboard side, abaft the starboard beam. Though seawater was coming through and none of the crew could see how long it had been flowing in, it wasn't viewed by the captain as a major problem as the pumps were easily handling it. However, because of the warm, dry air being continuously circulated throughout the dry bulk cargo tanks and other storage areas to keep dry everything from electronics and ammunition to yeast, a massive oven effect had been created, part of the fissure in the hull having penetrated the starboard walls as well as the bottom of tanks five and six, containing sugar and yeast.

It was a disaster that any housewife might have predicted but which the New York Port Authority, beset by a multitude of other problems, had, not surprisingly, overlooked. By 4:00 A.M. enough of the huge tanks of damp sugar and yeast had combined in the dry, warm air to create enormous pressures. And by the time the bridge sensed the buckling of the plates under the pressure within the tightly sealed tanks, it was too late; the longitudinal steel stiffeners reinforcing both the inside and outside plates retained their integrity, but the seams were stressed beyond their limit.

Soon, high-pressure pipes burst and there was a low *whoomp* from down below in the engine room, the needles of the "explosimeters," or gas-pressure gauges, for tanks five, six—and now tank four, buckling under the abnormally high "back" pressure of tanks five and six—moved into the red. Then, in the pitch darkness, there was a sound like a rocket taking off, but no flame, as one of the Butterworth fuel tank covers whistled high into the night and everything began shuddering, the *Nagata* listing hard astarboard, its four tank developing a deck blister on the starboard side of the ship.

"She's about to blow!" the starboard lookout informed the master. "Her weight's shifting like a beanbag."

The fuel tank didn't blow, but its seams gave way, the high octane spewing into the sea. The captain could do little, for like most of the big Combo carriers, which relied on shore-based suction pipes for loading and unloading bulk cargo, the *Nagata* had derricks only midships and at the forecastle, and these were surrounded by stacked and lashed containers. Helpless to do anything about the mountain of yeast and sugar now growing like some enormous amoeba, or vast cake overspilling its pan, shifting the ship's center of gravity dangerously, all he could do was try to vent some of the bunker C and more of the octane to compensate for the starboard list.

Twenty minutes later, at 0426, the *Nagata*'s master gave orders for his crew of thirty to abandon ship and, refusing to break radio silence, alerted the convoy leader by signal lamp, allowing only one repeat of his SOS, and then, opening all cocks, he scuttled his ship rather than run the risk of leaving her afloat as a half-sunken hazard to the other convoys en route to and from Fortress Europe. In obeisance to the ancient and unwritten law of the sea and the traditional precepts of the Japanese code of honor, he remained aboard, after seeing all his men safely off in the Beaufort rafts, and went down with his ship.

The loss in equipment was enormous, for while there were other spare parts for the A-10 Thunderbolts in the convoy, the *Nagata* had been carrying the lion's share of A-10 replacements—engines, ammunition, bombs, and electronic "boards." Enough to have reequipped seventy of the tank-killing Thunderbolts, which, coming in low at four hundred miles an hour, often no more than two hundred feet above the ground and loaded with six and a half tons of bombs with three-second BPSM—best possible safety margin—had proven critical in slowing the Soviet surge through the Fulda Gap.

Although they had managed to take out only two thousand Russian tanks, a third of the Soviet force, the Thunderbolts held a special place in the affections of the half million men in the British Army of the Rhine, the American Fifth, and the German Twelfth. Though the NATO soldiers had been pushed back almost a hundred miles from the prewar NATO/Soviet line, and though they were fighting for their lives in one of the fiercest combats ever recorded in modern history, they owed what life they had to the bravery of the Thunderbolt pilots and the astonishing maneuverability of an aircraft which, swooping down with its two high-mounted rear engines, could absorb the kind of punishment that would have downed the "supersonics" on the first pass.

The loss of the *Nagata* was a hard lesson for everyone, from John Brentwood at the New York Port Authority to the naval planners in Norfolk, Virginia. Reams of new instructions regarding the loading of mixed cargo were issued along with an order to all NATO and "associated merchant marine'' ships that ship's masters were not required to die with their ship. Captains, like pilots, were in short supply.

The consequence of this order would be a spread of what, ironically, became known as the "Nagata defense" in courts-martial where it was charged ships could have been saved had the captain and crew remained. It was an argument the counsel for the defense planned to use in the ongoing inquiry into the sinking of the fast guided-missile frigate USS *Blaine* off Korea. Ray Brentwood, however, refused to consider it, arguing that this defense would require him admitting that he gave the order to abandon ship when in fact he said that, to his recollection, he had not. The defense counsel, once again, had to resume the task of trying to find a witness who would corroborate Ray Brentwood's stand. It was thought at least six other men, including the OOD who thought he'd been given the order, were on the bridge when the North Korean missile had hit, but three of them had been killed outright, two dying later of burns to 80 percent of their bodies; the remaining sailor and ensign, Mahler, was still fighting for his life in Honolulu's Veterans' Hospital, having been judged too ill to be flown on to La Jolla's Veterans' burn unit.

Another outcome of the *Nagata* incident was that despite the heroic efforts of the convoys, the frontline soldiers, though representing only one-tenth of the total force, nine out of ten men required to support one soldier at the front, could no longer be guaranteed the regulation six pounds of food per man per day. And much of the bread the Western armies would be eating from now on would be flat. The loss of the *Nagata* also meant that the Dortmund-Bielefeld pocket would shrink further without the vital resupply for the tank-killing A-10s.

The other lesson from Convoy 24 was a reminder to all NATO commanders that any man guilty of self-inflicted wounds would not only be court-martialed, but his next of kin would forfeit receipt of all military pensions. The rule, of course, was already on the books of NATO's armies, but it was the most diplomatic way that ACLANT could think of conveying to their Japanese allies that choosing death rather than withdrawal or a surrender was not in the defensive interest of the Allied cause. The more enemy troops that the Allies could tie up with either delaying tactics or surrender, the better.

The difficulty of getting this message across, however, was

compounded by the fact that, following a failed counterattack by the German Second Army and the American First against the Soviet's southern flank ninety miles west of Prague, 321 American and West German prisoners of war had been summarily executed by the *Stasi*—the supposedly disbanded secret police of what was formerly East Germany, many of its members still working for Moscow.

CHAPTER SIXTEEN

IN THE DARKNESS of the drop, all David Brentwood remembered was lining up when the green ''go'' light came on, the steady shuffle to the Hercules' rear, the dark incline of the ramp-door disappearing into the vast blackness of the night. The master sergeant smacked him on the shoulder, then the jump. Tearing air so cold, he couldn't breathe. And coming up toward them, graceful arcs of red and green tracer, crisscrossing with unhurried fluidity. The surrounding darkness was so black that though he knew his five hundred comrades must be all around him, they were invisible for the first thirty seconds.

Then he spotted several figures momentarily silhouetted in flashes of antiaircraft fire, some slumped like small toy soldiers, dead in their harness. The air was rocking violently with AA shells exploding, the acrid smell of the cordite reminding David not so much of war as of the Fourth of July. The fumes of the antiaircraft explosions, together with the pungency of burning rubber tires from several of the airborne's Humvee trucks, threatened to overcome Brentwood as he neared the ground, his legs flailing the air in panic lest he hit stiff-limbed with his eighty-pound pack before he could take the roll.

Suddenly flares illuminated a field below, the burnt-out

hulk of a barn, dead horses strewn about, the dark plum gash of a cow ripped open, its head missing, and off to the left, short, sharp stabs of bluish-white machine-gun fire. The sound of the battle increased to a crescendo at times, then fell off, small-arms fire heard in the pauses between the screams and crash of artillery and heavy 120-millimeter mortars coming in from the outer fringes of the Dortmund-Bielefeld pocket. Here the American airborne, instead of having landed within the designated drop zone in the northeastern sector of the pocket, were caught by a sudden shift in the crosswind, which swept most of them beyond the perimeter into the very barrage of the British and German batteries that were supposed to have given them covering fire.

Though David Brentwood didn't know it then, over 270 men had been lost in the first three minutes of landing, caught in the deadly cross fire of a Polish motorized company. The irony was too grim to bear—the drop zone having been selected because intelligence overflights had confirmed that this sector, in the northeasternmost bulge of the pocket, no more than five miles across, was up against the Polish Sixth Motorized Rifle Division. The intelligence experts pointed out that the Poles, though supposedly once loyal members of the old Warsaw Pact, were, in the main, staunchly Catholic, detested the Russians, and would either desert "en masse" or at the very worst offer only token resistance and quickly surrender to Allied forces.

Such intelligence estimates proved disastrously wrong on two counts. No matter what the Poles thought, no matter how Catholic they were, how much they liked America and Americans, they and their cities were being pounded by the NATO bombers that had managed to penetrate the Soviet defense line, which now ran like a jagged cut bisecting Western Germany, swinging off to the southwest where the Soviet advance along the Danube and north to Munich had been the deepest. And no one had to tell David Brentwood after his stint in General Freeman's celebrated raid on the capital of North Korea barely two months before that when you are being bombed and strafed, you make no distinction between friendly and hostile fire.

In addition to this, Western intelligence did not know that the Sixth Polish MR division, quite apart from wanting to protect its own skin from the Allied bombers' counterattacks, had another much stronger incentive: the Soviet military police, who shot deserters or malingerers on the spot. It was a policy that the Russians had prepared years ago, during the *gody prostakov*—"sucker years"—of the Gorbachev revolution, which had swept the dizzy West off its feet. There was another inducement for the Poles to fight well.

This was called *semeynoe pobuzhdenie*—"family persuasion"—inspired in part by Beijing's successful policy of 1989 through which people were encouraged to turn in counterrevolutionaries in their own family. The Soviet refinement was to take a family member, usually the very young or the elderly, for "antifascist war work" in eastern Poland. This way the Russians had it both ways: The relatives would work in the factories producing everything from electronic print boards for the fly-by-wire Soviet jets to biological/chemical weapons, including the manufacture of Tabun and the other VX gasses. A drop of VX paralyzed in seconds, producing involuntary defecation and vomiting. The Polish workers also served another function. If any of the Polish armed forces lost ground, relatives would be hanged. Shooting was too expensive, wasting precious rounds that could be put to better use on the front.

If the Polish and other Eastern European civilian workers—the Hungarians were the worst, in Moscow's view—sabotaged anything, then the GRU simply reversed the policy and shot their kin who were serving in the armed forces. On the advice of Brig. Kiril Marchenko, adviser to the STAVKA, general headquarters of the VGK—the Soviet Supreme High Command—as well as to the Politburo, the next of kin in the armed forces selected to be punished were taken from administrative divisions wherever possible and not from the frontline spearheads.

It was a policy, however, that was not working well in Lithuania, Latvia, or Estonia, the three Baltic states where the populations were so small that hostages could not be sent back to Russia proper without severely weakening the already overextended civilian labor force, most of whom were forced to work in the shipyards and munitions factories of Riga and Tallinn.

But David Brentwood knew none of the politics behind the Polish motorized division and indeed had never heard of General Kiril Marchenko or his tactics. All he knew, and was grateful for, was a soft landing in what felt like a marsh, his knees and right thigh sodden as he rose.

Quickly unclicking the harness and going into the prone position, he tucked his chin in close to the V of his Kevlar flak jacket beneath the Kevlar helmet, his web harness distributing the weight about his torso, unlike his World War II forebears, who had so often found themselves weighed down below the waist by their packs of ammunition, grenades, canteen, entrenching tool, and sidearm.

Pulling the squad automatic weapon, or SAW, back along his right side, he felt for the plastic protector at the end of the barrel, and instinctively checked with his right elbow whether his sidearm was in position. It was a ritual he had followed ever since Korea, when he had seen one man's mud-impacted weapon blow up in his face, inflicting wounds that were worse than those suffered by his brother Ray during the North Korean missile boat's attack on the *Blaine*. David, a veteran after his drop and fighting withdrawal in the hit-and-run raid on Pyongyang, also carried an unofficial sidearm, a sawn-off five-cartridge pump-action shotgun in a closed, swivel-mounted canvas holster on his left side.

Waiting for the next flare, to get his bearings, he tried to listen through the crescendo of noise for the clinking sound of any of his buddies landing nearby. There was a burst of fire off somewhere to his right, sounding like the tearing of linoleum—a light machine gun. But Allied or Soviet, there was no way of telling. It was all so UFU—unbelievably fucked up. Then he heard the pop, like a champagne cork, a flare climbing unhurriedly to its apogee, its harsh, metallic glare casting a ghostly, flickering light a hundred yards across. From experience, he avoided watching the dark, serrated perimeter, where the flickering light could resemble the shapes of everything from a tank to a charging platoon to a machine-gun nest—when there wasn't anything there. Instead, careful not to move, he froze in the prone position, watching the center of the ever-decreasing circle of light now that the flare was falling, and saw, with fright, a patch of greasy brown only six feet from him, a wriggle of barbed wire across it: a body, American or Russian—perhaps British.

The rolling thunder of approaching artillery shells told him that he was in the line of a creeping barrage. His throat was bone-dry, and he'd already urinated from fear. Now he quickly looked about for any sign of his company and friend Thelman, who had gone through Parris Island and Camp Lejeune with him. There was no sign of them—only the dark mush he'd seen seconds earlier and which he now knew had been a man's face, the uniform that of a Russian SPETS commando, the outfit that had already been in place throughout Western Europe and had played havoc with the NATO depots the moment war had broken out. He saw what looked like the man's finger a couple of feet away, but the hands seemed intact—all the fingers still there. Then he realized what the finger was. Jesus . . . Jesus . . .

He thought he saw something move between the man's legs—or what was left of them—where an ooze of intestine had spread over where the man's testicles had been. The movement Brentwood had seen was a cluster of leeches so fat, they seemed like slugs in the flare's dying light.

"Yank?"

He swung the squad weapon around to his right, could see nothing, and then could feel the rain of hot earth coming down on him as the American 105-millimeter high-explosive barrage kept coming. He heard a man scream nearby but was too busy huddling beside the corpse, using it as protection, to know where the voice had come from, aware only that if someone didn't quickly stop the American shelling, he'd be as dead as the maggot-infested corpse filling his nostrils with the putrefaction of death. The scream he'd heard seemed not far away, but it was impossible to tell in the barrage, and David drew himself up into the fetal position, not wishing to see anything, the next barrage so close, he could feel the earth leaping about him, and he wondered if both he and the voice he had heard would be killed—or, if they survived, who would kill whom.

The falling dirt was so thick now, it drummed down on his helmet and cascaded like hot sand over his bronze goggles, which were designed to protect him from harmful ultraviolet rays. "Like we're going for a fucking suntan!" his buddy Thelman had said when they had been in training at Parris Island and then at jump school at Camp Lejeune. Where the hell was Thelman anyhow? David was getting mad at him—Thelman had only been two in front of him.

"Oh, Melissa . . ." he murmured, clutching the squad weapon, calling to his girl back home, wondering if he'd ever see her again.

Despite the rubberized earplugs, his ears were ringing so loudly from the shelling, he couldn't tell whether it had ceased or not. But no earth was falling. Thank God someone had gotten through to the U.S. artillery unit firing the howitzers.

Then the star shells started. Flares with parachutes lit up an area a quarter mile wide, but all David could see was the pockmarked field, as desolate as the moon's surface. He couldn't tell from which direction the star shells had been fired—from Polish or American artillery. He thought he heard something scrabbling behind him. It slowed to a crawl. David swung quietly away from the corpse but found he'd slithered down a slight depression, slippery with the dead man's blood. There was a tremendous explosion in the air—one of the drop transports? A fighter? He didn't know. He couldn't stop thinking about the Russian's pecker being blown off like that.

Now, in the star shells' light, he could see that beyond the pockmarked field, by the edge of a wood, inert bodies, some of them still strapped to their chutes, lay strewn about, one with only one arm and one leg. The wind was shifting again, the dead man's chute ballooning, dragging his remains across the battlefield. Behind David, about a hundred yards away, there was a shout. He knew only that it wasn't English. The next sound was unmistakable: bayonets being clipped on. Christ! They'd told him the bayonet was used nowadays only for opening cans and for ceremonial parades. Still holding his SAW in his left hand, he felt down for the parachute knife. "Hail Mary," he whispered, but couldn't think of the rest of it. Thelman knew the rest of it—he was Catholic—he knew it. Where the hell was he? David heard the slushing sound of boots about sixty, maybe seventy, yards behind him, advancing. Poles . . . He was sure they'd be Poles. They knew the Hail Mary, too . . . "Thelman, you bastard," whispered David. Whatever happened, the man who'd called out to him earlier would have to show his colors. There might be some joy in that. Sweet Jesus . . . it sounded like a whole company was moving.

CHAPTER SEVENTEEN

MPO CAPTAIN MALKOV had ordered a roundup of all informers, including those listed in the GRU files.

He was surprised. The informers were not helpful. It wasn't that they didn't want to be, but apparently they knew nothing. They could be forced to talk, of course, but then all you got was rubbish. An informer would tell you it was the bishop or his grandmother behind the munitions sabotage in order to save his own skin. Whoever was behind the *nerazorvav-shiesya*—"dud"—rockets and shells being sent to the *Yumashev*—and who knew how many other ships?—had planned it very carefully, as the duplicated serial numbers attested to. Malkov also suspected that several heretofore helpful informants had gone mute, after being bitten by the bug of Baltic nationalism that had broken out ever since *Baba Gorbachev*—"Auntie Gorbachev"—and his stupid "liberalization" policy.

Watching the swarm of gulls over Tallinn's Number Three dock, the birds diving and rising above the giant gray gantries screeching so loudly that his driver did not hear him telling him to stop, Malkov marveled at the principle of internal organization that must be in operation to prevent the birds from colliding with one another. Malkov's small, two-cylinder car was flanked by four armored personnel carriers. This much force he knew might not be necessary, but better to arrive with too much than too little. Nothing focused the mind more effectively than a .50 machine gun. For some, the stocky, brutish build of the captain and his rough informality were enough to make them feel intimidated, the joke on the docks being that Malkov had been chosen for his looks more than for his brains. Others said that becoming an MOP chief made you look like that anyway.

The simple fact that Malkov's car stopped ten yards farther on than he had intended meant that a dirty-boiler-suited riveter, his huge riveting gun slung over his shoulder like a small, silver lamb as he headed toward the tool shed, and his apprentice, who walked with him, were selected as hostages rather than two other men farther back who were just coming on shift. The captain's maritime troops had already sealed off the docks, and he had ordered two Pauk-class patrol Corvettes to ply the harbor fifty meters offshore in the event that anyone trying to evade questioning might attempt to swim farther down the docks. When the 230 workers, all but 21 of them men, had been assembled, the captain mounted a weather-worn dais used for new launches from the Tallinn yard. The gulls were increasing in number as more fish boats came in from the gulf, the birds' screeching now so loud, the captain was obliged to ask an NCO to fetch a megaphone from one of the armored personnel carriers forming themselves in a semicircle around the workers. A row of troops from the APCs flanked the dais near the edge of the wharf, where crates of ordnance were awaiting shipment.

"I will be brief," said the captain. "Sabotage has been committed against the Soviet navy—the navy which protects your children from imperialist aggression." He heard someone in the crowd making a guttural coughing noise, getting ready to spit.

"I want information," Malkov told them, switching from Russian to fluent Estonian. "*Now!* I should tell you we have Mustamäe Apartments surrounded."

There was a murmur, a sudden shift in the crowd. The captain's inference was clear.

"Come here!" the captain ordered the riveter and his apprentice. Reluctantly, a marine trooper pushing them with his rifle, the two men walked up the four steps to the dais, the apprentice stepping over a puddle from the rainfall dumped by an early morning shower that had washed the air so clean that for a while the rusting, polluted aspect of the docks had taken on a clean, sparkly look. It was all illusion. The riveter looked at the captain defiantly; the apprentice tried to do likewise but was clearly afraid that if he did so, he would be shot on the spot.

"The first choice of hostages," said Malkov, indicating the two men, "has been from the docks. Future hostages will be taken from Mustamäe." He looked at the sullen crowd of workers, his eyes seeming to take in every stare and turn it back on itself. "I will be in the dockyard office." With that, he walked down the four steps of the dais and, passing through the flank of troopers, nodded to the NCO, handing him back the megaphone. His car started up and a volley of shots rang out, blowing the riveter and apprentice off the dais.

The crowd of workers were stunned, surged angrily, then, under a long burst of machine-gun fire from the armored personnel carriers, stopped, yelling and screaming at the Russian troops, their voices mingling with the screeching of the gulls, several of which had also been hit by the machine-gun bursts, their lifeless bodies tumbling down through the gantries. Here and there, feathers fluttered like bloodied snow, eventually to fall softly on the wind-ruffled harbor.

At Mustamäe they were already loading the trucks now that the lists of whose family lived where had arrived from the docks. Priority in the roundup was being given to teen-agers, as Malkov knew from his experience as an MOP officer in Riga that the elderly were not worth the trouble. They were easier to round up at the beginning but prone to die on you in the cells, which only stiffened resistance among the workers rather than weakened it. Younger hostages were by far the best bet.

An MPO corporal returned to apartment 703. On his copy of the list, it said, "Family Jaakson." When she opened the door, the woman, Malle Jaakson, remarkably well preserved for her age, he thought, was wearing spectacles and had a book in her hand. "You told us," the corporal said, glancing down at his clipboard, "that Edouard Jaakson was at school."

"I—"

"He isn't," the MPO corporal said.

Either the woman had been telling the truth and the boy had left for school early, then hopped it, or he was in the apartment. The corporal brushed past her, through to the small nine-by-nine living room, his head turning, his concentration absolute as he checked the four small rooms of the apartment.

Another Hitler, Malle thought. She had been gripping the

book so tightly, she could feel her fingers going numb from the lack of circulation.

The corporal stopped and looked back long and hard at her. She blushed; the man's eyes were not accusing but rather roving over her trim figure, ill defined beneath a loose-fitting, rust-red cardigan but obviously more alluring to him for that. Instinctively she pulled the cardigan closed about her as if to shut out his view. Immediately she realized it had been the wrong thing to do, as if she were in fact showing herself off. Even worse, it might occur to him that she was trying to divert his attention. But then, if she *could* divert his attention—

"Would you like some coffee?"

"*Real* coffee?" the corporal asked, his surprise total. Like most of the troops, he was clearly fed up with drinking the bitter ersatz stuff made from barley and chicory.

"No," she said. "I'm sorry. I don't care for the artificial kind either. But I have some tea. I imagine you must be tired. You could do with a cup, I expect."

"Yes," he said. "Thank you, Mrs. Jaakson."

She smiled nervously as she picked up the kettle. "Is that a Ukrainian accent I detect?" she asked as if she liked it.

"You can tell?" Though she had not turned around from the gas stove, she sensed from his tone that he was pleased. She could feel him relax, as if the very air had changed, and heard him unbuckle his webbed belt as he sat down at the table. Filling the kettle, she could see outside that the troopers were still surrounding the building, some trucks, packed with civilians, leaving, and others, empty, arriving. But even the line of soldiers seemed more relaxed, their circle around the apartments sagging in places, confident now that no one had gotten out who shouldn't.

"Have you been posted in Tallinn for long?" she said lightly, turning up the gas, the stove's yellowish-blue circle of fire hissing softly, comfortingly.

"In Tallinn," he said, "a year. I like it. You can buy more things here. Not so good now, of course."

"No," she said, reaching for the tea and spooning it out carefully into the pot. She thought she heard a noise, possibly from the bedroom, and feeling herself stiffen with alarm, rather than let him see her reaction, took her time replacing the lid on the tea jar and putting it back on the shelf above the gas ring. She heard the noise again and quickly turned the tap full on, topping up the kettle, though it was already half-full, not daring to look at him for fear he might see the alarm in her eyes. "You have a family?" she asked, concentrating on the kettle.

"Yes," said the corporal, "I've been married now for three—four years. My wife's name is Raza."

The noise sounded again, like the rustle of a curtain.

"You must miss your family."

"I have no children. But yes, I miss my wife."

"Yes."

When she turned to face him, she gasped, almost dropping the kettle—his erection purple, swollen and rising like some huge fat earthworm, the most disgusting thing she had ever seen. He nodded toward the bedroom with a crooked grin. "I'll take the boy off the list," he said. She was transfixed.

"I don't care if he's joined the *Lesnye Bortsy za Svobodu*," he said, meaning the Forest Freedom Fighters. "Or with relatives, whatever. I'll take him off the list." He paused. "But you must be nice. Like you enjoy it, yes?"

Stunned, Malle lifted the kettle, which was so heavy it splashed, almost extinguishing the gas ring, making a loud, steaming noise.

"I can't hear you," he said.

CHAPTER EIGHTEEN

THROUGH THE MIST, the silence after the shelling screamed its presence, the pounding of the heavy guns having pummeled eardrums so badly that only the high tones were left, their ringing so intense that the sound of the dawn birds' song was lost to David Brentwood as he lay, muscles aching, his whole body tense, hands still gripping the squad automatic weapon, his eyes adjusting to the bronze dawn of his goggles until he took them off. The glare of the sun-infused mist was hurtful to his eyes, but now at least Brentwood had a wider field of vision across the cratered landscape, which he remembered from the aerial reconnaissance photos had once been a meadow backed by a wood of Lombardy poplar. The wood was now gutted, the few remaining poplars blackened and splintered, leaning at impossible angles, looking like burned Christmas trees, leaves that had no doubt once flickered gold in the autumn sun now gone, one of the starkly naked trees that remained reminding him of the gaunt "lynching trees" he'd seen in old movies, stripped of foliage, charred, only one leaf still defiantly attached, a hundred yards from him. It was on this leaf that he focused, at once amazed and buoyed by its resilience against all odds. Or was it less resilience and more sheer luck?

There was a flash to his right, sun on steel. He swung the SAW up and around, its burst driving the butt hard into his thigh, the gun now silenced, squashed into the mud and guts of the corpse next to him, the long, razor-sharp blade of a knife at his throat, motioning him up—the Russian, if he *was* Russian, in a long, black, zipped-up jumpsuit and black balaclava, frightening the hell out of him, the man's eyes almost impossible to see, and his hot, sour breath on Brentwood's face.

"Up!" he told Brentwood. "C'mon, quickly!" The ease of the man's English, its purely American sound, devoid of any foreign accent, was the next thing David noticed.

The craters were now alive with the black figures moving forward. He counted at least fifty of them as he was hurriedly taken back toward Russian lines, escorted by relay, stumbling dizzily at first, his muscles still tight from the trauma of the shelling. A quarter mile farther on, he passed over more heavily cratered ground littered with the rotting corpses of what had been the American airborne, whole bodies the exception, limbs savagely amputated by the 120-millimeter shrapnel—from friendly fire. Stomachs literally blown apart, unrecognizable organs and intestines were scattered all over the battlefield in various hues of decomposition, some invisible in the mud except when revealed as a moving mound of maggots, others surrounded by crows pecking almost disinterestedly, waddling like ducks, so gorged they were too heavy to fly. And over it all the revolting burnt-chicken smell of death.

But for all the horror, worse than anything he'd seen during Freeman's raid on Pyongyang in Korea, the thing that struck David most was the catlike grace with which the black-suited Russian commandos moved, up and over the deep craters, taking no notice of the human detritus about them, or if they did, not showing the slightest sign, pausing only at the butchered chunks that still had heads attached or stopping where a severed head lay encrusted with mud, bending down, removing the airborne's dog tags, which were sometimes still attached to the neck or pressed into the mush that had been a face. Now and then he saw one of the black jumpsuits pause, raising his hand moments later with a clutch of ID tags. A runner, one of the Poles brought up from the support battalions, would dash up, grab the tags from the Russian, and then head back to the Russian battalion's headquarters in a thick stand of pine, where David now sat silent with the other two-hundred-odd prisoners, a few British but most of them forlorn remnants of the disastrous airborne drop.

It was only after they took his own dog tags that he realized why he hadn't been killed on the spot. A very fit, no-nonsense, English-speaking Russian NCO in army greatcoat ordered them to remove their uniforms. Walking behind him was a private, his arms festooned with wire coat hangers, one for every prisoner, and a small plastic garbage bag for personal effects. A British private, peeling off his brown-and-green-splash combat tunic with the British Army of the Rhine shoulder patch, offered David a cigarette. David normally didn't smoke, but he took it. The Englishman, a cockney, brushed a sprig of sticky pine from his sleeve. "Don't want 'em all messy, do we?"

David looked puzzled.

"When they cut your froat," said the cockney. "Makes a mess of the uniform."

David nodded. His ears were still ringing so that the Englishman's voice seemed to come from a long way off and as if he were talking underwater. Putting the cigarette in his mouth, still dry from fear, he reached over to steady the cockney's hand as the Englishman flicked his lighter, but David found his hand was no steadier, both of them trembling.

David was surprised how good the tobacco tasted. He took

a piece of the loose weed from the tip of his tongue and flicked it to the ground. "Could've—" he began, but his throat was so parched, he had to begin again, and only now, as he took off his trousers to put on the hanger, did he realize his thigh was wet not so much from the blood of the corpse against which he'd cringed during the barrage, but also from water that had leaked from his punctured canteen. The bullet had penetrated halfway up the canteen. He took a sip from what was left, offering the rest to the Englishman. "Could have strangled us, though," said David. "Taken our uniforms there and then. Why march us back?"

"Nah, mate. You shit yourself then, see? If they strangle you. Have to wash your duds out. No—they want 'em Persil white." The Englishman paused. "Reminds me of when I was a kid: 'I'm no fool, I use Persil on my tool.' " He shook his head, forcing a grin, and put out his hand to the American. "Fred Waite's the name."

"David Brentwood."

"Schweig doch!"—"Shut up!" shouted one of the guards, a *Stasi*, from his red-gold-black shoulder patch, walking toward them on the soft, brown needles of dead pine, and coming from a command truck that was only now visible to David through the camouflage netting. *"Schweig doch!"* the German repeated, and David saw the shadows of others guards in the nearby pines looking over at them.

"Bit late now, Fritz," said Waite. It was clear that it wasn't only their talking but the apparent friendship between the American and Englishman which annoyed the guard. It was as he had been told: the British and Americans had no respect for authority. From Waite's response, he appeared to think the two prisoners hadn't understood his order and so switched to English and gesticulations, his English broken and not at all like that of the sleek, fluent jumpsuits, the first of whom were now returning after their quick foray into the crater zone, where Polish contingents were taking up positions, digging in.

"There is to be no talking already," said the guard.

David saw the guard was about his age, maybe a few years older, midtwenties, his eyes tired but awake with suspicion. Waite, sitting on his haunches, leaned forward, arms protruding from the poncho that, apart from their regulation khaki underwear, was all the half-naked prisoners had to keep them warm. He held up his hand, like a schoolboy asking permission.

"*Ja?*" said the guard.

"Listen, Fritz. What's going on?"

"My name is not this Fritz."

"What is it, then? Your name?"

"Asshole!" called out someone from the twenty or so POWs in a clump that was being guarded near one of the eleven-man Russian armored personnel carriers.

"Who said this?" demanded the *Stasi*, swinging about. "What is this name?"

"It's an expression of endearment," said one of the British Army of the Rhine, shivering in the cold under his poncho.

"Yeah," put in one of the Americans next to him. "Especially in San Francisco."

There was a round of laughter, some of the British in another group opposite David and the cockney clapping their appreciation.

The young guard, red-faced, unslung his AKM, right hand snapping back the sideways-folding metal butt, and stepped to within a foot of the twenty or so prisoners. "It is strictly forbidden to—to be abusing socialist soldiers already."

"Stop fucking around!" It was one of the black jumpsuits, a bunch of dog tags in his hands. In German he curtly told the guard to check if any of the prisoners still had their ID tags. No one said anything; the jumpsuit officer, a man of at least six feet, lean and wiry-looking, was one of the toughest men David had ever seen. As the guard snapped to attention and immediately began checking everyone's neck for dog tags, the officer unzipped and removed his boiler suit, folding it with such dexterity, it was clear to the NATO prisoners of war that it wasn't the first time he'd done it. Someone murmured something about a strip tease, but the weak ripple of laughter quickly died. He was standing in a well-worn uniform of an American airborne lieutenant, complete with dog tags.

"They get caught doing that," murmured Waite, "they'll be shot as spies."

"Maybe," agreed David, "but I'll tell you something, Ted."

"Fred."

"Well, Fred, would you think of pulling up a lieutenant for his ID?"

The cockney, finishing his cigarette, pulled out another and lit it from the first. "Suppose not, old cock—Jesus, they're gonna cause one hell of a lot of confusion if they get inside the pocket."

"Nothing to getting inside it," said David. "Everything's screwed up inside there anyway—units split up, some of our guys inside, most of us dropped outside. They won't be checking ID. These bastards'll get through, all right."

Waite nodded. "Afraid you're right, mate." He paused, cigarette held meditatively down in front of his knees. "They're after bloody Munster." He turned to Brentwood, his tone infused with the urgency of delayed revelation. "That's it, Yank!"

"David."

"They're after bloody Munster. Our prepo site! Christ, mate!" Waite was feeling beneath his poncho for his cigarettes, forgetting he had one on the go. "They blow that depot—it'll be a fucking slaughter."

"Unless our guys can get out first," said David. "Evacuate."

"Where to?" asked Waite, fidgeting with his lighter. "No fucking Dunkirk this time, matey—boats waiting. Last I heard was they got fucking armored all round us. Getting ready for a big push, they are—west of Hannover. Right down to the fucking Rhine and on to Bumsum." He meant Brunssun, south in Belgium, where the German operating out of headquarters dug deep in the coal mines. "And once we start crossing the Rhine," Waite added, "it'll be absolute fucking chaos. Sitting ducks. That's what our lot will be."

"Maybe not if the evacuation's orderly," said David.

Waite turned to Brentwood, his movement revealing white, bony legs like those of some overgrown chicken. "*Orderly?* No such fucking thing, Davey boy. It'll be a balls-up." They could hear artillery rumbling like thunder southwest of them from about twenty miles inside the pocket.

"Doesn't have to be a mess," said David, adding, "I've been in a pull-out."

"Where?" asked Waite, his tone that of an incredulous senior talking to a freshman.

"Pyongyang."

Waite raised an eyebrow. "You were with Freeman?"

"Yeah."

"*Freeman!* Well, me old son, hats off! You should know. What was it like getting out then?"

David didn't answer—the remembrance of the bloody retreat so vivid in his memory that for the last twenty-four hours, from the moment he'd hit the Hercules' slipstream, it had overwhelmed him, the reason he hadn't moved from beyond the crater, curled up against the protective carcass of the dead man. Waite was probably right. When they had got out of Pyongyang, there had been only fifteen hundred men to think of. And while it had gone much better than expected, they'd lost a lot going in. Trying to get out a quarter million men trapped in the pocket by a ring of steel would be a different proposition altogether. What had his father always told the three of them, Lana, too? "When the going gets tough—" It was old hat, but it made him feel ashamed of his recent loss of nerve. "Least it won't be an air withdrawal," he told Waite. "We'll have the bridges."

"*What?*" asked Waite, and David Brentwood knew instantly from the cockney's tone that some of the bridges must be blown.

"How many?" he asked Waite, who was now watching the *Stasi* guard shouting at a man in another group of prisoners for his dog tags.

"What—how many bridges blown?" It was another man's voice, also a cockney, sitting behind them, an eye partially covered with a blood-congealed bandage, the compress having slipped down on the man's cheek, revealing a pus-filled gash beneath the black-red swelling. "All of 'em, mate. Right, Waite? The whole fucking lot."

"Marvelous, in't?" said Waite as they watched the other Russians coming in, taking off their jumpsuits and looping the appropriate—British or American—dog tags about their necks. The *Stasi* guard was handing one of the Russians who was wearing a U.S. Army corporal's uniform—with a machine gunner's flash patch—a St. Christopher medal, which the guard apparently thought was part of the American's ID. There were guffaws from the prisoners and barely suppressed laughter from some of the Russians. Then the tall Russian, wearing the American airborne lieutenant's uniform, quietly walked over to the young guard, took the St. Christopher medal, and put it on.

"Then," concluded David, "we're going to have to swim across if all the damn bridges are blown." They could hear the artillery, Soviet or American, they couldn't tell, increasing.

Waite indicated the *Stasi* guards stationed around the edges of the pine wood. "Don't know whether you've noticed, me old darlin', but those Kraut goons 'ave got a nasty habit of shooting people. My advice, old cock, is to sit tight for the duration. You've done your bit. 'Sides, this lot's only going to last a couple more months, then someone's gonna threaten to push the big one and that's going to get 'em to the table." Waite glanced back at his wounded comrade. "That right, Bill?"

" 'Ope so," said Bill, his pallor like chalk, his arm, which he could hardly lift, making an unsuccessful attempt to keep the bloated flies away from his eye.

"I don't think so," said David, slowly, his gaze held captive by the curling twist of cigarette smoke disappearing into the mist that now shrouded the pines about the Russians' mobile headquarters. "No one wants to use nuclear weapons—they'll use up everything else first." He flicked the cigarette away, the tiny red ember dying in the mud. "Anyway, no war's finished when it was supposed to. Experts always get it wrong. After the second war, everyone said the next would be so high-tech, so mobile, it'd be over in no time. Hell, we're bogged down in that pocket worse than—" He glanced across at Waite. "You know, World War Two wasn't anything like as mobile as all the films make out. Soldiers dig in soon as they can. Then others try to root them out. Same old story. Look at our fighters—they can't break through to Russia, and the Russians can't break through to England. We're in the middle. I heard bayonets last night."

"Yeah," said the Englishman with the bloodied eye patch. "So did I."

"The Poles," said Waite.

"Ivans," put in someone else. "Shit—our sergeant told us bayonets were for museums and can openers. No one would ever use them again to—"

"Will you guys knock it off?" came a voice from the back. "Talking about the friggin' war. Talk about women or something, for Christ's sake. What I'd like now is a good lay."

The Russians were ready to go—in all, sixty-two had captured Allied uniforms. The one in the American airborne lieutenant's uniform was doing a last-minute check to see that none of the uniforms was too ill-fitting, making several men swap because sleeves were too short, pants too tight. Anything about the uniform that might draw undue attention was being weeded out. Next, he passed an American airborne Kevlar helmet along the line to collect their watches, followed by another in which prisoners' watches had been collected, each man double-checking that there was nothing engraved on the watches that might arouse suspicion if they were questioned after being infiltrated behind enemy lines.

"We have to escape," said Brentwood quietly. "Soon."

"You daft?" asked Waite. "You've got no chance. Besides, why bust your gut, mate? You've done your bit."

No I haven't, thought Brentwood. If he'd done his bit, he wouldn't have lain petrified most of the night; he would have moved down the lines, risking the deadly, albeit friendly fire, trying to get through to the pocket. Or had it been just common sense to stay put till the shelling was over? After all, no one would blame him for what he'd done. No one, that is, except himself—the man who'd won the Silver Star for bravery at Pyongyang. His father certainly wouldn't forgive him.

Something had happened since Pyongyang. Strange, he'd always thought you could divide people into the brave and the not so brave, but an awful possibility began gnawing away at him—that it might just be how you felt on any given day. But there was another reason, beyond honor, beyond regaining his sense of self-esteem, that impelled him to think of escape. "We've all seen it," he told Waite.

"He's right," said the man behind them, who, having lain down, was now propping himself up, trying to keep the head bandage on, grimacing in pain as the effects of the last morphine jab wore off. "Now we know what they're up to, they're not going to let us—" He didn't have to finish it.

"Christ!" said someone else. Brentwood looked behind him. It was a British lance corporal, terrified. "Hey, wait a minute—I mean, they could have done us already. Right?"

David shook his head. "Not before they got our uniforms. Waite's right. That would have got our uniforms all messy."

"Aw, bullshit," said another cockney. "They aren't going to shoot us."

"Why?" asked Waite.

"Well—too—too fucking close to the front, mate. Might draw a chopper strike."

The young German guard and the other guards began to *"Raus!"* them—getting everyone ready to move out.

"Where are we going?" demanded a British officer from a group on the other side of the clearing.

"Charing Cross!" came a Scottish voice.

One of the *Stasi* guards, an older man, waved them to their feet with his hand. The German had a weary look about him that worried David more than it might have comforted him. It was the look of a man who'd seen it all before, a man for whom nothing would be a surprise. A man who would follow orders to the letter, not because he hated Americans or British but because it was the easiest thing to do. "You will be taken back," the German said in passable English, "for the interrogation."

"See?" whispered a cockney triumphantly. "We're going to be interrogated—that's all."

"Oh, lovely," responded Waite. "That's just ducky, that is. I love being interrogated. My favorite fucking pastime, that is. Eh, Brentwood?"

"I can think of better things to do," answered David.

"So can I," said the soldier with the bloodied eye, his voice tremulous with fear. "Jesus, I can't see where the hell I'm—"

"Here," said David, getting up. "Hold on to my arm."

As the bedraggled column of poncho-clad prisoners started off through the gloomy wood, the wounded cockney asked his American friend what he thought their chances were.

"Watch it," said David, steering him around a jagged stump that was almost invisible in the mist-shrouded pines.

"What do you think, Waitey?" the man asked.

"Waitey—?" pressed the soldier, David steering him about a long, ghostlike branch that, stripped of its bark, had served as a toilet seat for the cesspool trench.

"I think," said Waite, "we're in for the high jump."

"What the hell's that mean?" asked one of the Americans.

"It means," said a Scottish voice, "he thinks they're going to hang us, laddie. Or shoot us."

"Jesus! Jesus—that's against the—"

"Geneva Convention," the Scot finished for him. "Aye."

"Anybody got a Mars bar?" asked an English sapper who'd been captured two nights earlier by a *Stasi* patrol sweeping the pocket's perimeter.

"Och," said the Scot. "Rot your teeth, laddie, and tha's a fact."

"You're mad," said the American. "You're all goddam mad."

"It helps," answered Waite wryly, adding, "Be careful now." He nodded toward the young guard they'd dubbed "Asshole." But for now the guard wasn't saying anything, looking as miserable as the prisoners. Even so, David was surprised they had let the prisoners talk at all—not when they were all supposed to be going to be interrogated. He remembered his DI at Parris Island screaming at them, "Never fucking let your prisoners talk. Why, marine? Because the fuckers'll make up the same fucking story. Are you listening, Brenda Brentwood?"

"Yes, sir."

"You listening, Thelma?"

David smiled at the memory of the DI yelling at him and Thelman—something David had once thought it would be impossible to smile about. Besides, he told himself, the Russians had probably already collected fairly reliable intelligence about the American, British, and German armies bottled up in the pocket. Hell, they were right there to pick up the airborne, or had they just been in the area anyway?

Try as he might, however, David could not help thinking of one of the great secrets of World War II: the massacre of thousands of Polish prisoners of war. Slaughtered by the Russians, deep in Katyn Forest.

"Leave it on," the corporal told Malle. She reclipped her brassiere. The way he'd said it only added to her sense of shame, as if she'd been caught wanting to exhibit herself and he doing her a favor—a small mercy—telling her to cover herself up. But now she guessed his real reason was the thick, raised scar of the mastectomy where they had taken off her left breast. At once she feared for Edouard, hoping, in spite of the revulsion she felt for the Russian, that the scar hadn't turned him off.

Tossing his cap onto the bedside table, obscuring the photo of Malle and her late husband, and pulling off his shining black boots, dropping them with a thud, motioning for her to come closer and smiling as one would coax a shy, frightened puppy, he patted the bed, dragging the two pillows down so they lay flat on the multicolored quilt.

"Come on, Malle. You've done this before, eh?"

She was shocked at his use of her first name and for a

moment stood holding her black slip protectively in front of her, suddenly frozen as she smelled the strong odor of camphor. No, she decided, of course he wouldn't wonder about the new quilt—lots of people used camphor to protect their clothing.

"You should call me Mitya," he told her, reaching out, hooking the slip's spaghetti shoulder straps, taking it away from her. "It's short for Dimitri."

She forced a smile, walking haltingly toward him, her left hand in his. It was sweaty and warm—cloying—her other hand fidgeting at her throat. His grip became stronger as he pulled her closer. She fixed her eyes on the crazy pattern of the quilt, vibrant reds flowing into deep blues, then orange and speckled brown swirls that made no sense and which, normally pleasing to the eye, now panicked her—everything swirling out of control. She braced herself. He became suddenly angry, releasing her. "What's the matter with you? You want me to pick up the boy? I can, you know. All I have to—"

"No, no," she said, "no—I'm—I'm sorry."

"You forgot something," he said, his tone surly.

"I—" she began, hands on her forehead, her head shaking, trying to think of what it was. "I'm sorry, I—"

"All right—" he said, sitting up from his slouch, grabbing for a boot, obviously about to stalk out in a mad huff.

Quickly she sat down on the bed beside him, her hand touching his shoulder. "What did I forget—please?"

The corporal stared hard at her, his tone still angry, undershot with petulance. "My name—"

"Oh—Mitya. Yes, of course. I'm sorry. I forgot." He hesitated for a moment, the muscles in his face and neck so taut that his face took on a knotted yet strangely adolescent expression. "It's very important you call me Mitya."

She understood now—her saying *"Mitya"* would make it all right. She could feel his whole body relax, except his member, which now looked so big, she knew it would split her, make her bleed.

"It's a nice name," Malle said.

"Kiss me first," he said, then pushed her away as her face neared his. "No," he instructed her. "There."

She hesitated, felt him tensing angrily again, and so, quickly, closing her eyes, she bent her head between his legs. He fell back onto the bed, bumping the headboard, but of this he was oblivious, his groan of pleasure filling the room. She almost gagged.

"*Mokree!*"—"Wetter!" he ordered her. "Much wetter!" Now his arms folded from him like wings, his hands grasping both sides of the bed, the quilt sliding beneath him. Above them somewhere there was a noise, a rustling sound. "What—" His eyes opened. They were glassy. He looked idiotlike. "What's that—" he began.

Malle lifted her head, brushing her hair away hastily. "The heating vent," she gasped. "Do you want me to stop, Mitya?"

"What—no, no. S'wonderful." Her lips encased him again, her tongue pressing, curling and darting, her saliva in danger of drying up, driving herself on frantically to keep him under the spell. "I love you," he said, his breath panting. "I love you, Raza . . . Raza . . ." Then, just when she thought it would be over, he told her to stop, kneel astride him, pushing her, shifting her as one would a piece of furniture for the best effect, telling her to sit on him, pulling her forward until her brassiere was so close, he could smell the perfume of violets mixing with the musky cinammon odor of herself. His eyes were closed. "Raza . . ."

She heard another noise, like a scrabbling, above her, and she rose, then drove herself down upon him, harder and harder until he was in a reverie, his head lolling, then whipping from side to side, his tobacco-stained teeth plainly visible, his mouth open like an ugly fish, eyes half-closed, the idiot expression becoming more pronounced so that it seemed his eyes were going to roll back into his head, his grip on the crazy quilt so powerful, he was now holding it up either side of them like the sides of a canoe, his wrist veins bluish in sharp contrast to his pale white skin. He was trying to talk, but it only came out as a series of short, gurgling noises and grunts, then the quilt sides fell from his hands, his body arched, arms locked about her, pulling her down hard against him, his body smacking her hard as spasm after spasm racked him, his crying like a child running terrified from some huge beast but the cries of ecstasy. Eager to get off, Malle felt him pulling her back, and he kissed her tenderly on the earlobes, stroked her hair, whispering how wonderful she was, how beautiful, his voice cracked and dry. "Did you come?"

Of course not! she wanted to scream. "Yes," she said.

He knew she was lying, but it didn't matter.

His breathing slower now, he pushed her away gently, asking her to bring him a towel.

When she returned, she had a housecoat on, and he avoided looking at her as, wrapping the towel about him, he walked unsteadily toward the bathroom. "Put on some coffee," he said, closing the door.

As Malle turned on the gas, the blue ring became a blurred circle and she used her sleeve to wipe away the tears. She must get control of herself, mustn't make him feel as if he'd forced her, for he could still turn on her. But what choice had she had? she asked herself. Turning the hot water tap full on—it was only lukewarm—she rinsed her mouth out again and again. For a moment in the bedroom when she had felt she couldn't bear doing it, she had thought of her husband as the only way of getting through it. Now the guilt of sordid betrayal weighed so heavily on her, she felt she could never look anyone in the face again.

She heard a surge of radio static. It so alarmed her, she swallowed and swung about, realizing it was only the corporal's walkie-talkie. Unhurriedly he pulled on his boots, turned down the squelch button on the walkie-talkie, and rising from the edge of the bed, picked up his cap from the bedside table. She thought she heard some mention of the Tallinn docks. The corporal glanced at his watch as he slipped it on his wrist, then clipped the walkie-talkie onto his belt. "The apartments are to be kept under surveillance," he said, adding apologetically, "I can't stay for coffee. We have to go to the docks."

"Oh—" She tried to sound convincing. "That's too bad."

He was out in the kitchen now, pulling on his tunic, looking smart, repositioning his cap in front of the small hall stand mirror, the green cap's green ribbon in gold lettering reading, "Infantry of the Border Troops."

"Never mind," he said, opening the front door and smiling back at her. "I'll come by tomorrow."

In Moscow there had been snow flurries all morning, giving the air a bluish-white tinge with a wind coming down from the Lenin Hills, making eyes water and noses run. Inside the Politburo chamber, all fourteen members and their aides present, the air was warm. It was too much so for Premier Suzlov, as he found, not yet halfway through the meeting, that his sinuses were plugging up. The minister of war was in favor of releasing twenty-five Far Eastern divisions, to be entrained at once from all points west of Ulan-Ude near the Mongolian border two thousand miles away.

"And if Japan enters?" asked Kiril Marchenko.

"Japan is already in it," said the minister of war, suspecting, though not saying it, that because one of Marchenko's sons, Sergei, had now qualified for fighter service and was based in Ulan-Ude in the Transbaikal, his father wanted to keep him out of it. The minister rejected the suspicion, however, as quickly as it had come in a moment of pique. Whatever else the Marchenkos were, they were not cowards. Sergei's gallantry during the bloody breakout at Fulda was evidence of that—for this he had been awarded the Order of Lenin, the Soviets' highest award for bravery. Nevertheless, the minister was confused by Marchenko's comment about the Japanese. It was as if they still had something up their sleeve.

"Yes, they do," answered Marchenko. "They are throwing in their lot with America but are not yet fully committed. Their defense forces are at America's disposal, but only in a support role so far, and in defense of our bombing attacks on their ports. I assure you, gentlemen," said Marchenko, looking down the long, green baize table toward Suzlov, "that Tokyo is nowhere near fully committed. My estimate—and it is supported, I should add, by the commander in chief, eastern TVD—is that they might yet throw in all their ground, naval, and air forces if they see the gate to their north unguarded. That is why I will vote against the motion."

"Rubbish," retorted the minister of war. "Beijing wouldn't let the Japanese walk into Manchuria. The Chinese navy would sink them before they got across the straits."

"It wasn't Manchuria I was thinking of," said Marchenko pointedly. "I am talking of *our* raw materials. Ore, oil—*our* Far Eastern holdings."

"Oh," replied the minister of war, "and what do you think our Pacific Fleet will be doing? Nothing?"

Kiril Marchenko pulled another Marlboro from his pack, taking his time to light it. Premier Suzlov appeared to be doodling, not paying attention, but Marchenko believed he was listening—intently.

"The Far Eastern Fleet will be attacking the Japanese," said Marchenko, shifting the gold Dunhill lighter close to the packet of cigarettes.

"Exactly, Comrade," said the minister of war, sitting back, relieved. "Exactly. So therefore why do we need so many divisions on the—"

"And the Taiwanese," put in Marchenko. "Our fleet will have to deal with the Taiwanese."

The minister of war shook his head. "No, my friend. Taipei hates the Japanese as much as the mainland Chinese do. And not just because Japan and Taiwan have been competitors in the capitalist system. No—it goes back much farther than that."

"I know," said Marchenko.

The minister of war was enveloped by the cloud of smoke from the American cigarette. "Kiril," he said slowly, leaning forward, short, stubby fingers clasped on the baize, "my good friend. Tokyo will never team up with Taipei to try for Manchuria or for our raw materials in the East. It would be the guarantee of a future war between them. Splitting the spoils. You know how these capitalists are."

"I disagree," responded Marchenko. "Tokyo will team up with the devil to get more materials, war or no war. Together with Germany, she is the powerhouse of the West. But her stockpiles, for all her cunning, are limited, Minister. Oil from the Middle East, cheap coal from Canada, bauxite from Australia. It must all come by sea. And—" Marchenko looked about quickly but intensely at everyone at the table, making sure the premier was alert to his point. "And all of it must come a long way—thousands of miles by sea." He shook his head knowingly and blew out a long stream of grayish smoke. "She is overextended, my friends. I agree that, for the moment at least, a Taiwanese attack on Manchuria is not likely. Our intelligence confirms that U.S. President Mayne has warned Taiwan not to do anything against China as long as China doesn't attack the U.S."

"Attack the U.S.?" asked the minister for war. "Where? China is five thousand miles from—"

"By sending Chinese troops across the Yalu," put in Marchenko. "Into Korea. Korea is stabilized now after the Freeman airborne attack opened it up for the Americans to counterattack. The Americans don't want any escalation of war in Asia."

"Then you are arguing against yourself," charged the minister of war. "There is no danger of Taiwan attacking. And if Japan makes a move against our Far East flank first, they will have to contend with our fleet of submarines and surface warships out of Vladivostok.''

"Very good," answered Marchenko, "but I think they might try for Sakhalin Island. It's rich in raw materials. You will recall that the Japanese called it Karafuto until we took it away from them at the end of World War Two. It is less than a hundred miles from Hokkaido. They could be there before our fleet way down in Vladivostok knew about it. And even if Vladivostok did find out, our fleet could never catch them in time. I can't think of a more opportune time for them to move—while we are preoccupied in Europe." Suzlov stopped doodling, looking up to see whether Kiril Marchenko's thesis had surprised the rest of the STAVKA as much as it had him. It had.

"We would annihilate them," said the minister of war confidently.

Marchenko leaned forward from across the table and offered the minister a Marlboro. The minister accepted it, smiling but nonplussed all the same. "Then," said Marchenko, lighting the cigarette for him, "you will need soldiers."

There was a silence invaded only by the intermittent clanking noise somewhere in the air ventilation system. Marchenko, holding his cigarette in the Western manner, unlike the minister for war, indicated the strategic map of the USSR across from them. It covered the entire wall: eleven time zones, its sheer vastness impressive even on paper. The war minister and everyone else at the table knew full well that once the Far Eastern divisions were raided for manpower and entrained westward—itself a logistical nightmare—the Far Eastern borders would be irrevocably weakened. Apart from Japan, there were the Chinese. There were always the Chinese. One point two billion of them at your back door. "Remember," cautioned Marchenko, "when Chairman Khrushchev threatened Mao over Damansky Island. He told Mao, 'We could invade China at a moment's notice. A press of the button and you will have a million dead,' to which the Great Helmsman replied, 'A million less to feed. You would drown in our blood.' ''

"Then what are we to do?" the war minister asked Marchenko irritably. "About the NATO front?"

"We are sending in SPETS now," put in the minister responsible for special forces. "Comrade Marchenko suggested we try further attacks behind their lines to take pressure off Marshal Kirov's forces while they are being regrouped and refitted for the final attack on the Dortmund-Bielefeld pocket.''

"And how do the SPETS get there?" asked the general for logistics and supply.

"They will walk in," said Marchenko, shifting his gaze west from Siberia to Western Europe. "In British and American uniforms."

"The Allies aren't fools," said the minister of war. "They'll catch on to that soon enough."

"Of course," conceded Marchenko, "but how long do you think it will take them, Minister? Hannover is sending in SPETS even as we talk."

"Where the American airborne were dropped?" asked a brigadier general.

Marchenko turned, making sure he would remember the face. The man was quick. "Yes," said Marchenko. "Exactly."

"I expect," said the minister of war, his tone tinged with sarcasm, "NATO will get onto it within a week. And then they'll refuse to take any of our forces prisoner in retaliation."

"A *week*?" said Kiril, smiling broadly, his cigarette jutting out from both hands, which were clasped in front of him as he smiled, positively buoyed by the minister's assessment. "A week! We estimate only three days, Minister. We only need one decent raid on the monster depot at Munster and the whole pocket will be down to eating rats and using slingshots within a week."

"*If*," put in the admiral for the Northern Fleet, "the convoys resupply them."

"Will they?" Kiril's speed in turning the admiral's question into a demand—almost an accusation against the admiral—took everyone by surprise. Suzlov was watching the admiral intently.

"I—I don't think so," replied the navy chief, clearly rattled but trying to rise quickly to the occasion. "We have a new strategy. Also—we have been—ah—gathering much better reports on shipping movements in and out of the English ports. Our intelligence agent networks in England are working extremely well. The more accurate the departure and arrival times, what ships are due where, the better chance we will have of sending in low air strikes across the English Channel . . . to specific targets . . . chop them up before they can even scramble their fighters.''

"Good,'' said Kiril. "It's imperative that we strike at both ends of the problem. At the convoys and at the pocket.''

"In a month,'' predicted the admiral, "their rollover convoys will have rolled flat and sunk.''

There was hearty laughter, much of it released from the tension between Marchenko and the minister for war. Nevertheless, Suzlov wanted to know what made the admiral so confident. Such promises he knew were not made idly; the man who said no one could reach Red Square without him knowing it was quickly replaced after the young West German, Rust, had landed on Red Square in a light aircraft.

"The plan for the convoys is classified 'for your eyes only,' Mr. Premier.'' It was the only answer the admiral could have given, but it aroused the curiosity of the other armed services so much that Suzlov decided to hear it along with the others. If he could not trust the STAVKA members, he could trust no one; besides, he was first and foremost a politician. He knew that a plan shared was responsibility shared, but when the admiral bared the plan from naval intelligence before them, Suzlov dearly wished he had kept his mouth shut. He would have preferred all the glory himself. It was a plan so stunning in its simplicity, so terrible for the Americans if it succeeded, that Suzlov knew it would win the war.

"Why have we not implemented this sooner?'' he demanded.

"Timing, Mr. Premier. All the instruments were there, but the players must perform under a single baton, orchestrated, otherwise we lose the initiative.''

Suzlov nodded his assent. "Yes, of course, you are right. When may I expect results?''

Marchenko was struck by Suzlov's use of "I'' instead of "we.'' A politician to his boot nails, thought Marchenko. Suzlov in an instant could take credit for something that others had been planning for so long. And it occurred to Marchenko that the admiral was almost as ambitious as he.

As Marchenko walked out to his black Zil limousine after the meeting, one of Suzlov's other aides caught up with Marchenko, his questioning about Japan so transparently having come from Suzlov that Marchenko could not stop smiling.

"What do you think Japan will do, Comrade Marchenko? Continue to play a passive role?"

"There's hardly anything passive in Japanese antiaircraft fire, Captain."

"No—no, of course not, Comrade. I merely meant—do you think she will commit herself more deeply?"

"It's a world war, Comrade," said Marchenko. His smile vanished. "You are either in it or you will soon be gobbled up."

"Some are suggesting that Japan has lost her aggressiveness. Not in commerce, of course, but militarily."

"Why are you so worried about Japan?" asked Marchenko, looking up at the dull autumn sky. "Do you have stocks on the Tokyo exchange?"

The aide was genuinely shocked. "Certainly not. But what—" The aide decided not to pussyfoot any longer and let Marchenko be so rude as to suggest that he, an aide to the Supreme Soviet, would be so guilty as to hold stocks in the—

"What the premier wishes to know," said the aide tartly, "is whether you think Japan wants war or will simply sit it out as best she can—as an ally of the Americans."

Marchenko made a face that said, "Who can tell?" yet he felt sorry for the aide. Besides, there was no sense in making enemies in a war that would see many dead—and many promoted. Had he himself not risen meteorically since the outbreak of the war?

Marchenko put his arm around the aide's shoulders. "Comrade—I was only joking, of course, about the Tokyo exchange. But to answer your question seriously, I would have to say that, after Hiroshima and Nagasaki, the Japanese people will be reluctant to commit themselves to anything like war on this scale. They will prefer to leave it to the Americans—who, after all, began it with their aggression in South Korea. And wait for us to finish it. Ultimately we must win. You see, for all their gadgetry—" here Marchenko wiggled his fingers in caution "—and, mind, I do not underestimate their technology. It is quite frankly the best. But the Americans do not have the staying power. They have not lost twenty million dead, as we did in the Great Patriotic War. This puts iron in the blood." He offered the aide a Marlboro. It was eagerly accepted, the aide putting it in his pocket for future use.

"Then," said the aide, "although you wish us to be on the safe side, to keep our Far Eastern forces on alert, you do not think Japan will go much beyond her supporting role?"

"No," said Marchenko. "I don't think she will."

Before his chauffeur closed the door, Marchenko handed the aide the packet of cigarettes. In case he was wrong.

Like Marchenko, many other strategic experts throughout the world had pondered the matter, believing themselves to have thought of every conceivable scenario and coming to much the same conclusion—that Japan would be America's handmaiden but not much more.

Another expert, though completely unknown at this time, was Tadanabu Ito, a graduate student recently arrived at Washington State University as part of the exchange plan from Wasada University in Japan. He held two Japanese baccalaureate degrees, one in the field of "macro" or large-scale economics, the other in plate tectonics, or the study of the shifting of the suboceanic plates upon which the continents rest. Ito had submitted the first draft of a Ph.D. thesis on the subject at Washington State University but was told by his adviser that his English, while it might have "squeaked through" the B.Sc. and M.Sc. level, was simply "not up to par" for the Ph.D.

Ito was so despondent discovering how, when you can't speak or use the language fluently, people automatically assume you're not as smart as they are that he didn't realize he was the only person in the world who, in his thesis, was predicting exactly what would happen vis-à-vis Japan. It was only a short chapter in his thesis—almost a footnote—and like a dream one has forgotten and only remembers later, he wasn't yet aware that he was in possession of one of the most important hypotheses in history. One that would directly affect the lives of David Brentwood, trapped in the Dortmund-Bielefeld pocket, his sister in the far-off Aleutian Islands, and Robert Brentwood and his crew in many of the same ways that it would affect the more than thirty million men and women in arms in the worst war in history.

In northwest Germany, 19 miles north of the 250-square-mile Dortmund-Bielefeld pocket, a crack regiment of Soviet SPETS commandos began to advance under the protective barrage that had kept the ill-dropped American airborne pinned down in the northern sector of the pocket.

In the early morning mist that clung to the waterways of lower Saxony and in particular along the Mittelell Canal held by the Soviet 207th Motorized Division and 47th Armored, the SPETS were being sent in to take advantage of the earlier gains made by the 11th Motorized and elements of the Soviets' 57th and 20th Armored Divisions. The Soviet tanks, though they had punched a ninety-mile corridor northwest toward the pocket through the American M-1s and the German Leopards, were now due for refit and resupply before the massive, and what Moscow hoped would be the final, assault by fifty divisions. In all, it would pit a million Russian troops against the two-hundred-thousand-odd beleaguered NATO troops in the pocket, who would first be pounded by simultaneous Soviet artillery and rocket barrages all along the now chopped-up snake line that had formerly been NATO's central and southern fronts.

The hundreds of SPETS and other underground cells that had infiltrated the West during the East German rush through the wire, or rather through the gaps in the wire that had been cut by the Hungarians in 1989, had already carried out highly successful sabotage raids on the railway marshaling yards throughout western Germany as well as hitting four of the huge "prepo" storage sites dotted about the central region, including two outside Göttingen and Fulda which had contained many of the central front's 150,000 military vehicles and nuclear warheads for 105-millimeter and 203-millimeter artillery. But not all of NATO's depots had been gutted in the early hours and weeks of the war, and the troops in the Dortmund-Bielefeld pocket were drawing on the deep underground reserve dumps of ammunition from around Munster, situated more or less in the middle of the kidney-shaped 250-square-mile pocket.

Soviet and East German bombers could not penetrate the NATO air screen thrown up around *avianosets Angliya*— "carrier England"—where, though exhausted by sometimes more than seven sorties a day, pilots of the RAF, USAF, and German Luftwaffe forming NATO's Second Allied Tactical Air Force continued to go up against the swarms of MiG-23–escorted "Backfire" and Badger-C bombers, the Soviet fighters carrying Kitchen and Kingfish air-to-surface missiles. Despite their pilots' fatigue and a crash rate of 5.2

percent—which didn't sound like much to the layman at home but which meant that after just ten sorties, you had only a fifty-fifty chance of coming back alive—the NATO air force commanders deep in the Börfink bunker before it was overrun had kept the Soviets at bay in the air. What the HQ of Second Tactical Air Force, now in the south at Ramstein, wanted—and what the U.K. Royal Air Force command in High Wycombe prayed for—was foul weather.

While this would complicate the already insufficient supply lines across the English Channel, including the floating oil pipeline, NATO preferred it because of the experience of the American pilots who had fought off Soviet interceptors in the night skies and bad weather during General Freeman's raid on Pyongyang. The American pilots, including Frank Shirer, had confirmed a long-held NATO article of faith: When it came to instrument flying with all visuals ruled out, American, British, and German fighters could outstrip their Russian counterparts.

Even during the daytime dogfights over northwestern Germany and over the area still held by NATO in the south around Mannheim and Heidelberg, the NATO fighters, particularly British and German Tornadoes and American F-11s and Falcon-18s, were outclassing the opposition. The problem was that the opposition had more planes and more pilots: an advantage of three to one in aircraft, two to one in pilots. It was a situation worsened by the spectacular success of the Soviet divisions in southern Germany, which had so badly mauled the Fourth Allied Tactical Air Force, SPETS attacks having penetrated as far as Bitburg, where forty-seven of the seventy-two F-15s based there were destroyed on the ground by "activated" SPETS groups who had easily infiltrated the sea of refugees fleeing westward from the Soviet juggernaut.

In Hannover, northeast of the Dortmund-Bielefeld pocket, the concern of the Soviet–Warsaw Pact was how to crush the pocket before NATO convoys could hope to replace what had been lost on the battlefields of Germany.

For the Soviet military accountants and logistical wizards in Berlin's subterranean headquarters, the problem was never calculated in terms of pain, of lives lost, because already the human face had become obscured beneath the wrap of high technology. Modern technology, contrary to public opinion, had not made killing any less barbaric, the twisted metal of modern munitions wreaking as much hacking and butchering as any of the barbaric wars of old. One of the "advances" in technology was bullets so heavy, yet so small—made of depleted uranium—and of such velocity that upon impact, they could vaporize a man's head in the way a piece of shell might have in the great artillery barrages of the First and Second World Wars.

For the HQ computer staffs, however, divisions were rectangles moved about on the computer screens, not a torso torn asunder, where arms and legs or stomachs simply disappeared and where carrion crows grew fat on the spilt innards of soldiers. Nor did the statisticians deal with the effect on morale of supersonic fighter attacks, or laser-guided antitank rockets, of the unimaginable nightmare of a cluster bomb bursting, bombs within bombs within bombs, releasing needle-sharp shrapnel. Nor did the statisticians deal with the overwhelming sweet stench of dead flesh that greased the treads of the tanks and APCs as men drove until they were exhausted or their fuel had been expended, many of them becoming nothing more than whimpering shadows of their former selves, their eyes bright with madness from high-tech stress levels beyond bearing.

In the Berlin bunkers, where the state had long held precedence over the individual, the Soviet military statisticians, many of them women, saw none of this—their job to coldly, dispassionately, estimate Allied losses and a timetable for Allied resupply. Bad weather to them was neutral; perhaps it would make the convoy safer, harder to find by visual means—on the other hand, the low mist and rolling fog banks of late fall could impede attack and aid defense on the land. For now, it was the matter of the convoys that Supreme Soviet Commander Marshal Leonid Kroptkin was concentrating upon. So long as the NATO fighter screen held over Western Europe, NATO supply lines through France and through Austria, if Vienna threw in its lot with the NATO forces, would sustain the Dortmund-Bielefeld pocket. And if supplies kept coming, the pocket could expand into counterattack. And so the top priority for Moscow and Berlin was to stop the convoys now heading for the French ports, from Dunkirk to Calais in the north to as far southwest as Dieppe, Saint-Malo, and Cherbourg.

"As long as this situation holds," the Soviet Western Theater of Operations C in C reported, "we have not won the war." It was not only the Allied submarine-escorted convoys that the marshal worried about, but the Allied capacity to air-drop supplies into the pocket if the NATO convoys succeeded in bringing in enough men and matériel to the ports. What the Russian commander wanted was massive reinforcements from the East preceded by an awesome artillery barrage of a thousand guns of the kind that had finally destroyed the Wermacht and swallowed up Berlin over fifty years ago. His losses had been staggering, the Allies exacting a terrible price, over 130,000 Russians killed while punching the hole through the Fulda Gap, and almost 200,000 Soviet troops wounded.

"There is talk of reserves coming up from Yugoslavia, Marshal," his aide, a colonel, reminded him, pointing on the wall to the alpine border between northern Yugoslavia and southern Austria. "Through the Ljubljana Gap and—"

"Yes, there is talk," said the marshal. "There is always a lot of talk, Colonel. And what if Austria does not come over to us and permit the Yugoslavs to pass through?"

"I think they will."

"Yes, *now*," said the marshal. "If it looks as if we are winning." He turned to the huge, three-dimensional contour table map, his hand sweeping down over southern Germany to Austria. "No, my friend—the Austrians are stuffing themselves full of pastries, eyes darting like parrots west to east, waiting. Their friends are whoever wins. No one can wait for the Austrians."

"The Yugoslavs could simply push their way through. Whether Austria liked it or not," proffered the aide.

The marshal was bending over the contour map, his finger tracing the long fold of the Danube valley eastward to the conjunction of Czechoslovakia and Austria. "I thought you went to officers' school. You should know better than to indulge in such speculation. If the Yugoslavs come in, they will first have to get through the Ljubljana Gap if they are to be any use to us."

A dispatch rider, goggles and uniform splattered in mud, came in, saluted, and handed the marshal a list of the latest positions of the retreating Dutch forces in Westphalia, north of the Ruhr. The marshal nodded and told the rider to give the report to his logistics aide. The colonel, though distracted for a moment by the sight of the dispatch rider in a room buzzing and crackling with state-of-the-art electronic communications, returned to the subject of possible reinforce-

ments confronting NATO's southern flank. "Even if the
Italians attacked on our southern flank, I doubt whether they
could stop the Yugoslavs, Marshal," the ambitious colonel
pressed on.

"Perhaps not," replied the marshal, his right hand alter-
nately opening and closing to a fist, leaving a finger pointing
at the Ljubljana pass. "But the Yugoslavs might stop themselves. With Serbs versus Croats. In any case, Colonel, by
the time the Yugoslavs reach southern Germany, the
Dortmund-Bielefeld pocket could have expanded. No—what
we need are more troops. And quickly—so that we can annihilate NATO." His arms swept across the Dortmund-
Bielefeld pocket. "Before they can catch their breath. We
need to destroy their convoys—and we need more men."

"You're thinking," proffered the colonel, "of the Far East
divisions."

The marshall nodded. In the Far Eastern military theater,
the Soviet Union, ever wary of the long-standing and often
bitter border disputes with China's one point four billion and
India's eight hundred million, maintained over fifty divisions, almost a million men, fifteen thousand tanks, sixteen
thousand artillery and mortar pieces, and more than fifteen
hundred tactical aircraft.

"I have already requested them," said the marshal.
"Whether I get them is another matter."

"I'm sure you'll get what you need, Marshal," said the
colonel optimistically.

"Why is it," the marshal asked no one in particular, running thick, stubby hands through thinning white hair as he
looked at the red-flagged bulge on the wall map that marked
the disposition of the Soviet armies' deep penetration of Germany, "that the young are so incurably optimistic?"

A soldier brought the marshal's tea. "Is it," continued the
marshal, picking up the hard cube of sugar, "because they
have no history? Or is it because they have not seen the
defeats?" He raised the glass of tea, sucking the hot, steaming liquid through the cube of sugar until it disintegrated in a
crunch of tobacco-stained teeth. "I think it is because they
have not smelled war," the marshal answered himself.

Until this moment the colonel had thought he had very
much been in the war, but the marshal's voice, utterly devoid
of sentimentality, hard in its every estimate, conveyed to him
the sudden truth that up till now, what he had thought was

war had only been war behind the front lines, in the relative comfort of albeit makeshift headquarters in the ancient German capitals. Suddenly the colonel felt *he* needed the comfort of knowing that more men were coming. That thousands would come to aid them—so as to crush the British, American, and Germans in one decisive stroke. To bury all uncertainty.

"Marshal?"

"Yes?"

"Sir—this is meant as no criticism, but I was wondering if it might not be more efficient if we carried out all disposition-of-forces information by radio phone rather than by dispatch rider."

"You're worried about our gasoline supply for the armor, eh? Well, so am I. Our supply line is overextended, and I realized that every drop—"

"No, sir. I meant, wouldn't it be faster—better—to rely on our electronics rather than—"

"Faster," said the marshal, "of course. But better?" He grimaced, but there was also the hint of a smile. "I don't think so."

The colonel was flabbergasted. Had the marshal not attended officers' school? But the colonel would later remember the incident as the turning point of his military career—the point at which the marshal had dragged him out of the twentieth century into the new age.

CHAPTER NINETEEN

FOUR THOUSAND MILES away, it was late afternoon, a stiff easterly clearing New York of its pollution haze, the twin towers of the World Trade Center reflecting the turquoise sky like two enormous slabs of green ice towering above the skyline. But the high wisps of cirrus cloud and the vibrant color of the sky went unnoticed by Adm. John Brentwood. The only reason he noticed the high winds was because of their baleful howling by his New York Port Authority office on the seventieth floor. The retired admiral had resisted the move to the Trade Center as long as he could, citing, truthfully, that even the confusion of the short move from the Port Authority offices around Battery Park would cause delay in the crucial matter at hand: his office's overseeing the loading and departure of the vital Atlantic convoys.

"No problem, Admiral," his secretary had concluded. "Everything's on disk. In the old days we'd need fifty trucks and a month of overtime. Now—we'll have everything up here, three days maximum."

"Three days we can well use here," Brentwood had grumbled, his pen skimming over the latest cargo manifest—nearly all ammunition and aircraft parts.

They had tried flying several replacement squadrons of Thunderbolts and F-111s over the Atlantic with extra fuel in drop tanks and midair refueling. But the Russians could see them coming across the Atlantic, and though the weather was worsening over the mid-Atlantic ridge, the Russian pilots had managed to intercept. For a while the Americans and Canadians were losing more pilots at sea than over European soil. Pilots downed in Europe stood a reasonable chance of chopper pickup, providing they didn't come down in enemy territory. But for those who were shot down over the Atlantic, the rescue rate was less than 5 percent, for even though the pilots' radio beacons had a minuscule failure rate, the Atlantic was simply too vast to patrol for lost pilots, when every spare available aircraft was being used to help ferry matériel or conscripted for antisub patrols.

Because of the high losses of combat pilots over the Atlantic, sixty-eight in the first two months of the war, women pilots—whom the army air corps had used in peacetime to ferry the vitally needed planes to Europe—were now, albeit reluctantly, being considered as combat pilots. An editorial in *The New York Times*, a usually harsh critic of Army General Freeman's "cowboy" tactics, now brought his name back to national prominence by praising him for having had the foresight to use women chopper pilots in the daring and successful raid in and out of Pyongyang, the editorial going on to severely criticize the Pentagon's failure to have trained women as combat pilots.

The *Times* also criticized the slow rate of convoy departures, so that while John Brentwood was happy that Freeman, his youngest son's commander and someone Brentwood Senior greatly admired, was being mentioned again, sending signals to Washington that "more aggressively innovative thinking" was needed, the retired admiral bridled at the implicit criticism of the Port Authority. And it didn't help John Brentwood or any of his colleagues when the *Nagata* joke had reached the "Tonight Show," the Port Authority becoming the butt of one of Leno's comedy routines. Leno suggested that maybe "what the New York Port Authority should do is put a congressman on every ship. With that much hot air aboard—no way it would sink!"

Now, high in his new office, Brentwood, his office's computer notwithstanding, was confronted by hills of files, piled upon and about his desk. No matter how many computers you had to punch in all the variables, from not stowing yeast, sugar, or rice cargos together to the myriad problems about where and how to get enough ships, in the final analysis the decisions often had to be made on an old sailor's gut instinct. The major problem was that the deficiencies of the United States' aging mercantile marine were now starkly evident, after having been virtually ignored by every administration since Reagan, despite persistent predictions by the Pentagon that the ten thousand merchant sailors in the United States were far short of the twenty-two thousand required in war.

For Brentwood, it meant requisitioning, cajoling, recommissioning anything that would float and help bolster the old fleet, most of which had been taken out of mothballs to be used for the dangerous three-thousand-mile journey from North America to the ports of France and Britain. But while many ships were called, and many willingly lent to the government for cash equity later on, only 30 percent of these craft were approved as seaworthy, the others, to the chagrin of many a proud yachtsman or sailor, not qualifying because they could not maintain the required seventeen-knot convoy speed.

There had been the public hue and cry for the admiral and his staff to "get off their butts," as the *New York Post* put it, and to use whatever was possible for the convoys. Many of his critics pointed out that some of the thousands of big yachts, for example, could do well in excess of seventeen knots. But Brentwood stood firm, pointing out in turn that it wasn't the yachts' speed that worried him so much as their ability to keep in convoy pattern while heading full into a force-ten gale amid radio silence. And sailing under strict convoy orders whereby neither naval escort nor other merchantmen could alter course to assist, thus giving a marauding sub a slow target. Even so, Brentwood insisted on considering all comers, the computer telling him in cold, hard numbers that not enough of the tonnage NATO so desperately needed was getting through. "Rollover" was failing, the deadly equations tipping decidedly in the Soviets' favor.

Six cups of coffee since lunch, his diet having held firm against the creamer until the last cup, Brentwood was surprised when he looked up and saw it was dark, the old familiar Manhattan skyline now drastically altered due to wartime fuel and energy conservation, including a blackout on all nonessential illumination. It had been suggested at first that the city go into full blackout condition, as in England and Europe, but this was ruled out on the assumption that if the Russians were going to attack New York, it would be with ICBMs or sea- and air-launched cruise missiles. They would have no need to see where the city was, the coordinates for such an attack already having been programed into the terrain contour-matching nose radar of the ICBMs aboard their "Boomers," as the giant Soviet Typhoon SSBNs were called. Besides, as the major pointed out, and few challenged him, if the city was blacked out, the crime rate would soar.

Even from the admiral's commanding view on the seventieth floor, whole sections of Manhattan were missing, only the blipping of the red aircraft warning light atop the Trump Building affording the admiral a sense of his old familiarity with the city skyline. Far below, the yellow ribbons of traffic kept flowing, red taillights shimmering in the warm air of car exhausts that rose from the skyscrapers' canyons. The admiral was so exhausted that at times he'd nod off. Upon waking, the red light on the Trump Building would cause him to start, taking him back to the other war long ago during which, his father had told him, many an exhausted American driver in the endless three-ton-truck convoys would suddenly jerk awake, momentarily panicking that he was driving on the wrong side of the road before realizing he was in England.

"More coffee, Admiral?" asked his secretary.

"No thanks, Janice. Feel like I could run a mile. We have anything back from San Diego on those three Japanese tankers?"

"I don't think so, sir. I'll check the fax." As she walked away, Brentwood watched her with a mixture of affection and lust. She was half his age, in her midthirties, a single parent with two children, yet the strains and stresses of working as well as raising children hadn't given her the battle-worn face of many mothers her age, and her trim bottom fitted his category of "grabbable."

The admiral had never made a pass at her, telling himself he never would, but she was divorced, and now and then, as he glanced up from the never-ending pile of files or in reaction to the weather pattern information changing on the TV monitor in front of him, he had caught her looking at him with what he believed was a mixture of admiration and warmth. But, he reminded himself, she was half his age, Lana's age, and besides, there was no way he would cheat on his wife, Catherine. Not only would it be dishonorable, but downright cruel. She was still trying to come to terms with Ray's condition. Already there had been ten operations—the last three purely for cosmetic reasons to try to reconstruct his face as something else than a horror mask that even Ray and Beth's children had found difficult to deal with.

And now David was missing—God knew where—in what the Pentagon was vaguely referring to as the "northern German" sector. The admiral was tempted to pull a few strings in Washington, D.C., to try to get details of exactly where the American airborne's rapid deployment force was. But that wouldn't help David if he had already been killed. Besides, the admiral detested that sort of back-door, special-favor nonsense. There'd never been favoritism on his ships, and be damned if he'd start asking for it now. And how the hell he could even think of monkeying around with some gal half his age while his family was in such turmoil was beyond him, though some navy shrink, he recalled, had once told him the sex drive knew neither the proper time nor the place, that often it hit you precisely when you thought it shouldn't: when you were exhausted, at a funeral, and certainly after combat.

Which was why the admiral had to make sure, without mentioning it to Janice, that as important as penicillin and all the other medical supplies were to the well-being of the men, condoms were an essential part of the cargo—usually cut sick bay lines by 50 percent. He told Janice, as he'd told his sons, Lana too, that more people had died in 1919 of the flu than all those killed in the bloodbath of World War I. These days it wasn't flu but the age-old venereal diseases that stalked the battlefields of every war. To avoid public disclosure that would only increase the anxiety of the womenfolk left behind, the condoms weren't listed as such but as sterile surgical gloves.

On the TV monitor, Admiral Brentwood saw that the red, skull-like pictures of the storm system over the Atlantic were changing again. Red patches invaded green, the storm having moved from force six to eight since midafternoon. He wondered if Robert was out there now in the middle of it. Maybe the *Roosevelt* was farther north, in the Irish Sea, part of the NATO force protecting England's western approaches. Or rather trying to.

"Admiral?"

He looked up at his secretary. Janice had the lips of a Raquel Welch and a body to boot, her curves flattered by a form-clinging emerald knit dress, the air around her redolent with the perfume of roses. His favorite flower. It struck him that she might know this, but he quickly dismissed the thought as mere conceit. She handed him a fax. "Admiral, San Diego regrets . . ."

"But they want the oil tankers for themselves?" he interjected, taking a file of letters she had ready for his signature.

"Afraid so, Admiral."

"I don't blame them," he sighed, taking off his reading glasses, sitting back, pinching the bridge of his nose. "The only oil Japan and the Sixth Fleet's going to get is from our West Coast, at least until Iran and Iraq stop shooting at anything that moves in the Gulf."

"We could fax Valdez," suggested Janice. "If there's a lineup there, we could ask Washington to intervene and release—"

"Yes," said Brentwood, leaning forward now, hands locked together, shoulders hunched from the long hours and stress of the job. "But if we fax Valdez to release a tanker for the Atlantic ops without going through San Diego, that'll only get San Diego's back up—not to mention the Sixth Fleet."

"And Tokyo," she added.

"You've got it. No—we're all running on a scarcity of ships, Janice. Everyone thinks their operational theater problem is the most important, their problems the most serious. But if anything happens to those tankers we have on—" he put his reading glasses on, peering through the dimmed light of the overhead neon at the transparent green "Ops" board "—Convoys Eighty-Three and Eighty-Four—we're in big trouble." Janice said nothing, and all he could hear for a moment was the soft sound of her breathing. "Look—let's request *one* tanker from San Diego. They'll look piggy if they insist on keeping all three. One's a compromise situation, and we can start moving it as a reserve. But double-check the draft on all three tankers, Janice—*before* we make the request. We don't want to do a Levins."

Janice laughed. "Yes, Admiral." Levins was one of Brentwood's colleagues in the New York Port Authority/Navy Logistics Liaison Office who had *"demanded"* a tanker from San Diego and had then become a laughingstock in the Pentagon and all up and down the West Coast after it was discovered the tanker he'd been thumping the desk for was two meters too wide for the Panama Canal. "Unless," a tongue-in-cheek advisory had come back from San Diego, "you intend sailing it round Cape Horn?"

"I think asking for *one* is a good idea," replied Janice. That'll hold us till there's a lineup at Valdez. Then we can offer to help relieve the congestion in Prince William Sound."

"And get another tanker," said Brentwood, smiling, shaking his head in admiration. He scribbled his signature on several letters and handed her the file. "You should be in Washington, Janice. DOD could use you in strategic analysis. You're wasted here."

"No, I'm not." She said it quietly, firmly, looking straight at him, holding the file close to her body as she spoke. "I'm very happy here."

Brentwood nodded, felt himself blushing, and mumbled something about being grateful. He could organize convoys of over a hundred ships, but damn it, how to handle this situation was beyond him.

A few minutes later, Janice returned, informing him, "San Diego's taking your suggestion under advisement, Admiral."

Suddenly he sat bolt upright, struck by the speed of her having sent the fax and receiving an answer. "My God, you didn't send it in plain language?"

"No, sir. Automatic code feed."

"Of course. Sorry, Janice. I'm going soft in the head. More tired than I thought, I guess."

She leaned over to put the fax before him, seeing his neck tendons tense from the long hours at the desk. "Admiral, you work the hardest of anyone I've ever known. You should relax more."

"What—oh, yes." He was unconsciously massaging his forehead, eyes straining over the reading glasses at the changing weather map.

"You have a headache?" she asked. "Can I get you an aspirin?"

"No. Irritates my—" He was about to say "gut" but instead said "stomach."

Her fingers trailed over the tense ridges of his shoulders. "You need a neck rub, that's what you need."

"Yes," he laughed, alarmed by her tone. Before he could reach for another file, he felt her supple hands on the hard, aching muscles and could immediately feel the tension start to drain from him. "Hmm—" he murmured, despite himself. "Damn—that's good." He hadn't felt so calm in days. "Hope they send us that tanker," he said.

"Shush—" she said. "Forget the tankers—they'll only make your headache worse."

As her hands kneaded the tight trapezius, the admiral felt his shoulders slumping, the tide of relaxation spreading down his body. With the hum of the computer terminal in the background and the soft hues of the changing weather pattern over the Atlantic playing across the desk, he felt drowsy, warm, aware only that her breathing was in harmony with his. He felt emotionally closer to her than he had ever thought possible—or was it the mere excitement of an elderly man? he wondered, intrigued by the flattering possibilities. She was half his age, he told himself again, and nothing would happen. Nothing should happen.

"That's better," she murmured, reaching from behind, undoing his shirtfront, her breasts, soft yet full, brushing against him as she spread his shirt over his shoulders so that her thumbs could reach deep beneath the scapula.

His eyelids grew heavy, opening and closing again, his vision fixed momentarily on the pinpoint of the flashing red light atop the Trump Building, until the red began to blur, the hum of the computer more soothing than before. He could always phone and tell Catherine he was staying over—which he had done more often than not when convoys like Eighty-Four and Eighty-Five, due to sail at midnight, had been bow to stern, choking the harbor in the final stages of loading.

A warmth enveloped him so deeply that he felt as if his entire body were wrapped in down, the faint smell of roses barely detectable but there, his thoughts more and more dreamlike, the surroundings of the office merging and melding into each other like a mirage shimmering on a summer sea. As her hands trailed along his shoulders, up his neck, taking the full weight of his head, her nails created a tingling sensation all over him, and she heard his groan of sheer pleasure, a boyish smile spreading over him, softening the robust features of his face. He turned and she kissed him. They did no more, and next morning he told her it had to stop before ". . . you know what." This made her inordinately sad about what could have been.

The admiral felt a guilt greater than if he'd lost another *Nagata* through negligence, haunted by the incomprehensibility of the betrayal to his wife. How he could have done such a thing, and when his youngest was missing, was beyond him. Oh, he had seen infidelity a thousand times in the navy, but that was always the weaknesses of other men. Just as his son Robert carried the responsibility of killing Seaman Evans aboard the *Roosevelt*, so his father labored under guilt, a guilt that to other men would have seemed disproportionate, to say the least. Though intellectually the admiral could see how it would be seen as nothing to other men, he could not shake the feeling of unworthiness, and it would become an even heavier burden as the war kept on, the admiral hoping that one day, somehow, somewhere, he could redeem himself.

Atop Hawaii's island of Maui, it was afternoon, the azure expanse of sea now darkening with no distinguishable horizon in sight, blue upon blue upon blue, silver winking of whitecaps soon indistinguishable, swallowed by the glare of the late sun's light. The uninterrupted aspect of the Pacific all about the Hawaiian Islands was a sight meteorologist Sam Ronson never tired of watching. As his four-wheel-drive Toyota took the last of the bending zigzag road up to the observatory, he flipped down the visor and wound down the driver's window, relishing the cold, icy blast of air.

His union had fought vociferously against the U.S. Weather Service scheduling only one meteorological officer for the six-to-midnight watch, arguing that six hours in the high, thin, pristine air was too hard on a single observer. The truth for Sam Bronson, however, and one he was careful not to reveal to the union bosses in Honolulu, was that for his part, he wouldn't have minded staying up at the observatory all night. He liked the solitude granted him by the astronomer, who was usually too busy to talk. For Sam, the spill of stars in the autumn sky was a sight that never ceased to awe. He wasn't sure whether there was a God or not, but if there was, then this night sky was more evidence of a supreme being than all the holy books. Night after night he had gazed toward the heavens, transporting himself to worlds beyond. The belief that there were no other beings in the universe seemed to him as silly as the belief that there was an up and down, an idea manufactured by men merely to comfort them in the huge uncertainty of infinity.

But even if he had not enjoyed the "nocturnal star gazing," as the astronomer on duty called it, Sam treasured this time away from his wife. She was his second and, after his first, his second biggest mistake. Sam didn't like partying or even talking much. After two wives and four children, what he wanted was to be left alone, to monitor the anemometer for wind speed, the seismograph, and rainfall—now called "precipitation" by the TV forecasters—and to marvel at the fact that within a few thousand feet, Maui's tropical rain forests were washed by rain that had been snow at the height of the observatory.

When he saw the stylus on the brown recorder jerk to five, registering a quake several hundred miles northwest of the outer island of Kauai, he didn't bother putting in a call to Honolulu as the information would automatically have gone through from the observatory via the SAT/bounce feed. But when the stylus went to 6.1, he initiated a manual as well as the automatic alarm, which was just as well, for, though he didn't know it at the time, the automatic sensors on Japan's west coast were being "fuzzed over" by an electrical storm sweeping down from Japan's northern island of Hokkaido. It meant that Sam Ronson's warning, via Honolulu relay and Australia's Tidbinbilla, was the first Tokyo center had of the quake and of ensuing tsunamis, the latter so often mistakenly called tidal waves, which were heading toward Japan.

The height and frequency of the tsunamis were being excited by a hurricane, moving northwest from the Marianas with winds in excess of 120 miles an hour. When the stylus jumped from 6.1 to 7.1, every digit on the Richter scale representing a *tenfold* increase in force, Sam Ronson again rang through the alarm. But by now Tokyo was being hit, and though no one realized it at the time, the thesis of Tadanabu Ito, joint degree holder and Ph.D. candidate, on "Tectonics and Economics" was about to become a reality. It would make Ito famous and explain the death of over three hundred thousand Japanese as the quake, the worst in Japan for a hundred years, reduced the financial center of Tokyo, despite all the "floating base" design of its skyscrapers, to a rubble of concrete and glass shot through with enormous natural-gas-fueled fires from ruptured mains.

To rebuild meant calling in, at the very least, the interest owing on the massive loans Japan had made to the West. In particular this meant calling in loans made to Brazil, Argentina, and Chile. Not yet combatants themselves, these countries and others like them who were required to repay Japanese loans in terms of raw materials could not repay even if they had wanted to, which they didn't, because of the Soviet sub packs roaming the south Atlantic and the Pacific, their prime purpose to play havoc along U.S./Australasian/Japanese sea routes.

The horrendous implications of such a situation had been unforeseen except for the obscure graduate student, Tadanabu Ito. His doctoral thesis on the economic and social implications of a Japan suddenly depleted of a steady supply of raw materials by natural disaster had predicted that a Japan starved for raw materials after her three-month reserves of iron ore, coal, and bauxite had run out would be a Japan open to the temptations of "military adventure." And that Tokyo, after her experiences in the thirties and forties, would not want another war with China. The only remaining source of such materials was the Soviet Far East.

At the end of November, Tokyo's full cabinet, with the emperor's approval, announced simultaneously to Washington and Beijing that in retaliation for increasing Soviet bombing of her western ports and the unlawful occupation of the northern islands, its defense forces would henceforth launch "surgical strikes" against Soviet bases.

This meant Vladivostok, farther inland at Ulan-Ude, and Cam Rahn Bay in Vietnam. The pilots of the Japanese "defense force," which had more F-18s than any country except the United States, were instructed, however, that under no circumstances must they enter North Korean air space, for this might be interpreted by Beijing as the prelude to a Japanese attack across the Yalu River into China.

CHAPTER TWENTY

THE STORM THAT had swept in over the Wash and down through England's Southeast, creating the torrential rain that Richard Spence and his daughters had driven through on their way back from St. Anselm's, had increased in ferocity Saturday night, kicking up so much debris that it had activated the IFRA—incoming fighter radar alarms—throughout the South of England. But early next morning it was difficult for Inspector Logan of the Oxshott constabulary to believe there'd ever been a storm. All Surrey seemed to be basking in sunlight, mists rising like steam from orchards and stubble fields.

Walking with a brisk pace, Inspector Logan relished the sudden rise in temperature that had alleviated his chronic arthritis. He could not remember the last time, at least not so late in autumn, when his tweed jacket and corduroy hat had actually made him feel so warm that he wanted to take them off, not that he would. Logan was an old-fashioned policeman and wouldn't have been seen dead without a jacket, tie, and hat. Besides, although he was perspiring, he was determined today to make no complaint about the weather, for while the pain in his hands and knees was still there, it had abated so much that he felt ten years younger, promising himself that he wouldn't be as irritable as usual.

The war had also helped Logan, pulling him, like so many others, out of early retirement to replace the younger men who'd been conscripted. He enjoyed the chance to shift his attention away from himself for a change so that now, as he walked toward the tree-wreathed cul-de-sac on the outskirts of Oxshott, there was more vigor in his step, and the smell of his pipe tobacco had seldom seemed so pleasant. He could see the two uniformed constables he had requested from the division over in Leatherhead waiting in an unmarked car parked beneath a large bare sugar maple on the road leading to the cul-de-sac of seven two-story houses. The Wilkins house was the one farthest away in the cul-de-sac, backed by a small meadow and then a dense line of oaks.

"Very quiet," said Police Constable Perkins, one of the two policemen in the unmarked car.

"Aye," replied his partner, PC Melrose, who was on the passenger side and who would rather have been home up north in the dales and the rugged wild country of Yorkshire, investigating livestock rustling by black marketeers, than down here in the lush, genteel green belt of stockbrokers and professionals. He didn't mind the natural surroundings so much, but the upper middle class were a bit too snooty for his liking. And Inspector Logan, whom Melrose now spotted in the rearview mirror, was an unknown quantity. "A little rusty," they'd said at the station. "Don't know why he didn't come in the car," said Melrose.

"Likes walking," replied Perkins, without taking his eyes off the Wilkins house. "I hope the other two are behind the house."

"They will be," Melrose assured him, "but I'm just thinking that the bastard might get away on us because Logan likes his Sunday morning stroll. See 'im coming a bloody mile, I could."

"No," said Perkins. "Where's Wilkins to go then? Out the window? Last thing you'd want to do if you were him is try to scarper. If he runs, he'll only confirm our suspicions. No, mate, I think we'll find Mr. Wilkins noshing tea and toast, reading the *Telegraph*."

The Yorkshireman made a face. " 'Twon't be the *Telegraph*. More likely be the Sunday bloody *Observer*."

"No," said PC Perkins with an air of unassailable self-confidence in these matters. "If you were a Commie spy, what would you be reading then? The very opposite, that's what. It'll be the *Telegraph*."

"You wouldn't like to put a wager on that, would you?" challenged PC Melrose.

"All right then. Ten p."

"Oh," grinned the Yorkshireman in mock alarm, "now, don't you go mad, lad. Come on, then—let's put a quid on it. And another quid Logan calls me bloody Melroad. He never did get it right." The truth was that Melrose thought Logan was over the hill; Oxshott should have waited until the storm-downed lines and battered microwave repeater antennae had been repaired and called London to send someone down.

"Not enough time, was there?" countered Perkins.

"C'mon," said Melrose. "You put a quid on the *Telegraph*, I'll put one on Logan calling me Melroad."

Perkins was about to answer, but now Inspector Logan had drawn level with the car, ruddy face, early sixties, puffing clouds of Erinmore Navy Cut into the car. "All quiet, boys?"

"Yes, sir," said Perkins. "Milkman's been and gone apparently." He nodded toward the house about two hundred yards away. "Bottles are still there."

Logan glanced at his watch. It was just after seven. "You sure Wilkins is home?"

"No, sir. But it being Sunday and all. Night shift said they saw the TV on late last night—till around eleven—then bed."

"How do they know that?" said Logan. "Blackout curtains would have been drawn."

"Aye," said Melrose, in his dry Yorkshire accent. "Apparently they were, but our lads could still pick up the TV winking on and off. At least it was a bluish light. They assumed it was the TV. Didn't want to complain about not having the blackout curtains drawn properly. Tip him off."

Logan grunted his assent. "You have the printout from Motor Vehicles?"

Melrose, on the passenger side, tore off the white slip and handed it to Perkins, who handed it out the window to the inspector. "Speeding ticket on the M1 a few months ago," said Perkins. "Apart from that—a perfect record."

"Phone tap?" asked Logan, his pipe gripped between worn-down teeth, the air rattling around the pipe's dottle. Melrose punched in the tap code to see if anything had come through since the last computer check-in. The small laser printer slurred. Melrose glanced at it before passing it to Logan. The inspector squinted at it, patting his pocket. To Melrose it looked as if Logan couldn't decipher the printout.

"One call in on the last shift," Melrose told Logan. "After the lines were fixed. A trunk call—reverse charges."

"Hmm—" murmured the inspector, the gurgling sound of the spittle in the pipe growing louder. He was frowning, trying to remember what part of the south coast was designated by area code number 703.

"Southampton," Melrose told him.

"I know that, laddie. *Where* in Southampton?"

"The docks, sir."

"Digest?"

Melrose took the clipboard from his passenger door latch. "Man called Ron—left a message on the answering machine telling Wilkins a convoy had just come in—a container freighter badly bashed in on the starboard side. Lots of cargo lost." Here Melrose had difficulty himself interpreting the transcript. "Sounded like Hum-V—anyway, Hum-V spare parts." It was typical, thought Melrose, the kind of unknown detail that gets even the most ordinary investigation off to a confused start. Never like it was in the cinema.

"What's a Hum-V?" asked Logan.

Melrose looked across at Perkins for help. Perkins shrugged.

"Well, find out," said Logan impatiently, taking what looked like a spiked thimble attached to a turnkey from his jacket pocket. He pushed it hard into the briar pipe, turning it, making a crunching-bone sound while PC Melrose called in, asking about a Hum-V. No one at the station seemed to know.

"Probably a Yank fighter," said Perkins. "Sounds American, doesn't it? Maybe it's Hummer, sir." Logan had his pipe cleaned now and was scooping the bowl deep into the tobacco pouch, the dark Navy Cut smelling like figs. "Well, we can sort that out later. Probably not important. Any calls out?"

"One," answered Melrose, this time reading from his notebook. "Mrs. Wilkins called the school hospital to ask about the boy. Didn't want to talk to her."

"Who?" asked Logan. "The boy or the headmaster?"

"The boy, sir."

The inspector knew that by now, if Wilkins was watching from the house, he'd be worried, which is just what he intended. Let Wilkins see them and the unmarked car.

"All right," the inspector said leisurely, sucking hard on the pipe, getting a good fire going. "You stay with the car, Perkins. Moment you see Wilkins's garage door open, you block the road—and get out of the car." The pipe was going fiercely now, tiny sparks hitting as Logan continued talking, the stem between his teeth. "You have a shooter?" he asked the two constables.

"Nothing about shooters, was there, Perkins?"

"No. Duty sheet just said surveillance. To assist Inspector Logan. Nothing about being armed, sir."

A stream of pipe smoke rushed up toward the bare maple. "Damn it! I distinctly told Leatherhead to issue sidearms. If this joker's a spy, he'll likely have one stashed in there somewhere." Melrose suddenly saw a gap in the inspector's assumption and moved to close it to protect himself and Perkins from the wrath of Leatherhead's chief constable. "Pardon, sir—but if this Wilkins chap is a spy, he's hardly going to carry a shooter. Dead giveaway if he's ever picked—"

"I'm not talking about a pistol, man," cut in Logan. "How about a bloody shotgun? Bird-hunting license, eh? That wouldn't be unusual around here. Lot of retired army chaps as well.''

"No, sir,'' said Melrose, deflated.

Logan looked again at the house, a magpie squawking somewhere nearby. The inspector didn't particularly like magpies. He felt the vest of his tweed jacket for his own standard issue—a Parabellum nine-millimeter. The holster was ill fitting. Last time he'd signed out a sidearm had been in the late eighties—a mental patient from nearby Holly Road Asylum, or Holly Road Mental Rehabilitation Center, as they called it these days. "All right,'' he sighed, taking Melrose's point, but not entirely satisfied. And keyed-up. "Well, we might as well go in.'' He hesitated. "I presume you *did* remember to bring handcuffs, Melroad?''

"Yes, sir,'' said Melrose.

"What's up with you?'' Logan asked, turning to Perkins, who sounded as if he was choking. "You all right?''

"Ah, yessir—something caught in my throat, that's all.''

Leaving Perkins at the car, Melrose and Logan started walking toward the house, shoes crunching on the steamy gravel. "Stay on your toes,'' Logan told Melrose. "My guess is our Mr. Wilkins is still in the land of Nod. But if not, it's conceivable he might try to run for it. Don't want to use the shooter if I don't have to, so be ready for one of your rugby tackles, Melroad.''

Melrose was surprised—how did Logan remember he played rugby but couldn't get his name right?

"Breakaway, wasn't it?'' asked Logan.

"Yes, sir.''

"Bit big for that, aren't you? Must have speed. That it?''

"Yes, sir.''

"Well, let's hope we don't need it this morning.''

"No, sir,'' answered Melrose, his sidelong glance at the inspector one infused with newfound respect. "Play yourself, did you, sir?''

"Yes. Century ago. On the wing.''

"Faster than me then, sir.''

"Not now,'' said Logan, bending down in front of the house to pick up the morning paper. *Telegraph*, Melrose noted.

Logan pressed the doorbell. "You hear it?'' he asked after about ten seconds. "Half the damn things don't work,'' Logan continued, this time reaching for the brass knocker. It was a coiled snake. "Must be a bloody lawyer," said Logan.

Before Melrose could comment, he saw the change in light on the peephole, heard the rattle of the chain, the door opening to a slit, and behind it he saw an elegant powder-blue housecoat. A middle-aged woman, brown hair and eyes, about five four, Melrose guessed, a little on the plump side, though that was probably the housecoat. Not at all bad-looking, really. Melrose tapped his police cap as Logan doffed his hat. "Morning. Mrs. Wilkins, is it?"

She took the chain off, her hands quickly moving to her throat, holding the satin lapels of her coat close together. "It's Graham—"

"No, no," the inspector assured her. "Your son's quite all right, Mrs. Wilkins. School hospital's taking good care of him. No, it's another matter, actually. Is Mr. Wilkins home?"

"Yes—I—I think so."

Logan nodded but managed to convey polite surprise.

"I mean—sometimes he comes home rather late and—" Embarrassed, she turned and called out, "James—"

There was no answer. She called again.

"He must be in the shower," she apologized to the inspector, moving a wisp of hair back away from her face. Logan smiled. It was an awkward moment, her eyes shifting to the constable.

"I wonder—" began Logan.

"Won't you come in?" she said quickly. "I'll go and fetch him."

"Thank you, ma'am," said Logan, taking off his hat, Melrose doing likewise, and both of them following her into the spacious, deep-carpeted living room, a large blue Persian rug at one end, Edwardian furniture, immaculate. Some photos on the mantelpiece—everything in its place, the smell of wax polish predominant. The kind of house, thought Melrose, you're afraid to sit in. Might disturb something. Logan's eyes lighted on a print that looked vaguely familiar, and on a small, round cedar table, dust-colored but clean figurines of the Chinese warriors dug up in Xi'an.

"I'll just be a moment," she said, starting up the long, curving stairway.

Logan's smile was fixed in a practiced graciousness. "Thank you, ma'am."

"What you think?" said Logan without looking back at Melrose.

"He might be going out the back."

"No—no," said Logan. "We've got the house covered. No, I mean the house. Marine insurance agent? Didn't know it paid this well."

"Maybe mortgaged," proffered Melrose.

"Possibly." Logan nodded, unconsciously patting the pipe in his left top pocket. "Or rented."

"Little too neat for renters, I'd say, sir."

Logan frowned disapprovingly. "You own your own place, do you?"

"No, sir—but I meant—"

"This *is* a Turner," said Logan, hands behind his back, looking closer at the painting. "Thought I recognized it— *Rain, Steam, Speed.*" His attention wandered back up to the mantelpiece—a wedding photo. Mrs. Wilkins was a lot thinner in the photograph, but it was her, all right, Mr. Wilkins in a tuxedo, a sharp dresser, mustache, and, or so it seemed in the photo, straining to appear as tall as his wife. Shifty, thought Logan. He was going on gut instinct, his voice low and unhurried. "Go and ask Perkins if there's been an out call since we've been here."

"Right you are, sir," said Melrose, taking a last glance up the stairs, expecting the woman to reappear at any moment. She'd sounded pleasant enough and totally surprised.

Logan pulled back from the print, confounded by its lack of definite line, moving left of the fireplace. If Wilkins was at home, and if he did have a gun, Logan was making sure his field of fire was much more advantageous than that of anyone who was coming down the stairs. The front door clicked softly as Melrose left. Then Logan checked to see whether there was another entrance to the living room behind him. There wasn't, and silently, the sound of an ornate cuckoo clock ticking woodenly behind him, he slid the high-backed Edwardian chair closer to the fireplace and in front of him. It would afford damn all protection, but was the right height to steady arthritic hands. He clenched and flexed his right hand several times to pump up the blood supply into his fingers. He was amazed—there was no pain in his knuckles.

The rear of the two-story house sloped down to a greenhouse, the blurred blobs of several enormous pumpkins and a run of what looked like cucumber barely visible through the steamy greenhouse glass. The two bored constables, watching from the base of the big oak trees seventy yards or so behind the house, saw Melrose, off to their left, heading back toward the car, then returned to their surveillance of the amphitheater of lawn and faded rhododendron bushes behind the house.

"Well, well!" said one of them. "What's going on here, then?"

A man in white shirt and gray trousers was crawling out of one of the upstairs windows and then began to slide down the main drainpipe to the guttering of the first floor, looking alarmed as he shimmied along the guttering just above the greenhouse roof, his left foot leading in a hurried, short shuffling movement to see if the guttering would hold before following with his right.

"Won't he be surprised to see us?" said one of the constables. "Didn't even take time to put on his coat."

"Would you?" asked the other constable, but his partner didn't answer, noticing the big aluminum TV dish, which, mounted on the west end of the house and not visible from the front, had several guy wires down to the guttering. "Be careful, Michael," he told his colleague. "This bugger might be carryin'."

"Yes—wish Melrose was round here with us. Could do one of his flying tackles."

"Not to worry, old son—he's coming right for us. All we have to do is step back and wait. I'll give him one of my half nelsons. That'll quieten—"

There was a yell, a tremendous crash of glass, and before the two constables had time to break cover, running for the house, Melrose was coming around the western corner of the house. Seeing one of the constables slowing, unable to go farther, Melrose assumed he'd been wounded but then realized the constable couldn't run for laughing.

"You see this?" he called out to Melrose. "Our boy's fallen into his ruddy pumpkins!"

By the time the three of them reached the greenhouse, the jagged edge of the broken glass panel was etched in blood, the man's face badly lacerated and bleeding as he tried unsuccessfully to extract himself from the pumpkins and kept falling back, each tumble making a bigger and bigger mess. Exhausted by the shock, he finally sat still, gazing up helplessly at the three policemen as Logan arrived on the scene. The constable who had been unable to run for laughing used his handcuffs to smack away a shard of glass that was dangerously close to the man's throat. "Fancy a little pumpkin pie, then?" said the constable.

"Be enough of that," said Logan sternly. "Go on, help him out of it. Melrose, go back in the house. Call an ambulance." It struck Logan as odd that Mrs. Wilkins hadn't appeared.

Staring down at the dejected pile of humanity before him, the inspector felt his pockets for his "rights" card. Fifty years on the force and he still hadn't memorized it exactly. The fact was that since his retirement, he'd found himself remembering less and less. Still, Logan doubted they'd throw out a spy case because your advisory to the defendant hadn't been word-perfect. "You are under arrest. I must warn you that anything—"

"Bloody 'ell—" The man's eyes were closed as he winced from pain, his left thigh bleeding badly. Logan saw Melrose coming down the half dozen steps at the rear of the house after checking inside, stepping over the broken glass and the remains of several cucumbers. "Did you call an ambulance?" asked Logan.

"On its way, sir." Melrose looked down at the man's bloody face. "Don't try to move, Mr. Wilkins. You'd better stay put until—"

"I'm not Wilkins—" said the man angrily. "Bloody 'ell." He grimaced. "Fink my knee's busted."

There was an amazed silence, the three constables looking at one another but carefully avoiding Logan's startled expression.

The man was moaning, "Oh, 'ell, me bloody leg's broken."

"Who are you then?" asked Logan fiercely.

"Corbett."

"Of course," said Logan sarcastically, thinking of the famous comedy team. "And I'm Ronnie Barker."

"Yeah—I get that all the time," moaned the injured man. "Very funny, I'm sure."

"All right then," said Logan harshly. "Show me your driver's license."

" 'Aven't got it. Didn't 'ave time, did I?"

"Where is it?"

"In my coat." He paused. "In 'ouse." He looked up in agony at Melrose. "I told you. Name's Corbett. I'm the—" He hesitated, eyes moving from one constable to another, then wincing. "I'm the bloody milkman. All right? Ask Mary—Mrs. Wilkins."

Logan nodded at one of the constables. "Ask Mrs. Wilkins to come out."

The moment the ambulance arrived and began the tricky business of first getting all the shards of glass out of the way, Logan heard one of the constables still chuckling about the squashed pumpkins. "It's no bloody joke," said Logan, upbraiding him. "Now we've tipped our hand, God knows where Wilkins'll be."

"Yes, sir," the offending constable said, and fell silent.

"You think it amusing," Logan kept on, filling his pipe from the pouch, tamping the tobacco in so tightly with his thumb that Melrose knew it would never burn. Logan waved vaguely south with the stem of the briar. "People are dying at sea because bastards like Wilkins are telling the Russians what ships are carrying what—departure times, how many escorts—the bloody lot."

"Sorry, sir," the constable apologized. "I didn't mean to make light of it."

Melrose, seeing the constable was about to burst out laughing again, quickly interjected, "Inspector?"

"Yes?" growled Logan.

"Well, sir—I doubt if Mrs. Wilkins'll tip him off. I mean, she'd have to tell him about Corbett—"

Logan was thinking about it, too. "Maybe not, but there's this bloody great shambles. . . ." said Logan, waving back toward the greenhouse debris with his pipe.

"The storm, sir," suggested Melrose. "We did have a spot of hail. Anyway, with the greenhouse behind the house, I doubt if it's the first thing he'll look at when he comes in. Can't see it from the cul-de-sac. And if she tries to phone out to tip him off, we'll know."

Logan seized on the idea, stopped for a moment to light his pipe, waving the match's flame back and forward over the bowl, his teeth sucking furiously, making a whistling noise.

"We could cut service," suggested one of the other constables. "Lots of lines went down in the storm. Station couldn't reach London. That's why we had to call on you, sir.''

Logan ignored the unintentional implication that he had been Oxshott's last choice.

"No," said Logan. "We cut the line and he tries to ring in—suspect something straight off.''

"The boy," one of the other constables put in. "We could move her out, leave a message on the answering machine saying she'd gone to be with the boy. Only natural the boy's mum would go to see him.''

"Does he know yet about the boy trying to do himself in?" asked the policeman who had been laughing before and was now trying for redress.

"Don't know," said Logan, sucking thoughtfully on his pipe. "I don't think so. She'd hardly risk having him barge in while she was entertaining our flying milkman, would she?" He turned toward Melrose. "Melroad?''

"Inspector?"

"Tell that ambulance crew I don't want that bloody milkman talking to anyone at the hospital. Call Oxshott and have them send one of our lads over there to stay with him.''

"Very good, sir." Logan saw the policeman he'd sent to the house coming down the back stairs. "She's in a right state," said the young constable. "Says she doesn't want to come out. Sight of blood upsets her.''

"I should bloody well think so," said Logan.

"We could tell her exactly what to say when he calls," suggested Melrose. "Make everything sound normal. I'm sure she'll be willing to go along with us. I mean, she won't want it getting out that she was having this Corbett character on the side.''

"No," said Logan, the tone of his rejection of the idea absolute. "They only do that on the stage, laddie—telling 'em exactly what to say. Doesn't work in real life. Man and wife have a hundred ways to convey to one another that something's up. No—we'll have to take her in. Slip a note through the mail slot saying she's at the hospital and then wait.''

Constable Melrose nodded his agreement. "Yes, but it's a sure bet he calls ahead when he's coming home. Otherwise she wouldn't have had Corbett in.''

"She's a smart one then," said one of the other two constables. "They might have arranged some external sign in the driveway or at the entrance to the cul-de-sac."

"Of course, it's possible," said Logan, "that she doesn't know what her husband does—I mean, what he does in addition to being a claims agent."

Melrose looked doubtful. "I'm not sure about that, sir. Not much is kept secret between a man and wife, is it?"

"Speak for yourself," said Logan, the comment slipping out before he had a chance to rein it in. He was sending dense clouds of sweet-smelling Erinmore into the still morning air, which was now heavy and pungent with the smell of fresh earth venting the rain. "Some of these jokers never tell their wives. Part of the cover, y'see. Don't think Philby's wife ever knew. I mean not until—" His voice trailed off. "Melroad, ask the duty sergeant in Oxshott to draw up four-on, four-off watches here around the clock. No cars visible. Don't use the house phone. Have Perkins call it through."

"Yes, sir."

"C'mon, you two," the inspector instructed the other two constables. "Let's have a look in the house."

When Melrose reached the car, he shook his head at Perkins, telling him the newspaper they'd seen on the porch was the *Telegraph*, so that Melrose now owed him another twenty p.

"Rubbish," said Melrose genially. "He's called me 'Melroad' about six times. *You* owe *me* a quid."

"Not likely, mate. I never took the bet."

"Welcher," said Melrose. "Well, anyway, you can chalk one up to our Wilkins, wherever he is. Logan's in a right pickle."

"Wasn't his fault," said Perkins.

"Balls. Should've let London in on this first up. Special branch. Cloak-and-dagger boys. But he wanted glory. Local lad lands big fish."

"Well, he couldn't call early last night, could he?" said Perkins. "Lines were down. Besides," Perkins added philosophically, "if Wilkins shows up, Logan could still come out smelling like roses."

"And if he doesn't?" asked Melrose. "The CID'll eat old Logan alive—pipe an' all."

Perkins made a pouty face, conceding Melrose's point. "Course, the Wilkins kid might be making it all up."

"You think so?"

"Melroad!" It was Logan, calling from the house. When they got there, the first thing they saw was Mrs. Wilkins, sitting boldly in the lounge chair by the fireplace, looking very pale. Logan beckoned them to follow him into the dining room.

"Feast your eyes on this," said Logan. He opened up a Marks and Spencer shopping bag. There were neat bundles of one-hundred-pound notes. "Must be twenty thousand at least," said Logan. "All used, looks like. Nonsequential."

"From the bedroom?"

"Just where the lad told us."

Melrose glanced over at Mrs. Wilkins, still in her housecoat, eyes downcast, fidgeting with the ribboned edge of her robe.

"No way she didn't know," said Logan quietly. "Course, she says she knows nothing about it."

"Course she doesn't," said Melrose, the uncharacteristic informality between inspector and constable a product of their mounting excitement. "Everyone leaves twenty grand hanging around the bedroom," he said. "Pay the milkman."

The inspector chuckled. "Good. Very good, Melroad. Well, lads—all we have to do now is sit tight and wait. I've got a call in to Leatherhead for a turnoff check. Nothing's come through yet, but as soon as his car turns off the M1, we'll have a half-hour warning."

"How about our friend, Mr. Corbett? Did he leave his coat, like he says?"

"Yes," said Logan. "He was telling them the truth after all. Here he is in glorious Technicolor."

Melrose saw from Corbett's National Health Plan card that he worked for Southern Dairy.

Melrose couldn't help feeling sorry for Mrs. Wilkins. Two men in her life, and neither of them any good. And she just didn't seem the type—the kind of person to betray her country. But then, none of them ever did, he reminded himself. That was the whole point. He saw her get up, and one of the two constables blocking her way. She stopped, cleared her throat, her tone braver than he would have expected under the circumstances. "Am I allowed to go to my own bathroom?"

Logan didn't bat an eyelid. "Of course, Mrs. Wilkins. As soon as the constable checks it out."

"What on earth for?"

"Razor blades—that sort of thing," said Logan, unfazed by the rising contempt in her voice. "We wouldn't want any other member of the family trying to do an injury to themselves, would we?"

She said nothing but folded her arms defiantly, turning her back on Logan, waiting, going into the bathroom, firmly shutting the door, after the policeman had emerged, holding a shower cap with several Bic safety razors and three bottles of pills inside it. Logan read the labels. One was for blood pressure—the other two tranquilizers. "As needed," Logan read from the tranquilizer vial before dumping it back into the shower cap. "I should think she needs them every time she lies to her husband. Not that I feel sorry for the swine, mind, but I can't abide a woman who cuckolds a man."

It was such an old-fashioned expression that it took Melrose by surprise, and for a moment he wondered if Logan's methods were just as old-fashioned, especially when Logan, a moment later, told him to take the pills out to the unmarked car as possible evidence. How tranquilizers might help the Crown's case, Melrose didn't know, and as he made his way to the car, it occurred to him that now they'd found a swag of money—something concrete—they should be calling in Special Branch—if the lines were up. If Logan didn't, maybe he should do it himself. It might save him some grief, put him and the others in the clear in the event that Logan botched up and missed nabbing Wilkins. On the other hand, Melrose knew, going over your superiors' head wasn't exactly cricket. And no matter how grateful Special Branch might be for the information, the word would be out.

Melrose rejected the idea and decided to wait, to do it Logan's way. If they were lucky, Wilkins would walk smack into the trap. It was only then that Melrose remembered the two bottles of milk he and Perkins had noticed outside the house when they'd first arrived. The two bottles were still there. If the milkman was her lover, surely he would have taken them inside with him. "Bit of a puzzle," Perkins conceded, but added, "Maybe he couldn't wait to dip his wick."

"Maybe," said Melrose, looking uneasily across at Perkins, "he isn't the milkman."

"Bloody hell," said Perkins, his head jerking around. "Then he *was* Wilkins?"

"What—no," said Melrose. "Christ—he couldn't be."

"Why not?" pressed Perkins, the tone of alarm growing. "He didn't have ID on him. Said it was inside the house. Anyone find it yet?"

"Yes, calm down. That's right. We did find his ID."

"But we didn't have any mug shots of Wilkins, though, did we?" continued Perkins. "All we were given, squire, was a man and his address. No priors."

Melrose tried to think hard, what Corbett's face was like. Was it the face in the photo of the married couple on the mantelpiece? He tried visualizing the man in the greenhouse, but all he could see were shards of bloodied glass.

"Forged ID?" he said.

"I think," said Perkins, "we'd better tell the inspector."

"You tell him," said Melrose.

"Not me," protested Perkins. "You thought of the milk bottles, mate."

"Bloody 'ell," said Melrose. "You think it was forged ID. Right?"

"Don't ask me. I never saw it."

Suddenly Melrose relaxed, slumping into the passenger seat. It would be easy enough to check. The man would be in hospital. Where was he going to go with a broken leg and—

"Oh Christ—" All they had seen was a lot of blood and the man moaning. A mustache meant nothing—shave the damn thing off in two minutes flat. Even less. Melrose tried to get through to the ambulance, but he couldn't, the waves "frying"—sizzling with the static of jammed frequencies— a Russian bomber raid under way. From the unmarked car Melrose watched the neighbors in the cul-de-sac peering from behind their curtains at the collapsed greenhouse, and he felt irrationally angry at them, as if it shouldn't be any of their business, when in fact he knew it was everyone's business.

CHAPTER TWENTY-ONE

CAPTAIN MALKOV WAS not getting the cooperation he'd expected at the docks, so now a different tack was called for. The border troops in dark winter uniform with matching fur caps that made them appear more menacing than usual selected two hundred civilians off the streets of Tallinn as "witnesses" and marched the two hundred, four abreast, through the winding streets of the city's old town toward the Viru Gate.

The column slowed when those at the front saw a roadblock of army trucks up ahead beyond the gates of twin towers, but the Ukrainian guards kept them moving. The burnt-brown cone tops of the twin towers were shiny, polished by the earlier rain, myriad raindrops on the evergreens like tiny diamonds as the foliage shimmered in the Baltic breeze. The fall air, too, washed by the rain, was cleaner, more invigorating, than Paul and Katrin Valk could remember. Two of the "witnesses," a young couple in from the country for market day, they were afraid that a terrible mistake had been made and that, like the two men whom Malkov had murdered the day before, they were going to be shot. Traffic had stopped, and beyond the shuffling sound of one another's feet on the blacktop over the ancient cobblestones, a silence was growing.

Katrin, her dark blue head scarf, dark as her eyes, catching the breeze, turned to the guard nearest her. "We have children."

The guard, a Ukrainian, said nothing but merely looked back over his shoulder for stragglers. "We are from a *Kolkhozy*—'collective,' " she pleaded, Paul tugging her back, wanting her to say anything to set them free but fearful that too much pleading would have the opposite effect, that if they were in fact being herded as witnesses, any more pleading by Katrin would put them in with the victims—whoever they were. Paul was ashamed, too, that they were trying to curry favor while the rest of the two hundred had said nothing, trudging toward the gate with the grim resignation of beasts being led to slaughter.

There was a sound like the rustle of paper, a muffled thud. A few rows back, the crowd had come to a stop before the guards waved them on again, around the fallen man. An elderly woman, perhaps the man's wife, was helping him to his feet, a guard motioning them to hurry up. It could have been Paul, Katrin thought, or her—in a rising panic, she seemed to recognize everyone.

"Run for it!" shouted a young boy from somewhere farther back down the street. Paul could hear the clicks of the safety catches coming off the AK-47s. The boy who had called had now taken flight, chased by four of the Ukrainian guards, one yelling for him to stop. There was a burst of automatic fire. Some of the two hundred in the column didn't even bother turning around, and Paul Valk felt sure he and Katrin were doomed, as sure as the Estonian republic, which for so long had been under the Russian heel—sure as his resignation of defeat had been bred in the bone during the long years of the Russian conquest. He thought of his ten-year-old boy, Juhan, and his "little songbird," Ellen, who had just turned six, both of whom, thank God, had stayed at home on the collective this day with their grandparents.

There was a scuffle, only this time ahead of them—an elderly woman having fainted, walking stick clattering on the roadway. The MPO guards would not let her be carried out. They knew that old trick. The Ukrainian guard, a sergeant, whom Katrin had been talking to was now watching her intently. Trying to keep her lips from quivering, she nevertheless looked plaintively at him and opened her arms as her mother, a staunch believer, had once done beneath the great spire of St. Olav's. "Please," she implored. "We have children." She fell to her knees.

"Katrin!" said Paul, his head bowed, lips a tight line, as he bent down to help her up. "Come, Katrin."

"We all have children," said the guard.

Katrin slipped on the road as Paul hauled her forward. "We have cognac," she said. "Armenian cognac."

The guard looked down at her. "My brother was on the *Yumashev*," he said bitterly. "Get back into line! Anyway, it's up to him." The guard indicated a speckled green and brown half-track truck, its horn bipping loudly, people moving sullenly out of the way to the narrow sidewalks, where they were now roped off and prevented from spilling back onto the road. Malkov was sitting next to the driver, his left hand gripping the windshield, the other lifting the megaphone. His voice, however, came across as a hollow, scratching sound as the megaphone went dead. Malkov looked at the megaphone and shook it.

"Vene Vark!"—"Russian shit!" shouted someone.

Malkov took no notice. He tried the megaphone again, and when it didn't work, had the driver stop and stepped up on the front seat, with one foot on the track. "We want information on the saboteurs and any other persons involved in anti-Soviet activities. Twenty thousand rubles for any information leading to the arrest of these criminal elements."

"Captain?" A middle-aged man stepped forward, his face as hard as rock, like one of the fifty thousand other small farmers who had defied Stalin's order to collectivize and been deported to die in the Siberian camps.

"You have information?" asked Malkov.

"No, Captain, but I beg of you—let the women go."

"Where do you work?" Malkov asked.

The man nodded his head eastward. "Rakvere," he answered, nonplussed.

"Oil shale factory?" asked Malkov.

"Yes," the man answered, looking at those nearest, trying to figure out the relevance of the question.

"Then you're lucky," said Malkov. "Like the shipyard workers?" not bothering to keep the contempt out of his voice. Oil workers had the green card—essential to the war effort. Before the man could answer, Malkov gave the order and an explosive roar of machine guns followed by screaming filled the air—acrid blue smoke going this way and that, choking the narrow street.

Not all of the two hundred were dead, some still lying in blood-drenched heaps, breathing their last—a few, Malkov saw, not even hit, struggling against the weight of the dead. Malkov and three noncommissioned officers made their way, stepping carefully over pools of blood, to finish the job with pistols. Soon only the woman Malkov had seen badgering his Ukrainian sergeant remained. He moved toward her, her eyes looking up at him doelike, her lips moving, but no sound coming from them.

He shot her.

The stink of urine was so acidic that several of the guards were complaining it made their eyes water.

The posters, most of them defaced within half an hour, that Malkov and his MPO troops distributed throughout the city proclaimed that two hundred a week, selected at random, would be shot until the saboteurs were delivered up to the authorities. There was also a reward of twenty thousand rubles. Malkov was convinced that it was the only way. A thousand or so Balts were small change compared to the life of the entire Northern Fleet and whoever else had been supplied with Estonian munitions.

That night Malkov signed the chit for extra vodka rations. This was always necessary, he found, to calm some of the men down. Besides, they needed all the sleep they could get, for until someone informed, there'd be much more work to do.

It was not until three days later that Malkov realized his mistake. Telling the inhabitants of Tallinn, and the other two Baltic capitals, that hostages would be taken randomly only encouraged them to remain silent, the odds against any particular individual being picked up quite high. Now he had lists of two hundred names posted. Except for a few, the well connected, escape from the city would be impossible, the pressure on those remaining, enormous.

CHAPTER TWENTY-TWO

IN THE FIRST five days of the war, back in August, in the rapidly converging pincers of Russian armor that encircled

Berlin, over two hundred thousand fleeing West Germans had been trapped, then ignored. Of no great strategic interest to the invading Russian generals, the fall of post-Gorbachev Berlin, or rather its instant collapse, as Kiril Marchenko knew, was of enormous psychological and political importance to Moscow. The holy words of John F. Kennedy, though ridiculously ungrammatical, as Marchenko happily pointed out, the phrase meaning "I am a beer" the way the U.S. president had used the words, had once electrified the West. It had been a statement of unrelenting determination by the West, before and after Gorbachev, to maintain its presence in Germany in the hope that one day the two Germanys would be united. Now, playing on Kennedy's misuse of the phrase, the Russian political officers were reaping a propaganda windfall.

One of the refugees was Leonhard Meir. He had been in West Berlin only a few hours when war broke out. The fifty-seven-year-old shoe salesman from Frankfurt had been sitting at a sidewalk café off the Kurfurstendamm, sipping a "Berliner" Motte, savoring the taste of the cool, frothy beer, when the first shots of the war in Europe were fired.

An hour later in a rented "Golf" and with two elderly couples who'd waved him down, Leonhard Meir was on the autobahn fleeing the city. The famed air of Berlin, said one of his four passengers, was a "trifle unhealthy" this evening. They were all silent for a second, but the famed Berlin wit, never far from the surface, suddenly exploded and the car was rocked with laughter tinged with hysteria as they headed west with the thousands of other cars, having no option but to go as fast as possible along the 120-mile autobahn through what in the old days West Berliners called the *Ozean*, the ocean of what used to be East Germany.

One of the women kept talking about the wonderful follies she had been watching at the Europa-Center Ice Rink and how just as a beautiful butterfly number "suspended in the air" was about to begin, all the lights had gone out. She told the story three times in as many minutes, and in the darkness of the car, her husband finally took her hand, pointing out at the ethereal moonlit countryside. "Deep in my heart," he said, "there has always been only one Germany." He turned to the others. "Is that not so?"

"Of course," they all agreed, though Meir didn't quite know what the hell he meant.

"Some of the fools have turned off their lights," Meir said. "They think the Russian pilots don't know where the road is." He told them he was worried, too, about his son in the army.

"Where is he stationed?" one of the older men asked.

"At Fulda."

"Mulda?" said the man's wife. "Oh—I have a friend—"

"Nein," said her husband, "he said *Fulda*."

"Oh—" It was the furthest extension of what had been East Germany into the West.

No one spoke until Leonhard himself broke the silence. "They'll probably leave the autobahn alone."

"They have other roads," said one of the women, but Leonhard didn't know what she meant. Did she mean that because there were other roads westwards, the Russians wouldn't bother bombing the autobahn, or did she mean that because there were other roads to carry the Soviet supplies to the west, they could *afford* to bomb the autobahn and cut off the main escape route from Berlin to western Germany?

"It really was a wonderful show," the other woman started up again. "So fluid, so graceful, when all of a sudden—"

"Ja, ja!" cut in her husband.

"Shh!" said the other woman, looking out the window into the moonlit sky. "Aircraft?"

"Tempelhof is closed," said her husband irritably.

"That's what I mean."

The traffic began to slow despite the strictly enforced German law, enacted after several shootings years ago on the autobahn, that forbade anyone to stop or get out of a vehicle. Finally all traffic stopped and drivers were getting out, doors slamming, horns beeping.

"Such language," the ice rink lady said.

"The Havel," said the other man. *"Mein Gott!* They have bombed the Havel crossing!"

"We don't know that yet," said his wife.

"Then you tell me," said the man. "Why do they stop us?" Over sixty years ago, when he was just a boy, he'd been in Berlin when the Russians had entered and he had seen his mother and sisters raped. "My God, they have broken the Havel Bridge," he repeated.

"Of course they haven't," said his wife sternly. "There have been no bombs."

"Zurückgehen!"—"Go back!" ordered the motorcycle

police, their blue and white pinion lights illuminating their
crash helmets as their motorcycles came up the line.

One by one the cars were pulling out and making their
U-turns, and when Meir's turn came, he could hear people
calling out, "They've closed the Corridor."

Who had? wondered Meir—the German police or Soviet
bombers?

"One by one, please," said the policeman. "No rush.
Orderly now. Go back!"

"I told you," said the man in the backseat. "It's just like
them, you see. First they give you hope, then they close the
road. The bastards. I'm not going. Stop, mister. I'm not
going back."

"Fritz, don't—please." They had difficulty holding him
back from opening the door, and as Meir swung the wheel
about, his headlights picking up the high wire fences either
side of the road, he could hear the old man weeping—his
wife making clucking sounds like a grandmother comforting
a baby. "Shush now. Everything will be all right," she said.

"Of course it won't be!" shouted the old man. "We are
finished."

The Dortmund-Bielefeld pocket was faced with either surrender or "elimination," as spelled out in the propaganda
sheets dropped all along the forty-mile front: "The French
are not coming, Englanders," proclaimed the pamphlets.
"You have now been fighting for two weeks and they are not
here."

"There will be no convoys," they were telling the Americans, the messages printed on poor-quality unpolished paper, which the GIs and Tommies found useful as toilet paper,
having been out of it for a week already. It had gone up in
flames with other NATO supplies in one of the explosions
that destroyed over ten thousand tons in prepo sites all over
Germany. So many of the supply depots had been hit by the
SPETS teams that their smoke, together with the smoke of
the battlefields, turned sunsets into the most beautiful reds
and oranges over Western Europe, some of the palls so dense,
however, that at times it seemed like an eclipse.

Had it not been for the American Thunderbolts, the *Wun-
derzeug*—"wonder planes"—as the Germans were calling
the remarkably maneuverable planes, the situation would have

been hopeless. Time and again the Thunderbolts' tank-killing nose cannon and antitank bombs had been thrown into the breach where the Soviet armor found holes in the precarious dyke of the Allied defense.

There was another cause, seen by most NATO commanders as fortuitously accidental, that might yet help the Allies to stiffen their resistance enough to slow the Russian colossus. As well as blowing bridges and rail crossings on the borders between France, the low countries, and Germany to further impede any British reinforcements that might get across the Channel, the SPETS teams, unintentionally or otherwise, had cut off the evacuation of several hundred thousand American and British dependents.

This meant that the British and American troops fighting in western Germany knew they were not fighting just to defend Europe but for their loved ones. Some French intelligence sources hinted that a ranking officer in the Bundeswehr, long unhappy about the fact that American and British civilians, "even their pets," were to be given priority on preordained evacuation routes, had purposely dispatched a battalion of Einzel KA MPF—West Germany's Ranger troops—to blow the bridges. But as in all wars, rumors abounded, and whether the French were correct, it was impossible to say.

Rumor or not, the predicament of the British and American dependents was certainly stiffening their resistance. The question was, however, would beleaguered American and British divisions fighting side by side with the Bundeswehr, Dutch, and Belgian troops be sufficient to turn the tide?

The rapidly changing fronts over the entire length of Germany were new in the annals of war, for while fast-moving armor and motorized infantry had been the most marked feature of modern wars to date, especially the Arab/Israeli Wars, never had armor or infantry moved so quickly on such a vast scale. And never had men had to endure such sustained and furious attack on a battlefield bristling with such a range of terrible weapons. The old definitions of "battle fatigue" were no longer useful. The stress levels were so intense, yet so fluid, that save for the Battle of Britain and the lot of German pilots attacking the aerial armadas of American Superfortresses in the final days of World War II, this kind of stress was hitherto unknown in the history of battle. It meant that whereas in the 1940s men could, in a pinch, be left on the battlefield for weeks, even months, now endurance was measured only in days—often, as with the tank crews, in hours.

CHAPTER TWENTY-THREE

FOR OVER TWO months Leonhard Meir and the two elderly couples he had tried to take out with him had lived in a roller coaster of uncertainty as the normally well-ordered *Stasi* police did not seem to know what to do with them. At first they were told they must stay inside, a twenty-four-hour curfew in effect, but then they had been issued brown passbooks allowing them to go outside but no farther than two kilometers.

At Allied headquarters in Brussels, the punishing cost in pilots trying to keep the Soviet-supply lines through eastern Germany closed could no longer be justified. It was clear that if NATO kept losing pilots at this rate, the equation would turn, especially with the enormous stockpiling of arms and matériel SATINT showed was going on in Berlin, the Russians in effect holding the Berliners as hostages in as cold-blooded a calculation as the NKA's General Kim had made in his advance down the beleaguered Korean peninsula.

From southern Germany Second German Corps, consisting of a badly mauled armored division and mountain brigade, fighting next to Seventh and Fifth American Corps, were requesting WFS—weapons-free status—for the mobile, nuclear-tipped Lance missile batteries, which, other than chemical weapons, were considered NATO's land weapon of last resort. Permission was denied, though the Lances were authorized to fire as many conventional warheads as "deemed necessary," NATO's way of signaling its commanders that stockpiles were rapidly diminishing.

Ironically, 130 miles behind the western front, Berlin had been one of the safest places in the opening stages of the war. The Soviet divisions and fighter squadrons situated between the city and western Germany protected the inhabitants from NATO bombing—the area so heavily armed that as well as the central front being festooned with SAM sites, some farmers, members of *Stasi* reserves, had been issued with the deadly hand-held Soviet SAM-7Ds, so that low-level attacks had become increasingly dangerous. And yet NATO HQ knew the buildup of supplies in Berlin must somehow be checked.

Battling his boredom, Leonhard Meir had started to take much more notice of his surroundings and discovered that the northern suburb of Lübars, where he was being kept along with his elderly acquaintances, could actually take on the air of a rural village, its crossed wooden gateposts and ornamental fences reminding Meir of his country childhood.

Perhaps it was the air, the pervasive smell of stored hay in the farms all about the city, with the soft tones of autumn, that reminded him of another age. If you ignored the jets— the two elderly couples seemed to have no trouble doing this—you could even delude yourself at times that you were on a farm.

At first Leonhard felt ashamed because the older people seemed more able to stand the strain of not knowing what was going to happen. Even the old man who had panicked in the car and had not wanted to return to the city now seemed calmer than he. But what Leonhard Meir didn't realize was that the old peoples' hearing had deteriorated to the point that they simply didn't hear many of the jets. Even so, Meir saw things *were* changing; morale began slipping rapidly in proportion to the depletion of their canned food stocks and the introduction of severe rationing, all farms' produce being claimed by the Russian authorities. For a while, supplies of canned goods had held out, and the fall having been reasonably mild to this point meant that some of the late vegetables were also available, though these, too, very quickly ran out. Still, for a time, the Berliners' renowned sense of humor, never entirely understood by most other Germans, who had never lived surrounded in a Communist sea, had held. Then, when all reserves were gone, shops looted, the sense of humor began to wane—even around the outer suburbs such as Lübars, closer to farms than the inner suburbs. It became evident that "old" Berliners, especially those who had lived in what had once been the old, Western sector, were expendable.

It was on a Friday morning, one of the old men complaining again about how they had become prisoners in their own apartment, that Leonhard first sensed a resentment of his presence. Once grateful to him for trying to get them out of Berlin, the two couples now saw him as merely another mouth to feed.

Going for a walk to let things cool off a little, Meir pondered how long it would be, if ever, before he'd have any knowledge of his wife, daughter, and grandchildren, let alone his son, who had been stationed at Fulda. But he was determined not to let the depression overwhelm him, always telling himself that tomorrow would see some small improvement. Surely the war couldn't last much longer. All the experts had said that another war couldn't last very long. Just as they had told the world Adolf Schicklgruber wouldn't last long.

Meir heard the village clock strike noon and set his watch ten minutes ahead, an old habit he'd developed on his shoe salesman's route to make sure he was never late for appointments.

At that moment a squadron of twenty-four British Canberra Mk-8 bombers were taking off from Greenham Common in southern England, their yellow lightning flash insignias either side of the RAF's blue-circled red bull's-eye streaked with water from a passing shower. Their target was Berlin.

MiG fighters scrambled in northern Holland, flying out over the hook high above the North Sea.

Seeing the blips of ten MiGs fifty miles east of him, the squadron leader of the twenty-six Canberra bombers crossing the North Sea called for interceptor assist. This wasn't necessary, however, as RAF ground radar on England's south coast had already dispatched six aquamarine, bullet-nosed "Tigers" out over East Anglia into a fish-scaled sky to do battle with the MiGs. The Canberras' commander looked out across his bomber's wide, stubby-looking wings and, seeing heavy cloud cover over Holland, instructed his pilots that the squadron would detour farther south, below the hook of Holland, which arced like a left-handed scythe toward Germany, then go in for the attack south of Hannover. The Canberras' navigators recalculated, under instructions from the wing commander to use Magdeburg, twenty-three miles east of the old West/East German line, as the IAP, initial aiming point, for the bombing run on Berlin.

Of the nine remaining Canberra bombers that had survived the German Roland missiles, three were hit by SAM-16s, the advance hand-held Soviet surface-to-air missiles in plentiful supply along the Berlin Corridor. One Canberra crew managed to bail out over the Havel River in Grunewald Forest in what used to be the American sector of West Berlin. He pulled the cord for his inflatable vest well before he hit the water, but the carbon dioxide cartridge was a dud. One of the coolest of the cool in aerial combat, the pilot, Kevin Murphy, an Australian born and raised in the outback, had a dread of water, and was now desperately telling himself to calm down, which he did after a few anxious moments, unhitching the chute harness and breaking free before beginning to blow into the mouthpiece of the Mae West. Now his uniform, particularly the elastic G suit, was beginning to soak up water at an alarming rate. His finger slipped from where he was holding the mouthpiece. He grabbed for it and resumed blowing as he heard a power boat start out from the shore. He was going under.

The *Stasi* people's patrol boat dragged the river for two hours: slow, monotonous work, a crowd gathering on the eastern shore by the picnic tables to see whether they would find the "terror bomber."

"Why bother?" said one of the three men aboard the patrol boat.

"Because, you *Dummkopf*," said the oldest comrade in charge of the boat, "it is important."

"Why?"

"Because, you *Dummkopf*, headquarters wishes to know what squadron he is from. This is vital intelligence."

The crew member, a youth in his midtwenties, made a rude noise at the acne-faced teenage boy who was the third member of the crew. "Intelligence, nonsense," said the crewman. "We know what squadron they came from. Three of them crashed out near Lübars. Can't you see?" He was pointing north.

The older man in charge knew he was correct, but the thick, coal-brown smoke that was rising and flattening over Berlin was coming not from the Allied bombers that had crashed but from farther in than Lübars, from Tegel Airport and from around Schönefeld Airport to the east, where storage sheds, hit during the raid, were burning out of control.

"So," pressed the crewman, "why do we waste our time dragging the river? Let the fishes have him, *ja*?"

The people's captain, a thickset man with a game leg, was kneeling awkwardly on the deck, face showing the strain, untwisting one of the lines on the chain-weighted drag. When he looked up, his face was beet red from the effort. "If you don't wish to be sent to the Fulda Gap, my young friend, you'll help me and stop your complaining, *ja*?"

"They cannot send me," answered the crewman insolently. "I have medical exemption."

"Ah," said the people's captain, pushing himself up from the gunwale. "And if the Americans counterattack? If their ships do come? What then, eh?" Before the crewman could answer, the people's captain spat into the lake. "That is what your exemption will be worth, Comrade. Nothing."

"Their ships will not come," answered the other boy sharply. "And even if they do—where will they land them? We have all the ports. Bremen will fall in a few days. You'll see."

"They will use La Rochelle and Saint Nazaire," said the captain. "They will not need Bremen or Hamburg if they land there. It will also save them two hundred kilometers."

This gave the two boys food for thought, but the one who had started the argument was not deterred. "Paris will not permit them to use the French ports."

The captain had straightened out the drag line. "If one of our bombs lands on French soil, France could be at war with us overnight," he said, turning, suddenly hearing the drag tackle go taut. But it was only one line, the others still loose. He sat back on the seat behind the steering wheel of the plywood boat and put it on "idle," letting the current push them—the way it would push anything else.

"You think the French capitalists are that stupid?" challenged the youth. "To let a stray bomb bring them to war? No, Comrade. The French are not idiots. If you bombed a whole French city, they would not come in—they would say it was a mistake. They are waiting like the giraffes, the French.''

"Giraffes?''

"Yes . . . scavengers . . . you know.''

"You mean hyenas!'' laughed the old man. *"Giraffes!''*

"Whatever you call them,'' the youth replied angrily.

"And what if we bombed Paris?'' asked the old man. He saw the lines go taut. "Hey then, Comrade? What if Paris was bombed?''

"Paris is different,'' conceded the younger man. "That's quite another matter.''

When they finally found the dead pilot and pulled him aboard, they discovered the air bag, what the "terrorist fliers'' called a "Mae West,'' had a small tear in it. They delivered the Australian's body to headquarters in the old Karl Marx Allee and were cheered by some former East Berliners, including several of the Turkish migrant workers unable to go back home but enraged nevertheless by the NATO bombing. The military commander, flanked by *Volkspolizei*, personally came out to congratulate the people's patrol.

As they were leaving, the crewman who had been arguing with the people's captain noticed a police corporal handing the older man what looked like a voucher of some kind. Now he understood why the people's captain had been so determined to find the flier. Marx was right, he said to the boy. Money is a corrupting force. Nevertheless, if the party had offered a reward—

He went up to the captain and demanded his share, right there and then. And got it.

In Lübars, on the city's northern outskirts, a gaping bomb crater thirty yards wide was still steaming with burning debris near the remains of the two four-story apartment blocks. The two elderly couples befriended by Leonhard Meir, who was out at the time, had been in one of the apartments when the six Canberra bombers struck.

With an efficiency they were famous for, the Berliners immediately began to clear the rubble, looking for survivors, moving as quickly as caution would allow around the debris, especially a staircase teetering near the edge of the crater, though it was quite clear they did not expect to find anyone who would be easily identifiable. The strangled horn siren of the *Volkspolizei* put an end to the clearance, however, as police arrived, quickly cordoned off the area for "investigation."

"Investigation of what?" asked an elderly Berliner, his wife still shaking but with presence of mind enough to pull him away.

"Investigation of crimes against the state!" answered the policeman.

The old man Berliner threw his hands up in disgust. "Crimes against the *state*! Against those Russian pigs, you mean. Don't forget Moscow in your *investigations, Kamerad*!"

"Silence!" shouted the policeman, and despite the death and destruction that had come upon them like a cyclone, several people began laughing, others joining in, mocking the official's officiousness. Several small boys were playing war, running around the crater and the cordoned-off debris, one with a plane in his hand. It was an American F-15, ghost gray with U.S. Air Force insignia.

"Whose child is that?" demanded the policeman.

"Mine," said a woman rather timidly.

"Stop him. It is not permitted."

"What isn't?" cut in the old man again.

"Antisocial behavior," answered the *Volkspolizei*.

The old man spread his hands again, staring at the sky, his faded coat ballooning about him like a clown. "*You* talk of antisocial behavior!" He pointed angrily at the crater. "*You* are the cause of this! You—you fascist!"

The *Volkspolizei* took him away, his wife screaming as he was hustled inside the small Volga sedan.

In the second apartment that had been split open as if struck by an enormous ax, several suites were open to the air like a doll's house, a body visible and still near the lip of the third floor. And, astonishingly to most of the onlookers, a radio was blaring with news reports of the *"brüderlicher Hilfskrieg"*—the "fraternal war of assistance"—the boys around the crater fighting now over who would be *Bombermannschaft*, "bomber crew," and who *AA-Flak*, "AA battery commander."

After a while another *Volkspolizei* returned and checked off names against those on record as having lived in the two apartment blocks. They managed to identify some by wedding rings, medical bands, odd podiatric shoes, and so forth.

There were still eleven people unaccounted for, among them the temporary permit holder, Leonhard Meir.

By nightfall Meir had decided to try again to escape from Berlin. At first he felt somehow responsible for the old couples' death, for not having been there with them, for having left, all of them in a bad temper. But soon guilt gave way to his determination to reach the west. He had hatched the plan on the way back from his work after having seen several dead *Stasi*-led AA battery crews near Tegel Forest. All that remained of one battery after a direct hit from one of the Canberras' iron bombs was strips of flesh dangling from tree branches like sodden toilet paper. But nearby, the headless corpse of one man was still sitting upright in the sidecar of an army motorcycle, the dark blue boiler suit and AA armband the man had been wearing bloodied and lacerated by shrapnel. Meir also noticed that several other corpses nearby which were not burned and were dressed in the boiler suits looked as if they were in their fifties—about his age.

Racing against what he knew would be the imminent arrival of the ambulances, their Klaxons wailing in the distance, Meir quickly stripped a boiler suit from one of the corpses, snatched up one of the helmets strewn about the edge of the wood, and made his way over to the motorcycle. He kicked the starter pedal. Nothing. He kicked again and again until he was exhausted, then gave it what he told himself would be his last try. The bike coughed and promptly died. "Shit!"

Now he could hear a car, perhaps a hundred yards or so away down by the lake, and voices coming toward him. He ran back to the gutted battery and into the wood. The voices receded, going farther down the lake. Back at the bike, Meir kicked the starter again. It spluttered, coughed, and rattled to life. He unscrewed the petrol cap and stuck his finger in it. It felt ice-cold. Full tank. He had no excuse—it was either now or never. A dash for freedom down the Corridor or wait. Would the Allies come? Or would it be slow starvation in the occupied sector? No one knew. He let the engine die. If stopped by the GDR *Polizei* or the *Stasi*—with nothing but his "enemy alien" card, it would mean torture and interrogation.

He hesitated, got off the bike, moved around, looking for a piece of ID, finding an identification card on one of the dead. The card's photo, even in the pale, shimmering moonlight over the lake, looked nothing like him. *Entscheide doch, Meir!*—"Make up your mind, Meir!"—he told himself. *Brio!* Do it with *brio!* He kicked the starter pedal again and, as it gained power with a throaty roar, switched on the slit-eye headlamp and tightened the chin strap of the AA helmet. Slipping the bike into gear, easing out the clutch, he sped over the grass down toward the lakeside road and from there headed out for the autobahn, singing, his voice rising, though drowned by the noise of the bike and sidecar, "La Donna è Mobile" louder and louder, trying to drown the fear that kept telling him to turn back, a heavy drone of Russian bombers overhead. He had strapped on a holstered gun but had absolutely no idea how to use it, wondering if it had a safety catch or not.

CHAPTER TWENTY-FOUR

ON THE OTHER side of the world, a flooded green rice paddy below, outside Munsan, heading north, though still five miles south of what used to be the 150-mile-long DMZ between North and South Korea, the loud rotor slap of the Seventh U.S. Army Cavalry choppers could be heard above eight escorting Cobras. The latter's chin turrets, whose chain machine guns were slaved to the pilot's helmet eyepiece, kept moving side to side, up and down, like a mosquito's proboscis.

The usual thin head-on silhouettes of the Cobras were fattened this day by the thirty-eight rockets on each side of the stubby wings, giving the eight choppers a bug-eyed appearance, their tails higher than their bodies. Each of the 304 rockets was armed with a fragmentation head to provide covering scattering-shrapnel fire for the ten Hueys following and the sixty soldiers of the air cavalry aboard them. Their task was to steal the southern end of what was hoped would be a successful encircling movement against a company of North Korean regulars that had ambushed a U.S.-ROK convoy the previous night en route to Kaesong, north of the old DMZ.

All across the Korean peninsula, 120 miles wide at this point, hundreds of such missions continued to press home the U.S.-ROK counterattack against the NKA, a counterattack made possible by Gen. Douglas Freeman's daring hit-and-run airborne attack against the North Korean capital. Like David Brentwood and many others who had fought and been decorated for the raid that stunned the world and bought valuable time for the fleeing U.S.-ROK forces, General Freeman was no longer in Korea. On leave after undergoing a violent allergic reaction to a tetanus shot, Freeman had, despite his protest, been taken off the active list for some weeks, and now there was concern that without him, the counteroffensive in Korea would bog down.

In the lead Huey, Major Tae, liaison ROK-U.S. officer for the Seventh Cavalry, a man whom Freeman had never met but who had been among the first to see action on the DMZ, was gripping the open door's edge so tightly, his knuckles were white. The sound of 152 smoke-tailed rockets from the Cobras near him, streaking toward the scrubby side of the paddy, along with the howling rumble of the twin chin turret guns, each gun spraying out 550 rounds of 7.76-millimeter per minute into the scrub, was so loud that even though Tae was plugged in to the Huey's intercom, he had difficulty hearing the pilot telling him and the six American cavalrymen in the chopper that they were about to put down on the south side of a long east–west irrigation ditch.

Some of the cavalrymen in the chopper, also veterans of the U.S.-ROK counterattack against the invading North Korean army, took no notice of Tae, his eyes watering with the wind, his viselike grip on the doorframe nothing more to them than confirmation that the South Korean major was as apprehensive as they were. The truth, however, was much different.

Before the war, Tae, an intelligence officer in the ROK, had conformed exactly to the ideals of West Point. A gentleman in every sense, he seemed to some more American than the Americans, despite his short, slim build. Indeed, Tae, though not nearly as widely known as Freeman and not known in America at all, had become something of a legendary figure throughout the U.S. Army in Korea. Interrogating the usual peacetime quota of would-be NKA infiltrators who had been captured while trying to slip into the South, Tae, who forbade torture of any kind, was struck not by anything the NKA prisoners said but by the fact that the chopsticks found in the NKA infiltrators' kits were shorter—fourteen inches long rather than the standard seventeen. From this he had deduced that the North Korean army, in a country with an acute shortage of timber, was stockpiling wood. In a calculation that merely amused the U.S.-ROK headquarters in Seoul and made no sense to the U.S. officers born and bred in a throwaway consumer society, Tae had predicated that the North's saving in wood, given the millions of chopsticks used, was probably going to the manufacture of *chiges*. These were the NKA militia's famed A-frame backpacks, on which they carried all their ammunition and food, including the shoulder roll of ground pea, millet seed, and rice powder, which, mixed with water, would sustain them and which made the North Korean regular much more self-sufficient than the more elaborately supplied-from-the-rear U.S.-ROK forces.

Despite his prediction of an impending invasion of the South by the North in August, Tae's warning was not heeded, in the main because an invasion during the monsoon was a no-no in any self-respecting army manual. Even the most junior U.S.-ROK officer knew that your heavy armor would simply bog down in the rains.

In the early hours of August 16, the morning following the South's annual Independence Day celebrations, the NKA had struck, overwhelming the U.S.-ROK forces all along the line, the NKA's light, Soviet-made fourteen-ton PT-76 tanks able to move much faster and with more maneuverability than the much heavier and mud-bound fifty-five-ton American M-1s.

Behind the armor, tens of thousands of NKA regulars came pouring out of the tunnels that had been painstakingly dug under the DMZ over several years during North Korean and U.S.-ROK maneuvers when normally sensitive ground noise sensors were rendered useless by the smothering noise of the maneuvers themselves. The United States had found three tunnels in the 1970s and cemented them up, with machine guns at each exit, but the NKA had dug others, which had gone undetected. Many of their troops streamed out in a massive feint that successfully engaged the bulk of the U.S.-ROK forces on the DMZ. This allowed the NKA's famous Fourth Armored Division, whose forebears had spearheaded the NKA invasion of the South in 1950, to make an end run, breaking through down the Uijongbu Corridor, only eleven miles north of Seoul. Most of the long-standing U.S.-ROK booby traps on the eleven-mile stretch to Seoul had been neutralized by NKA commando teams, while other widespread and synchronized sabotage by "in place" NKA cells effectively gutted the crucial American chopper and fighter bases in the South.

In the face of the NKA's *byorak kongkyok*—"lightning wars"—U.S.-ROK communications in a shambles from the sabotage, there had been panic in both the American and South Korean regiments. On the DMZ, Tae had fought bravely in his intelligence headquarters outside Panmunjom, but with the NKA having encircled him and threatening to annihilate everyone in the area unless he surrendered, Tae had been captured.

But if the NKA's General Kim had succeeded in wreaking a humiliating defeat upon the Americans, his army was about to receive a rude shock. Douglas Freeman, his career looking as if it was about to be eclipsed by the younger men who had inherited the chronic instability of the post-Gorbachev world, devised and led a raid on Pyongyang. Confounding all military logic with a nighttime air cavalry attack on the North Korean capital launched from F-14-escorted choppers off carriers in the Sea of Japan, Freeman's raid cut the NKA's overextended supply line to the South. In doing so, Freeman bought precious time for reinforcements from Japan to reach the embattled U.S. and ROK forces, who, their backs to the sea, were fighting a bitter retreat along a fan-shaped perimeter running east-west for eighty-three miles from Pusan to Yosu on Korea's south coast. Once reinforced and regrouped with an infusion of the fresh troops from bases on Japan's west coast, the American army and the ROK were soon able to launch a counterattack over the next seven weeks during which they had retaken Seoul and crossed the DMZ, now entering the area around Kaesong where the U.S.-ROK overnight convoy had been attacked.

But while Freeman's daring attack had electrified the world, as had Doolittle's on Japan in 1941, and made it possible for the U.S.-ROK forces to retake the DMZ, the American troops that liberated the Uijongbu POW camps and set the then emaciated Tae free had come too late for Tae's family. His wife and eight-year-old son had been strafed and killed, his nineteen-year-old daughter, Mi-ja, captured, betrayed by a boyfriend, Jung-hyun, who, an active member of the SFR—Students for Reunification—had talked her into the huge student demonstrations against the Americans that had preceded the NKA invasion. Jung-hyun, like so many from the SFR, was now believed by the U.S.-ROK intelligence to be an NKA officer somewhere in the North.

Now, amid the roar of battle, looking down on the wind-flattened green of the rice paddy, Tae was braced to jump but knew he must wait—watching long, dense trails of white smoke rising from where the Cobra escorts had dropped smoke canisters to curtain off the paddy from the thick scrub on the northern side of the east–west ditch. The scrub was erupting with dust from the fragmentation rockets and tracer from the 7.76-millimeter, so powerful, it was cutting saplings clean through, branches trembling, then falling to the ground, creating more dust, on fire and adding to the smoke.

Tae lifted his squad automatic weapon and waved the six other men to follow him out. Heads lowered, rivulets of water spreading away from them through the violently shivering grass, the men spread out, the splashing sound of their canvas-topped boots lost amid the whistle of bullets and machine-gun fire coming from beyond the scrub through the smoke screen, the shuffling noise of the big 120-millimeter mortar adding to the scream of the Hueys' engines as the choppers hovered a foot or so from the ground while they unloaded, bullets thwacking into the fuselage. But Tae was unafraid, already well ahead of the squad, traversing the ditch and, to the other squad members' astonishment, going straight over its protective wall into the thick smoke cover.

"Jesus!" shouted one of the air cavalrymen. "He's crazy!"

The soldier was right. Something had happened to Tae the night that the North Korean major had brought in what he called a *soltuk*—"inducement"—for Tae to reveal the names of the top three KCIA counterinsurgency chiefs in the Pusan-Yosu region.

Tae had withstood the initial beatings, steeled himself enough to get through the unrelieved panic of the NKA soldiers holding him down, one of them stuffing a filthy rag, stinking of gasoline, into his mouth, pushing him underwater, then tying him to a chair, blindfolding him, suddenly tipping the chair back, catching it, setting it upright, tipping it back again to increase the panic. And then, as four men held him, another taking the pliers to his testicles. But this last torture had its own answer—a half second after they began, he blacked out. They'd left him for two days—back in his cell—giving him plenty of time to think about the pain next time, his strength fading, his only food a scum-rimmed rice cup of watery soup, a small piece of rancid meat flung into it. It was white and they told him it was fish, but he knew it wasn't, having seen dozens of rats scampering through the cells and feeling them scuttling over his face and stomach during the night. When they brought him into the tent the third day, the major had asked him if he had enjoyed the meal. Tae, his arms pulled back and pinned by the guard, looked at the NKA major and, with his voice hissing through the broken teeth and raspy from dehydration, replied, "Very much. Thank you."

"I'm glad you did," said the NKA major, walking over and smiling down at him. "It was one of your allies."

Tae did not believe him until he was dragged back into the cells again for refusing to identify any of the KCIA section chiefs. He knew that the NKA guards, as UN troops had discovered in another Korean War long ago, were regarded as the cruelest possible captors, surpassing even the brutality of the Japanese. Still, he was not prepared for what he saw. A white man, limbs tied to an upright mattress frame that was propped against the shell-pocked remains of the Uijongbu Catholic church, was being used for bayonet practice—the man still alive. It turned out that the man was not one of the Swedish UN observers from the DMZ but a young American from a signals corps captured near Uijongbu. What Tae remembered most about the man was how long it had taken him to die. A squad of NKA militia, having cut a crude U.S. of A. flag on his stomach, had bayoneted him again and again, literally disemboweling him, then, once he'd been cut down from the frame, hacked him to death, in the same way as in the 1979 "incident" when NKA troops had stormed across the DMZ and murdered two Americans who had been trimming a tree for a better view across the line.

The next evening, Tae had been taken back to the dimly lit interrogation tent. He would never forget the cloying smell of the flickering paraffin lamp, the enormous shadows of the interrogator and the guard, or the fragrance—of something so sweet, so familiar, that even in the semidarkness, heavy with terror, he knew it was his daughter.

The North Korean officer had asked Tae once more for the names of the KCIA agents. Tae said nothing and tried to smile at his daughter, but when she saw what they'd done to him, she began to cry. The NKA major gave an order and the guard jerked Tae's head back against the chair, gagged him, and taped his eyelids back so that he was forced to watch his daughter.

Tae gave him the names and the NKA major raped her. After, as the NKA major stumbled breathless, satiated, back from her discarded form, Tae, in an agony the likes of which he had never known, heard his daughter whimpering like a dog in the far darkness of the tent, huddled in the corner, clutching her muddied clothes.

The NKA major gave her to the troops to do as they would.

It was the last Tae had seen of her. The NKA major was one of those reported killed during Freeman's raid on Pyongyang, the name of the young American soldier who had shot him, Brentwood, one that Tae would never forget.

But it was not satisfaction enough. With the madness that turns sorrow to rage, all Tae wanted to do now was to find Mi-ja and to kill every NKA he could find. Most of all he wanted to kill Jung-hyun, who had betrayed his daughter. And though he had already had more search-and-destroy missions in the last week than anyone else in I Corps, he had particularly wanted to go on this mission. Intelligence had received information that the company of NKA the air cavalry was now engaging was led by officers formed from the South Korean chapters of the Students for Reunification.

Ahead, through wafts of acrid white smoke beyond the slight rise of an irrigation ditch, Tae could see the wooden stock of a RPK 7.62 machine gun, surrounded by concertina wire, sweeping through a wide field of fire. Their bursts were too long—the barrel would overheat. But if you rushed the wire alone and tried to go through it, it would wrap itself around you faster than any concertina. And too far for a grenade. The choppers had all gone. If the air cavalrymen didn't move now, they would lose the advantage of the smoke screen.

Tae checked to make sure that the barrel of his SAW wasn't clogged with paddy mud. He waved for two air cavalrymen to come up to his position. One man, steadying his helmet with his left hand, mouth parched with fear, drew level with him behind the ditch.

"Thought we were gonna get some F-14s up here," the American said, eyes squinting skyward. "Off the carriers."

"They're busy," said Tae. "Carriers have all been called up North."

"Fuck!" said the cavalryman. "*We're* up north!" Despite the heat of the battle, it struck Tae that the American private would never speak to an American officer like this. But he didn't mind—all he cared about was the NKA.

"Russians are moving against the Aleutians," Tae explained.

"Fuck the Aleutians. Send the Tomcats here."

"They don't see it that way," said Tae. "I want you to cover me."

"Where are you goin'?"

Tae indicated the machine gun still stuttering away. "They'll have to change a drum soon."

"Yeah—" said the cavalryman. "That'll take 'em about two seconds flat."

"You ready?" asked Tae.

"Down!" yelled the cavalryman. The air filled with a *shooshing* noise, then an explosion that shook the earth, a hole blown in the wall of the irrigation ditch, a spume of dirty-colored water rising high in the air. Tae pulled the two smoke grenades from his pack and threw them upwind—the smoke cover the Cobras had laid almost gone.

"Ready?" asked Tae again. "We'll have to do it without the Tomcats."

The cavalryman nodded, his mouth too dry for him to speak.

CHAPTER TWENTY-FIVE

MALLE KNEW THERE was nothing she could do but submit to the corporal. Neither her daughter-in-law nor son had returned from the docks, and she, like everyone else in the Mustamäe apartment complex, had heard the tearing sound of machine-gun fire down near Viru Gate, and feared the worst.

Unable to closet her grandson, Edouard, in any of the other apartments for fear of Party informers in the building—there was always at least one on each floor—Malle had tried to explain it to Edouard, telling him that for now, until the nightmare was over, whenever the corporal "called by," he would have to be ready to go straight up to the crawl space above the double bed in her son and daughter-in-law's room.

Malle had tried to lead the corporal away into her room, but he said he liked lots of room "to move about," raising his eyebrows in unison like a gypsy, meaning to convey an all-knowingness and sexual prowess he did not have; his impatience, his ripping and slobbering whenever he mounted her and took his pleasure, reminded her of hogs she had seen out on the collectives. Above all, she despised his cowardice—not simply the bullying rape in exchange for not launching a search for her grandson, but the cowardice evident in his gasps for "Raza! Raza!"—his wife's name. For Malle, it wasn't that she was a stand-in for Raza that angered her—thinking of someone else while making love to one's partner was a common enough thing, she thought. What did disgust her whenever he called his wife's name was that it clearly wasn't a cry of separation from his wife so much as a primitive ploy for absolution—that somehow the utterance of her name while he was raping another woman would lessen his culpability.

Before the corporal had "called by" the second time, Malle had sat down, feeling unclean, contaminated, but determined and with a sense of obligation to explain it all as best she could to young Edouard—yet how could he understand that she had no option?

To her surprise, he said he understood very well. Then, his eyes burning with hatred, he told his grandmother that next time he'd kill the corporal.

"No—" she begged him. "Edouard, no—no. Don't you see he'll—Edouard, he is the only one who knows you haven't been taken in for questioning. He doesn't care about searching for you as long as I—"

She was talking to him now as one adult to another, the hatred in his eyes having evicted the innocence of childhood forever.

"Edouard—" She clasped his hands in hers, his coldness frightening her. "Edouard, if you do anything—" She closed her eyes at the horror of it, shaking her head, wishing it away, holding him close. She felt him draw away from her. "If you do anything like that, they will kill you," she told him. "And your mother and papa."

"They already have," said the boy, speaking in a tone so seemingly detached from his body that he seemed to be talking to someone else. It was a voice she had never heard before.

"We don't know that," Malle said quickly.

"You heard them outside," he said evenly, looking straight at her. "You heard them screaming, Nana."

Nana! She seized upon the word of endearment as a desperate soul grasps for the slenderest hope. "Edouard," she pleaded, squeezing his hands, which were still cold and unresponsive. "They will take your Nana and you—all of us." She tried to smile, the smile of the brave, showing that if *she* could accept it, then surely—

"Be patient," she told him. "Soon they will find who it is they're after and leave us alone."

He said nothing for a moment, and his silence was thick with accusation. Finally she could bear it no longer, her head bowed, shaking from side to side, her age at once ashamed and prostrate before his youthful impatience. "You *must* see we have no choice. They would go to your school, your friends, until they found you, then—"

There was a knocking on the door.

Edouard, the muscles taut in his face, looked from her to the door and back at her from the precipice of decision. "Go!" she whispered hoarsely, then walked out into the hall through the kitchen toward the door, her eyes frantically searching again for anything that might betray Edouard's presence in the apartment, catching her breath as she spotted one of his socks, having dropped from the dirty wash basket. She snatched it up and stuffed it back into the basket beneath slips and lace underwear—of various designs which the corporal had insisted on her wearing to make it "different" each time. He had complained bitterly of her "peasant" attire, and she had been forced to borrow some of her daughter-in-law's more daring lingerie to keep him happy.

One hand at her throat, the other on the doorknob, she steadied herself for a moment. Putting on what she shamefully called her "collaborationist" grin, she opened the door.

He said nothing—the moment the door was closed, his hands were already under her skirt, bunching it about her waist, where he used it to pull her toward him, his lips smothering hers wetly, his garlic breath so strong, it made her want to throw up. He mumbled for her to try and stop him. She tried to push him away but couldn't, his game becoming her panic, yet knowing she must yield. Backing her up against the hallway wall, he pushed against her so hard that the mirror of the hallway hutch shook, throwing their reflections in a quivering embrace. "Pull it!" he told her. She closed her eyes, buried her face into his neck, which he took as arousal. "You like it, eh?" He smiled, looking down at her, feeling her trembling. "Excited, eh?"

Surely, she thought, he must know how repulsed she was, that no amount of force could ever change her hatred for him and his kind.

"Come on, Malle," he said, smacking her bottom. "To bed, eh? Turn around!" When she did as he commanded her, he grabbed her left hand and held it between his legs. "Pull," he said. "Hey!—Wait!" He laughed roughly. "You don't know your strength, Malle."

No, you swine, she thought, you don't.

"That's better," he sighed. "Whoa—steady, horse!" He

made her stop by the small refrigerator, opening the door and peering in. "No beer?"

"No. We haven't been allowed out to buy—" She had completely forgotten that he had brought two cans the day before and that in her distraction, she had put them in the small freezer section, so that now the cans were distorted.

"Ah—" he said, annoyed, taking them out and setting them on the small kitchen counter. "Soon they would explode. Like me, eh?" he said, laughing.

She didn't hear him—her eyes riveted on the slightly opened cutlery drawer. She couldn't be sure, but it looked as if the big serrated bread knife was missing.

"Hey, Malle!" he bellowed. "What is it?"

"What—oh, I'm sorry. They're frozen."

"What?—oh, the beer." He pulled her close to him again. "But I'm hot, eh, Malle?"

She stopped. His expression had changed. He was looking high up in the kitchen. She felt her carotid artery pounding like a taut cable. Had he seen something? Oaf that he was, he had a natural animal instinct. But he was looking above the counter at the meagerly stocked shelf. "Like honey?" he asked.

Suddenly she thought she heard Edouard moving in the crawl space above the master bedroom only a few meters away to the right of the hallway. "Yes—yes I do," she answered hastily. "Why?"

He let go of her hand, walked over, and brought down the small can of Danish honey, turning to her with a leer. "I'll bet you do." It took her a moment to realize what he meant, but didn't know how long she could go on debasing herself. For as long as it took, she supposed, for as long as it took him and his barbarians to find whom they were searching for and leave the apartment block. For as long as she could prevent them from searching for Edouard. As he levered the lid off the can of honey, Malle moved back toward the single drawer.

"What are you doing?" he demanded. For a split second she saw suspicion in his eye. It was the same look he'd given her a day before when she'd tried to lure him away from the master bedroom.

"Why," she said, "getting a towel. The bedspread'll—"

"All right, but hurry. I have to be back by four. It's already three."

As she took the hand towel hanging on the small chromium rack beside the refrigerator, she glanced quickly in at the cutlery drawer. The knife *was* gone. She closed her eyes, her breath caught in her throat. No, she implored Edouard, as if by the sheer power of her mind she could forestall him from protecting her honor, from getting them all killed.

"Malle!" the corporal shouted impatiently from the bedroom. She could hear him undressing, the sound of his suspenders thwacking the bedside dresser. Taking a deep breath, she walked into the bedroom. He had a pillow under his knees, and it was staring at her like a one-eyed snake, and she knew that directly above them was her grandson.

"You want it, don't you?" he asked. It was part of the game. He knew she didn't. How could anyone think she wanted to?

"Yes," she said.

"Say 'I can't wait.' "

"I can't wait."

He handed her the small, opened can of honey. "Put some on me."

She dipped her finger in the honey—trembling. She could not have him here another day. Edouard was probably right—his look had told her he believed his parents had been executed by the Viru Gate. And she knew that even when the troops left the Mustamäe apartments, the corporal would not stop "calling" on her. Edouard would always be a hostage to the corporal. How many other women was he doing this to? She put the honey on him.

"All round the top," he instructed her, guiding her hand, groaning with pleasure. She made her decision. She would be especially nice to him, then ask him to take her to Kadriorg Park, and put an end to it.

"Now," he said. "Be a good bear, eh?"

She smiled quizzically at him. "A bear?"

"Lick your honey," he explained.

Tossing her head to one side with an abandon the corporal had not seen in her before, Malle pinned her hair back so as to keep it out of the way, then, her tongue moistening her lips, her eyes closed, she lowered herself to him. She would make it the best he'd had.

CHAPTER TWENTY-SIX

BEFORE THE WAR, the kill ratio on the NATO books was six to one—that is, six Soviet combatants had to be killed for every NATO combatant if NATO was to hold. Within four hours of the Fulda Gap, becoming the Fulda "Gash," the ratio changed dramatically to ten to one, the armored spearheads of the Soviet divisions, a half million men in all, first crossing the Polish plain with a speed that surprised even General Marchenko. He had long held that the "fatal flaw" in NATO's armor would be the West's bourgeois reluctance to engage "other elements," by which he meant the West's reluctance to kill civilians. And he believed it would work in the Soviets' favor.

He was right. The army of refugees fleeing west of Fulda, and indeed, all along the north–south axis that had been NATO's central front, impeded NATO tank reinforcements. No matter how "hard-nosed," as the Americans called it, NATO's troops had been trained to be, most British, American, and particularly Dutch tank regiments found it unacceptable to fire point-blank into the human tide of refugees that clogged the roads. Some of the Allied tanks, seeing a blur of red, the treads of Russian T-90s mercilessly rushing and chopping through the screaming columns of refugees, did open fire. The belch of the M-1s and Leopards, their 120- and 105-millimeter guns sending white-hot, dartlike armor-piercing tungsten through the tightly packed refugees in efforts to stop the Russian T-90s, only added to the carnage. The air sleeve alone surrounding the armor-piercing needle, traveling and discarding its sabot, or shoe, at over forty-five hundred feet a second, was so hot that it alone seared people for distances up to two or three meters from the trajectory path. Even so, the molten discarding sabot rounds and the HESH—high-explosive squash heads—of molten metal that were deadly as tank killers, effective on both sloped as well as flat armor, were not the rounds that caused the major casualties among the refugees. This dubious honor was left to the high-explosive antipersonnel rounds which were favored by both sides, as much to destroy supporting infantry as the tanks that spearheaded them.

In the first twenty-four hours following the Soviet breakthrough to a megaphone-shaped two-hundred-square-mile area west of Fulda, there were over seventeen thousand civilian casualties, most of these women and children. In the raging cacophony of the battle, involving five thousand NATO and Soviet tanks, the inability of NATO Medevac choppers to get through the dust, smoke, and cross fire meant that many wounded civilians and combatants perished who would otherwise have survived had they been treated at MASH units within the first two critical hours of having been hit. This was particularly the case among the elderly, many of them disoriented—some gone mad from the sight and smells of bodies blown apart and from the ear-shattering screams of shellfire and the gut-punching sound of earth exploding all about them. Utterly confused in the tumult of the highly mobile battle, positions of friend and foe shifting rapidly from one moment to the next, and dazed by indiscriminate artillery and mortar fire, some of the elderly were separated from loved ones, and wandered about, dazed, blinded by dust and smoke, suffocating in gasoline-drenched air and then crunched beneath the advancing Soviet and defending NATO tanks.

The breaching of the gap by the Russian army divisions had come much faster than expected, not only because bad weather over the Polish plain hampered Allied air attacks, but because of a single piece of equipment, vastly underestimated by the Allies.

As reports came through to Allied HQ in Brussels, it quickly became evident that the T-90s, having been fitted with thermal imagers of a quality underestimated by NATO intelligence, had created havoc during nighttime battles. In addition to mixtures of expensive laser and Stad R stereo coincidence and optical range finders, neither of which was proving as good in actual battle conditions as in maneuvers, when the cost of real shells had precluded thorough testing,

the Russian T-90s and T-80s had a thermal sight. Originally
made under contract in South Korea, and later copied in East
Germany, it proved remarkably resilient, whereas the other,
more sophisticated, laser imagers used by NATO had run
into unexpected trouble after the sustained shock of actual
combat.

Although Maj. Kiril Marchenko had played only a relatively minor role in advocating the thermal sight, he nevertheless managed to take a lion's share of the credit. And it
was true that the purchase of the much less expensive thermal
imagers did fit with his advocacy of the *svyatye dvoyniki*—
"holy twins" of the Soviet High Command. The first tenet
was that overwhelming numbers in the Soviet armies would
have to make up for qualitative superiority in the West. And
secondly, this meant you had to win quickly—before NATO
could rally and/or resupply.

In turn, a quick war meant that not only must sabotage be
ruthlessly stamped out in the republics, as General Brodsky
in Tallinn had finally realized, but armored columns had to
be trained to fight as well at night as in the daylight. Accordingly, at Marchenko's urging—a very unpopular move at the
time—T-90 and T-80 tank regiments had been trained on the
vast Russian steppes *first* at night, then in daylight maneuvers. Indeed, the division of 270 tanks in which Marchenko's
son, Sergei, had fought before winning his transfer to the air
force academy and his posting to the Far East station had
itself trained first at night. And during these night maneuvers, commanders insisted on tanks maintaining the Soviets'
punishing twenty-five-meter margin between each tank, a
much narrower one than that used by the German Leopards,
American M-1s, or British Challengers, who disdained such
distances for fear of attracting high-density antitank artillery
fire.

One advantage the NATO tanks did possess was a gun
depression of nine and ten degrees, twice that of the Russian
tanks, so that whenever NATO armor was given the chance
to withdraw to defensive, hunkered-down defilade firing positions, they exacted a deadly price for any S-WP advance.
Still, the sheer numbers of the Russian tanks that had poured
through the Fulda Gap, a ratio of four to one, had overwhelmed and continued to overwhelm NATO. And this despite the carnage visited upon the massed Russian armor by

the high-tail-engined American Thunderbolts. Once thousands of tanks were joined in close battle, often at ranges of less than a thousand yards, the deadly hail of the American Thunderbolts' armor-piercing twenty-millimeter cannon fire was lost, for in the confusion of night battles particularly, where a T-90 and an M-1 became indistinguishable on the pilot's infrared, NATO's air superiority in ground attack aircraft ceased to count.

Out of the melee a report, initially lost or simply disregarded in the avalanche of incoming signals, reached an Allied intelligence officer in Heidelberg. It would forever change the nature of war, and strike down the prejudice of renowned tank commanders like Gen. Douglas Freeman.

Recovered from his hospitalization and riding high on his Korean exploits, Freeman, over the objections of most of the Joint Chiefs of Staff, had been ordered by the president to take over command of the Dortmund-Bielefeld pocket. Freeman, known to even the European troops as "George C. Scott" after his successful attack on what he called the "verminous pad of the runt"—Kim Il Sung's Pyongyang—had stunned his officers during the Pyongyang raid by using women volunteer chopper pilots in the lead assault on the North Korean capital.

At a time when American-ROK morale was rock-bottom in Korea, Freeman had paradoxically reversed his previous stand against using women in combat roles. He had asked for women volunteers to pilot the lead choppers—and had got them. In one stroke he had ended debate in America about women in combat and shamed reluctant male conscripts to "volunteer." Even so, a prejudice Freeman held close to his bosom and took to Europe was his belief that no matter how successful women might be as chopper pilots or superb ground crew, there was no place for them in a tank. The Dutch Forty-Second Mechanized regiment now trapped in the Dortmund-Bielefeld pocket had been the first to raise the matter. Freeman's objection, in a confidential memo to the Pentagon, was now part of the growing Freeman legend.

"A tank battle," he had written, "is no place for a woman. Forty sixty-pound rounds may have to be hand-fed into the main gun if automatic load malfunctions. I do not subscribe to the common theory that a woman aboard a tank will make the men softer—cause the men to be more concerned with protecting the weaker sex than with killing enemy tanks. Nor do I believe they are the weaker sex in terms of their ability to sustain high-level stress. On occasion I would argue they are superior in this regard. Nevertheless, a woman aboard a tank is unacceptable because it is a matter of hygiene. No one in the Pentagon seems to realize that in battle, a tank crew cannot make *rest* stops. For a tank to stop in the kind of sustained and highly mobile battles we have been engaged in to date would make the tank a stationary target, and as we have discovered with the Russian night sights, the enemy needs only a five-second fix on a stationary target to blow it to pieces. Besides which, the interior of the tank is a highly charged, fume-laden atmosphere in which the necessary body functions only add to an already unpleasant situation. In short, defecation and urination will in most cases have to be undertaken, as they have traditionally been, in helmets until the opportunity for jettisoning such material presents itself— which may not be for many hours. It is not only the severe discomfort and unpleasant atmosphere which I have in mind in strenuously arguing against women tank crews but rather a sensitivity to their need for privacy, which simply cannot be accommodated aboard an armored fighting vehicle.''

Col. Maureen Davis of the USMC replied that ''General Freeman's objections to women tank crews no doubt arise out of his sincere concern for hygiene and practicality. He need not be so concerned. No doubt the general knows a great deal about tanks, and in being so occupied with this, it appears that he has not kept pace with the results of an astonishing study which shows a woman's anatomy allows her to drop her pants as quickly as any male, and in any event, women find it easier to relieve themselves than their male colleagues, who, as I understand it, often have difficulty in aiming.''

''Cheeky bitch!'' Freeman had thundered, and was not won over until the intelligence officer in Heidelberg personally requested three minutes of the general's time after Freeman's intense briefing of the disastrous NATO situation.

''What's your name?'' snapped Freeman.

''Norton, sir. Major James Nor—''

''All right, Norton. You've got one minute. Shoot!''

''Sir, I've been tallying destroyed tanks by crew composition. Those Russian tanks with mixed crews are scoring better than all-male crews.'' He paused.

"You've got thirty seconds left, Major," growled Freeman. "I'm not a goddamned mind reader. Shoot!"

"Sir, it seems that our assumption that women would inhibit aggressive action—that male crew would want to protect the women and therefore withdraw—is incorrect. All the evidence suggests the opposite. With a woman aboard, male crews are afraid of being seen as, well—"

"As cowards!" said Freeman. "Yellowbellies."

"Yes, General."

"What's your name again? Norton?"

"Yes, sir."

"All right, Norton. We'll put gals inside the turrets." It was the kind of decision that endeared Freeman to field officers—the ability to cancel his own prejudice on the evidence and to waste no time in implementing a new tactic or strategy. "Mind," added Freeman, "none of them over thirty-four."

Norton was nonplussed.

"Their tits," explained Freeman, pulling the glove on harder, riding crop dangling freely from his wrist as he smelled the change in the air, still dusty and cordite-filled, blowing in from the battlefields to the east, but much colder, more bracing. "No big tits," he continued. "Get in the way of the laser sights. Can't get close enough to the eye cup."

Norton looked for help from Col. Al Banks, the general's aide from his Korean days, but help was not forthcoming. Sometimes Al Banks didn't know himself whether the general was being serious or making a joke.

"Norton?"

"Yes, General?"

"We've got to do something about this Dortmund-Bielefeld pocket. We need every man, woman, and jackrabbit we can get. Appreciate your report."

"You're welcome, General."

Freeman was already walking back to his staff Humvee, buttoning his coat collar against the sudden drop in temperature that had resulted from an Arctic front, when he turned to Norton. "Major? How'd you like to be in my G-2? Get your ass out of that castle in Heidelberg to where the action is?"

"That'd be fine, sir," Norton lied.

"Good man. Al, you see to it."

"Yes, sir."

"Norton, when you get yourself to Arnhem, I want you on aerial reconnaissance. Not afraid of flying, are you?"

"No, sir," Norton lied for the second time that night.

"Good. You're the kind of man who sees detail. Any ass can draw arrows on a map, but what I want is attention to detail. That right, Al?"

"Yes, sir."

"You know about Tae and the chopsticks, Norton?"

Norton looked blank.

"Well—never mind. I think you'll work out fine."

As he was getting into his Humvee, Freeman could hear the rumble of Russian artillery in the Oden Wald to the east. Like the bad weather also to the east, it was getting closer. Driving out of Heidelberg to catch his plane to Arnhem, he said to Banks, "Al, I want all aerial photographs for the last twenty-four hours at Arnhem HQ."

"You've got that look again, General."

"Have I? Well, I'll tell you what else I want—a plan for a fighting retreat. Regimental level."

Banks wasn't sure he'd heard correctly. "Retreat, General?'

"What's the matter—you got sand in your ears?"

"No, sir, but—well, sir, you've never pulled back before."

"I've never been surrounded by four thousand Russian tanks before. And, Al, when we do start using women in the tanks, I don't want anyone playing Sir Galahad and getting out of the tank for a leak. That's an order, and I want it circulated to all commands. Northern, Central, and Southern NATO commands—what's left of 'em."

Al Banks tried not to smile, but Freeman caught him. "Think I'm a rude son of a bitch?"

"No, sir, I just don't think the men are going to obey an order that involves unzipping in front—"

Freeman's voice grew cold. "Any man *or* woman who leaves a tank to urinate or defecate in action will be fined five hundred dollars and I'll flail 'em alive. Those Russian thermal detectors'll pick up a 'hot shimmer' at a thousand yards." He paused. "You know how I know? Because I *bought* one of the sons of bitches. On the black market when the Berlin Wall was getting holes punched in it and all the goddamn liberals and fellow travelers were having orgasms over 'Gorby' and thought it would be peace ever after. I'm not losing a single Abrams, not a goddamn one of 'em, because some joker's too embarrassed to piss inside his helmet. That clear?''

"Yes, sir."

"One more thing, Al. Those casualty lists we saw in Heidelberg show six crewmen killed because in defilade they spelled one another off. All six were crushed because the ground under the tank suddenly gave way under the weight. I don't blame them. Underneath a tank's as good a shelter as any. Besides, they'd just been shipped over—so didn't expect it. Different geology than California. Still, their commander should have known better. We need every goddamn tank and man we can get. Now our G-2 tells us the Russians are stockpiling oil supplies in our own underground depots they've captured outside the pocket—safe from aerial attack. Meanwhile the bastards are pounding the shit out of our Atlantic oil and supply convoys. They keep getting clobbered, we could lose this thing for the want of a shell.''

Banks said nothing. As usual, the general was exaggerating—and as usual, he was right.

CHAPTER TWENTY-SEVEN

"MORNING, COMRADE GENERAL," welcomed the captain of security.

Marchenko grunted and kept walking down the long, crimson corridor of the Kremlin's Council of Ministers building to the first deputy prime minister's office. The general was in no mood for pleasantries, and his lumbago was starting to act up again, a sure sign that winter was on its way. When he arrived in the waiting room outside the deputy minister's office, the general informed the secretary he must see the minister at once.

"Is it pressing?" the immaculate major asked, his red shoulder boards vibrant in the pale shafts of sunlight.

Damn protocol, thought Marchenko. "It's not pressing," he retorted. "It's critical."

The major, unperturbed—it was always "critical"—put the ivory desk phone on "conference." Often the minister could deal with it over the phone without wasting his time in the office. "General Marchenko here, sir," the major informed the minister crisply. "He wishes to speak with you."

There was a slight hesitation. "Very well," said a voice resonant in the tinny-sounding speaker. Marchenko could see, through the beige-draped panel of the glass door, that the minister wasn't coming to meet him, so that the general was required to walk the twenty meters down the long, rectangular office to where the deputy sat talking on one of the seven white phones to his left, waving Marchenko to a chair as a headmaster to a prefect. Marchenko bristled—after all, he was the senior adviser to Premier Suzlov, and yet the deputy minister wouldn't meet him halfway. At the end of the row of chairs down the wooden-paneled wall to the minister's right, a young, nervous executive type sat waiting apprehensively below the sepia-toned portrait of Marx.

"Comrade," said the deputy minister. A small, squat man with a shock of graying hair, he pushed himself back from the semicircular cutaway in the elegant desk and rose, extending his hand. But Marchenko felt it was more protocol than heartfelt. The general envied the minister—he'd always wanted a desk like that, where documents were all around you, rather than where you could never reach them. "Comrade Deputy," said Marchenko, simultaneously indicating the glum, nervous man sitting below Marx.

"It's all right," the deputy reassured him. "He is one of my advisers. We all need advisers, eh, Comrade?"

Marchenko was a recognized expert on military matters, but the nuances of superiors often bemused him. Was the deputy reminding him of the Kremlin's pecking order with his comment or was he merely being polite?

"So—what's critical, General?"

Marchenko gave him both barrels at once. "The Japanese fleet is in La Perouse Strait. Sailing north."

The deputy said nothing, his face impassive.

"Between Japan and Sakhalin," continued Marchenko.

"The Japanese call it Karafuto, you might recall." Still the minister made no comment. Indeed, he seemed rather bored.

Containing his exasperation, Marchenko went on to explain, "They're obviously strengthening their western flank. Northern Sakhalin is a perfect springboard for an invasion of Siberia."

"Oil," said the deputy.

Unconsciously Marchenko gave a sigh of relief. "Among other things, Comrade, yes. Oil and our Siberian bases, from which our bombers have been hitting their west coast."

"You are sure it's an invasion force? I thought you were the one who doubted Japan would escalate her involvement militarily."

Marchenko looked straight at the deputy. "I was wrong. There are a dozen transports at least," replied Marchenko. "A carrier, helicopter, ships as well, and a screen of fighters and surface vessels. Thirty vessels in all."

"Can we stop them?"

"I don't know," said Marchenko. "If we were only fighting on one front, yes, of course."

"But the Japanese defense force, I didn't think was all that—"

"*Defense* force?" cut in Marchenko, eyebrows raised. "It's as offensive as any other force. *'Defense'* was mere propaganda because they were forbidden to call it anything else under the surrender terms with the Americans in 1945." Marchenko paused, and the deputy noticed the general looked more worried than he had ever seen him.

"We could muster enough troops in Vladivostok and ferry them over, but we haven't the time and there are only two divisions on all of Sakhalin. It's as big as Japan's north island. But our main concern, Comrade Deputy, and this is why I've come straight to you for your support in the Politburo, is that even if we repulse the Japanese landing—and this may be possible with our fighters out of Yuzhno-Sakhalinsk in south Sakhalin—so long as Japan continues to get oil from the Americans, she will be able to harass us along our eastern flank. We've got to stop the oil coming to her from Alaska. Even if their fleet is a feint to—"

"What about our submarines?" interjected the deputy. "We surely have enough of those out of Vladivostok?"

"So do the Americans, Comrade Deputy. And quite frankly, the U.S. hydrophone arrays—underwater microphones—are so good in the Pacific, they pick us up way ahead. At the moment, we can't get near those tankers because of Shemya and Adak.''

The deputy glanced up at his wall map at the Aleutians arcing like a sickle toward Russia's Kamchatka Peninsula, with only the two Soviet Komandorskiye Islands between Kamchatka's ICBM sites 190 miles to the west, and the westernmost U.S. island of Attu 250 miles east of the Komandorskiyes.

"So we have to take out Shemya and Adak?" proffered the minister.

"Adak would do. It's the U.S. submarine listening post and base.''

"*Can* we do it, General? If there are so many American submarines in the Pacific—"

"No, no," the general was quick to tell him. "Not by sea. By air. It's the only way, given the time problem. Fighter attacks to soften the island base up—then paratroops.''

The deputy minister frowned. It was now evident why Marchenko was seeking his approval so urgently. He would need a majority of Politburo supporters on this one. "General—I am not as adroit as you in military matters, but I would doubt the Americans will fail to see you coming. An attack on the island by our fighters flying below enemy radar can be done. This I know. But when you take in paratroops, the radar will surely see them.''

"Not if our fighters knock out the American radar first.''

"And what if they don't? As I remember from your reports on our air-to-ground rocket raids on England, radar installation masts can be notoriously difficult to knock out. Almost as difficult as bridges, I believe. But if I am correct, Shemya Island, as well as being one of the most heavily armed places on earth, is between Komandorskiyes and Adak?''

Marchenko nodded. "And if we wait, we could have the American Pacific Fleet to contend with. Elements of it are already heading up from the Sea of Japan, where they were providing carrier fighter cover for the U.S.-ROK counterattack in North Korea.''

"Then how do you propose dealing with the Adak submarine base?''

Marchenko walked to the wall map, extending his hand out from the Komandorskiyes. "We will fly due east two hundred miles north of Shemya—midair refueling for the MiG-29s. Then due south to Adak.''

The deputy minister nodded approvingly. ''Then what about the Americans' antiaircraft missile batteries on Adak Island?''

Marchenko permitted himself a smile of anticipated satisfaction. ''We have our covert trawlers commanded and manned by disaffected Aleuts—descendants of our fur traders. Some of them still believe the Aleutians are theirs—very much like the American Indians and—''

''We have them, yes, but can they do the job?''

''It's already proven, Comrade. One of them has already downed a Hercules off Unalaska. The Americans thought it was volcanic ash from Mount Vsevidof. The Aleutians are a chain of volcanos. The trawlers will be 'fishing' off Alaska. Very rich fishing grounds, especially off Adak.''

''The American shore batteries on Adak will blow them out of the water.''

Marchenko shrugged. ''Of course—*after* the trawlers have wreaked havoc on Adak Station. Our paratroopers will finish the rest, and we will have secured a stepping stone to Alaska. Most importantly, we will have neutralized the American advance warning station for their submarines just as the Japanese neutralized their Wake Island station in the Second World War. Our submarines will be much freer to attack oil tankers en route from Alaska. In addition, this—''

''Will take the pressure off our western front,'' said the deputy, ''and allow us time to deal with the Japanese.''

''Exactly,'' said Marchenko. ''Will you support me in the Politburo?''

The deputy's fingers were tapping his blotter. ''You really think it will work, Marchenko?''

''Comrade Deputy, my son is stationed in the Far Eastern Theater. In Ulan-Ude. I fully expect him to be one of the fighters in the attack on Adak.''

''If you're that confident, Comrade,'' said the deputy, ''I'll support your proposal to the premier.''

''Thank you, Comrade Dep—''

''One thing,'' cut in the deputy, pushing himself back from the desk. ''I take it the Americans had a board of inquiry into the crash of their Hercules. Do you think they are convinced it was—what did you call it, 'volcanic ash'?''

''I have taken steps to cover that eventuality, Comrade.''

"How?"

"Sir, the officer in charge of covert operations is an Aleut— Bering—no relation to the explorer. He has things well in hand. The trawlers carry Grail surface-to-air missiles. Infrared homing. Fired off the shoulder. Bering's trawler brought down the Hercules."

"And the Americans never picked it up on their radar?"

"That's what I mean—he's very resourceful. He fired it off a volcanic caldera. There is often volcanic ash clogging the engines. But Bering is very careful. He 'volunteered' to the American Commander to look for possible Soviet missile sites on the nearby islands. Not surprisingly, he's found nothing. That's what I call initiative."

The deputy minister concurred. "So you're sure he will be able to neutralize the Adak radar and communications installation? I hope he has more than Grail AA rockets for that."

"He has," answered Marchenko. "We pay him very well. He'll keep Adak Naval Station *more* than occupied while our paratroopers are landing elsewhere on the island and closing in."

"When do you suggest we initiate the plan? If I'm to support you, I'll need documentation and—"

Marchenko reached into his vest pocket and extracted a five-by-seven satellite photo of a carrier and battleship battle group. "The carrier is the *Salt Lake City*. The battleship, we are almost certain, is the refurbished *Missouri*—the Seventh Fleet off Korea. Elements of the Third Fleet from Hawaii are also en route from Hawaii. Strictly speaking, the Aleutians are the Third Fleet's responsibility. So you see, the very fact the Americans are also taking one carrier battle group, the *Salt Lake City*, from Korean waters shows how serious they are in trying to thwart any attack from us on the Aleutians. The only way to beat them is to go in *now*. With paratroops."

The deputy minister nodded slowly. "Very well, General. You've managed to convince me. I'll support you in the STAVKA."

Marchenko sat back, relieved. "There is one thing I should tell you before the meeting is called, Deputy—"

"Yes?"

"Two of our airborne assault brigades are already on their way from Petropavlovsk on Kamchatka Peninsula—en route to the Komandorskiye Islands. They'll make the attack from there.'' He paused. ''Minister, I had to put my neck out—there simply wasn't enough time to go through channels.''

The minister's tone was quiet. ''Be careful, General. People who stick their neck out too far are likely to get it cut off.'' He smiled and extended his hand.

Marchenko rose and returned the smile. As he left the deputy's desk for the long walk out to the waiting room, he heard the telephones start ringing. ''General—''

Marchenko turned around. ''Comrade Deputy?''

The deputy minister was holding a receiver, one hand over the mouthpiece, waving it censoriously at the general. ''What about the two divisions you have put on full alert in Khabarovsk? *Without* my approval? You never mentioned those.''

For the first time in years, Kiril Marchenko felt himself blush with embarrassment. ''Ah—reinforcements, Minister.''

''But you don't think we'll need them, do you?''

''No. I don't think they will be necessary, Comrade Deputy.''

The deputy sat back in his swivel chair, hand still over the receiver. ''I hope not, General. For your sake.''

CHAPTER TWENTY-EIGHT

WHEN CONSTABLES MELROSE and Perkins checked the Oxshott emergency ward and discovered that the man who had given his name as Corbett was indeed Mr. Corbett and a ''milkman to boot,'' as Perkins put it to Inspector Logan, there was relief and embarrassment all around. Relief for Logan because he hadn't completely bungled the attempted catch of Mr. Wilkins, whose wife had lied about him being home to protect her milkman lover. Embarrassment for Mrs. Wilkins, who, following the inspector's threat to charge the milkman, admitted to Logan and the two constables that her husband was in Southampton, where he was ostensibly assessing damage wreaked upon a convoy for the purposes of apportioning government reimbursement to the shipping lines whose merchant ships had been requisitioned.

Logan and the two constables took the 6:20 to Southampton. They were delayed at Woking because of track torn up by a Russian rocket attack between Woking and Basingstoke, necessitating a detour via Farnborough and Guildford and a late arrival in Southampton at 10:30 P.M. A light drizzle was falling through the blackout as they got out of the Southampton police car and approached the Westward Arms pub on the Southampton dockside. The contrast between the cold, bleak darkness from which they had come and the hearty, warm, noisy pub was striking, Logan commenting that he hadn't seen such thick clouds of cigarette smoke since prewar days.

"Whole ruddy navy must be here," said Perkins.

Wilkins was well dressed in a brown suit, but even his tailor couldn't hide his beer belly.

" 'Ello, 'ello!" someone called out at the sight of the policemen. "Anybody smell coppers?"

There was ragged laughter, someone else shouting, "You're for it!" to the bar in general. Wilkins was turning, with a pint of Guinness in one hand and a gin and orange in the other, when he saw the inspector in his tweed jacket, cap still on, and the two constables by his side. His face changed from a merry pink to ash white.

"Mr. Wilkins? James G. Wilkins of Herries Street, Oxshott?"

Wilkins nodded, someone shouting at him, "I want you to 'elp us wiv our inquiries?"

Logan had the charge card out and was reading Wilkins his rights, Perkins and Melrose watching their flanks. It was a tough crowd—mostly merchant seamen getting well and truly sozzled after the harrowing Atlantic run.

"Come along," Logan told Wilkins. Wilkins looked pained. "What'll I do with these?" he asked plaintively, looking at the drinks.

"I'll 'ave the Guinness, mate," said a distinctly Australian drawl. "Who's the lolly water for?"

"It isn't lolly water," Wilkins said.

"No worry," said the Australian, "I'll drink it, too."

Perkins drew the inspector's attention to a young woman getting up from one of the cubicles. Logan nodded, and Perkins made his way through the drinkers toward her. Wilkins was still standing immobilized, holding the drinks.

"Might as well give them to Ned Kelly," Logan advised him, indicating the Australian. "We'll give you a chit for them if you like," Logan added, intent on following procedure to the letter.

"Jesus," said the Aussie, laughing, "free booze!"

Logan feared a rush on the bar. "Cuff him, Melroad."

Melrose did as he was told and, amid a solid chorus of boos and "You bastards!" led Wilkins out.

"I'm innocent," said Wilkins, looking about in the darkness, feeling the pull of the handcuffs.

"Of what?" said Logan as he hit the cold, bracing air.

Wilkins looked from one policeman to the other. "I don't know."

"Well, that's a start," said Logan. "Eh, Melroad?"

"Yes, sir," replied Melrose dutifully.

"You have the lady, Melroad?" asked Logan.

"Yes, sir."

"Good. Into the car, then."

Logan was jollier than Melrose thought he had a right to be. They'd darn near botched what Oxshott station was already dubbing the case of the "pummeled pumpkin." Nevertheless, Melrose felt a sense of achievement himself, and the warmth from the "lady" against him helped. Then, as they were leaving the dockside, he caught a glimpse of one of the ships in the convoy, her list near to capsize point, and he wondered how many men had died on her because of spies. He heard Logan calling in Scotland Yard's CID. The Criminal Investigation Division would add an extra shine to Logan's glory. If Wilkins talked.

In Berlin's Alexanderplatz it was 11:45 P.M. and also raining, but here no rights were being read to the prisoner, and the crowd of one of the suburban "committees against terrorism" were a sullen lot, dragged out in the rain as witnesses to what happened to anyone found spying against the newly declared people's German Democratic Republic. Behind them, there was the smell of chicory from the ersatz coffee being brewed in the police station.

What made the charge even more serious than usual was

that the prisoner had been found wearing a uniform of the people's antiaircraft battery. The Alexanderplatz was chosen because, while it was some distance from the point of arrest, it afforded the authorities maximum propaganda value, for television cameras were already installed overlooking the Platz, and the population at large could see the penalty for actions against the state.

"Could I please," asked the prisoner with great dignity, "leave a message for my wife and family in Frankfurt?"

"No," answered the *stabfeldwebel* who had arrested him at the roadblock, "you may not."

As they blindfolded him, Leonhard Meir thought of his son, who had fought at Fulda Gap, and wondered whether he was alive or dead. As the *stabfeldwebel* pinned the white paper disk on Meir's boiler suit, Meir started to say something, but his throat was so dry, no sound came.

As the shots rang out across the vast Platz, the citizens of Lübars had already turned to head home.

CHAPTER TWENTY-NINE

"I'D RATHER YOU volunteered your help," snapped La Roche, his lean, tanned frame reclining in the ultramodern chair that overlooked Pearl Harbor from his top-floor office of the La Roche Building.

Two Forrestal-class carriers, though in the safety of the harbor, were surrounded by a swarm of destroyers and fast-guided missile frigates, loading up with supplies. Though it wasn't general knowledge, La Roche knew this battle group would be the second to head for the Aleutians, his sources in Washington informing him that while the war in Korea was going well for a change, Japan's move north to protect her western flank meant that the United States' "back door," the Aleutians, might be endangered as the Soviets sought to isolate Japan from the vital supply routes to and from the United States. He'd heard that already elements of the Third Fleet out of Yokosuka were steaming toward the far-flung islands. Whichever way it went, Jay La Roche was satisfied he was in the right place at the right time, Hawaii being the supply hub for America's Pacific war.

"It's not that I'm unwilling to help," replied the congressman, adjusting his tie of dark maroon and blue stripes against the starched white shirt that contrasted with the blue striped suit. "But this trouble with your wife—" He was very careful not to say "ex-wife." "Well, what she did up there off Halifax—I mean, it's a very touchy subject with the navy. They're sticklers for discipline, as you know, and if she suddenly transferred out of there—to here—well, Waikiki's hardly a hardship posting. It'll look awfully suspicious."

"Suspicious to who?" asked La Roche angrily, using his letter opener as a drumstick on his desk of Carrara marble, the same kind, he told all visitors, that was used by Michelangelo.

The congressman shifted uneasily. "It would be suspicious to everyone stationed up there."

"I don't give a fuck," said La Roche, his drumming on the marble increasing. "All I'm interested in is getting her the hell out of there. And back here."

"I understand your feelings, Mr. La Roche. . . ."

"No you don't," said La Roche. He was tired of one-night stands. There was nothing after. He wanted her back, damn it. Way the world was going, you never knew. You had to take what you wanted when you wanted it, otherwise it might be too late. He'd promise to behave—cut down on the booze and dust. "I can get you unelected, Congressman. Easy as I put you there. Anyway, why the fuck should you care what a bunch of stumblebums in the navy thinks anyway—"

"Mr. La Roche, my boy's fighting in Korea. If I can't get him out—"

"You can get him out."

The congressman tried to look La Roche straight in the eye. It was difficult; La Roche's eyes bored into you with more experience behind them than most men accumulated in a whole lifetime. "I don't . . ." continued the congressman, "want to pull special favors for my son."

"Then you're a goddamned fool. Anyway, if you have a

quiet word with the navy—sweeten it with the promise of increased appropriations or whatever—who's going to know?''

"I will," said the congressman quietly, his voice seemingly swallowed by the vastness of the plush gray-pile-carpeted office.

"I don't mean your kid, for Chrissake," said La Roche, temper rising. "I mean, who's going to know about my wife?''

"Word gets out.''

La Roche opened a drawer, pulled out an Irish bond envelope, and walking closer to the panoramic view, slid the envelope across the marble desk. "No, Congressman. Word doesn't get out—not if you pay enough. Now, how much do you want?''

The congressman was surprised. La Roche was smarter than that; he'd banked from New York to Shanghai. He should have known that on some things, even congressmen can't be bought. "I don't want money," he told La Roche.

"Course you fucking do. Ten grand? Twenty? You're already a whore. All we're talking now is price. I've bought your way to Capitol Hill and you know it.''

"I like to think that some people voted for me," said the congressmen evenly.

"Think what you fucking like—but I bought the commercial that bought you the vote. Mr. Fucking Nice and Clean—Robert Redford from the Sunbelt. Don't give me a dance.''
La Roche walked back to the desk and slid the envelope closer to the congressman. "Go on, have a look." La Roche spun the envelope opener, which, in the fluorescent light, threw a series of long white slashes on the high ceiling. "I know your boy's in Korea," he said. "Americal Division. Near Racin. Port for Pyongyang—or it was until our bombers pounded the shit out of it." The congressman tried to hide his surprise at the extent of La Roche's knowledge about his son.

La Roche shrugged nonchalantly, sat down, and swung his high-backed leather chair around toward the harbor, watching a fog bank that was moving inshore. "You shouldn't feel out of it," he told the congressman. "You're not the only—'' He almost said "gofer" but used "connection" instead.

"Then why don't you have your other connection fix the

transfer?" asked the congressman, looking down at the unopened envelope.

La Roche was watching the fog starting to roll as the warm land eddies rose from beneath the cooler air of the sea. La Roche spoke without turning back to face the congressman. "He's in Japan at the moment. I can hardly fax him, can I? Besides, he's busy over there. If we don't watch it, we're going to lose our supply of China crude."

The congressman lifted the envelope. It was heavy. As he began opening it, he had to admit to himself that La Roche certainly was well informed. The fact that the United States, because the fighting in the Mideast had effectively dried up Arab shipments of oil, depended for up to 30 percent of its oil supply on China crude, was a little-known and carefully unpublicized statistic in the United States.

La Roche turned away from the window and stood behind the congressman, looking down at the contents of the envelope. "I like the redhead," Jay said. "How old's he? Sixteen—seventeen? Hard to tell with you on top of him. His face is in the shadow, but that's you, all right, isn't it?"

The congressman's head didn't move. "Where did you get these?"

"I got them. That's the point, isn't it? Now get the transfer."

"Ah—" The congressman couldn't go on, his voice cutting out.

"You need a drink," said La Roche, moving over to the mahogany wall, pressing the panel that opened with a quiet whir, revealing a bar twinkling in its opulence. "Jack Daniels—crushed ice. Right?"

The congressman didn't answer.

La Roche returned and held out the drink. The congress man hesitated, but then his body slumped and he seemed to shrivel. As he took the drink, he could hear the quiet tinkle of the ice collapsing, the smell of La Roche's minty breath overpowering. "I suppose you have copies?"

"No," said La Roche, "not of that lot. But I've better photos of you than that."

The congressman didn't want to look at the photos anymore, but he was shocked doubly by the fact that they were Polaroids, that someone must have used a flash. But how—

"You were so pissed," said La Roche, anticipating him

in a matter-of-fact tone, "you probably thought the bright light was a fucking sunrise."

The congressman felt something on his shoulder. La Roche's hand.

"Relax," intoned La Roche, sipping a crème de menthe. "You're all right. Should be a bit more careful, though. Use someplace you know—somewhere you've checked out. I always do." La Roche's other hand was on the congressman's shoulder, massaging his neck.

"Christ!" said the congressman, slumping forward now, his head buried in his hands.

La Roche kept up the steady massage. "It's a bastard, isn't it? Still—we have to keep it in the family. Right? I mean— for the family's sake." Outside, the fog had become a gossamer of gold swallowing the carriers.

CHAPTER THIRTY

THOUGH THE AFTERNOON was overcast above Tallinn, it could not dampen the corporal's spirits. For him it was a day of singular victory. Were Malle any older, it could have been embarrassing. Normally it wouldn't do—a man courting a woman ten years his senior—but she kept her figure well. It was the first thing he'd noticed on the day he'd knocked on the door of her apartment in the Mustamäe complex. He had commented on her beauty often, especially after she undid the tight bun and let her hair cascade down. And the more he told her how beautiful she was, the more he convinced himself that having sex with her was a completely natural outcome of their first "meeting," as he called it— rather than rape. In his eyes she had confirmed as much herself, asking him after they'd made love the day before to go with her today for a walk in Kadriorg Park, explaining that with the MPO's Captain Malkov continuing to arbitrarily take hostages from the street until he rooted out the munitions saboteurs in Tallinn, she was terrified to go out alone.

"I would be honored," he had told her, the very idea of his comrades seeing him with a vivacious woman on his arm pleasing him immensely. Indeed, he regarded his being posted to Estonia as the best thing that had happened to him since he'd been conscripted, his liaison with Malle confirming his belief not only that things work out for the best in the long run but that at heart women craved a *palochku*—"bit of stick"—even though they would never admit it. And what if anyone in his MPO company saw him and blabbed about it to his wife, Raza, back home? Then, he determined, he would merely tell Raza that Malle had been another suspected Estonian saboteur he had been ordered to—well, that would be a bit thin, he thought, but it was highly unlikely someone would mention it in their letters. Besides, the company censor would be quick to black out anything that might cause consternation on the home front.

They were strolling beneath the copse of linden trees, the pigeons walking about more skittishly than usual—pigeons were fresh meat in a time of severe rationing. "You are very quiet today," he said to her, smiling.

"Yes."

"You look sad. I thought you would be pleased to be out in the park again, yes?"

Two MPO guardsmen passed by, one of them giving him a knowing leer. "Well—?" the corporal pressed. "Why are you sad?"

"Because," she began, looking pensively ahead at the denuded chestnut trees etched black on the gray sky, "of the war." She fell silent.

"Don't be so glum," he said, slipping his arm about her. He was surprised she didn't resist—most women did, in public at least. It made him even surer of himself. "Sometimes the war brings good things," he said. "I like you and you like me. Not at first, but you see, strange things happen in the war. Things we have no control over, yes?"

"Yes," she agreed, slowing down by the rest rooms, the grass about them knee-deep in fallen leaves that were spilling out onto the cement pathway.

"Wait here for a moment," she said. "I have to go to the rest room."

Waiting for her, the corporal pulled his gloves on more tightly, something he always affected when he felt in a particularly good mood. Problem was, if Malkov ever found his damn saboteurs, the corporal knew he'd be moving out, probably reassigned, God help him, to guard duty around the mines in east Estonia. The backside of the Baltic. He hoped Malkov would never find the saboteurs, but anyway, he would turn the boy in then. Did Malle really think he hadn't figured out the boy was tucked away in the crawl space? He could smell him. The kid was probably masturbating every time they did it.

The corporal's attention was on a motorcade; the big boy, Admiral Brodsky, was down from Leningrad, and word had it that he wasn't happy with Malkov's failure to root out whoever had been sabotaging the munitions that had gone to the *Yumashev* and God knew where else. The MPO had already taken over six hundred hostages, with no results. It was said Brodsky was also under pressure from the STAVKA to settle the problem, and quickly—an artillery battery in Germany had come across several duds in what was supposed to be high-explosive 120-millimeters. It was all going to mean more hostages, most likely. Pray, thought the corporal, that the saboteurs, whoever they were, would hold out and give him more time with Malle. But he doubted they would. Some teenagers, like Malle's grandson, had been shot in the last few days.

Suddenly it occurred to him Malle had been gone a long time, though Heaven knew women always took an age in the—maybe there was a rear door? He started toward the washroom.

"What's wrong?" It was Malle, coming out, her hair no longer in a bun but about her shoulders, her coat over one arm. Her hair shocked him—she only did that when they were about to make love. It was as if she were undressing in public. She took his right arm with her left and pulled him close to her.

"My God!" he said. "You want to do it *here*?" He looked about, half-ecstatic, half-inhibited. "Here—in the park?"

"Not in the open, silly," she said, smiling, and led him up the incline by the pond into the thicket of linden trees. Out of view, she turned to him, looked expectantly in his eyes, pushing her thigh into him.

"My God," he said, his voice a hoarse whisper in his excitement. "My God, Malle, I love you."

"I love you," she said, her expression unchanged, and as they embraced, her coat fell among the dead leaves, the long hat pin piercing his heart, blood spurting over her bodice. Staggering back, wiping the hair from her eyes, she picked up the coat, put it on, and trying not to hurry, walked away—then she was running. She slowed down, breathing quickly, intent on not looking at all conspicuous, unaware that when she had brushed her hair from her face, she had left it smeared with his blood.

The COMPAC—Commander Pacific—was in his Pentagon office when Congressman Hailey's call caught up with him. It was on the scrambler, and the congressman was talking about a Wave, a nurse, La Roche, L.—née Brentwood. Separated.

Given the fact that her younger brother, David Brentwood, was MIA in northern Germany and another brother, Ray, ex-captain of the FFG USS *Blaine*, was badly burned and undergoing restorative surgery in La Jolla Vets', would it be possible "for the family's sake" to have her posted to a non-combat area? To Honolulu, to be specific. On an unrelated matter, the congressman would like to get together sometime with COMPAC to discuss increased naval appropriations from Congress.

"I'm afraid," the admiral informed the congressman, "I'll have to forward the request to the chief of naval operations in Washington. Computer here says there was a disciplinary problem."

"Yeah, I realize that," replied the congressman. "Little indiscretion off Halifax. But surely she's paid for that, being posted up there in Siberia. Anyway, we still have the siblings policy, don't we? One missing or killed, the other is called home?"

"It's voluntary, Congressman."

"Hell," said the congressman, "you don't think she'd volunteer to get out of the Aleutians?"

"Well, congressman, we need everyone we can muster, and none of Admiral Brentwood's children have been killed."

"Jesus!" shot back the congressman. "What d'you want? One kid's a goddamned monster in La Jolla Vets' and one kid's MIA. I'd say that was a fair contribution to the war effort."

"Very well, Congressman. I'll put the request through normal channels."

"Shit—I don't want you putting through anything. It'll get lost in a sea of paper. That's why I'm calling you. When you come up for congressional approval for the post of CNO, I'm not going to be wading through normal channels."

"I'll check it out, Congressman."

"Fine. When can I expect to hear from you?"

"Oh, I'd say a week or two."

"Jesus, Admiral—I mean today. Tonight."

"I'll get back to you, but I can't promise—"

"Appreciate it," said the congressman. "You boys are doing one hell of a job."

"Thank you, sir."

When he put the phone down, the admiral was shaking his head, passing a slip of paper to his aide. "A Wave—La Roche, L. What some guys'll do for a bit of poontang. We're trying to fight a war and he's trying to get his favorite piece of tail to Honolulu. I thought I'd seen everything. Put it through normal channels. I don't give a damn if the son of a bitch doesn't confirm me."

"Yes, sir," said his aide, a balding, world-weary officer who'd served two other COMPACs. When his boss left, the aide faxed the request for a transfer to Washington. Strictly speaking, it wasn't worded as a request, but the aide was long schooled in not saying what he was saying. His boss could afford to take the high road, at least officially, but the aide knew a quick response to the congressman would do COMPAC no harm, and aide to a CNO was one of the most powerful positions in the country. Either way, COMPAC had to deal with it. He was going to get a lot more of this bullshit. If the truth be known, the aide thought, it was probably old Admiral John Brentwood behind the request, using the congressman as a front.

CHAPTER THIRTY-ONE

IN THE HEAVING darkness eleven hundred miles northeast of Japan, the rain-lashed flight deck of the U.S. carrier *Salt Lake City* was a roaring blaze of blue-white light, slivers of red, yellow, and green piercing the frenzied air. The carrier battle group of ten warships centered about *Salt Lake City* was thirty-six hours, less than halfway from the Aleutians, but its airborne screen and combat air patrols had been up since leaving the Korean waters.

As one of the pancake-rotodomed Hawkeyes, part of the carrier's early-warning airborne screen, came in to land, three twin-engined ''electronic countermeasures'' Prowlers were warming up for the waist catapult, their bent ''bee stinger'' refueling nose rods casting strange shadows on the deck.

''He's tired,'' said the assistant LO, the landing officer in his yellow ID vest waving off a second Hawkeye for another run around, the plane already in its bolter pattern.

''Tired gets you killed,'' yelled the LO, hand over his extended throat mike. The Hawkeye was coming in again.

''Looking good for the three wire,'' said the ALO, the plane approaching in low over the fantail.

''Clean trap,'' confirmed the ALO, the Hawkeye's nose dipping, power off, lurching to a stop. Seconds later its three moles, electronic warfare operators, came out. Arms extended, grasping the shoulders of the men in front of them, they were led through the blaze of light like blind men, their eyes not yet readjusted after the hours of near total darkness in the windowless aft of the Hawkeye's electronic cave. As the seaman led them out of harm's way across the hose-strewn deck, green-jacketed men checked the arrester cable, a blue jacket driving his yellow ''mule'' out to push the plane as quickly as possible to the "parking lot." Another Hawkeye, its rotodome already up, well above the fuselage, turned about at the refueling station, as a "grape" jacket, with earmuffs, quickly hooked up a wire-wrapped pressure hose, pumping a load of JP-5 fuel into the aircraft. Two men, green shirts, sprinted through the rain to Frank Shirer's F-14 Tomcat as he and his radar intercept officer stood by, trying not to look upset. The two green jerseys, maintenance men, flicked up an access panel and replaced a black box.

"Try it!" one yelled at the top of his lungs, and the second man watched the cockpit as the Tomcat's HUD lit up.

"A-OK!" the man screamed back, thumbs up.

"Thanks," said Shirer, his voice drowned in the fury of a Prowler, a blast sheet up as the plane roared off the waist catapult into the rain-driven night.

On a mission to try to protect Shemya Island from an ominous buildup of Russian fighters and bombers at Petropavlovsk on the Kamchatka Peninsula, no one admitted to being scared. They were too busy thinking about what they had to do. Next to submarine duty, working a carrier's flight deck was the most dangerous job in the navy, made especially so this night by the line of squalls sweeping in all the way from the Sea of Japan. Screaming across the carrier's deck, the wind gusts and shears combined with the back-blasts in a fierce hodgepodge of crosscurrents that could blow a man off the deck like a tumbleweed. The only good thing about this night was that the smell of Avgas wasn't so astringent, the winds whipping fumes away as soon as they rose.

The first wave of fighters having taken off to go ahead and cover the carrier's "Wild Weasels," the advance electronic-jamming Prowlers, it was now Shirer's turn as leader of the second wave. His cockpit closed, the Tomcat's two twenty-thousand-pound Pratt and Whitney turbofans in high scream, preflight check completed, Shirer asked his RIO—radar intercept officer—if he was all set.

"Ready to go, Major?"

The Tomcat's light gray fuselage appeared angular, ungainly, from the carrier's island, the two intakes cumbersomely boxlike, until the plane turned under the lights, presenting its streamlined profile, the two flyers' names stenciled alongside the cockpit bright white as Shirer lined her up with the starboard bow catapult track. A yellow jacket, both his flashlights arcing, walked back as the jet fighter inched forward. Two red-jacketed ordnance men appeared in front of the plane and shone their flashlights directly onto the tips of the Tomcat's Sidewinder missiles. Through his headphone Shirer heard the faint burr, its sound like the run-down battery sound in a car. The heat-seeking missiles were now armed and live. The Tomcat's nose settled, its chin gently nudging the catapult's hook as the latter was attached to the nose wheel's strut. Across, left of him, through the rain- and steam-filled night, Shirer could see his wingman lining up on the port bow catapult.

The twin exhausts of Shirer's F-14 turbofans wailed in zone three, having changed from red through crimson to bright orange, harsh on the deck crew's eyes, and now moved to zone four, purplish white, and then, with the engines in the high banshee of zone five, the exhaust turned to screaming white circles edged in icy blue.

The catapult officer saw both men had "hands off" instruments so as not to interfere with catapult launch. Shirer saw the yellow-clad catapult officer drop to the left knee, right hand extended seaward. The shooter in his "dugout" pushed the button. Shirer sucked in his breath for the "kick," the F-14 shooting forward from zero to 180 miles per hour in three seconds. Shirer, feeling his whole body slam back into the seat, ejaculated under the G force as they were hurled aloft, then took back the controls, the white slab of the carrier tilting crazily downhill in the rear vision, flecks indicating the nine ships in the carrier's screen coming up on the RIO's radar.

On the carrier, where he was one of the team of professionals handling up to forty jet aircraft in various stages of takeoff, loading, refueling, and arming on a slab of steel shorter than most commercial airport concourses, a ground crew plane captain, brown jacket sodden with spray and wind-driven rain, jumped down from checking a Tomcat's Martin-Baker rear eject seat. He saw the left bow cat's blast deflector up, and bent down, head low, hand on his helmet to be on the safe side. A weapons trolley, low to the deck and unloaded, lurched, smacked him on the thigh, pushing him just left of the deflector. A quick-thinking ordnance man hauled him down on the deck, but a wind gust caught him in the slip of the jet's blast and he was gone.

"Man overboard!" came through to the bridge. The "air boss" in the tower kept his eyes on the plane-crowded deck, the two men on the situation board moving the small magnetic plane models according to their new disposition—there were still twelve Tomcats to launch, the second wave of Shirer's arrowhead formation. The huge, ninety-thousand-ton ship would not turn, nor would it stop. It was up to the "rescue" department to pick up the man, either with its launches or silver Sea King chopper hovering a safe distance off from the carrier, its red and green lights blinking, hardly visible, however, in the black void beyond the ship's undulating apron of light.

Ironically, the light from the carrier so flooded the sea immediately about her hull that the plane captain's saltwater-activated safety light, normally quite visible in darkness, was not seen. The captain of *Salt Lake City* had never met him—there were six thousand men aboard.

They called up his file from SHIPCO—ship's personnel computer—and gave the details to the executive officer, it being his job to write the boy's parents, farm people in Springfield, Missouri.

Already sixty miles from the carrier, Shirer, on strict radio silence, checked his head-up display and vectored in the present tail wind, which would be against them coming back—if they came back. Even with drop tanks carrying enough fuel for a maximum two-thousand-mile round trip, the computer was telling Shirer and his RIO that they would have only four minutes over Shemya Island. Still, last intelligence reports to the carrier relayed by the pick-up station at Adak Naval Station east of Shemya reported that everything was quiet on Shemya and that in what was a crucial game for the pennant, the New York Yankees had doubled the Boston Red Sox four to two.

When the phone burred, Jay told the girl to get out of bed and go and answer it. "I left it in the bathroom," he said.

"You should turn it off," said the girl. She was seventeen—consenting age. Jay La Roche was very careful about that.

"Don't you fucking tell me what to do, you little tight-ass," said La Roche, using his foot to push her out of the bed. He watched her walk away with an indifference bred of boredom.

"Just a moment," he heard her say. She brought in the

phone. Jay snatched it, cupping the mouthpiece. "You can go. There's a hundred by the lamp."

"We didn't even start," she said.

"No, well, I want a real woman. You don't know your ass from your tit. And put on the lock when you go out."

He turned back to the phone. "La Roche here," he said, pulling a Kleenex and wiping his nose.

"It's me," said the congressman, careful not to give his name.

"That was quick. So what's the story?"

"Listen—I did the best I could—"

Jay scrunched the Kleenex into a tight ball. "What are you telling me, Congressman?"

"Jesus, don't use my—"

"What are you saying, damn it?" pressed La Roche, throwing off the covers and getting out of bed.

"Look, there's some kind of flap going on up there."

"Up where?"

"The islands. COMPAC said he'd put the request through, but there's nothing he can do right now. She and a bunch of other nurses have been sent to some naval base hospital. Adak, I think it was."

"You jerkin' me off?"

"No, hey, wait a minute. I did my best."

"You did fuck all. I want results. You're the big politico. You'd better get me results, Congressman, or you're going to lose your friggin' reelection committee. I meant what I said. Now, you get to it. I *want* her, you hear me? I want her *here*. In Honolulu. In a fucking week. Otherwise—you're in the morning edition. Photos and all." La Roche slammed the phone down and looked at himself in the mirror for a few moments, admiring his lean physique and how well hung he was. He made his way to the bed, opened a drawer in the night table, and took out her photo. Like a brunette Marilyn Monroe, someone had said. She wasn't, but her lips—yes, Jay would give her the lips and the figure, but her eyes were so different, shy yet not timid. How much had she changed? Touching the photo, he got into bed and, in a rage, started to weep.

Suddenly he sat bolt upright. It was time to kick ass. He wanted her now—goddamn it, she could be killed up there. Snatching the phone, he got up and walked over to the globe on the plush burl coffee table, and in the soft peach light, looked to see if he could find Adak. Christ, it was just a spot in the ocean. To hell and gone. All he'd heard about was Shemya and the big early-warning radar there. What if the Russians hit this Adak as well as the base on Shemya? Had anyone thought of that?

Admiral Brodsky's motorcade had passed by the Kadriorg Park as Malle was halted by the MPO guardsmen who had seen her earlier with the corporal. Distraught, so weak she'd collapsed and had to be carried out of the park, where a crowd was gathering, she was taken to MPO headquarters across the street in front of the old city hall, and charged with murder.

Alarm spread throughout the MPO and other occupation troops. If a fifty-five-year-old woman, one of the normally passive Estonians, the "handholders," as they'd been dubbed since 1989, when they'd helped form a human chain with the other Balts to protest Russian hegemony, could strike so wantonly and brutally against the occupying troops, the situation was getting out of hand.

The matter was brought to Admiral Brodsky's attention at once, though the woman's name was not mentioned. Was she a suspected saboteur? he asked Malkov.

"No, Admiral, but that doesn't mean—"

"Don't tell me what it doesn't mean. You've let these Estonian renegades run rampant. STAVKA's still receiving reports of dud ammunition all over the place. When I initially recommended you, I thought you were tough enough to put an end to it. I was persuaded that the MPO could handle it better than the GRU. Obviously I was misinformed."

"With all due respect, Admiral," replied Malkov, "we've shot over six hundred hostages already in an attempt—"

"In an attempt, yes. But it obviously isn't working, is it?"

"I believe it is, Comrade Admiral. Informants are telling us for the first time that there is enormous internal pressure on the saboteurs to give themselves up for the sake of any further hostages. I believe it is only a matter of days before—"

"Captain Malkov," Brodsky cut in, "I am officially taking over this operation." He looked at his watch. "Sixteen forty hours. From now on it will revert to GRU jurisdiction under my command. You will be reassigned to Riga headquarters."

Malkov waited for more details, but Brodsky had nothing further to add.

When Malkov stormed out to his half-track in front of city hall, his mouth was set grimly, eyes brimming in such temper that his driver could tell it was going to be a bad day, or rather, what was left of it. He hesitated to say anything at all to the captain, but a call had just come through on the radio from the docks.

"What's it about?" snapped Malkov.

"I don't know, sir. The lieutenant asked me to—"

"All right, all right," growled Malkov, "give me the phone."

"Lieutenant—Malkov here. What is it?"

"Sir, it seems that your hostages are cracking the silence. We received an anonymous message this morning from number three shipyard. Six men are willing to talk, but only on condition that we will recognize them as members of the Estonian Liberation Front. That is, they want us to treat them as prisoners of war. And no more hostages are to be shot."

Malkov sat back in his seat, the driver, having overheard the conversation, equally relieved.

"Tell them," said Malkov, "we will agree to that on one condition. We want *all* saboteurs to come forward by ten hundred hours tomorrow. Otherwise we will continue to take hostages and they will have lost their chance. From then on, they would be treated as spies and shot on the spot."

"Yes, sir."

Beaming, Malkov handed his driver the phone. "To barracks, Igor. It's time for a drink."

"Yes, sir."

The following morning at number three shipyard, fourteen men and five women gave themselves up, but Malkov did not get the credit for it, as the official documentation showed he had been relieved of his assignment at 1640 the day before the surrender was made, under Brodsky's reign of authority. Furthermore, Malkov's agreement that they would be treated as POWs had no legal standing under military law—not that he had intended to keep his word anyway.

Brodsky fed the prisoners well and told them he expected a full list of all saboteurs in three days, or five hundred hostages he had ordered rounded up would be shot along with the nineteen.

The dam broke and over fifty names were presented to Brodsky. One day later, Brodsky signed an order that the saboteurs be sent to the shale oil fields around Kohtla-Järve, ninety miles east of Tallinn.

"I made at least twenty duds on the day I gave up," declared an old man defiantly as they were taken on their way. "I scratched 'MJ' on them, too."

The others obviously didn't know what he was talking about. "That women who shot that corporal bastard. Her name was Malle Jaakson—MJ, see?"

"Huh," grunted one of the others, his tone surly. "A lot of good it'll do her."

"Or us," added another. But soon the tensions among them and the animosities over whether or not they should have surrendered after all were lost beneath the overwhelming fact that they'd had no choice but to give in if they didn't want to see the slaughter go on. The emotional strain had been tremendous, and to revive their spirits, some of the oldest aboard the trucks began singing the Estonian national anthem. The convoy stopped for a while in the forest outside the city of Rakvere, and the prisoners were machine-gunned.

As Brodsky asked to sign the death warrant for the murderer of the MPO corporal and unscrewed the cap of his gold Parker pen, he noticed the first name of the woman was Malle. When he turned the page in the file and saw her photo, his hand froze. "Has this woman been interrogated?" he asked his aide.

"Oh, she confessed," the aide assured him. "There's no doubt about it, Admiral. Claims it was rape, of course. Trouble is, she was apparently having it off with the corporal for some time."

"Where is she?" Brodsky asked curtly.

The aide was confused—where else would she be but here? "Here, sir. In cells."

"Bring her to me."

"It wasn't a forced confession, sir. The woman fully admitted to having—"

"Bring her to me!" Brodsky repeated.

The aide had never seen him so agitated. The admiral rose

and seemed to grow angrier by the second. "Don't you understand a simple order?" he shouted.

"Yes, sir."

"Immediately!"

"Yes, Admiral."

The aide was utterly perplexed. It was a shut-and-closed case. No matter what the circumstances, it was murder. The penalty—death.

CHAPTER THIRTY-TWO

"SNEG!"—"SNOW!" IT was the one word in Russian that gave pause to Soviet commanders all the way from the northern reaches of the Kara south to Bavaria.

"Sneg nemozhet byt' neytral'nym"—"Snow is not neutral"—was one of the maxims of the Frunze Military Academy. Only fools thought it an equal impediment to friend and foe alike. Snow was regarded by the Russian armies with the same passionate intensity as that with which a priest might look to the Holy See. Time and again fate had used it to preserve their destiny, to deliver them from the darkest hours of their history. It had defeated Napoleon in 1812 and Hitler at Stalingrad in 1943. If you were a Russian, you did not complain about the snow, you melded in with it, became part of it, used it, your Russian "greatcoat" enfolding you, and you kept *moving*, for you understood snow better than anyone on earth, save the Eskimos. You could tell better than anyone else the temperature by the white-blue aura of the northern light, how falling powder snow was the best for attack, the worst for defense, whiting out one's vision, the great soft billows hiding you from the enemy and muffling the sound of your tanks.

Preceded by a barrage of over a thousand guns for two

hours, the Soviet divisions under Marshal Leonid Kirov led the attack on a hundred-mile front against the north–south sausage-shaped pocket. Surging ahead with their four-to-one advantage, the tanks converged in thousands, refugees and tens of thousands of farm animals scattering pathetically before them.

With only twenty miles to go, Marshal Kirov estimated that if all went well, his forces would reach the outer defenses of the DB perimeter in the next two hours. The British and Americans, Marshal Kirov assured the Russian premier, would be dug in, in defilade positions, and with thermal imagers in addition to their laser range finders, would take a heavy toll of Soviet tanks. But dug in, the NATO armor would be loath to risk leaving their defilade positions and revetment areas in deference to the sound military axiom that defense was easier than attack—especially in such foul weather. On the other hand, the only pause his armor had to make, reported Kirov, in the sudden change in the Arctic front from heavy rain to snow, was for some of his most forward tanks to make the switch from summer thirty-weight oil to winter ten-weight.

This was achieved with remarkable efficiency by the crack Soviet armored divisions coming down on the Dortmund-Bielefeld pocket from the north and those coming from the far south, where the Tyrol was already blanketed by early snowfall.

The very mention of snow, even to those Russian troops in the green flats of the Palatinate, was welcome because, except for the odd Canadian contingent in the pocket, it was more their element than the Americans' and British. And it was this point that General Marchenko pressed home to his political officers in charge of morale. Oh, certainly the NATO forces had run maneuvers in the Arctic, but that was a stop-and-start affair compared to the Russian soldiers, who'd been raised to it and who, like those from Khabarovsk, knew what it was to go fishing in the ice-covered lakes, not for sport but for survival. It was this edge, Kiril Marchenko confidently assured the STAVKA, that would finally tell in the Soviets' favor.

Marchenko also brought them good news about the last-minute Allied airlift out of Heidelberg. Here, Hungarian divisions had outflanked NATO's Southern Command's Wermacht divisions with such unexpected speed, it was reported that paper shredders had overheated and caught fire in the haste that verged on panic during the Allied withdrawal. That the Hungarians had achieved such a success was no surprise to Marchenko and other Soviets old enough to remember the Hungarians' tenaciousness in battle, but it was around Heidelberg that one of the most pervasive Allied illusions was shattered. Namely, it was the belief that because Hungarians hated Russians, they would either turn against Marshal Kirov's forces or surrender in droves to the Allies. And yet any cold, objective analysis of the prewar situation would have shown what would happen with Russia literally behind them, virtually holding Hungary as hostage. In an otherwise complex world, the answer was as simple as it was brutal: If the Warsaw Pact did not win, the Russians would raze eastern Europe in their retreat. The Russians' *strategiya vyzhzhennoy zemli*—"scorched earth policy"—would turn the Hungarian plain into a slaughterhouse such as the world had never seen and which, in its utter desolation as a base from which to wage war, would as likely stop the Allies just as it had Hitler.

For the Hungarians, there was no choice—better to be on the winning side. In any case, the West could not be relied upon. The martyrs had called upon Britain and America and all the other democracies to help them when they'd rebelled against the Soviets in '56 and then were brutally crushed by Russian tanks as the West looked on in paralyzed horror.

CHAPTER THIRTY-THREE

UP AGAINST THE eccentric but brilliant American General Freeman, Marshal Kirov and his sector commanders were determined to avoid North Korea's fate, when General Kim's rapid advance down the peninsula outstripped his sup-

ply line, which in turn had made Freeman's attack on Pyongyang so effective. Indeed, Kirov was convinced that it was
precisely this kind of SPETS-like interdiction that had been
the intent of the American airborne drops behind his lines.
The shock exhibited by some of the captured American paratroopers, the marshal's intelligence units had told him,
seemed to indicate otherwise—that the American airborne
had simply been blown off course.

"Yes," commented the marshal sarcastically, "just like
our SPETS units behind NATO lines. Blown off course and
in American uniforms!" This got a belly laugh from the
cluster of officers pressing in around Kirov, determined to be
in the newsreel the Ministry of Propaganda was taking. It was
a decisive moment in history—the impending and massive defeat of the American and British armies a certainty, something
that one could look back on with one's grandchildren.

"And this time," the marshal announced, "we won't be
as stupid as Hitler." Everyone laughed knowingly, including
a young colonel of artillery who really wasn't sure what the
marshal meant. The colonel looked about for someone lower
in rank. He saw a major on the marshal's staff, standing away
from the map table, hurriedly signing for receipt of
motorcycle-borne field reports. For a headquarters, it struck
the colonel as being as hectic as usual—an outsider would
think it chaotic—but it was relatively quiet, given the slight
radio traffic, all the important orders concerning the imminent attack on the Dortmund-Bielefeld pocket being issued
and received, at the marshal's express order, by motorcycle
companies. It struck the colonel as terribly old-fashioned.
The colonel waited until the cameraman had finished at the
map table, then walked over to the major.

"What does the marshal mean about Hitler?"

Normally the major would have deferred to the colonel,
but a headquarters major in effect outranked a field colonel.

"You should recall your antifascist history, Colonel," the
major told him. "In 1939 Hitler pushed the British and the
French right to the sea. At Dunkirk. They were trapped.
Hitler could have—" The major glanced quickly at a requi-
sition handed to him, scribbled his signature, and continued,
"Hitler could have driven them into the sea—annihilated
them. But he didn't."

"Why not?"

The major shrugged. "The fat man, Goering, wanted glory and persuaded Hitler to let the Luftwaffe bomb the Anglo-French into submission. Air force types always think bombing will do it—like the American LeMay in Vietnam, eh? Anyway, while Hitler halted his armor to let the Luftwaffe have its day, a British armada—everything from destroyers to sailboats—plucked the British and French off the beaches and took them back to England. The marshal won't halt our armor, Colonel—or our artillery. You'll be going all the way to Ostend. It's the nearest port for NATO withdrawal. So you'd better get lots of sleep. Once the offensive begins, there'll be no stopping."

In Munster Town Hall, its walls already scarred and pockmarked by the big long-range Russian guns, Freeman walked past the ruins of what had been the foyer down into the basement headquarters of the Dortmund-Bielefeld pocket, which had once been used to store the city records. With the cacophony of noise, a babble of radio traffic, of motorcycle messengers for the lines that had been cut and for the areas that had been jammed by the enemy, the scene was faintly reminiscent of the blue-versus-red games fought in the hot, stuffy headquarter tents of Fort Hood in Texas.

But there was something new, something he had never experienced before: the smell—not of men and women perspiring in high summer heat or overheated winter quarters, but the vinegary stench of impending defeat, heavy in the air. People were moving so fast that he could see panic was gripping many, only a few officers aware of his presence, perfunctorily saluting. His eyes took in the situation from one glance at the situation board, a long, snaking line of red pins marking the ever-expanding easternmost front of the Dortmund-Bielefeld pocket running north to south, the diagonal crisscrosses of Soviet armor creating a sharklike mouth, its jaws either side of the 250,000 men from the British Army of the Rhine, Bundeswehr, and what was left of the U.S. X Corps trapped inside, the Rhine behind them.

"It's snowing heavily twenty miles east of us," said a British brigadier, his face drained, eyes red with fatigue. "Might slow them down a bit, I should think."

"Who's commanding their northern sector?" asked Freeman. "Yesov?"

"Believe so, General," answered the brigadier.

"Believe so or know so?" said Freeman sharply, taking off his gloves and helmet, dropping them in the nearest "IN" tray without once taking his eyes from the map of northern Germany, seeing the northernmost point of the 240-square-mile pocket, still held by the Allies, barely five miles away.

"Yesov," confirmed the brigadier.

"Marchenko's stable," said Freeman, taking out his reading glasses, using the metal case to tap the area sixteen miles northeast of Bielefeld. "What we have to do is kick their asses back here beyond Oeynhausen—across the Weser."

"May I ask what with, General?" said the brigadier pointedly, fatigue overriding caution.

"With determination, General," Freeman told the brigadier, "and tanks."

The brigadier was too tired to bristle at the inference, restricting his utterance to a description of what he called a "devil" of a logistical problem. SPETS commandos had apparently been reported in the area, and the two major fuel depots for the pocket had been blown.

"You mean we're outta gas?" Freeman said, turning on him.

The brigadier called over his supply officer. "You have the figures on that petrol, Smythe?"

"Yes, sir," answered the British major. "We've enough petrol for our most advanced tanks to run four or five miles out from the perimeter."

The brigadier looked down at the major's notes. "You said we had more than that."

"You've lost the depot at Ahlen," said Freeman, without taking his eyes from the board. "You also have fewer tanks than you had yesterday. Nine hundred approximately."

The brigadier said nothing, feeling he had been set up by the American to reveal the deficiency of his own intelligence reports. Still, the brigadier was relieved that Freeman was, as the Americans would say, "on the ball." He was equally resentful of the fact that while elements of the United States, Bundeswehr, and the British Army of the Rhine had been fighting and dying for almost five weeks in various stages of retreat, since the breakthrough at Fulda in the South, no one outside the pocket seemed to know just how punishing this high-tech war of movement had been on the Allied troops. Meanwhile the troops waited, apparently in vain, for NATO's air forces to be resupplied enough so that they could do more than simply harass the Russian armor.

The war they had thought would be a quick push-button affair wasn't quick, nor was it push-button. You pushed buttons, all right, but often nothing happened. For all the training in peacetime, the accuracy of laser beams standing in for cannon fire to save the exorbitant cost of live ammunition, there was no substitute for the terrible punishment of a high-explosive shell hitting an M-1's reactive armor packs, which blew up and destroyed the shell but which couldn't do a thing about the jarring impact that set sensitive electronic and computer circuits awry. Time and again the brigadier had seen high tech fail the retreating troops as the more simple, brutish Russian armor kept on coming, losing more tanks than the Americans, but with a four-to-one advantage, the Russians could absorb it.

"We can't just sit here," said Freeman. "Yesov's a mover. Not the old Zhukov at all. He won't wait for too much longer before he attacks. He'd prefer a steady buildup of men and matériel before he hits us, but given this snow cover for attack, he won't wait."

"Then," said the brigadier, "he'll run into our mines." The British major couldn't suppress a wry smile at his superior's ready response. The mine fields beyond the perimeter were ample evidence that the British Army of the Rhine hadn't exactly been sitting on their derrières. The brigadier had spread his hand eastward out from the BD pocket, indicating the fan shape of the mine fields.

"He'll clear," said Freeman.

"If I may say so, General," replied the brigadier, "I don't see how. Oh, certainly—he'll use his 'roller' and 'flail' tanks to move ahead, but that's a slow business at the best of times. In this weather—I grant you he'll clear here and there, but we've got two-man mobile antitank units to close them up again. Even if he gets through, he'll pay an awful price. I daresay it would give him pause, General—if not stem the assault altogether."

"You don't have to justify stopping and seeding mines rather than standing your ground, General," said Freeman evenly. "It was your decision and I wasn't here, but if our intelligence reports are right, Yesov has at least a three-to-one, possibly four-to-one, tank advantage. We can gobble up as much of his steel as we like and he'll still have enough to break through, spread north and south—split our forces in two, then eat them up—just like they did at Fulda. Russkies aren't shy about repetition, General. If it works once—they'll do it again."

Freeman's knuckles rapped an area on the map ten miles northeast of Hereford. "Reconnaissance has Russian tanks converging on a twenty-mile front about Bielefeld."

On a tank-to-tank basis, Freeman knew that the M-1s had an edge on the T-90s, for though the Russian tanks had good laser and thermal range finders, the M-1s dug in with a much better defilade angle, or what the GIs called the "angle of dangle." Freeman also knew the British brigadier had acted correctly, ordering the NATO tanks to dig in under camouflage nets, using the mine fields as a protective moat with mobile platoons of three tanks each, ready to rush any gap through the mile-wide mine field. But if the Russians should somehow break through the mine field on a wider front, the dug-in NATO tanks would quickly find themselves surrounded, and the mobile NATO reserves would be in danger of hitting a NATO tank for every Russian T-90 they missed.

The greatest danger wasn't only to the men trapped inside the DB pocket, but a rupture through the mines would allow Yesov an end run to the Rhine. "If they cross the Rhine—" began Freeman. He did not need to say anything more, but he did, ordering, "All tanks and APCs to prepare for immediate counterattack. We'll open the narrow channel through the mine field and break out—hit them with all we've got before they roll over us." Freeman glanced at his watch, then, taking a blue marker pen from below the map, slashed three broad strokes at ten-mile intervals along the eastern side of the DB pocket. "I want them ready to roll at oh four hundred."

"General," said the brigadier, "a word—"

"What?" grunted Freeman. A word? He realized the Englishman wanted to speak with him in private.

Walking away from the babble and surging static of the "OPS" table, Freeman, his hands on his hips, waited impatiently for the British brigadier to make his point.

Surely, the brigadier told Freeman, their best hope was to simply keep "dug in," let the storm slow the Russian advance. The Allies' best hope, he argued, was to effect a stalemate behind the mine field, to buy time for NATO reinforcements of men and matériel. To hold out a few days—a week even—until what the brigadier flatteringly called "the clear genius of the American air force to resupply by air" would allow a NATO buildup.

Agitated, Freeman turned back to the wall map, thumping it with such violence that some of the blue NATO pins popped to the ground. A Bundeswehr corporal quickly picked them up again, but not before a sudden and noticeable silence ensued, as all operators' eyes momentarily turned toward Freeman. The brigadier's jaw was clenched, not in anger so much as in shock, while Freeman's eyes, far from indicating any embarrassment, swept over every man in the headquarters basement. "Now, you listen to me. This isn't a command post. This is a goddamned Tower of Babel, and it's all about how the Russians have got us on the run. Well, we're going to change that in—" he looked at his watch "—approximately six hours from now. At fourteen hundred hours. We're going on the attack. Those tanks that run out of gas will siphon fuel from the APCs, those men in the APCs will ride on or behind the tanks. Do what the Russians do—rig up sleds. Prisoner intelligence tells us Ivan's low on gas, too. Recon flights show they're carting refueling drums, just as they did in all the prewar maneuvers. That means, gentlemen, his supply line's overextended. Tell your battalion commanders that I want to see some initiative or tomorrow they won't be commanders. I'll break the sons of bitches to sergeants—every goddamned one of 'em."

Freeman stopped, but it wasn't for breath. He wanted to make sure every man in the hut had his eyes fixed on him. They did. "Now I'm gonna tell you something else. It's the last thing Yesov will expect. Every goddamned tinhorn reporter is telling everyone that the DB pocket is on its last legs." He turned to the brigadier and the other British officers who had gathered to watch the mad American. "Why, last night even your BBC were telling your own people we're about to fold. Well, we're not going to fold." He snatched up his helmet and gloves, pushing them sharply in front of him to underscore his point. "We are going on the offensive!"

There was silence; even the crackle of the radios seemed to have died. There were no cheers, no *"ja!"'s* from the

German officers present, one *obersleutnant*, lieutenant colonel, commenting to his colleage, *"Kindlicher Quatsch!"*—"Nonsense." Did Freeman, they wondered, really think that this "silly American football pep talk" would have any effect? Would he expect the headquarters company, most of them career officers, to be suddenly filled with elation?

Freeman certainly didn't expect it. He knew that an order to the top-echelon commanding officers, no matter how forcefully delivered, was not enough to galvanize a dispirited army, and so within minutes he was in his command Humvee, its driver peering through the smudge of windshield as the wipers howled, heading through the blanket of softly falling snow to visit individual battalion commanders, Freeman noting the increase in Russian artillery, their distinctive thuds louder than the quieter thump of American artillery. "Cheap gunpowder," he told his aide, Col. Al Banks. It was almost certainly the softening up before what Freeman believed would be a massive Russian frontal and flank assault. The NATO artillery battalions were firing intermittently, their supply of ammunition dictating restraint, one that could not help but be noticed by the Russian divisions, boosting their morale even further.

"We have to keep telling our boys," Freeman shouted over the high-gear whine of the Humvee, "that concentrated fire is far more effective than blanket random fire." His aide found it difficult to concentrate with the rolling, crunching noise of the creeping barrage coming toward them from the Russian artillery around Bielefeld. The racket made it even more difficult to hear Freeman, who, as usual, insisted on standing up in his Humvee, gripping the top of the windshield, his leather gloves now covered in snow, the general seemingly oblivious to the increasing menace of the enemy's artillery, the whistle of shot above them and the clouds of cordite, burning rubber, and fuel that, wafting westward, smudged the white curtain of falling snow. Freeman's expression, beneath the goggles, was one of eager expectation.

"Looks like a kid at a fairground," grumbled a GI, one of the bedraggled remnants of a reconnaissance patrol making its way back wearily to their battalion headquarters.

"He's mad," said one of the loaders in a cluster of 120-millimeter howitzers, the harsh, metallic aspect of the discarded shells now softening, melding into a mound of virginal white as the black spaces between the brass casings filled with snow.

With the Humvee nearing the perimeter, Al Banks heard the splintering of timber and an eruption of black earth only a few hundred yards ahead of them, his eyes, like those of the driver, frantically searching either side of the road for some kind of shelter, the pines of the forest too close together for the Humvee to hide in them. The road turned sharply to the left. Ahead they saw a small bridge had been taken out, one of the bridge's elegantly carved wooden posts miraculously intact, its dwarf's face smiling sweetly beneath a hiker's hat capped with snow.

As the shelling increased, Banks thought that for a moment enemy intelligence must have somehow found out where Freeman was and "bracketed" his position, ordering its artillery to saturate the area. The driver, seeing a small forester's hut in a clearing a hundred yards to the right of the bridge's ruins, wasted no time in pulling the Humvee off toward it, the other two Humvees, one front and back of the general's, braking and following.

Approaching the hut, Freeman saw it was unlocked and what he thought was movement inside. He spotted discarded ammo belts and empty cans. He saw the movement again—something orange. Drawing his pistol from the shoulder holster beneath his camouflage jacket, he flicked the safety off and opened the door. Inside the gloom he heard a huffing sound, like someone out of breath, as if they'd been running. Then he saw a blackened face gazing up, terrified, from a pile of Hessian sacks. The soldier, an American, didn't move; the woman—her green-and-brown-splotched Bundeswehr jacket open, breasts rising and falling rapidly beneath her khaki T-shirt—reached quickly for her trousers, crumpled by her side. Looking first at the soldier as he grunted and rolled off her, she gazed up in terror at the general. Freeman saw the flash of Day-Glo orange, the woman clutching her trousers.

"Sorry . . . sir . . ." began the GI, his camouflage greasepaint catching the light from the snow as he scrambled awkwardly to his feet, two feet in one trouser leg, falling and knocking over a pickax and shovel in the corner of the hut.

"Where the hell's your squad?" asked Freeman.

"Don't know, sir. We got separated . . ."

The general holstered his .45. "Well, son, finish up here and get aboard one of our jeeps. We're going up to the front.

You—'' He looked across at the German woman''—and your young lady friend can come with us. If that isn't too inconvenient?''

The soldier was too frightened to answer. Freeman left the hut. "Goddamn it, Banks!" he said. "I've been in this man's army for over forty years, and the incompetence we harbor never ceases to amaze me."

The shelling seemed to have subsided, or at least passed beyond the immediate area, the Humvee drivers taking the opportunity to brush off as much snow from windshields and windows as possible.

"Take a message," Freeman told Al Banks. "Immediate and confidential. SACEUR.''

Is it necessary to compound the danger to our fighting men by the issuance of Technicolor rubbers, which can be seen by the enemy at a thousand yards in snow conditions? The resulting injury to our men from enemy fire would be far more hazardous than that which you seek to avoid.

The message puzzled both Supreme Allied Command Europe and Commander in Chief, Channel Forces, in Northwood, England, until it was explained by an American liaison officer that "rubbers" were *not* "erasers" but American slang for condoms.

"Oh—" replied a brigadier. *"Oh!"*

Mirth in the British officers' mess aside, SACEUR realized that the American general had a point quite apart from the fact that over 12 percent of all casualties in all armies were due to venereal disease—often higher than the casualty rate suffered in combat.

In any event, the story of the general's encounter with the battlefield lovers swept like wildfire through the decimated ranks of American X Corps and other contingents around the perimeter, including those among the American airborne who had not been blown off course into enemy territory beyond the drop zone. By the time the story had reached Dortmund, only fifty miles in the rear, it was attaining mythical proportions and was completely changed, the story now being that Freeman "comes across one of our guys humping a fräulein and says, 'What the fuck are you doing, soldier?' Well, this dogface looks up at Freeman and says, 'This little honey bee if she'll let me, General.'' So Freeman says to his aide, 'Al,

you'd better promote the son of a bitch. Any man that quick
on all fours deserves a battlefield citation.' So his aide says,
'You want him made a sergeant, General?' and old Freeman
says, 'You make him a lieutenant. And that's an order!' ''

Back at his headquarters in Munster, Freeman was told the
story and, though he smiled, was curiously ambivalent about
it. On the one hand, he told his aide, the story would probably do more to raise Allied morale in the pocket than a
dozen speeches. On the other hand, the distortion that the
story had undergone in the retelling disturbed him, for it was
as clear an example as you'd want, he told Banks, of how
"screwed up the simplest verbal exchange gets as it's passed
down the line." No matter how sophisticated the communications equipment, all the more vital in a war of rapid
movement, it often came to naught when messages had to be
relayed verbally. The general state of communication glitches
that had been reported from Heidelberg, before it fell, was
one of the reasons he was so determined to reestablish personal contact with as many units as possible within the chaos
of the shrinking perimeter. He particularly wanted to rally
the airborne, who had taken a terrible beating, many of them,
like young David Brentwood, who had fought with him in
Korea, now reported missing, apparently having come down
on the wrong side of the drop zone. Well, there was nothing
he could do about those out of reach.

In the rear, the media army, most of them safely across
the Rhine, were clamoring for interviews with Freeman once
they'd heard the fräulein story. Freeman's press aide suggested to the general that it might be prudent before he spoke
to any of the reporters to "rephrase" his response for home
consumption.

"Hell, no!" was Freeman's response, too busy in any case
with trying to figure out how he would meet what he was
sure would be Yesov's massive and final assault upon the
perimeter. "Doesn't matter what you say," said the general
as he held out his hand impatiently for his map case. "Newspapers screw it up anyway."

Freeman placed his forefinger on Bielefeld and, moving
the second finger to form a divider, checked the rough measure against the map's scale. It was twenty-seven miles east
from Bielefeld to the Weser River. If only there were some
way he could push the Russians back to the river, to suddenly
reverse the position, to buy time for NATO reinforcements

to pour in from the convoys that he hoped were now unloading at the British and French ports. The Russians had damned good Leggo bridges, but if they were forced to withdraw, the crossing would slow them down, giving the Allies a vital pause so that RAF, USAF, and Luftwaffe fighters could bring all the firepower they still had from their fast-dwindling supplies to bear onto the smaller, concentrated areas of the bridges. With hopefully devastating results. "You know," he told his press aide without looking up from the map spread out before him, "that James Cagney never said, 'You dirty rat.' "

"No," said his aide, somewhat nonplussed. "I didn't know that."

Freeman ordered the Dutch mobile infantry to close on what he believed would be the northernmost right-handed punch of the Russian armor. The Dutch had always been a concern for prewar NATO HQ. But recognizing the implications of being stationed farther away from the front line, they'd made up for it, developing a speed that had won the respect of even the Bundeswehr. "Well," Freeman told his press aide, trying to boost morale with a little trivia, "Cagney didn't say, 'You dirty rat.' What he *did* say was 'Judy! Judy! Judy!' "

When the press aide saw Al Banks walking toward the command bunker, the snow was falling heavily. As Banks took off his coat, the aide noticed he had a somber, pained look about him. The aide poured a mug of coffee for him and, handing it over, asked, "What the hell's the general on about—Judy, Judy, Judy?"

"What—?" asked Banks, cupping the coffee mug in his hands. "Listen, we've just got Stealth infrared overflight photos that show the Russians are moving in three more tank regiments under this blizzard. Another two to three hundred tanks."

"Jesus—"

"I think they're just trying to frighten us," said Banks, laughing. There was a hint of fatigue-craziness to it that unsettled the press aide.

"T-90s?" asked the aide.

"No. PT-76s apparently."

"Well, that's not as bad as the 90s."

"Yes it is. I think the old man hates them more than the 90s. Nineties are like our M-1s. Great when everything's going great, but one good bang and out go half the electronics. With the 76s, we're down to VW Beetles versus Cadillacs. Sometimes the simpler the better—in weather like this.''

"Easier to repair," said the press aide, eager to show he knew more than the usual media "flak."

"Yes," confirmed Banks, pouring more sugar into the steaming coffee. He could see Freeman at the situation board, a corporal, with a plug-in wire trailing from his headset, writing in the estimated strength and position of the Russian armored buildup with his marker pen. They had been using the small, magnetic block stickers, the kind civilians use for sticking messages on refrigerators, but they'd had a major foul-up near Heidelberg because the magnets on the big "tote" board had wiped a nearby computer disk clean. The result was a rifle company misdirected and lost. It was the sort of unpredictable screw-up that haunted all the commanders, Freeman especially, who confided in Banks that it was the "accidents of history" that worried him more than the enemy—the little things upon which great events can turn, despite the best-laid plans.

"Another thing about the PT-76s," said Banks, "is they're about half the weight of our tanks, Kraut Leopards and British Challengers included. Don't get stuck nearly so easily in the slush. That's why the North Koreans caught us with our pants down. Gave 'em the edge.''

"This wet snow isn't going to help them," replied the press aide.

"Nope. What we need now is it to get a damn sight colder—drop well below freezing. That way we'd have hard ground.''

"That how we beat 'em in Korea?''

"That and an uninterrupted supply line from Japan," replied Banks, the worry lines in his face so deep, they made him look like a man twice his age. "If we don't get a full NATO convoy through in three weeks—we're sunk.''

"Jesus!" said the aide. "You really think we'll lose the perimeter?''

Banks looked down at him. "Where've you been, Larry? We could lose the *war*. If I were you, I'd have a press release ready in case they bust through.''

The young press aide was visibly shaken. "Christ, I didn't think it was *that* bad.''

"You've been reading your own press releases. No one

else but the old man, our G-2, and those poor bastards right *on* the perimeter know. I'm just saying that meanwhile you'd better cover your ass. Not too much about our gallant boys at the front. If you pump up the public back home, they'll turn on you if we get our butts kicked back behind the Rhine. Why do you think the old man won't allow any TV cameras on the perimeter?'' Banks drained the coffee cup. ''It's going to be the biggest attack since Fulda Gap.''

''I dunno if I can keep the media off that,'' said the press aide, shaking his head. ''Those TV guys are pretty persistent. Already there's a stringer on the loose. One of my guys said he put on a groundsheet—no press insignia showing. We've lost track of him.''

''What's his name?'' asked Banks.

''Rodriguez.''

''There's a thousand Rodriguezes. You have his accreditation number?''

''Yes—why?''

''We don't want him doing a Vietnam on us. Not now—when we're down.''

''I don't see how we can stop him, Al. He'll be hard to spot. I mean those hand-held videos these days are no bigger'n a Hershey bar.''

''Never mind,'' said Banks. ''You get MPs out after him *now*.'' Banks had a faraway look in his eye. ''I haven't had a Hershey bar for—'' He couldn't remember since when. ''And a Coke,'' he said wistfully. ''Not that goddamned flat shit they pump into paper cups. I mean a bottle. Glass. No friggin' plastic. Just turning to ice—not quite. I mean, just about to.''

Depression was not unknown to Gen. Douglas Freeman, but it was rare. He was a believer in seeing the glass half-full, not half-empty. As a British commander of submarines had told him, in the end the best equipment could not stand up to the best morale. Witness the outmanned, outgunned Vietcong in the Vietnam War and the outnumbered ''outradared'' Nazi U-Boats in '44–'45. Nevertheless, Freeman's habitual optimism, with which he imbued his troops, like the young Brentwood boy in Korea, was sorely tried when all Stealth overflight photos of the enemy prepo sites were presented to him as his mobile Humvee command post headed out for another sector of the front north of Munster.

As the machine-gun-mounted jeep bumped around the bomb-cratered road, Freeman found it difficult to focus the 3-D overlay on the latest aerial photos just taken within the last two hours. Perhaps, he told Col. Al Banks, there *were* the ubiquitous extra fuel drums on the Soviet tanks in the photos, but he couldn't spot any. They had definitely been there in the photos from the earlier overflights.

He ordered the Humvee to stop, to look more closely and steadily at one of the T-90 turrets that the Stealth had picked up by infrared through the low ceiling of pea-soup stratus. "A lot of skirting around this turret, Al. Looks like some kind of spaced or reactive armor. Soon as one of our shells hits it—blows itself up. Most they get inside is a headache. But damned if I can see any extra fuel drums on the back. You have a look."

"No, General, no fuel barrels I can see."

"Goddamn it! Russkies always carry extra fuel. Two things you know about Russian armor is, those bastards break down sooner than ours and their matériel support isn't anywhere as good as ours."

Banks said nothing, and the general did not speak for several minutes, confirming to Banks just how worried his boss was. The general got out of the Humvee and, pulling his lamb's-wool collar high about his neck, walked ahead, slapping his leg with his gloves. As he turned back to the truck, Banks slowly keeping pace behind him, the look of disgust he'd had when he'd gotten out was still there. "Damn it, Al! I just got through telling my field commanders—damn it, my whole strategy was based on telling our boys to pull back to defilade positions. Suck Ivan into thinking we're turning tail— conserve our ammunition. Get those Commie sons of bitches overextended till their spare fuel drums are empty, then we go on the offensive. Hit 'em with everything we've got."

"I don't understand, General. I thought you'd be pleased they're not hauling extra fuel tanks. Limits their range."

"I know, I know," replied Freeman, his hand in the air irritably brushing Banks's observation aside. "Gas drums are normally their most vulnerable spot. But in this fight they'll outnumber us, Al. Four of their tanks to every one of ours. There are only so many you can stop like that—then the rest are all over you. No—what worries me is that no auxiliary gas tanks means they don't *need* auxiliary tanks. Means they've got lots of gas, more than we thought, stashed in that prepo site south of Hannover.''

The general climbed back into the Humvee. ''I've got to think of something else. Fast.'' He was looking straight ahead, three other Humvees behind him and an armored car in front, but Al Banks was betting that what the general was really seeing was a map of the DB pocket.

There was a whoosh of air somewhere above them in the low cloud, followed by the chatter and rattle of machine guns.

''Holy—'' began the Humvee driver, his voice drowned by the feral roar of an AA missile hitting an Apache gunship, the bug-nosed chopper momentarily visible in the orange ball of flame engulfing it. The Humvee driver put his foot down, swung the truck away from the deep pothole, and straightened it, oily smoke curling toward him. They hit the Humvee in front of them hard on its left rear fender and rolled.

By the time the men in the Humvees behind reached them down a steep embankment whose vegetation hid a drainage ditch, the driver was bleeding badly from multiple lacerations to the face. Al Banks was dead, his neck snapped, apparently in a swing blow from the barrel of the Humvee's swivel .50 machine gun. Freeman was unconscious, his left arm looking as if it was broken.

''Watch it!'' one of the soldiers cautioned. ''Don't move him.''

''Are you serious? I think he's bought it,'' answered another.

''General!'' the sergeant was shouting, ''General, can you hear me?''

''He's dead,'' said one.

''No he isn't.''

''Close enough, Frank.''

''C'mon. Where's that fucking medic?''

CHAPTER THIRTY-FOUR

OUTSIDE KAESONG, ROK Major Tae jumped over the irrigation ditch, burst through the thinning smoke, his squad automatic weapon spewing flame, its tracer tattooing the NKA machine-gun position twenty yards from the ditch wall, the U.S. cavalryman giving him supporting fire, spraying the paddy to their right, the rice stalks trembling under the hail of the 7.62-millimeter bullets.

When Tae reached the machine-gun post, he saw it was abandoned, one NKA dead, the top of his skull blown off, the Soviet-made RPK 7.62 gone. Tae felt several spent casings. They were still hot, and he waved for the six-man squad from his Huey to advance.

"Where the hell have they gone?" asked the cavalryman, relieved but surprised. "Hot damn, those bastards can melt away on ya!"

Tae saw one of the cavalrymen off to his left prod a dead NKA down by the irrigation channel.

"Don't touch him," cautioned Tae.

The cavalryman by Tae's side was signaling the other sixty-odd troops behind him on the search-and-destroy mission. He turned to Tae. "They wouldn't have had time to booby-trap their dead, Major."

Tae was down on one knee, clipping a new magazine into his SAW, surveying the paddy field, wisps of cover smoke still obscuring his view.

"Where the hell have they gone?" repeated the cavalryman. "Underground?"

"Not unless they've got scuba suits," said a sergeant, moving up to join Tae and the other cavalryman. "Nothing but flooded paddy out there."

"They're using reeds," said Tae. "They wait till we pass."

"Then we'll go around it," suggested the sergeant.

"They could've rigged sticks," put in another, referring to the camouflaged pits of spikes so often set by the NKA.

"So what do we do, Major? Get our feet wet? Sitting ducks or do we risk 'sticks'?"

The major ordered a fifty-fifty split, half the force—about thirty men—in a broken line to go across the paddy, the remaining thirty to sweep the flanks beyond the paddy, requesting an air strike ahead of them to clear.

Within ten minutes an F-4 Phantom came in low over the hills, strafing the bush area beyond the paddy a quarter mile away and dropping two napalm canisters, which turned the jade-green countryside to orange-black, leaving the once bushy area denuded. A swarm of insects had started to bother the men while they had been waiting, and several in the paddy pulled on head nets over their helmets before they moved forward, still tense but feeling better now that the air strike had pummeled the area before them.

The major was moving cautiously but was so far out front that one U.S. cavalryman dubbed the once shy major "Hound Dog." Every one of them now knew the story of his daughter being raped before his eyes and sympathized with his obsession for vengeance on the NKA, but they weren't keen to be part of it. Tae's obsession was making him altogether too dangerous, in their eyes.

They slowed as they approached a second area, where they saw the remains of four NKA, one man's limbs charcoal, two of the faces black jam already seething with insects. Tae was annoyed the napalm had burned off all unit patches or any other kind of identification that might have confirmed they were against one of the units led by Students for Reunification traitors like Jung-hyun.

The men on the flanks were resting on the slope up from the ditch when they heard the spitting of light machine-gun fire. Hitting the ground, no one knew where it was coming from until two cavalrymen dropped in the paddy fifty yards behind them, the high waterspouts dancing amid the stalks of rice. The Americans around Tae were unable to return the NKA fire for fear of hitting their own men in the paddy, and it wasn't until two more Americans had been killed in the paddy and an NKA was seen floating that the firing ceased.

Seeing two of his men badly wounded, staggering from

the rice field, the air cavalry lieutenant was on the PRC-25, calling in a Medevac chopper. Major Tae ordered the others into a tighter defensive perimeter. There was a scream off to his left, three men hit by a "Malay whip," a long, six-inch-thick dead log rigged to a trip wire, slamming down like a swing trapeze. Two men were killed outright, the other, his back broken, screaming in agony—someone yelling at him to shut up, the lieutenant pulling a violet flare, its purple smoke designating the landing zone for the chopper and also alerting any NKA nearby to the Americans' position.

It was then that Tae saw two badly burned NKA, fifty to sixty yards away, crawling into unburned brush, a whiff of burnt flesh and wood smoke in the air. One of them tried to turn and fire what looked like an AK-47, but either he was out of ammunition or the gun jammed. The other NKA, all but naked, save the singed rags of what had been a drab, olive-colored uniform, kept crawling toward the brush.

The cavalry sergeant caught up with him, and the man, though beaten, was staring up, eyes alive with hatred, his breathing labored and wheezy, eyebrows gone and a gellike pus where napalm had eaten into his left thigh. But there was no mistake, and Tae recognized him at once. Jung-hyun— his daughter's onetime boyfriend and SFR activist who'd turned on his own country.

The cavalry lieutenant could tell at one glance that Tae had found his man. "About time, eh, Major?"

If Tae heard, he gave no indication, but while the lieutenant was preoccupied with organizing covering fire for the incoming Medevac, Tae handed his squad weapon to the sergeant, then, bending down, drew his knife from its leg sheath. The chopper was coming in, sporadic NKA fire erupting from the bush. "Where is Mi-ja?"

Jung-hyun refused to answer. Tae grabbed Jung's tattered collar, bringing his head close to the blade. Once more he saw his daughter across the interrogation room—the smell of her perfume, and the rape as real to him as if it were happening now. And for her he could not kill Jung. As he stood up in the stinging dust of the Medevac chopper, whose rotors were beating the air into a maelstrom about him, Tae's anger at his inability to do that for which he had stayed alive overwhelmed him and he kicked Jung in the side. Jung's body rolled. There was an explosion—Tae's body seemed to jump, sending him crashing into the sergeant, the grenade's shrapnel killing the sergeant outright and mangling Tae's feet, his boots, shredded with splintered bone, streaming blood.

In the American camp south at Uijongbu, the instructors used it as an example of how an officer, Tae, well trained and knowledgeable about booby traps, had, in a case of what the instructor called "emotional overload," forgotten the very thing he'd just told a U.S. air cavalryman a few minutes before: "Never move close in to an NKA body, live or dead." One of the oldest NKA tricks in the book was to pull a grenade's pin and shove it under the weight of your body. As soon as you're moved—down goes the striker. "Boom!"

Had it not been for the Medevac getting Tae to a field hospital within half an hour, said the instructor, the ROK major would have lost his life rather than having to be in a wheelchair for the rest of his life.

"Would have been better off," said one of the pupils.

CHAPTER THIRTY-FIVE

"SCHNELL!"—"QUICKLY!" SHOUTED one of the *Stasi* guards. The POW column had slowed momentarily while a salvo of high-explosive shells whistled overhead, every one of the British and American soldiers hitting the forest floor. The guard was waving an AKM submachine gun, its black folding butt and tangent sight a stark contrast to the falling snow. The powder snow had stopped for a while over the northernmost part of the Teutoburger Wald, and now, with the temperature only slightly above freezing, the flakes were big and damp, disappearing on contact into the blankets that were being worn as capes by many in the column who had had their uniforms taken by the SPETS.

Now, with other prisoners being picked up along the way,

the British and American column being force-marched to Gobfeld, eighteen miles north of Bielefeld and forty miles southwest of Hannover, had swelled to more than three hundred men. As much as the prisoners resented the bullying guards, most of them, like David, realized that ironically, in the Russian's haste to move the POWs out of the way of their advancing echelons of armor-led troops and motorized regiments, the Stasi guards were in fact keeping some Allied prisoners alive who would have otherwise died from hypothermia had they been allowed to stop for any length of time.

Even so, the cockney's earlier comment to David Brentwood and Waite that they were all "for the high jump"—execution—made the prisoners reluctant to keep up the punishing pace. "Hope the bastard that's got my uniform is warm," complained a U.S. engineer. "I'm sure as hell not."

"Least you've got your boots, mate," said Fred Waite, the British private who had teamed up with David Brentwood. "Least your twinkies won't fall off."

"Speak for yourself. Anyway—"

"*Schweig doch!*" yelled a guard.

"Shut up your fucking self," said Waite, turning to Brentwood, his breath steaming the air. "That Kraut's getting on my tit."

Brentwood said nothing, glancing anxiously about as another stream of POWs, thirty or so Americans, up ahead were being melded into the main column heading for Gobfeld. For a moment David thought he recognized Thelman, but the main POW stream quickly swallowed up the new additions before Brentwood could know for sure. Dizzy, like so many of the other prisoners, from lack of food and sleep, and the effects of the cold, David found it necessary to muster all his strength merely to keep going in the column. Nevertheless, he tried to increase his pace.

"Easy, Davey, old son," cautioned Waite, his breath no longer visible in the air, his body losing the battle. "Not the World Cup, you know."

"Thought I saw a buddy of mine," answered David.

"Yes, well relax. Husband your energy, old son. That's the—" Waite wanted to say "ticket" but couldn't go on, gasping for air like an exhausted swimmer. Brentwood took the Englishman's left arm and draped it about his shoulder, taking his weight. "You okay, Fred?"

"No."

"Schnell! Schnell!" one of the guards yelled, soon joined by several others shouting at the stragglers on the flanks. Brentwood heard the shouts of an altercation several yards behind them. The snow muffled the tramp of the column, and the voices seemed unusually loud, bouncing off the pine trees. *"Schnell!"* the guard kept shouting. Brentwood saw it was the Englishman with the badly injured eye. The bandage had slipped down from his eye, the blood now a dark plum color against the snow. The man was sitting on a stump, winding up the bandage and telling the guard to "stuff it!"

Several prisoners stopped, including David, and within seconds it was looking ugly; a *feldwebel* was running down the side of the column, with two other guards trying to keep up with him, other guards yelling for prisoners to stay in column, prisoners retorting, some of them derisively clapping the *Stasi* guards. "Run, girls! Run, you sausage guts!"

The *feldwebel* stopped by the Englishman, drew his pistol, and ordered the man to get up. The Englishman refused and the *feldwebel* shot him. There was silence, then a bulge of prisoners forming around the dead Englishman, his bandage fallen, like a streamer in the snow. Guards either side of the *feldwebel* held cocked Sudayev submachine guns. Suddenly David saw Thelman fifty yards ahead of him, also looking back at what was going on. The tension hung in the air like icicles. The *feldwebel* shouted and a few prisoners shuffled forward, the outrage still thick in the air, but the submachine guns were staring the prisoners down at point-blank range. "Any soldiers stopping," shouted the *feldwebel*, "will be shot. You understand!"

"Christ—" said Waite, the bottom seeming to drop out from what David had thought was the Englishman's reservoir of high morale. "I'm—I'm for the knackers," confessed Waite. "Like bloody running downhill—once you slow down, you're buggered."

David had tried to get Thelman's attention, but he had disappeared into the column in front of a tall flyer, one of the glider pilots who'd overshot Munster, coming down too close to the Teutoburger Wald.

As the POW column emerged from the wood a few miles south of Gobfeld, the prisoners were surprised to see a convoy with ten olive-green army trucks with Russian markings on the rear bumper.

"Bloody 'ell," said Waite, his teeth chattering, as they were ordered aboard the trucks. "This is more like it."

"Yeah?" came a doubting voice from behind. "Where are they taking us?"

"If they wanted to do us in, mate," said another Englishman, "they could have done it in the woods."

The doubting voice was silenced, but Waite himself gave David a very cool, practical reason why the woods wouldn't have been a place of execution. "Not enough open space to bury three hundred of us, unless they used 'dozers." As if to underscore his point, Waite now remarked on the fact that they were loading the dead Englishman onto one of the trucks. "No evidence," said Waite.

"Take cover!" shouted one of the prisoners. Three Thunderbolts, terrifyingly close to the ground, swept out of the cloud above the trees, a short burst from the lead Gau cannon, its rotary barrel spewing a narrow cone of thirty-millimeter tracer, exploding three trucks in less than two seconds. The men aboard the trucks, half of them on fire, dropped from the tailgates, rolling in the snow at the roadside.

The other two Thunderbolts, pilots so near, they were plainly visible as they whooshed by, withheld their fire the moment they recognized Allied POWs waving them off—NATO's Thunderbolts' supply of thirty-millimeter tank-killing ammunition dangerously low due to the heavy convoy losses.

The *Stasi* guards, short of trucks now, were already quickly selecting the fittest of those who had survived, loading them onto the other vehicles. David Brentwood and Waite, already on one of the other trucks in the middle of the column, found themselves squashed hard against the vehicle's cabin by the press of newcomers.

"Stumble-Ass!" It was Thelman, face lighting up the moment he spotted Brentwood.

"*Schweig doch!*" shouted one of the four guards assigned to the truck, but in the confusion, no one took any notice.

"Buddy of mine," explained David, grinning for the first time in the last seventy-six hours. "We were at Parris Island together. Same DI. Called me 'Stumble-Ass'—Thelman 'Thelma.' He was a son of a bitch."

"Charming," said a cultured English voice.

When they reached Gobfeld, the convoy roared on through the town.

"Thought someone said we were stopping here."

"You've been misinformed, old boy," came the English voice. "We're going to a holiday camp in Stadthagen."

"Where's that?"

"Seven miles farther on, I believe."

As the truck bumped its way north over the artillery-scored road, snow started falling again, but this time more densely than before.

"What's in Stadthagen, Fritz?" asked one of the Americans. The guard said nothing. "Anyone speak Kraut?" asked someone else. The cultured English voice, which Brentwood could now see belonged to a junior lieutenant in the Royal Engineers, owned up to knowing "a few words" of German. In fact, he was fluent, and the rest of the men fell silent so that he could talk to the guard, but it was still difficult to hear above the high whine and rattle of the convoy.

"He says," the Englishman reported to his eager audience, "that there are no girls in Stadthagen and that it will be hard work."

"What will be?"

The Englishman asked the guard to be more specific. "He says there is a 'store' there. A very big store."

"Macy's?" suggested Thelman.

"Harrods?" said another.

David was pleased to see the morale picking up now that they were off their feet, at least for a while, and in the relative warmth of the truck, even if they were destined to work hard at whatever it was in Stadthagen.

"I think," proffered the English engineer, "that he rather means *stores*. I should think he's alluding to a prepo site of some kind. Did we have one at Stadthagen?" He looked about the truck.

"Yes," answered a British lance corporal, wearing the insignia of RAF ground crew. "Ruddy great petrol dump."

"Ah!" said the engineer. "Then, chaps, we'll 'roll out the barrel'!"

"And we'll have a barrel of fun," a few voices chimed in. But the hilarity collapsed beneath the rumble of more massed Soviet artillery than any of them had heard before.

CHAPTER THIRTY-SIX

IN PITCH DARKNESS, flying low over the sea six hundred miles southeast of Mednyy Island, the smaller of the two windswept Komandorskiyes, or Commander Islands, Col. Sergei Marchenko's attack wing of fourteen MiG-27 Flogger Ds, with three drop tanks apiece, were now turning due south toward Adak Island seventy miles away. With a jagged, rugged coastline and topography, the U.S. island, one of the Aleutians' chain of forty-six volcanoes, looked large enough on the map, but in reality it was at no point more than twenty miles wide. Marchenko was glad they were on satellite navigation. At their attack speed, it wouldn't take more than two minutes for the entire wing to pass over the island.

With almost half their fuel for the 1,553-mile round trip gone, they would have approximately five minutes over Adak Naval Station from the initial aiming point of the thirty-six-hundred-foot-high Mount Moffett. If all went well, they would drop over ninety-two thousand pounds of iron and laser-guided bombs on the remote American submarine base. A half hour later, Adak radar out, one thousand SPETS paratroopers, already in the air aboard seven Candid transports from both Mednyy and Beringa in the Komandorskiyes, would be chuted into the remains of Adak to take over the bomb-gutted submarine listening and provisioning base that threatened the entire Soviet east flank.

It would be strictly hit-and-run, with high losses expected. And though Sergei Marchenko's wing would not run from a fight, the orders from STAVKA via Khabarovsk command were very specific. No aircraft were to be sacrificed in dogfights with either the advance U.S. carrier screen fighters or the relatively few American fighters on Adak. Dogfights usually meant going to afterburner, and fuel suddenly sucked up at twenty times the normal rate, leaving the Floggers with insufficient fuel to make the return journey.

To lend weight to STAVKA's order, Sergei Marchenko, during engine start-up on Mednyy strip, had stressed that even if the enemy carrier *Salt Lake City* picked up the MiGs' departure from the Komandorskiyes on satellite, the range to and from the American carrier meant that the danger of running low on fuel would be as much a problem for the Americans from the carrier battle group as it was for Marchenko's wing. Though the American jets had greater ranges than their Soviet counterparts, the Americans had farther to come and could afford only a very short time over the Aleutians. This was particularly so given the fact that the Americans would most likely be drawn away from Adak by the feint of nine shorter-range but faster MiG Fishbeds now approaching Shemya four hundred miles west of Adak.

Hopefully all the enemy fighters between Adak and Shemya would be drawn in, the Americans logically assuming that as the prelude to any Soviet invasion of the Aleutians, the first Soviet target would be the massive early-warning radar arrays on Shemya, which was only 350 miles from the Kamchatka Peninsula ICBM sites.

Four hundred miles east of Adak, one of the huge phased radar arrays on Shemya, looking like some great wedge of black cheese in the night, was picking up six surface vessels. Either big Japanese trawlers or possible hostiles, they were bearing 293 at a distance of 150 miles. Coming in behind them at five hundred feet were nine blips traveling at Mach 1.05. Undoubtedly fighters. To cover a possible invasion force? wondered Shemya's CO.

There were other unidentified aircraft Shemya had been tracking, but they had been much slower, possibly a long-range reconnaissance sub-hunting force. In any case, they had now passed into Adak's radar envelope well to the east. The CO quickly turned his attention back to the faster blips and the six ships. If it was an invasion force, it was a small one. On the other hand, if the ships were chopper and VTOL—vertical takeoff and landing—fighter carriers, it would constitute a major fleet attack.

The commanding officer, or "Gatekeeper," as he was known because of Shemya's strategic importance, was taking no chances. He ordered eight F-4 Phantoms aloft to intercept the suspected hostiles, withholding his fourteen much faster swing-wing F-111Fs in the event of other attacks that might be coming in on the deck, successfully evading his radar to the north, south, and west of him.

The thing that puzzled CO Shemya most was that if the Soviets were going to try to take out Shemya's early-warning capability, why hadn't they used an attacking force of their long-range supersonic Blackjack swing-wing bombers? The duty officer, however, turned to the vast, triangular area of ocean covered by Shemya in the west, Adak four hundred miles to the east, and the *Salt Lake City* carrier force nine hundred miles south. He pointed out that it wasn't enough merely to knock out the radar station on Shemya; you had to occupy it and make sure it stayed that way, otherwise the U.S. Navy would immediately send in their Seabees to repair the damage. This convinced the CO that his first hunch was right, that the six blips and accompanying fighters were an initial invasion force coming at him, to be followed by many more once, and if, the base was secured. He ordered "engine start" for the fourteen F-111Fs carrying the combinations of iron bombs and TV-guided Maverick air-to-surface missiles.

In fact, the commanding officer was half-right about the Soviets using Blackjack bombers. Six of them, from the Kurile Islands base south of Kamchatka Peninsula, each replete with over thirty-five thousand pounds of bombs, the most sophisticated electronics in the Soviet Air Force, and with a range of over eight thousand miles, were now approaching the *Salt Lake City* battle group far to the south of the Aleutians. Their crews were in high spirits after having so badly mauled the Japanese "defense fleet" the day before and knowing that over half the *Salt Lake City*'s fighter screen was well away from them, flying combat patrols to cover possible attacks on Shemya.

CHAPTER THIRTY-SEVEN

TWO HUNDRED MILES south of Ireland, a bulge suddenly appeared on the surface of the dark blue Celtic Sea. The next moment the bulge erupted in a phantasm of white, the "boomer," in this case the USS *Roosevelt*, bursting through the surface, white smoke as well as spray pouring from her from a fire in her aft engine room, where the crew had been working on the MOSS. No one knew exactly where the electrical short had occurred as several of the monitoring circuits were themselves out of action following the severe concussion of the *Yumashev*'s depth charge attack.

It was the submariner's worst nightmare, and Robert Brentwood knew that the acrid smoke pouring from the sub's sail would alert the enemy for a hundred miles around. Yet he was the epitome of calm as he kept his men moving through Control up the sail, where he had posted his executive officer. If the fire was uncontainable, he had to get as many men as possible out and into the inflatables before setting the destructive charges that would be sure to destroy code-safe and disks along with the sub. In any event, with the carbon dioxide scrubber system out of action, the men had to get fresh air. Several off-watch crewmen, asleep when the fire had broken out, were unable to get their masks on in time and were asphyxiated by the highly toxic fumes. In the face of their loss, the thing Brentwood was most proud of, as he stood in Control, overseeing the evacuation through the dense smoke, was that there was no panic—he might have been a coach welcoming his team back to the dugout after a losing but hard-played game.

Up in the sail, Executive Officer Peter Zeldman saw men were also coming out of two of the six-foot-diameter hatches, one forward above Command and Control, the other leading up from the reactor room. But no one as yet was exiting the stern hatch above the turbine/drive space, and he reported this to Brentwood.

Brentwood knew there was a fifty-fifty chance that the fire-fighting party, having sealed themselves off in one of the forty-one cylinders that, welded together, formed the sub, might extinguish the flames if they could get in quickly enough behind the panels. But as captain, he couldn't have taken the chance of staying submerged with the lives of over 100 men in his hands. He called up to Zeldman, "Officer of the deck, I want every available man on deck acting as a lookout. Don't load the inflatables till you get my word."

"Every man a lookout. Don't load inflatables. Aye, sir."

Next Brentwood called through to the chief of the boat in charge of battling the fire. "What are we looking at back there, Chief?"

A young voice came on, rising above the hollow roar of the fire. "Sir, this is electrician's mate Richards. The chief's—" Brentwood waited—either the circuit had gone or the seaman had also been overcome by the toxic fumes—a defective mask seal, the mask knocked askew by falling lagging—anything could happen.

Brentwood pulled a man out of the line of sailors waiting to go up to the sail and guided him toward the ladder. "Give me your mask, sailor."

Brentwood informed Zeldman he was going aft so that should anything happen to him, Zeldman would take over. "Give me five minutes, Pete," Brentwood instructed.

"Five minutes. Aye, sir. Mind how you go."

Brentwood strapped on the mask, his throat already raw from the smoke, his voice nasal inside the mask as he entered the smoke-choked passageway. "On your left, make way. On your left . . ." As he walked through "Sherwood Forest," the smoke was swirling thickly about the huge missiles like the set of some fantastic opera.

CHAPTER THIRTY-EIGHT

BY THE TIME the bulk of Mount Moffett, the initial aiming point fifty miles away, started bipping green in Sergei Marchenko's head-up display, the Flogger D automatically started to climb in preparation for bomb release. Knowing he was going to be in full view of Adak's radar as he gained altitude, Marchenko released his *khlam*, as did the other thirteen fighters in his wing.

The chaff, aluminized glass fiber strips cut to lengths corresponding to those of Adak's radar band, immediately started sowing havoc with Adak's radar, the screens a frantic dance of "fly shit." As the fourteen Soviet fighters passed between Mount Moffett, massive but invisible on their right, and the two-thousand-foot Mount Adagdak to their left, Marchenko saw the snow-framed mirror of Andrew Lagoon racing toward him, and beyond it, the soft glow of the "marker" fire indicating the command and control center of the naval base.

Below, off to his left, he could see long arcs of red and white tracer disappearing eastward over the black void of Kulak Bay. Though Marchenko only glimpsed the trawler intermittently in flare light reflected off the snowy peaks surrounding the icy blue crescent of the bay, he was more aware than any of the other pilots of how much they owed the crew of the trawler for having set the bonfire marker and now firing Grail missiles at virtually point-blank range into the Kulak Bay defenses.

Despite his high state of tension, Marchenko was content to let the Flogger D have its head, trusting entirely to its contour-matching radar, its computer automatically selecting wavelengths to be different from those being jammed. It was at once exhilarating and frightening.

He saw the target growing on his infrared screen and took over the controls, Adak base directly ahead, its cluster of long huts, all the same in appearance, looking in the snow surprisingly like a camp he'd seen in the Gulag. Between the huts there were shimmering figures—people running for cover.

The computer had already selected the Flogger's "exit" trajectory, the shortest vector away from the point of bomb release, as the large sub base, its pens outlined now on the infrared TV screen above the main instrument panel, came in on the "zoom" frame immediately below the larger screen. He felt the shock wave bumps of antiaircraft fire but ignored them, releasing only when he heard the bip.

Bombs released, turning hard right, he heard the chatter of American voices on the radio, spotted an American Tomcat in his HUD, and went air-to-air. The American passed out of sight above the sudden light of the exploding inferno beneath them that had been Adak Naval Station. Marchenko turned left, rolled hard right, trying to center another Tomcat. A wing edge slipped into his HUD. He fired a missile, but the American had gone down and now was probably going around, trying to get into the Flogger's cone, to take him out from behind. He saw another Tomcat on his radar coming for him, then breaking off, down, for a stern conversion. He went to afterburner and climbed high.

Shirer's Tomcat was on warning yellow—weapons hold status—fourteen miles from Adak, having been halfway to Shemya before they heard Adak's call for assistance. "Master arm on," he told his RIO in the backseat. "Centering the T. Bogeys ten miles. Centering the dot."

"Bingo!" It was his wingman on the halfway fuel mark, breaking off to head back to the carrier.

There was a rush of static, then the RIO's voice came through, "You got the tone?" to confirm whether the Tomcat's Sparrow missile was ready.

"Got it," answered Shirer. "Centering the dot . . . Fox 1." Shirer felt the twelve-foot Sparrow release.

"Bogey at three o'clock," called the RIO. "Bogey . . ." Shirer hit the afterburner. The RIO felt the sudden G, like steel against his chest.

Shirer saw another Bogey climbing fast, crossing his HUD's green lines. He centered. "Fox 2." This time a Sidewinder took off from the Tomcat, heading for the Flogger's exhaust.

"Angels 2," said the RIO, telling Shirer they were at two thousand feet. Shirer hit the afterburner again; the steep wall of fire that was Adak base slipped downhill from him into the darkness. He was in cloud. He glimpsed the flames again—they were making tiny shadows on the fading patch of snow as he entered more cloud. The Flogger D had exploded, its orange ball curling to black.

"Outstanding!" the RIO yelled. "That'll—"

There was a ragged crimson streak in front of them—a Flogger D's six-barreled rotary cannon spitting out twenty-three-millimeter tracer, a Tomcat exploding to Shirer's left. The Flogger D passed into Shirer's HUD for only a millisecond, but Shirer's reaction was automatic, the Tomcat slid, its rotary cannon in the port side erupting in a long, blue-white flash, the reflection dancing madly in the cockpit. A sound like tearing canvas. Then the Tomcat went crazy, Shirer doing everything he could but realizing he was quickly slipping into an inverted spin.

"Eject!" he shouted to the RIO through his mike as he tried every trick he knew, released the break chute—nothing worked as the plane continued yawing, pitching, and rolling simultaneously, its engine flamed out, the blood roaring from feet to head. "Eject!" he yelled again.

Elbows in, head tucked, he pulled the release, felt the kick of the rocket assist, then blacked out.

An F-16 and Flogger collided over Andrew Lagoon as the four F-16s that Adak had scrambled tried to beat off the surprise low-level Soviet attack. Two of the remaining three F-16s in the flight were destroyed on the Davis runway. The other one was destroyed by one of the Tomcats' Sidewinder missiles after having been mistaken for a Sukhoi Fitter C, which, like the F-16, was also a single-engined fighter.

The engagement, involving all planes, had lasted 4.73 minutes, the Adak base by Kulak Bay gutted, rendered ineffective. In the light of the fires from the oil and food stores, those among the two thousand civilian and military personnel still alive saw the shoreline around the C-shaped bay littered with the bodies of hundreds of dead fish and gannets, some of the birds coated with the sheen of high-octane from the ruptured storage tanks, but most of the wildlife killed by the concussion of several off-target bombs exploding in the bay.

The commanding officer of Adak was trying to contact Shemya, four hundred miles to the west, and Dutch Harbor about five hundred miles to the east, but could reach neither. Meanwhile the duty officer was informing him that the SOSUS, the underwater hydrophone sound surveillance system, was out. Whether the underwater arrays themselves about the island had been damaged by depth bombs or whether it was the connection between shore and the arrays that was the problem, there was nothing but "garbage" coming in. Adak was on its own.

"Then our first priority is to get those fires out," replied the CO. "Unless we do, we'll all die of exposure in this weather. Contact our Wave contingent and see what they can rig up if the hospital huts are gone, and make sure every available pump hose is—"

"Sir?"

There was a crackling noise in the distance, above the noise of the nearby fires. "What's that?" demanded the CO.

"Probably the Aleut shacks that are—"

"By God," said the CO, "that sounds like small-arms fire to me."

It was the first sign they had that Soviet paratroops were descending on Adak.

CHAPTER THIRTY-NINE

ROBERT BRENTWOOD AND the chief of the boat collided outside *Roosevelt*'s galley, the smoke so thick, they couldn't see more than a few inches in front of them. But the fire was out, and a six-inch coil suction hose was rigged to the hatches to vent the smoke.

"Am I glad to see—" the chief began, but couldn't continue, his coughing going into a dry retch.

"Come on, Chief," said Brentwood. "Let's get topside with everyone else."

As the chief and his fire-fighting party emerged from the forward hatch, there was a smattering of clapping on the deck and the sound of several sailors being violently seasick in the heavy swells that were slopping over the *Roosevelt*'s deck. The moment his gas mask was off, Brentwood looked skyward and at the whitish silver of horizon between the sea and cumulonimbus that was piling up like bruised ice cream, heading farther away from them in the direction of the Bay of Biscay. "Officer of the deck."

"Sir?" responded Zeldman.

"Soon as we clear this smoke, get everyone below. I'm going down to assess damage. Chief says our automatic scrubbers have had it, but we can break out crystals—run a few days on those. Even at three and a half knots, we should get to Holy Loch in another seven days. I think the water supply will—"

At the same time as the *Roosevelt*'s lookouts spotted them, Brentwood also saw the long line of more than thirty ships southeast of them, the sub's surface radar not having picked them up because its circuit, like that for the passive underwater sonar receivers, had been shut down due to the fire. Once they got under way, the consoles would be operational.

Brentwood felt strangely calm yet vulnerable, the rolling deck twenty-five feet below him more than ever looking like some great whale pushed back and forth by the gray swells. On the other hand, there was the disadvantage that the sub's position was almost certainly known now by satellite bounce-off, for even without infrared, their smoke trail had now spiraled thousands of feet above the Celtic Sea. It was an "unenviable situation," as his father would have said wryly. Knowing that now he would almost certainly come under attack, Brentwood decided to rule out any thoughts of reaching home port at Holy Loch.

"We'll set course for Falmouth," he instructed Zeldman. "Even with our present drag-ass three and a half knots, we should make it in plus or minus fifty-five hours—a hell of a lot sooner than if we tried Holy Loch now we've been spotted."

"Maybe no one's picked us up yet," said Zeldman.

"Right, Pete. And elephants fly."

"Well," said Zeldman, indicating the line of ships on the horizon, "we've received no fire from them."

"Which is why we know they're ours. They're not the ones I'm worried about, Pete. It's what we haven't seen that concerns me."

The lookout was reporting two Sheffield-class British destroyers in the horizon line, confirming Brentwood's hunch.

"Very well," responded Brentwood, and for a moment, seeing as their smoke was undoubtedly being picked up above cloud level by satellite, Brentwood elected to use the above-water high-frequency antenna for a quick transmit to SACLANT—Supreme Allied Commander Atlantic—via ACCHAN—Allied Commander Channel—to arrange for a tow as soon as possible to reduce their transit time to Falmouth.

For a moment it struck Brentwood that it was possible the war had ended between the time *Roosevelt* had been attacked by the *Yumashev* and now. The reply from SACLANT, decoded in seconds, immediately disabused him of any such notion. A tow could not be sent for at least four days, and *Roosevelt* was instructed by SACLANT, via sat bounce from Norfolk, Virginia, that she was to maintain her position and provide a defensive umbrella in the area for the convoy—now only seventeen hours from the port of Brest in the Bay of Biscay.

The war message stressed the DB pocket was so critically short of supplies that several squadrons of NATO's Thunderbolts were waiting at Brest, unable to fly effective missions against the Russian armor because of the lack of thirty-millimeter depleted uranium ammunition. The message ended, "Imperative you give max assist to convoy. Convoy notified."

"I thought," said Zeldman, "the Royal Navy would have the Channel approaches bottled up."

"Obviously not, old boy," said Brentwood in a bad imitation of an upper-class English accent.

"Course," added Zeldman, "the Russians will have come out from Kola, around the top."

"Captain?" It was the chief. "We have three casualties aft. Lost 'em in the smoke coming out."

"All right, Chief. Take the tags, have a deck party put them by the hatches. Then back quick as you can."

"Deck party to put casualties by the hatches. Aye, sir."

The chief didn't hesitate. It might seem to others a cruel decision, but *Roosevelt*'s job was to fight, and she needed all tubes free for firing to help make up for her lack of speed and helm response time.

Zeldman was on constant lookout as the deck party heaved the body bags up through the hatches and laid them on the deck. They were in what the NATO sub captains called "Sarancha Gulch," Saranchas being the fast, small missile boats operating from "Milch Cow" auxiliary mother ships. Highly maneuverable and bristling with surface-to-surface sixty-mile-range N-9 missiles and surface-to-air N-4 missiles, the boats were perfectly suited for this kind of last-minute attack around the Bay of Biscay and the other western approaches before the convoys reached Brest, or the relative safety of Land's End, Falmouth, and the Channel.

As Zeldman came down the ladder into Control, he heard the hatch close behind him, a seaman beginning the holy litany of the dive. "Officer of the deck—last man down. Hatch secured."

Zeldman took up his position as officer of the deck. "Last man down. Hatch secured, aye. Captain, the ship is rigged for dive, current depth one ten fathoms. Checks with the chart. Request permission to submerge the ship."

"Very well, officer of the deck," said Brentwood. "Submerge the ship."

"Submerge the ship, aye, sir." Zeldman turned to the diving console. "Diving officer, submerge the ship."

"Submerge the ship, aye, sir. Dive—two blasts on the dive alarm. Dive, dive." The wheezing sound of the alarm followed, loud enough for the crew in Control to hear but not powerful enough to resonate through the hull. A seaman shut all the main ballast tanks. "All vents are shut."

"Vents shut, aye."

A seaman was reading off the depth. "Fifty . . . fifty-two . . . fifty-four . . ."

One of the chiefs watching the angle of dive, trim, and speed reported, "Officer of the deck, conditions normal on the dive."

"Very well, diving officer," confirmed Zeldman, turning to Brentwood. "Captain, at one-thirty feet, trim satisfactory."

"Very well," answered Brentwood. "Steer four hundred feet ahead standard."

Zeldman turned to the helmsman. "Helm all ahead standard. Diving officer, make the depth four hundred feet."

They were just flattening out at 390 when Brentwood heard, "Sonar contact! Possible hostile surface warship, bearing two seven eight! Range, fifty-three miles."

Brentwood turned calmly to the attack island. "Very well. Man battle stations."

"Man battle stations, aye, sir," repeated a seaman, pressing the yellow button, a pulsing F sharp slurring to G sounding throughout the ship.

Brentwood turned to the diving officer. "Diving officer, periscope depth."

"Periscope depth, aye, sir."

Brentwood's hand reached up, taking the mike from its cradle without even looking. "This is the captain. I have the con. Commander Zeldman retains the deck."

Beneath the purplish blue light over the sonar consoles, the operator advised, "Range fifty-two point six miles. Classified surface hostile by nature of sound."

"Up scope," ordered Brentwood. "Ahead two-thirds."

"Scope's breaking," said one of the watchmen. "Scope's clear."

Brentwood's hands flicked down the scope's arms and, eyes to the cups, he moved around with the scope. On the Compac screen Zeldman could see the dot, moving so fast at forty knots, it had to be a hydrofoil.

Brentwood stopped moving the scope. "Bearing. Mark! Range. Mark! Down scope." Above the soft whine of the retracting periscope Brentwood reported, "I hold one visual contact. Range?"

"Forty-four point five miles," came the reply, placing the hostile forty-four miles northwest of *Roosevelt*, the convoy ten miles to the southeast. The sub was between them.

But Brentwood had a problem. To fire a cruise missile with its nuclear warhead was out of the question unless he wanted to start a nuclear war, and yet the sub's state-of-the-art Mark-48 torpedoes had a maximum range of twenty-eight miles. With the hostile still over forty miles away, he would have to wait. To make matters worse, it was unlikely that the convoy had seen the hostile—their sonar not as good as the sub's, their radar not picking up the hostile, which, because of its small size, would be lost in sea clutter.

"Range every thousand yards," ordered Brentwood.

"Range every thousand yards, aye, sir. Range ninety-one thousand yards."

"Ninety-one-thousand yards," confirmed Brentwood. The hostile would have to close to at least forty-five thousand before he could fire. At its present speed, this would be in 14.7 minutes. However, it was now that Robert Brentwood showed why he had been chosen as the skipper of the USS *Roosevelt*. "Officer of the deck, confirm MOSS tube number."

"MOSS in tube number two, sir."

"Very well. Angle on the bow," said Brentwood. "Port four point five."

"Check," came the confirmation.

"Range?" asked Brentwood.

"Ninety thousand yards."

"Ninety thousand yards," repeated Brentwood. "Firing point procedures. Master four five. Tube one."

"Firing point procedures, aye, sir. Master four five. Tube one, aye . . . solution ready . . . weapons ready . . . ship ready."

"Final bearing and shoot—master four five."

The sonar operator announced the *Roosevelt* was now bearing three four nine. "Speed four."

"Up scope!" ordered Brentwood. "Bearing, mark! Down scope."

The firing control officer responded, "Stand by—shoot."

"Fire," said the shooter, pushing the lever forward.

The firing control officer watched the screen, the torpedo running, monitored. The tension in Control was palpable. No one spoke except for the sonar operator reading off the range, watching intently to see if the hostile would go for the bait of the MOSS—mobile submarine simulator—its sound disk having been altered, according to Brentwood's orders, to duplicate the new sound signature of the *Roosevelt* following the *Yumashev*'s depth charge attack that had bent its prop.

The hostile vector was unchanged, the sonar operator now confirming its signature as that of a Sarancha hydrofoil—armament one thirty-millimeter multibarrel close-in gun, four surface-to-surface Siren antiship missiles, two surface-to-air N-4 missiles. Then suddenly its radar dot seemed to blur, as it changed course, heading to intercept the MOSS. It went to a small dot, then shuddered on the screen, the sonar operator announcing, "Hostile has fired surface-to-surface. Trajectory two seven four."

The Siren was streaking toward the convoy.

Several hundred miles to the north, James G. Wilkins, having been arrested and brought to London for trial, now found himself standing in the dock in London's Old Bailey, looking ashen-faced before a jury as he heard the verdict of "guilty." He was convicted of fraud—the money he was stashing at home being "kickbacks" from several shipping companies whose "marine loss" claims, as the magistrate pointed out, "were assessed by Mr. Wilkins as being substantially higher than in fact they were." The difference between the claim paid by the government to the shipping companies and the actual value of the goods lost had been split by what his lordship described as a "mutually convenient agreement between the defendant and various members of the mercantile establishment."

Rosemary Spence was there out of some vague sense of responsibility toward young Graham Wilkins, who, although he had clearly charged his stepfather out of malice, and had been wrong about any spying, had nevertheless enabled the government to arrest and convict a war profiteer and to make an example of him.

The magistrate sent him "down" for three years and three on probation and commended Inspector Logan of the Oxshott, Surrey, Constabulary. Mrs. Wilkins looked relieved.

"More fun with the milkman now," Melrose told Logan as they walked out of the central courts.

"I suppose so," said Logan. "Can't say I envy him. She seems a hard woman."

"The son's the hard one," put in Perkins. "Didn't even blink when the beak sentenced his old man."

"Stepfather, though," Logan corrected him. "Not his real pater."

"Still," put in Melrose, "you'd think he'd show some emotion. The schoolteacher—the Spence woman—she was more upset than anyone."

"Well," said Logan, "she's the type. Worrywart. See it a mile away. Cool outside, but underneath—quite churned up, I expect."

"Probably worried about her boyfriend," commented Perkins. "Engaged to some Yank, I believe. Navy type."

"Ah!" said Logan, as if that made everything clear. "Well then, that explains it. Separation and all. Bad days for the navy. Dicey business on the water. How about you, Melrose—you a sailor?"

"No, sir." Actually, Melrose had done some sailing in his youth, but he was so shocked from Logan getting his name right at last, he didn't really think about the question.

"You and I won't be needed then," said Logan knowingly. Perkins glanced across at Melrose and shrugged.

"Ostend," continued Logan. "That's where we'll be pulling them off this time. Nearest port to the pocket."

"You think it's that bad?" inquired Melrose.

"Yes I do, I'm afraid. That's one thing I'll say about old Professor Knowlton. He faces facts."

"Professor Knowlton!" laughed Melrose. "Isn't he the old bloke who keeps on about hair dryers? Conserving electricity on the home front, et cetera?"

"That 'old bloke,' as you so impudently call him, Constable, knows what he's about. Mark my words." Logan dropped his voice, looked around, and continued, "Just between you, me, and the gatepost, I can tell you all about that hair dryer business."

"Oh—?" said Melrose, winking at Perkins.

"Yes," said Logan. "Harriers!" He said it as if the word alone would explain all.

"Harriers?" said Perkins, willing to go along as he eyed two young beauties emerging from Barclay's Bank.

"Yes. Going to be the RAF's last defense, the way the Russians are knocking out our airstrips. You know how they put the wings on Harriers?"

"Stitch 'em on, I should think," answered Perkins.

"Don't be bloody clever," said Logan. "They're made of carbon wafer, special epoxies, among other things. Stuck together. Found the same thing with the new models as with the original Harriers. The drying, I mean. Has to be done by hand, you see. It's a craft—just can't stamp them out like ruddy milk bottles."

"You're joking," said Perkins.

"I most certainly am not. Without enough hair dryers, we don't have enough Harriers. They're more important to us than the Spitfire was in the last show."

"Crikey," said Melrose, "so the old blighter isn't so potty after all?"

Logan eyed him irritably. "Just because you get to retiring age, Melroad, your brain doesn't stop working."

"Of course not—sorry, Inspector."

Logan slowed as he neared the entrance to the tube station. "At the risk of sounding immodest, Melroad, you'll note that this old 'bloke'—" he pointed to himself "—wasn't so dim that he couldn't crack this Wilkins case."

"No," conceded Melrose. "You're right there, sir."

"Tooraloo," said Logan heartily, heading down into the Temple underground station.

Melrose touched his cap in farewell, smiling and muttering to Perkins, "No, you silly old twit—you just nick villains instead of spies. Minor detail. I think I'll get my name tattooed on my forehead. Think he'll remember then?"

Perkins shook his head. "Doubt it, Melroad."

The air raid sirens were starting up again, and people were running for the shelters. At the beginning of the war, they'd affected a traditional British calm and disdain for any panic, but this time it was very different—the rockets so fast, you had absolutely no idea where they would hit. "A bit like the old V-2s," Logan had told him. "Only much worse."

"Hang on!" Melrose called out to a couple of callow youths, almost running an elderly woman down in their eagerness to get below. Suddenly the underground sign vibrated, the railing below it shaking; people were falling, and in the distance, above the Mall, there was a high spume of brick and sandstone, now falling in a deafening hail.

"Bit close to the palace," commented Perkins as they hurried, without trying to appear as such, into the shelter outside Blackfriars Station. "What do you think?"

"I think it *was* the palace."

"Bloody 'ell! They should have left London—like they were told."

"What—and leave everyone else to take the shit while they're nice and comfy up in Windsor? Not bloody likely. I'm no monarchist, mate, but that's one thing I'll say about old Charles. He's no coward."

Heading for Oxshott, the train Rosemary was on stopped near Wimbledon during the rocket attack. The engineers had found that the Soviet pilots always favored a moving train, assuming that because it *was* moving, it was carrying vitally needed supplies to try to stem the impending catastrophe in northern Germany. But Rosemary believed that the fact that the enemy pilots went after moving passenger or goods trains had less to do with strategic considerations than the fact that a moving target was more exciting to kill. The mere thought that Robert was at the center of such hazard at sea over-whelmed her, and when the conductor asked for her ticket and she discovered she'd lost it, she burst into tears. What made it even more terrible was that in that moment, she was sure she felt their baby move, which she knew was impos-sible so early in her pregnancy.

"Up scope," ordered Brentwood. "Ahead one-third."

"Scope's breaking. Scope's clear."

In the scope's circle Brentwood could see an orange speckle, one of the convoy's screen destroyers afire, its crew abandoning ship. He swung the scope about and saw the Sarancha. At its full speed of sixty knots, its hull clear out of the water, foil-borne, the boat was obscured by a cocoon of spray, in weaving pattern, closing on the convoy. Behind it were three more.

Well, thought Brentwood, Mark-48s can weave, too. "An-gle on the bow," he said, "port, point four zero."

"Check," came the confirmation.

"Range?" asked Brentwood.

"Forty thousand yards."

"Very well," replied Brentwood. "Firing point proce-dures. Master four zero. Tube three."

"Firing point procedures. Master four zero. Tube three, aye . . . solution ready . . . weapons ready . . . ship ready."

"Final bearing and shoot—master four zero."

A seaman announced, "Bearing three four one. Speed six."

"Up scope," ordered Brentwood. "Bearing, mark! Down scope."

The firing control officer responded, "Stand by—shoot."

"Fire," came the confirmation as the shooter pushed the lever forward.

The firing control officer watched the screen, and con-firmed the torpedo was running and being monitored. *Roo-sevelt* repeated the procedure three more times. One after another, the dots of the Saranchas on the screen swelled, then vanished. Because of *Roosevelt*'s interception, only five transports in forty were lost, the remainder safely reaching Brest.

As the gray dawn fog swirled about the Aleutians, scurrying over the spindrift like the cape of some primeval beast about to devour the islands, the fighting on Adak was confused and bloody.

Because of the natural amphitheater on the northern part of Adak Island formed by Mount Moffett and Mount Adagdak, only four hundred of the two thousand civilians and military personnel escaped injury. Those not killed outright by the blockbuster bombs used to destroy the runway, which filled the air with everything from auto- to fist-sized concrete fragments traveling at hundreds of miles an hour, fell victim to the cluster "Bee" bombs, which opened up midfall, releasing hundreds of smaller bombs, each in turn filled with thousands of razor-sharp steel darts. Filling the air with their distinctive buzzing sound like a swarm of bees, the darts sometimes would kill outright but more often than not inflicted terrible wounds. Kiril Marchenko, and others in the STAVKA responsible for efficient defense spending, favored the Bee bombs for such missions, for casualties in the field required many more support troops to transport and care for them than did corpses. And the Americans were notoriously obsessive about getting their wounded out to the nearest MASH field hospitals—all of which meant fewer troops who could actually man the front.

At first, the rugged terrain surrounding the base favored the survivors, for it was taking time for the Russian paratroopers to descend from the hillsides through the deep snow. But soon the terrain would work against the shell-shocked survivors of the Adak raid because their only means of escape was either eastward, through the six-mile valley between the mountains to Shagak Bay, or Kulak Bay immediately behind them to the west.

Only 63 of the 115-man marine company assigned to airstrip guard duty were still alive at dawn, and these moved out to intercept the paratroopers, but though the marines were superbly equipped, they had had no cause to be issued white battle coveralls. These weren't the drill for guarding the runway at night, when the only danger had seemed to be sabotage from the sea—white coveralls on the darkened runway being perfect targets—and those they had in stock had gone up in flames in the bombing anyway.

As the sixty-three marines moved out east from Kulak's C-shaped bay, the fighting was not yet at close hand. Indeed, most of the small-arms fire that the Adak CO had heard shortly after the bombing attack had fallen off during the night as the paratroops were presumably trying to form into a coherent force before attacking what was left of the base. Nevertheless, sniping had continued from the foggy mountainsides, and more than a dozen marines and civilians fell to this sporadic but deadly fire. In an attempt to use the thick, gray fog that was rolling down the sides of the mountains to their advantage, the sixty-three marines moved out a quarter mile west of the base to form a semicircular perimeter.

Meanwhile the CO of Adak was trying to assemble the civilian survivors as best he could down by the shore of Kulak Bay and to find enough boats that were still seaworthy enough to take them out beyond Sitkin Sound, through Asuksak Pass, and on to Atka Station a hundred miles to the east. Many of the women who had rushed out from the burning huts clad in no more than night attire were in the early throes of hypothermia, which only added to the commanding officer's problems. As if this weren't enough, Atka could not be raised on the radio by the communications officer, as the microwave repeaters on the island had been destroyed in the raid, along with the sea-to-shore SOSUS connections.

One of the mothers, whose children, oddly enough, were contentedly playing amid the ruins of the base, approached the commanding officer, asking him what she could do. The CO paused, not knowing what to tell her and, for want of anything helpful to say, directed her toward the MASH tent down by the bay's edge, where dozens of casualties still lay awaiting attention from the overworked staff, many of whom were also injured.

"It'll be a hell of a squash," the communications officer reported to the CO after the woman had left. "I've done a quick check on the waterfront. Most of the fishing boats are holed."

"We'll just have to do the best we can. By now the boys on the *Salt Lake City* will sure as hell know we've been hit. Their combat patrols should keep those bastards busy. If we can hold out till they come, we should be all right."

The communications officer didn't say anything but thought

maybe the CO should go down and join the line outside the MASH tent. Hell, even if the *Salt Lake City* sent every fighter they had, there was nowhere on Adak they could land now with the runway destroyed. Anyway, every marine left on the island—there wouldn't be enough boats for them—would be a hostage. If the Tomcats bombed, they'd kill as many marines as Russians.

Suddenly the valley was filled with the staccato echoes of machine-gun fire—firefights breaking out as the marines engaged the Russian paratroopers. But the Russians had the overwhelming advantage in that the dark camouflage of the American marines' uniforms, so ideal in the summer months on the wild, windswept islands, was disastrous for them now.

In a desperate defense, the marines began to dig in, but the SPETS had planned the operation with great detail, and soon a telltale shuffling sound in the air above them gave them only seconds warning of a murderous heavy mortar attack from the mountainsides.

Spumes of dirty snow leapt high in the air, and the screams of the wounded could be heard above the muffled thumps of a fire so concentrated that it was evident to the commanding officer as well as the hysterical civilians in the ruins of the base that they would soon be either killed or taken prisoner. A mortar bomb, exploding barely twenty yards from the MASH tent, sent a hail of shrapnel, killing two small children, one of the bomb's fins slicing through the tent and decapitating a surgeon who had been in the final stages of suturing a stomach wound.

As a hospital corpsman and two others carried the doctor outside, the Wave in charge of nurses called out brusquely, "Brentwood, finish that suture, then lend a hand here."

So busy she didn't have time to be afraid, Lana moved quickly to take over the surgeon's task, using the suture gun to finish up, then, turning the patient over to the junior nurses for postop, she turned to the next casualty in line.

"This one's in a coma, Lieutenant," said the corporal. "Some facial lacerations. X-ray shows a sprained wrist, but can't find anything else. I've taped the wrist."

Lana knew there wasn't much she could do for the man, his face bloodied and dirty with gravel rash, his cheeks swollen. They could come out of a coma within twenty-four hours or stay in it forever. "Next one," she called out to the medical corpsman. Quickly glancing at her watch and grabbing the admission sheet, she jotted down, "O814—superficial lacerations. Coma."

The corporal reached for the dog tags from beneath the man's flying suit. "Shirer—" he said. "Frank J."

Lana suddenly felt immobile, aware only of his face, trying to see if it *was* him or merely the same name.

"All right, everyone," boomed a chief petty officer. "Down to the wharf. We've got to get these wounded loaded fast as possible. We're pushing off."

"Load 'em on what?" someone shouted.

"Whatever floats. We'll do the best we can. Women and kids first, then the wounded. Let's move!"

"Where the hell are we going, for God's sake?" a frightened orderly asked.

"Anywhere," said the petty officer, throwing open the flap of the tent. "One of the other islands nearby. All I know is the CO wants everybody down there on the double."

"Watch that IV!" called out the head nurse, a saline pouch swinging wildly on its stand.

"Is he dead?" Lana heard someone say. "*Lieutenant Brentwood!* Did you hear me?"

"What—yes. Sorry, Major. No, he's in a coma."

"Then get him out with the oth—"

The MASH tent shook violently, and outside, Lana could hear the screams of wounded and children and return fire from the few marines who were left, and a shattering, ringing noise as the Russian heavy mortars, finding the range, began pounding the beach. Now she could see white figures moving in the gray fog through the smoking black remnants of the base. Russian paratroopers.

CHAPTER FORTY

THE TRUCKS CARRYING the POWs had stalled outside Stadthagen, the snow falling so heavily and the temperature dropping so fast that by nightfall, black ice covered the snow-plowed road from the huge fuel depot twenty miles behind the front, so that the prisoners were made to get out and push the trucks up a long one-in-twenty incline. The guards were yelling at them to work harder, but to no avail, as prisoners like David Brentwood, Waite, and Thelman, despite loud exclamations of intent, merely leaned against the trucks, grimacing ferociously but doing as little as possible to aid and abet their captors. Military police were in evidence everywhere, directing convoys of tank refuelers moving slowly out of the dump of countless drums of fuel hidden under enormous camouflage nets in woods several miles north of Stadthagen.

David Brentwood was surprised to see, in lines of other prisoners all wearing distinct white POW armbands, hundreds of Bundeswehr troops. Before the American airborne had left for their ill-fated drop outside the DB pocket, they had been told that the only NATO troops they might run into, should they be blown off course, would be members of the Dutch Forty-First Army.

"Looks like the whole German army surrendered," Brentwood said casually, blowing on his frozen fingers. He had no idea that his comment to Thelman about why there were so many Germans would trigger a series of events that would have a profound effect on his life and thousands of others' in a chain of fate over which he had no control.

"Yeah," added Thelman. "Thought we were told we'd

only be running into the Dutchies. Where'd all these Krauts come from?''

"Germans to you," said someone amid the scrabble of boots and curses of men clambering back into the trucks, their breath in the frozen air creating a mist that momentarily made the four *Stasi* guards look as if they were in a steam bath.

"All right," said Thelman. "Germans. No offense."

"How the hell should we know where they came from?" retorted an infantryman grumpily. "What is this—'Let's Make a Deal'? What's it matter? We're all in the same boat."

"Actually," put in the English lieutenant, "I think they're from the Territorials."

"Who are they when they're at home?" asked Waite in his cockney twang.

"Reserves," the lieutenant replied. "Damn well trained, too. Not frontline troops, of course."

"Like us!" said Brentwood. It got a good laugh.

"Touché," said the Englishman. "No, what I mean—"

"Schweig doch!" one of the four guards called out.

"Up your doc, too!" said Thelman.

The guard began shouting again, but the British lieutenant ignored him, as the other three guards didn't seem to care one way or the other.

"Bundeswehr Territorials," the lieutenant continued as the truck skewed dangerously on a patch of black ice before straightening. "Territorials were assigned to man and maintain all NATO transport in Northern Command. Unfortunately, they ran out of gas—thanks to our SPETS friends, who got behind our lines and cut both Amsterdam and Rotterdam pipelines. Ergo—the Territorials in our midst."

"Like Doug Freeman did in Korea," said one of the Americans.

"He didn't use enemy uniforms," said David.

"Well," said the English lieutenant wryly, "I don't think Americans look much like North Koreans, do they?"

"Suppose not," answered David, not quite knowing whether the Englishman was being sarcastic or merely gently matter-of-fact.

"How do you know he didn't put South Koreans in gook uniforms?" asked a disgruntled signaler.

David felt the man was less interested in finding out than

in venting his spleen against the SPETS who'd deprived him, like David, of his uniform and who'd left him near death with cold.

"He knows," Thelman said, pointing to David. "He was there."

"Really?" asked the Englishman somewhat haughtily.

"Yeah, *really*," replied Thelman. "Silver Star."

Brentwood was acutely embarrassed, but the Englishman's voice lost any trace of haughtiness. "I say, well done! Brentward, isn't it?"

"Brent*wood*," said David, feeling conspicuous.

"Silver Star and no fucking brains, right, Brentwood?" an American ribbed him. "Signed up again."

"Right!" said David boyishly, grateful for the laughter that swept through the truck and started the guards shouting again. This time all of the guards were joining in, one of them waving the AKM as the truck slowed a hundred yards from the main entrance to the fuel dump, which was almost obliterated in the swirling snow as lines of prisoners carried 160-liter drums on stretcherlike pallets to waiting trucks on the opposite side of the road. A *Stasi oberst* approached the truck, tiny balled snow bouncing off his uniform like fine hail. "English? *Amerikaner*?"

"Yes," answered the lieutenant, being the most senior rank.

"You will be issued with armbands, which you must wear at all times."

"When are we to dine?" asked the Englishman.

"Who are you?" asked the *oberst*.

"Lieutenant Grimsby, Royal Engineers. And you are?"

"*Oberst* Hoffer."

The lieutenant jumped down from the tailgate and gave a snappy salute. "Very well, Colonel Hoffer. I must request that these men be fed as soon as possible. We've been traveling all day and, as I'm sure you're aware under the rules, specifically agreed to by both NATO and Warsaw Pact under the Gorbachev Protocols—"

David wasn't listening. He was far more interested in the fact that the fuel dump wasn't in the old NATO prepo site after all but had been cunningly moved. No wonder the NATO bombers had been unsuccessful in penetrating the old prepo sites.

What would Freeman do? Not sit on his ass whining about

the next meal, that's for sure. It was a God-given opportunity. The idea literally caught his breath for a moment, the row developing between the *Stasi* colonel and the disdainful Englishman over the issue of "appropriate apparel" and "victualing" passing over him. Why hadn't he thought of it earlier? he wondered. But that was easy. His only concern, like everyone else in the truck, had been to survive. "Defensive driving," Freeman used to call it derisively drilling them that defensive thinking was "a disease for the timid . . . defensive tactics excuses for not attacking. A goddamn torpor looking for reasons to fail."

David could still see him aboard the chopper carrier before they'd lifted off on the Pyongyang raid against "Kim Il Runt," as Freeman had called the dictator Kim Il Sung. David hadn't known what torpor meant until he'd heard the general use it.

There was a sudden crack, silence, then bedlam in the truck, the guards outside firing into the air. "What the—" began David. In the pale yellow light of the tailgate, he could see the Englishman spread-eagle in the snow, a dark pool round his head, a look of utter amazement on his face.

The *oberst* slapped the pistol back into his holster. *"Ja!—"* he was saying, a smile on his face that David recognized immediately as the mad look spawned of sustained battlefield stress. *"Ja*—now you see. You will do as you are told." He turned to the guards, one of whom looked as astounded at what had happened as the dead Englishman, and rattled out a series of sharp orders. Turning to the prisoners in the truck, he informed them, "You will go over to the depot. Two men to each drum, and you will load them back into this truck. Is this understood?" No one answered, and as the guards motioned them out and they dropped down to the snow, one by one they looked down at the dead Englishman, no one speaking out of respect and fear.

In the distance, muffled by the snow, they could hear the steady crump of Marshal Kirov's thousand guns that kept pounding away in a massive creeping barrage through the DB pocket, to stun the already battle-weary Americans and British, as the Russian advance moved inexorably westward. Now and then the sound of the guns would change as the creeping barrage shifted, when the Russian gunners, after having "bracketed" an area, laid the shells down in a different sector to confuse and undo any of the defenders' attempts to predict where they would be hit next.

David, clutching his blanket and shivering, plaintively held up his hand, reminding Thelman of a timid student asking for permission to go to the washroom.

"Ja" asked the *oberst* brusquely.

"Sir—may I bury him?"

"You want his clothes, his boots, *ja*?"

David shrugged ingratiatingly. The *oberst* nodded to one of the guards and then told Brentwood, "Be quick. We must be loading the trucks in twenty minutes."

"Could I have a spade?" asked Brentwood.

"Use your hands," said the *oberst*.

"But, sir," David started to protest, then stopped himself. "Thank you, sir." The *oberst* had turned away from him, heading across the road toward the entrance to the dump.

"Schnell!" said the guard whom the *oberst* had ordered to follow Brentwood, waving the machine gun toward a ditch and the snow-covered field across from the truck in the opposite direction to where the prisoners were being marched.

David motioned to the guard that he needed help carrying the lieutenant off the road across the ditch. The guard obviously understood his gestures but wasn't going to help, instead indicating brusquely that Brentwood should hurry up.

By the time Freeman was out of the field hospital's OR, the advancing thunder of the Russian guns was barely twenty miles away east of Bielefeld, the Russians having already penetrated the defenses south of Bielefeld beyond the Weser River. Simultaneously other Soviet tank and helicopter surges out of Frankfurt-am-Main to the south were hammering at the fragmented NATO line, forcing what was left of the Belgian Sixteenth Armored, Bundeswehr Second Mechanized, and the American Third and Eleventh Armored to try to contain the ever-widening arrowhead of the enemy advance swelling and curving north from Fulda in a left hook encircling movement, heading toward Krefeld and Gelsenkirchen.

If this left hook coming from the south was successful, Supreme Allied Command Europe knew that the hundred-mile-long Dortmund-Bielefeld pocket could not retreat, the Rhine behind them cut. Yet SACEUR, in having to commit NATO forces to the south, were forced to deny the pocket vitally needed reinforcements which could provide rearguard actions to effect withdrawal from the pocket.

* * *

"You can't give the general that!" Major Norton advised the doctor as he prepared to give Freeman a shot of Demerol to ease the pain after the operation he'd had to relieve complications of paresis.

"Why not?" asked the harried doctor.

Major Norton, whom Freeman had seconded to his G-2 staff, did not know everything about the general yet, but Al Banks had made a point of telling him early on that the general was a man who eschewed medication, boasting on occasion that the strongest pill he'd ever taken was an aspirin and that anything stronger than the medical corpsman's APC was for "goddamned sissies."

"Are you serious?" asked the exhausted doctor scornfully. "The pain's acute after that surgery."

"What exactly's wrong with him?" asked Norton.

"He's got paresis. Insufficient blood supply to the spinal cord. It's a partial paralysis, but he'll get over it. Meanwhile I'd like to make him as comfortable as I can."

Freeman stirred, his eyes opening briefly, then closing again, his voice slow, raspy with dehydration. "Al?"

The doctor looked down at him, loudly informing him, "General—I'm going to give you a shot. It'll ease your discomfort."

The general tried to turn his head. "Al—what the hell's—" He slipped back to unconsciousness. The doctor gave him the shot.

"I hope that won't make him confused when he wakes up," Norton admonished him.

"Well, without it, he won't be thinking at all, Major. Anyway—it doesn't really matter, does it? No one's getting out of this abattoir."

For a moment Norton thought the doctor was talking only about the hospital—until he realized the doctor meant the entire pocket. Norton had to admit to himself that the latest batch of aerial reconnaissance photos still showed no sign of Russian tanks with fuel drums attached. It confirmed Freeman's last-minute discovery on the way back from Heidelberg that the Russian tanks were not short of gas. As soon as the front wave of Kirov's tanks were on empty, rather than having to stop, sitting ducks for the stationary NATO tanks dug in defilade positions, already low on ammunition and with no fuel reserve, a second wave of Russian tanks would sweep forward in echelons to cover the first as they refueled.

The other members of Freeman's staff told Norton that it was the first time in Freeman's career that the general had ordered a defensive strategy, hoping to convert it to an offensive one when the Russians' overextended supply line brought their tanks to a stop. Southern Command was pressing Freeman's staff to release the tanks, arguing that they might as well rush the breaches in the DB perimeter. But without oil and the tank-killing Thunderbolts, it was adjudged by Freeman's staff that any such move would only trade short-term gain for a massive overall loss, as well as giving away the defilade positions to the Russian choppers, which, though hampered by the blizzard conditions, were on infrared, the vacated defilade positions merely providing the Soviets with more gaps in the line.

"There are too many holes in the dike," conceded Norton, "and not enough fingers to plug them."

The final blow to the already rock-bottom morale of the American, British, and Bundeswehr divisions fighting for their lives in the pocket was the news that Soviet SPETS who had infiltrated the rear areas had blown up fuel reserves west of Munster and that Freeman's mine field/defilade strategy was not working, the Russians driving prisoners before them to clear the mine fields. The choice for the prisoners had been a stark and simple one: run for your lives or get shot. In some places to the south, particularly near Leverkusen, it didn't work, prisoners refusing to be used as human detonators. But in other areas they ran toward the lines, blown into oblivion, opening corridors for the Soviet armor-borne troops to pour through.

Allied helicopters, roughly equal in number to the Soviets' were, in general, superior fighting machines, and for the most part, the Allied pilots could literally fly rings about their Russian counterparts, but as in the Thunderbolts' case, the Allied choppers were short of ammunition and missiles of all types. Compounding NATO's problems in the first few hours of Marshal Kirov's attack was the Soviets' dropping of nonnuclear EMP—electromagnetic pulse—bombs, knocking out all radio communications, every microchip circuit within a twenty-mile radius blown, leaving NATO's frontline commanders without communications while Kirov's divisions stayed in close touch with each other via Kirov's superbly trained motorcycle courier battalions. The DB pocket *was* becoming an abattoir.

On Marshal Kirov's general staff, only the marshal was worried. He held the awesome responsibility if anything went wrong, and he understood better than any of his subordinates that for all the years since World War II, and especially after the defense cuts of the Gorbachev years, the Soviet Union's victory in the West had to be a *quick* victory—a victory of quantity over quality—before the Americans and their damnable ability to resupply had a chance to make any difference. Still, as the battle wore on, the fact that the NATO forces were now being split in two raised to a certainty the possibility of driving them into the sea before the Americans could muster the wherewithal for a counterattack.

Shaking with cold, David Brentwood had quickly dug a shallow grave in the snow. As he dragged the Englishman's body into the depression and removed the Englishman's clothes, he felt as unobtrusively as he could for a cigarette lighter. There was none. Maybe it was inside the boots. But here, too, he drew a blank. He was sure he'd seen the Englishman smoking, but perhaps he'd got a light from one of the guards. He looked about for anything that he could make a rude cross from, but there was nothing. The guard was telling him to hurry up again. Quickly putting on the Englishman's uniform and taking the Englishman's dog tags, he heaped up the snow and placed a bramble as the only marker he could find for the makeshift grave. He bowed his head for a moment and then trudged slowly back to the ditch, slipping the dog tags over his head, forlornly carrying the snow-sodden blanket with his left hand, jumping the ditch, breaking his fall with the right.

As he got up, he threw the blanket into the guard's face, shoved the AKM up into the air, and kicked the man in the groin. He heard the explosion of air from the *Stasi* as the guard fell back into the ditch, cracking the ice, David falling with him, bringing his knee up to the guard's chin. There was a crunch of bone, and for a second David didn't know whether it was his knee or the guard's jaw. Either way, he finished the job with the butt of the AKM. Quickly he took the dead guard's coat off him, but the man's torso fell back into the broken ice so that when Brentwood reached for the man's undershirt, it was sodden, as was the rest of his uniform. "Damn!" said David under his breath, but he did find a lighter. He could do it, he guessed, by cutting out a strip from the truck cabin's plastic upholstery, but the problem was, he didn't know how long it would take.

He heard voices as the men started to return from the dump. He wouldn't have enough time to hot-wire the truck—they'd cut him down before he got behind its steering wheel.

"All right," he muttered to himself, determined to do a little SPETS number of his own, "it's time we evened the score." He tore off the guard's dog tags, and inside thirty seconds he'd put on the guard's sodden coat, stuffed the two grenades the guard was carrying into the coat pocket, put on the helmet, and started running to the last truck in the line. He could hear the colonel's voice and the muffled thud of an oil drum and a guard shouting at the two men who had dropped it. His back to the other prisoners, now, he guessed, about fifty yards off, he lifted the collar of the guard's coat high around his neck and fired a long burst across the ditch into the field, screaming, *"Amerikaner! Halt!"*

Behind him he heard prisoners dropping to the ground, the other guards running through the snowstorm to join him at the end of the line of trucks, and the *oberst* shouting orders. He moved quickly back down alongside the ditch to the first truck, unscrewed the gas tank cover, snapped the AKM's swing butt hard on the stock, and using its bayonet, cut through the neck of his T-shirt to make a wick for the gas tank.

But the guards were closing faster than he'd thought, and he still wouldn't have time to get into the truck. He stuffed half the T-shirt strip into the tank, lit the bottom of the taper, and slid down the embankment toward the ditch, running as fast as he could away from the line of trucks. He guessed it would be no more than five seconds before the truck would blow, and instinctively everyone around it would hit the road for a few minutes, afraid to go to any of the other vehicles behind it. He slipped on the ice, crashing headlong into the snow-covered side of the ditch, the blizzard swirling about him, and glanced back the fifty yards or so—the trucks dim blots in the rolling snow.

There was no explosion—maybe the taper had been too long and they'd seen it in time, or maybe it hadn't been as dry as he thought. He kept running, and although hot from

the effort, the sodden clothes turned his perspiration to ice.
He paused to catch his breath. The unexpected, the DI had
always told Thelma and Stumble-Ass—go for the unexpected.

Gasping, the icy air searing his lungs, he wondered how
far he could get before they recaptured him. He heard shouts
coming from the direction of the parked convoy and then an
ominous silence, except for the howl of the blizzard. Crawling up to the top of the embankment, he looked for the trucks
again, but they had vanished in the white-out, and though he
knew the dump was opposite him, a hundred yards or so
across the road, the loss of depth perception in the white-out
created the dangerously comfortable illusion that because he
couldn't see his enemy, he was safe.

Then, beneath the wail of the blizzard, he heard a swishing
noise, faint yet distinct—coming closer.

CHAPTER FORTY-ONE

WHILE, IN THE port of Brest, the convoy, minus one mer-
chantman and one of its destroyer escorts, was docking, Gen.
Douglas Freeman, beside himself with frustration, was raging against his immobility, which prevented him from being
at the front during the attack. "Here I am trussed up like a
mummy, and my boys are dying like flies." Increasing his
sense of failure, Freeman's headquarters received a message
via a ham operator, using an antiquated radio set that, operational because it used vacuum tubes instead of up-to-date
printed microchip circuit boards, picked up a BBC broadcast
of the nine-o'clock news reporting that a strike of dockworkers was under way in several of the French Ports, including
Brest. Freeman ordered Norton to grab the nearest F-16 pilot

at Krefeld to take a message to Brest that the French strikers were to be shot on the spot.

"You threaten that, General," Major Norton advised him, "and we could have one hell of a problem with France. They're allowing us to use—"

"Allowing us nothing," snapped Freeman. "They're allowing us and the British and Germans and every other poor son of a bitch in that pocket to die. Only dying they'll do is to protect France. And if the NATO commander in Brest is too cowardly to do it—I'll order air strikes on French forces and make it look like the Russians hit them. You see how quickly things'll loosen up then. I want those supplies and I want them now."

Norton was appalled, staring wide-eyed at the general, convinced that when Freeman had been thrown out of the Humvee, he'd lost some of his marbles as well. "We can't do that, General. I mean, there's no way—"

Freeman, his face contorted with pain, eyes smarting, nevertheless managed to fix Norton in his stare. "Watch me! If I'd had my way, I'd bomb the sons of bitches myself to get them into the fighting. Now, are you going to transmit that order or do I have to shoot *you*?"

As the general's Apache helicopter rose to ferry Norton to Krefeld, its rotor slap momentarily drowned the noise of battle, but he knew it was an illusion and that, like it or not, the general had a point. If they lost Western Europe, it was all over.

Freeman called for the doctor.

"Yes, General?"

"I want another shot of that painkiller."

The doctor tried but couldn't hide a smirk of satisfaction that said, So you're human after all?

"I may be—" Freeman began, but for a moment he couldn't go on. "I might be stubborn, Doc, but I'm not stupid." He turned to his logistics aide. "Charlie—you got a manifest for the convoy that's due in Brest?"

"No, sir, but—"

"Get one."

"I know there are twenty-four merchantmen, all over twenty thousand tons. There's a hell of a lot of stuff—if it got through."

"Well, if it did get through, I don't want any screw-ups down there. Ammunition and fuel, Charlie. Ammunition and fuel. Onto the Hercules and up here. At least we've still got fighter cover. Bring me a map of North Rhine–Westphalia."

"Fox 1 . . . Fox 1 . . ." Shirer was calling, the nose of the MiG plainly visible in the flash of an exploding Tomcat, then he was falling. Gradually he became aware of someone holding his hand and a rush of sensations all at once, the stink of a boat's diesel fumes and a stringent antiseptic smell and perfume, the hand holding his warm and reassuring, the woman's face indistinct, warping in and out of focus as if through a glass tumbler, swaying to and fro with the motion of the boat. And somewhere in the distance, above the rhythmic throbbing of the marine engine, the chatter of machine-gun fire, and other wounded all around him. The perfume was a memory to him, and he couldn't quite match the face in his mind, but it awakened a desire in him that transcended everything else around him.

"How's he doing?" a man's voice asked.

"He'll be all right," she said. "He was in a coma at first and we thought his arm was broken. But he was lucky. The marines who brought him in said his chute was a little twisted, but he came down all right, and the snow helped."

"Can't keep a good man down."

"No," she answered, smiling. Now Shirer could see her clearly.

"You know him?" the man asked.

She turned to look up at him as she answered, and Shirer knew the profile at once. "Lana?" He was grinning like a schoolboy.

"Well," said the man, straightening up, arms akimbo, "I guess that cuts me out!" It was a tone of good-natured resignation. "And here I thought I'd hit pay dirt with a pretty navy nurse. If you'll pardon me, I'm going to try my luck elsewhere—surely there's one nurse who'll take pity on a lonely sailor."

Lana laughed easily in reply, and in that moment Shirer knew beyond the shadow of a doubt that if he did nothing else in this damned war, he'd take her, hold her, and never let go.

"Captain—" Lana called out, "thank you for all you've

done. If you and the others on that beach hadn't got us off—''

''Ah—'' he said, waving aside any thanks. ''No problem, Lieutenant. Fish weren't running yesterday anyways—and don't call me Captain. Makes me feel like *I'm* in the navy.''

Shirer watched her effortless laugh, as entranced by her beauty as when he'd first met her. Only she was more mature-looking now—more confident than the girl he had known before the war. And if he could, he would have made love to her right then and there. Her hand was still in his and he said, ''My God, I never thought I'd be glad to be shot down.''

''Neither did I! You *are* feeling better, aren't you?''

''More than you know.''

Soon they were talking as if they had never parted.

''Where are we headed?'' he asked her.

''To Atka,'' she answered. ''It'll be about five hours. From there they'll probably fly us back to Dutch Harbor and you'll—'' Her pause conveyed more to him than she realized. Both of them pretended that they would have more time together once they reached the safety of Dutch Harbor, but both of them had seen enough of the war to know that as soon as he was able, he would be flying again, as every effort would be made to gain air superiority over Adak as a prelude to retaking the island in order to protect Shemya, four hundred miles east of Adak, before it was permanently cut off and overrun by the Russians.

The head nurse, coming down the companion ladder from the wheelhouse, where more of the wounded had been crowded in, noticed Lana was still with the same patient. ''Lieutenant Brentwood—could I see you a moment please!'' Her tone was admonishing. ''We need help on deck.''

Lana rose, taking her hand from his. ''Uh-oh. I'm in trouble. I'll see you at Dutch Harbor.''

''Lana?'' he asked.

''Yes?''

''Are you still afraid of pirates?'' For a second she didn't know what he meant.

''They wear eye patches.'' He grinned.

She was buttoning up her parka before going on deck. Her voice was subdued, yet quietly joyful. ''I love them,'' she said.

* * *

"You were very palsy-walsy with that pilot," the head nurse commented sharply. "Do you hold hands with all your patients?"

"He's an old friend."

"So I gathered. But I'd appreciate it if you could spare time to attend to some of the other patients. We have several cases of—"

"Yes, of course," replied Lana. "I'm sorry. It was selfish of me."

Surprised and mollified by Lana's apology, the head nurse put Lana's lapse of duty down to the battle fatigue they were all feeling. Adopting an equally conciliatory tone, she asked Lana if she would help her secure all the medical supplies they'd had to put on deck to make room below for the wounded. "We'd better hurry," she told Lana. "Captain Bering says we'll likely run into some squalls before we reach Atka."

On the other side of the world, Major Norton, bearing Freeman's message to Brest, had just finished a terrifying flight with zero visibility in a storm sweeping in over the Ardennes. He had sat, white-knuckled, in the electronic systems operator's tandem seat in a Luftwaffe Tornado out of Krefeld, eyes closed throughout the 530-mile flight, which the Tornado made in thirty-eight minutes, often flying less than five hundred feet above the ground, courtesy of its contour-scanning radar.

As Norton deplaned, his legs almost buckling under him, the Luftwaffe pilot apologized effusively, telling him, "I am sorry we took so long. But you see, Major, the STO"—by which the pilot meant the Smiths/Teldix/OMI head-up display—"is a little off, you understand, so it was necessary for us to go a little slow." Adding insult to injury, when Norton arrived at NATO Brest HQ with Freeman's threat, he discovered that there had been such an uproar from the French public about the dockside strike that the unions were back at work within the hour and the convoy's supplies were already en route to NATO's beleaguered Northern Army.

"You wish to go back now?" asked the tired but eager young Luftwaffe pilot.

"No," said Norton. "I think I'll sit a while."

As he headed farther away from the trucks, following the line of the ditch parallel to the road, David Brentwood heard the swishing noise increasing, and now there seemed to be more than one source of the noise. Skis? He crawled up the sharp incline of the embankment but slid back, a hump under his foot giving way. Looking down, he saw it was a child's body. He hesitated, held the child's frozen hand, a little boy. Though not expecting a pulse, David checked anyway. There was none. Realizing he could do no more but unable to leave the tiny corpse, he turned the body facedown, the savagery of it all overwhelming him. Unmarried, no children of his own, he found it difficult to judge how old the little boy might have been, but he guessed no more than five or six.

The swishing noise was louder now, and he thought he saw a flashlight through the thick curtain of the blizzard. He touched the boy's head, the hair frozen stiff, eyes closed, and was about to make his way up to the top of the embankment again when he noticed several more humps in the snow, scattered along the shoulder of the road. One body, a woman's, was covered by that of a soldier who had obviously fallen on top of her, trying to protect her. The soldier's uniform was that of the Bundeswehr. Why the advancing Soviet forces had perpetrated such a massacre, he had no idea. Perhaps it was nothing more than that civilians posed inconvenient delays.

Looking back down the road, he saw four figures with flashlights, the black barrel of their slung weapons in contrast to the falling snow. Sliding back down toward the ditch, he ran for another twenty yards or so, and when, glancing back, he could not see them, he quickly crossed the road, ready to slide down the ditch on the other side. There was none, and so he kept running into a snow-covered field. The unexpected, he told himself again. They would not think of looking for him on the dump side of the road.

He saw the dim shapes of trees about a hundred yards ahead of him, a wood, and at the edge he crawled beneath the snow-laden branches. Looking back across the field, he watched as the search party, four of them now, continued down the road. One of them stopped—looking down at what David guessed must be the child's body. Damn! He shouldn't have touched the body, disturbed its blanket of snow, because now they knew—

But then they began moving again, stopped, and turned back. Jesus Christ! he admonished himself. You dumb bastard! You stupid, dumb bastard—

They had seen his footprints, and given the heavy fall of snow, they would know he must have crossed the road shortly before. Heaving himself up under the weight of the coat, he began moving through the woods, then paused. Calm down, he told himself. So they were better-equipped, better-armed—and they were already starting to cross the field, following his footprints toward the wood. But he realized it would be much easier for them to pick up his footprints inside the wood where the snowfall was not nearly so windblown. He turned back toward the edge of the wood, unslung the AKM, thought about himself and Thelman on the range at Parris Island, and eased himself into the prone position, seeing the DI, not shouting for once but calmly telling them, "You've got time. Relax. Get your breathing under control. You're going no-where—and the enemy's advancing. Don't panic and start spraying everything in sight. Waste your ammo. Deep breaths! Stumble-Ass, I said deep breath. Exhale, not all of it. Hold—that's it. Now *squeeze* the trigger—not your cock, Thelma. Fire, and don't keep looking at the target. You're not at the county fair. No dollies or box of chocolates. Move your aim straight to the next one or he'll move you. You got that, Stumble-Ass?''

David cupped the barrel in his hands, letting what warmth he had in them thaw the snow that now might be ice inside. He'd come too far to kill himself. If he was to die, they were going to have to do it for him. Far over on his right, down the road, he heard the trucks starting up, the convoy, he expected, warming up, getting ready to head back to the front as soon as loading was completed. He flipped up the rear tangent sight, set it for fifty meters, aligned it with the front protected-post sight, and moved the bayonet scabbard from where it was digging into his belly.

When the first man filled the sight, David squeezed off a burst. Snow fell from a branch overhead from the air vibration and he shifted the AKM to the right, firing again. The first man was already down, the second thrown back till the safety bindings gave on the skis and he toppled into the snow. The other two were down, returning fire, bullets thwacking into the timber above and around him, but so high and wide, he doubted they had any precise idea of his position. Getting up behind the cover of the branches, sticking a twist of hand-kerchief into the barrel, he headed through the wood toward the dump—if he was still within the dump's precincts. He was making much better time now, the snow in the woods nowhere as deep as in the field behind him.

In a few more minutes, having left the sporadic fire well behind him, he saw the trees were thinning. He was out of the wood.

"Halt!"

The *Stasi* trooper had his rifle up. David dropped to the ground as he fired a wide, sweeping burst. The man's legs buckled, snow flicking up around him, and David felt his left shoulder stinging like crazy. He heard a loud panting noise coming out from the wood—too close for the other two to have caught up with him.

Then he felt the hot rush of air, a flurry of snow. Instinctively his left hand flew up, but the Doberman had it between his teeth, fangs crushing through the thick coat, crunching to the bone. David reached for the AKM but couldn't find it. He tried to roll the dog over, but the Doberman had him pinned. His left arm bleeding profusely, David shoved his right into the coat's right hand pocket, felt the lighter, and grasping it with all his strength, flicked the flint. The blue-orange propane flame shot up, and David pushed it at the dog's eyes. Astonishingly, the Doberman hung on, jaws still clamping down on David's arm, trying to shake the life out of him. Then suddenly the dog jumped back, skittering a short distance away, his paws frantically wiping his eyes. David saw the stock of the AKM and pulled it toward him. Its barrel was jammed with icy snow. Getting up, he flipped the butt down, lifted the gun by the barrel, and felled the dog.

The voices in the wood behind him were getting closer now. Stumbling through the snow, David reached the dog's handler, who was making a noise as if he were snoring, something wrong with his breathing. David, almost passing out from the pain in his arm, removed the two M42 screw-threaded stick grenades from the man's belt, as well as two banana clips of 7.62 millimeter, stuffing them into his coat's pocket, then headed toward what looked like a barn fifty yards away, a horse trough nearby congealed with ice.

Then, beyond the barn, he saw what he'd been after from the moment he'd seen the Englishman dead in the snow and had asked the *oberst* permission to bury him. For once the snow was helping, firm underfoot, packed down, presumably by the boots of prisoners as they'd marched in from the trucks. The huge, snow-laden, camouflaged canvas-and-netting roof formed a strikingly beautiful and symmetrically scalloped pattern like the awning of some vast, expensive garden party marquee. Behind him he could hear the two men crossing the field and was about to turn to see if he could spot them when, seventy yards in front of him, away to the left, he heard a truck slowly coming to a stop, and the sound of more dogs. Without hesitating, he fired the whole magazine at the truck, the barrel so hot, the steam rose all around him. The truck's engine was now in the high whine of reverse. He knew that now was his only chance. The AKM slung over his right shoulder, he ran the fifty yards toward the black wall of fuel drums. Kneeling, unscrewing the stick handle from two grenades, screwing them together, forming a demolition charge, he pulled both pins and threw them as far as he could into the gap between the canvas roof and the stacked fuel drums.

Running fast through the blinding snow, he estimated he would have five seconds. He was wrong. On a three-second fuse, the grenades blew, and the next instant he was lifted off the ground, the force of the explosion throwing him forward at least twenty feet, behind him a mountain of orange fire and dense, black smoke, the air like a desert wind, fantastic shadows playing across the snow, men running farther down the road from rivers of lighted fuel spewing out into the snow like molten lava. David dragged himself up, stumbled and fell, rose again, not knowing where he was heading so long as it was away from the fire. He heard screams and the futile spinning of truck tires trying to grip on snow that in seconds had become a bubbling sludge. More men somewhere off to his right were running, throwing weapons down, clambering aboard what looked like half-tracks in a desperate exodus as more and more of the drums exploded, adding to the towering flames, leaping hundreds of feet into the air, visible to NATO positions as far south as Bielefeld.

Hauling himself to the wood's edge, it was not until about a quarter hour later that David realized the back of his head had been singed and the coat covered with the burns of airborne cinders. He knew he could run no more. If they got him—the best he could hope for was that he'd make them pay. He put the AKM across his lap and felt for the other two grenades, making sure no snow had iced up on them. Last thing he needed was the pins to freeze.

CHAPTER FORTY-TWO

THE GERMAN ARMY would call it the "Time of Deliverance," the Americans, the "Bust-Out," the British, "About Bloody Time." But whatever name they gave it, the American-driven counterattack was something to behold.

Ironically, the first man to witness its beginning was not a combat soldier at all but a Bundeswehr surgeon. Assigned to the field hospital west of Munster, the surgeon had always admired the Americans for their inventive know-how, especially the revolutionary MUST—Medical Unit, Self-Contained—hospital that had been first designed in the 1980s. Seemingly rising out of nothing, inflated within twenty minutes by sterile compressed air from portable generators, and air-conditioned throughout, the fifty-two-foot-long, twenty-foot-wide, and ten-foot-high ward of six operating tables and inbuilt equipment had greatly reduced the fatality rate. The only fault the German surgeon found with it was that, as in all American installations, the thermostat was set way too high.

Stepping out at around 1600 hours on the day of the convoy's arrival in Brest for a blast of cold and invigorating air between operations, he heard a thunderous roar overhead in the blizzard that had blanketed the front from lower Saxony as far south as Heidelberg. He hoped it was an American plane, for if not, there was nowhere to go for shelter—the slit trenches dug earlier in the day were now snow-filled, every available man having been sent to the perimeter in the desperate last-ditch attempt to stop the Russian advance. The roar of the aircraft had barely abated when out of the blizzard

he saw a dark square the size of a house descending several
hundred yards away above the airstrip designated "Munster 1," but dubbed by the Americans "Monster 1." As he
watched the object, a vinelike mesh dangling from it, and
saw the four ghostlike chutes above, he realized the mesh
was the cargo net about a resupply palette.

The blizzard, so welcomed by Kirov's divisions and which
Kirov's staff had predicted would bog down the Americans,
was proving no impediment. From the Bielefeld line to the
Danube three hundred miles to the south, the American
M-1s, German Leopards, and British Challengers were about
to be given new life. The airlift from Brest would fly in more
supplies than in either the famed Berlin airlift of '48 or the
resupply of Khe Sanh in the Vietnam War. In the blinding
white-out, American ingenuity, German organization, and
British doggedness came together like old friends called to
the bedside of a critically ill relative. In the snow the Americans' high-tech instrument flying constantly amazed the Soviet divisions that had broken through, rolling toward what
they had thought was certain victory.

With fighter cover provided by RAF Tornados flying out
of southern England and American F-111F swing-wing fighter
interceptors, dozens of the giant 245-foot-long, 65-foot-high
American C-5C Galaxies, flying out of Brest, delivered fuel
and ammunition to the hastily prepared prepo sites west of
Munster. The giant transport's normal load of 121 tons was
increased to 150 tons, the Galaxies able to cut down on their
own fuel load because of the short sixty-eight-minute, five-
hundred-mile flight from Brest to the Dortmund-Bielefeld
pocket.

Almost none of the Galaxies landed in the pocket; most
of their intermodal CONCAR—containerized cargo—having
being taken straight from ship to plane, was dropped low by
chute-braked palette. The cargo of ammunition and fuel
drums from the hundreds of forty-eight-foot-long containers
was heading toward the front within twenty minutes of a
palette skidding to a stop, the snow helping to brake the
palette's slide in a shorter distance than usual.

The massive resupply drop had no noticeable effect for the
first six to seven hours, the NATO-sown mine fields Freeman
had relied upon to slow the Soviet armor breached by Russian divisions pouring through gaps where the mines had
been rendered useless in the heavy fall of snow. Because of

this, a British infantry battalion and an American Ranger regiment were overrun southwest of Bochum, over three thousand taken prisoner. Many of them were shot out of hand for no other reason than that the Soviet supply line—already stretched for the final attack on the besieged Allies—had no containment areas or food allocated for prisoners. After U.S. M-16 and M-60, and U.K. SLR 7.62-millimeter ammunition had been stripped from the British and American bodies, they were left to be covered by the snow, Kirov and his staff regarding the fuel necessary for a bulldozer to dig mass graves too vital for their armored and mechanized divisions. The early discovery of this by an American airborne battalion led to some of the most vicious fighting anywhere on the perimeter.

Six hours after the airlift had begun, around 2200 hours, the snow-filled sky over the pocket became brilliantly incandescent, with blossoming patches of ruby-red and ice-cream-white flares shot through with green and orange parabolas of tracer as refueled Apache and Cobra gunships, flying in excess of 150 miles per hour, swarmed across the outer reaches of the chaotically shifting and segmented front, firing thousands of Hellfire—fire and forget—antitank missiles. Though equipped with infrared sensors far superior to those of the Soviets, the initial Hellfire attacks were not as effective as hoped because of the lack of laser-beam-equipped forward air controllers to guide each missile to its target. NATO choppers, with pods of eight TOW-tube-launched, wire-guided missiles, were more effective against the enemy tanks, the TOWs not requiring anyone on the ground to assist. Soviet Hind and Havoc helicopters, having had it their own way for the last forty-eight hours because of NATO's rapidly dwindling fuel supplies, were now faced with a far different situation, scatter fragments from the exploding warhead of the Sidewinder missiles proving deadly to the Soviet gunships.

Much of the credit for the destruction of the Soviet choppers was due to the contour-imaging guidance radar aboard the American Apaches, which permitted their pilots NOE, or "nap of earth" flying, the choppers able to skim less than fifty feet above ground, tree, or water contour even in the worst snow conditions. NOE flying was especially easy over the flatter southern sector of the DB pocket.

* * *

By the time Major Norton had returned from Brest to Freeman's hospital HQ outside Munster, he found the general, though still rigid in his brace, very much alert, looking up at the maps of Lower Saxony, North Rhine–Westphalia, and the Rhineland Palatinate that were taped to the field hospital's ceiling. The general's exhausted yet attentive staff clustered about the bed, the mood of new hope evident from the sheer vitality that radiated out from Freeman, who was holding forth a telescopic pointer, stabbing at the ceiling. "Ah, there you are, Norton. What d'you think of my chapel?"

Before Norton could say anything, Freeman raced on. "If Michelangelo could do it on his back, so can I, eh?"

"I guess so, General. I heard on my way up here that we've stopped our withdrawal."

"Stopped!" It sounded like an obscenity. "By God, Major, we're moving. We are going on the attack! Their advanced dump—the bastards had it hidden away up here in the goddamned woods—has blown up in their faces." The general moved the pointer north of Bielefeld. "Outside Stadthagen." Freeman's face was so flushed with optimism that at first Norton thought the general had had some kind of adverse reaction to the pain shot. "Now," Freeman continued, lowering the pointer and looking around at his staff, "the shoe's on the other foot. Kirov—" the general paused, savoring the moment "—is running out of gas, gentlemen. Here, Norton," said Freeman, passing him a bulging manila folder. "Feast your eyes on these."

They were infrared aerial reconnaissance photos. At first Norton thought they had been badly overexposed—everything seemed white—almost no contrast at all to the wooded area around the edge of the photographs. Then he realized what he was seeing. "My God, General, that's some bonfire. It must be—" Norton glanced down at the scale line.

"Over two thousand yards," Freeman cut in. "They must have had enough gas—*our* gas—there to fuel Lord knows how many divisions." Freeman paused and looked about at his staff. "God is on our side, gentlemen. We shouldn't get too damn cocky about this. Least not until we're in Moscow."

"Well, General," said Norton good-naturedly but clearly skeptical, "I think it'll be some time before we get to Moscow. There's the matter of eastern Germany, Poland—"

"Norton," Freeman responded, "you're a good G-2. You've got an eye for detail that surpasses anyone I know.

That's why I seconded you to my staff, but you're too conservative in matters military. Because we've been losing up
to this point, you want to hold back. Consolidate. I understand your caution, but it would be fatal. It's un-American.
Their tanks are chugging to a stop, and within twenty-four
hours we'll have every one of our tanks gassed up and ready
to go. Instead of sitting on our butts in defilade—our only
option till now—we can move out in force. Kick their ass all
the way back to the Volga. At this moment, gentlemen, we
have a confluence of forces that will not visit us again—our
navy's secured Atlantic resupply of troops and matériel, the
enemy's supply line is now overextended, out of gas, and we
have air superiority. With our Thunderbolts killing their tanks
by the bushel, it'll be a *rout*! We'll grow stronger as they
grow weaker—'' Here Freeman paused, fixing each man in
turn with what his commanders called the ''Patton look.''
''If we strike *now*—while they're confused—out of steam.''

Freeman's assumption that Kirov's army was confused was
incorrect. As relayed to the world by the TV reporter who
had earlier defied Freeman's ban on media at the front, the
truth was that the Russian armies were stunned—not only by
the refueling and resupply of troops and tanks all along NA-
TO's front but above all by the A-10 Thunderbolts. The snow-
filled TV pictures were often blurred but nevertheless plainly
showed the subsonic Thunderbolts coming in low, often at
acute angles of attack, their maneuverability holding even
the supersonic pilots in thrall. At times almost in a stall, nose
down, the high-mounted rear jets making them look like
enormous insects, the Thunderbolts sent down an orange
rain of depleted uranium tracer. This fusillade from the
thirty-millimeter cannon lasted for only a second or two
but, streaming down at a rate over four thousand rounds
a minute while the pilot sat protected in the titanium-
sheathed seat, passed through the Soviets' main battle
tanks and anything else in the way like a hot poker through
butter. Exploding the tanks' fuel, if it had any left, or
igniting the fifty-odd rounds of tank ammunition, it blew
the tank apart.

Most of the more than one thousand T-90s and 80s were
destroyed in the ensuing forty-eight hours by the Thunderbolts—long before NATO's tanks were refueled and ready to
move. Ironically, had the NATO tanks been moving, the

Thunderbolts would not have been anywhere near as successful. For, as in the dust-shrouded battle of Fulda Gap at the beginning of the war, identification between friend and foe in the blizzard would have been extremely difficult, with many Allied tanks destroyed as a result.

The American public and all those watching the TV reports—now Freeman was offering transport to media reps wherever they wanted to go—did not realize that the reason for Freeman's order to keep his tanks in defilade was that his decision had been dictated by the critical shortage of gas. Nor was NATO's Supreme Command anxious to let them know how close the entire NATO front had come to irreversible disaster in the DB pocket. What viewers saw before their eyes on every news report in a jubilant America was yet another example of the tactical genius of "End Run Doug," as the more sensational papers were calling him. And even *The New York Times*'s in-depth reporting could not detract from his glory. It was clear to everybody from Florida to Alaska that Freeman had gone on the offensive when lesser men would have counseled caution. The reputation of the once unknown one-star general who had been close to retirement when he'd led the raid on Pyongyang was now secure, it seemed, in the Pantheon of American heros.

While a prisoner, dressed in *Stasi* greatcoat and helmet, with *Stasi* identification tags, and captured by the Coldstream Guards during the British advance on Stadthagen, was claiming he was an American called "Brentwood," General Douglas Freeman was receiving a congratulatory call from the president of the United States.

Four days later, when it was confirmed by a Private Thelman and others who'd escaped when the fuel dump at Stadthagen had "blown" that the man who said he was David Brentwood *was* in fact David Brentwood, Freeman's headquarters was informed.

David, weak from pneumonia and en route on a hospital train to Lille in Belgium, oblivious to the fact that news of his exploit was now being broadcast around the world, was greeted ecstatically upon arrival in Lille by normally reserved Belgian civilians, who a week before had thought they would be under the heel of Soviet occupation. In the hospital's admissions office, a pretty, young female clerk asked

David, pronouncing every English word with painstaking exactitude, "This honor medal you will be getting—it is made of gold?"

David, sitting down, his breathing labored, feeling so tired, he could fall asleep that instant, nevertheless managed a wink. "It had better be," he said. Her name tag, he noticed, was Lili.

"You will be famous, no?" she asked. "Like your General Freeman."

He liked the way she said "General"—sounded cute. "Don't tell anyone," he said, pausing for breath, "but I taught him all he knew."

She laughed, and he with her. It was the first time he had done so in a long while. He watched her, trying not to be too obvious, as she completed the form. No rings, he noticed. It reminded him of the last letter he'd had from Melissa telling him as gently as she could that perhaps they shouldn't be too hasty about marriage plans. After all, she reminded him, his brother Robert hadn't become engaged until he was much older than David. Lili was looking better all the time.

CHAPTER FORTY-THREE

COLD AS IT looked, rising bleak and forbidding out of the fog, Dutch Harbor was a welcome sight to Lana and the evacuees from Adak after hours of force-six winds, more than enough seasickness to go around on the boat, and air sickness on the Hercules flight from Atka.

When they got ashore, the news of the American-led breakout from the Dortmund-Bielefeld pocket was general knowledge, but as yet, news of David's action had not been received. In fact, the only news about her family was a letter from her mother, its postmark showing that it had been mailed a week before.

At first, after Frank had left her to report to the base commander, Lana had looked forward to reading the letter, but before long it had made her feel thoroughly depressed. Her mother told her how excited she was about Robert's imminent marriage to Rosemary Spence, lamenting the fact that none of the family could be there, all together again. She was naturally worried about David but reported that Ray was "coming along" and that "your father is still doing too much and has started bringing work home with him after some 'tiff' at the office."

Lana rushed through the remainder of the letter, feeling more angry than grateful. It was good to hear from home, but her mother had started using a kind of Pablum code with her ever since Lana had had what her mother called her "little problem" with Jay—as if avoidance of discussing anything unpleasant would make it go away. She had never been like that until Ray was so badly burned on the *Blaine*. What did her mother mean, she wondered, by Ray "coming along"? And what *exactly* was Father's "tiff" at work?

When Lana finished reading the letter, she realized that what was really eating away at her was what would happen to Frank. They had hardly stepped ashore when he was requested to report to Colonel Morin. She was afraid that he would have to report back to the carrier as soon as possible. She told him he wasn't ready, that after what he'd been through in the last few days, he needed rest—and that she didn't have any qualms about telling Morin that.

But he'd gone all macho on her and said that if he had to go, he had to go, that "someone owes those marines back there."

And she knew he was right. But the thought of losing him, just when she'd felt her life was coming together again, filled her with such anxiety that although all she wanted to do was sleep—she couldn't.

When Shirer came back from Morin's office, he told her he didn't have to go back to the carrier—at least not immediately, not until he and the squadron of F-14s being ferried the following day to Dutch Harbor had flown an attack and reconnaissance mission over Adak.

As wind-driven rain swept the runway at Dutch Harbor, the red-vested ordnance man stepped out from beneath the wing of Shirer's F-14, holding the red streamers up, showing Shirer that all safety wires had been removed—the bombs and missiles now ready. Shirer gave him the thumbs-up okay, and within a minute the afterburning thrust of the twin Pratt and Whitney turbofans had the Tomcat aloft, leading the other nine in arrowhead formation for the 450-mile mission to Adak. Climbing fast, they leveled out at ten thousand feet, keeping subsonic, wings on full spread to conserve fuel for the nine-hundred-mile return trip. This would give the planes well over an hour above and around Adak, where each plane would drop its concrete Divers to crater the runway, hopefully rendering it unusable for the Russians until a U.S. seaborne and combined-ops invasion could be mounted. Any dogfights, of course, would drastically decrease the time over target to a matter of minutes. With the afterburners kicking in, the Tomcats would consume a third of their fuel in less than four minutes at full war speed.

As Dutch Harbor slid back on the snail-gray sea, Shirer, for the first time since his carrier sorties in the Sea of Japan, worried if he would return. Yet he was not so much afraid as impatient. No other woman had made such an impression on him—merely to be near her was exciting, an excitement only increased by anticipation. Having been unable to spend any time with her since their arrival in Dutch Harbor with the rest of the evacuees from Adak, he found it difficult now to think of anything else. Last night he'd dreamed of having her, but each time they embraced, she drew away from him— shy or afraid, he couldn't tell. Perhaps both. He told himself not to get all hung up about it—to expect too much. If war had taught him anything, it was that. And a relationship took time, or so they said. But who had time in a war?

At fifteen thousand feet, they were over Umnak, a hundred miles west of Dutch Harbor, and he could see the white cone of Okmok Caldera and the black patches that warned of the turmoil below the surface. The next instant they were in thick cloud, which had ballooned up under the pressure of a westward-flowing millimaw, covering the western Aleutians all the way from Atka to Amchitka Island. Even the most experienced pilot was leery of going into soup on passive radar and radio silence, but any signal emanating from the Tomcats could provide a homing beam for an enemy missile.

Keeping on radio silence, not even talking to their RIO in

the backseat until the last possible moment, Shirer and the other ten pilots began their descent toward Adak, instruments telling them they were okay but every pilot wanting to see for himself the IAP of Cape Adagdak on the northern side of Mount Adagdak, which would bring them over Clam Lagoon and Kulak Bay to the left of Andrew Lagoon, where they would pass between Mount Moffett on their right, Mount Reed to their left, exiting over Shagak Bay and Adak Strait on the western side of the island.

Coming down through the cloud, his cockpit in a constant slipstream of moisture, Shirer saw the weather clearing and switched on the active radar, jammers, and the four cameras in the nose.

Suddenly the cloud broke, Adak dead ahead, the sea a shining cobalt blue shot through with silver, three dots—fishing boats, most likely—far left on Kulak Bay.

Almost immediately the sky started to smudge with AA fire, the gutted remnants of Adak Base, like some vast, scattered campfire, racing toward them at over six hundred miles an hour as their first bombs toppled and they climbed to avoid the shock waves. He saw an orange wink from one of the fishing boats and his alarm was flashing—the trawler had fired a missile. Shirer released chaff and flares to thwart its trajectory, felt his Tomcat buffeted, the F-14 to his right gone.

"Bogey four high, four high!" someone was yelling. He glimpsed the MiG closing, reduced speed, slid left in a defensive break, hoping the Russian would overshoot. Instead the Russian stayed with him, diving down, as Shirer went into a rolling scissors, the two fighters turning fast around each other, waiting for a shot. Suddenly Shirer found himself in the MiG's cone of vulnerability, the three green arcs on Shirer's HUD not yet cutting the MiG's image, the bars widening, Shirer gaining but the MiG still outside the impact lines. The Russian wiggled left, right, high left, but Shirer was still on him, the sea a blue wall far to his left.

"Angel Two, Angel Two . . ." came his radar operator's voice, warning him he was at two thousand feet. He hauled the Tomcat into a steep climb, saw the Russian behind him, then dropped like a stone, the HUD's circle on the MiG's tail for a millisecond. Shirer pressed the button and felt the staccato tug of the twenty-millimeter multibarreled cannon. The tail was gone, the MiG's cockpit flashed in the sun, the pilot ejecting, his chute ballooning now miles behind the Tomcat.

By now Shirer was fifty miles out to sea, and as he headed back toward Adak, he saw the palls of smoke from the bombs of the other eight fighters. Swooping low in one last pass, coming in west of the island, he saw the trawler lost in a thick smoke, but it hadn't been hit, the smoke camouflage of its own making. The cockpit went milky, and for a moment he thought he'd hit a seabird, but the radio officer told him it was tracer coming up from the trawler.

Climbing, banking hard left now out beyond Sitkin Sound east of the island, he came back in, upwind of the trawler, its smoke no longer affording it as much protection, its tracer still feeling up toward him. He centered the dot and gave the trawler a one-second burst, his tracer dancing on the deck, shattering the wheelhouse, but still the trawler kept firing, Shirer recognizing it now as the boat that had evacuated them from the island.

"That thing must be armor-plated between the bulkheads," said Shirer's RIO. Now everything slid into place, explaining the tracer he'd seen pouring in from the sea to Adak Base the night he was shot down.

"Maybe he's got a titanium hull?" the RIO half joked.

"Not for much longer," said Shirer. The trawler was centered, and Shirer released his FAE-fuel air explosive—the trawler engulfed in an ovoid canopy of fire.

As he climbed down from the cockpit, thanked the ground crew, and walked across the tarmac toward the debriefing hut, the weather was piteously cold, some of the worst he'd ever seen, but he couldn't care less, for Lana was waiting. Though he knew that shortly he and she would be part of this new war in the Aleutians, for now at least they would be together, and just as when he was in the air, high above the earth, where time was measured not by the hour but by the second and life rushed in the vein, it was the quality of the time they would have together that was important, not its duration. Not even the fact that the camera recon showed that the Flogger he had shot down had probably been the one that had brought him down particularly interested him. There was no doubt the Flogger's logo—a Russian name that translated as "Marchenko" above a rampant black bear crushing a bald eagle in its claws—would stay with him. And it was certain that the two air forces would clash in battles yet to come. But until then, he would spend as much good time with Lana as possible.

CHAPTER FORTY-FOUR

HER FACE DRAWN, beside herself with worry about Edouard and his parents, her sense of self-dignity and worth shattered by the humiliation of her jail cell, Malle Jaakson was lost for the first time in her life. For the past fifty-odd years she had been a model citizen of the republic of Estonia. To her, people who ended up behind bars were the ne'er-do-wells of society. Even political prisoners, automatically assumed by the West to be innocent of all wrongdoing against society, had been regarded by her as fundamentally troublemakers, the kind who would not be happy in any system. And now, here she was inside the damp, cold cell—the smell of it the odor of ageless despair. No matter how you were when they brought you here, the degradation of that moment would never leave. Forever after, a part of you would feel dirty.

It was not the charge of murder that overwhelmed her; of this she knew she was guilty—she had seen no other way—and would pay the ultimate price. What had struck her with the most force was the indifference of her jailers. She had feared they would beat her, and they had not. At first she thought this was because she had no information to give, that they assumed she knew no saboteurs in Tallinn—which was true—but it quickly became evident to her that she did not matter to them because she was a mere thing, one of the countless thousands of Balts they had processed through these cells over the years. They had photographed her, given her a number, checked her file for previous crimes against the state—there were none; indeed, she had an honorable discharge from the Baltic Fleet's signal school—then locked her up and left her to herself. She had found this bad enough, but what was worse was the mundane but dreadful formality of having to surrender her stockings, her bra, the belt of her coat, the laces from her low-heeled shoes, and her glasses. Having not said a word so far, she now asked them why this petty humiliation was necessary.

"To stop you," answered one of the guards, his voice one of tired boredom, "from trying to kill yourself."

Do you care? she had wanted to ask, but the cell gave her the answer. It was merely a rule they were enforcing, like that of having to use the bucket in one corner of the cell. To move it was punishable by solitary confinement. They issued her prison garb: a coarse black-and-gray-striped woolen dress, supposed to fit all sizes and which, without a belt, made everyone look pregnant. How, she wondered, did the men's prison "pajamas" stay up? surely they were not fitted with a belt. She remembered seeing trials on TV of those charged with crimes against the state, the prisoners required to stand before the prosecutor, allowed only one hand with which to clutch the waist. Sometimes one of the more frail prisoners, who could not keep his balance, would falter, and the pajamas would drop—the packed courtroom erupting in laughter—the three judges warning the gallery they would not tolerate such outbursts.

After she had been so suddenly taken from the world above to the world of the cells, the effect of her first few hours, an old man, a "psychiatric criminal" in the next cell, telling her what he would do with her, was devastating. She was terrified, not of what she had done but of how quickly her self-confidence had been shattered by the most banal loss of dignity.

Malle had always believed she was made of sterner stuff, but now, with the suddenness of revelation, she understood how so many confessions had been obtained by the secret police. Most of the public, she thought, felt as she did: that apart from admissions of guilt extracted under duress, most other confessions, especially those given in the first twelve hours, when the ink was barely dry on the charge sheet, were true. Now she understood how, in those first hours, the psychological collapse could be total. You were ready to confess to anything—just to get your shoelaces back.

During the night she had been unable to sleep, the terror

of her impending death mounting in her, the madman in the cell quiet. Asleep or dead, she did not know. She called to him and there was no answer. She listened vainly for the sound of breathing, but there was none, or if there was, it was muffled by the hollow clanking of the pipes. In that moment the certainty of the firing squad made her so weak that she longed only for its finality—the end of her suffering—and, sobbing, she clung to the bars.

"You!" She thought it was a new guard she hadn't seen before, but without her glasses, she was unsure. She could hear the crunching of boots on the cobbled courtyard above her and the click of the rifles' bolts.

"Come on!" the guard hurried her. Instinctively she looked about for her glasses, then remembered they had been taken. Walking in front of him, she heard the crash of the volley, the clicking of rifles, and the crunch of the boots again. Barely able to stand, clinging to the banister as she was ordered to the second floor, her mind numb with fear and unable to see the edge of the steps clearly because of her shortsightedness, she was nevertheless vaguely aware of the guard changing his deportment, and brushing what appeared to be dandruff off the shoulder boards of his baggy uniform.

Inside the room, she squinted in the brightness of the northern sun that was streaming in, its beams of light giving the room's sparse but elegant furniture a surreal look. But there was nothing surreal or imaginary about the Russian officer, his back to her—an admiral, from his splendid uniform. He turned as the guard slid the chair behind her, told her to sit down, clicked his heels, and left the room, the echoes of his footsteps hollow and hard. She sat down.

"Why?" asked the admiral, looking out the window, standing behind his wide, baize-covered desk, a ray of sunlight slicing the air between them, dust particles dancing crazily within. "Why did you kill the corporal?"

"He did unspeakable things to me."

"He raped you?"

"Yes."

"How many times did this occur?"

"Does it matter?" She marveled at her defiant tone.

"Why did you not come to the authorities?"

"He *was* the authorities," she said. It was as if her inner voice, against all odds, demanded to be heard. "He came to my city. Like you all come and do what you want."

"You knew no saboteurs? He was investigating—"

"None."

"Your son, daughter-in-law. Were they saboteurs?"

She wanted to say no, but instead she said, "Perhaps. I don't know. They went to work one morning and never came back. Shot along with all your other hostages, I expect."

It was several seconds before the admiral spoke again. "You have a grandson?"

She said nothing—sensing danger.

"He was caught last night," said the admiral. "Trying to storm the jail. It was very silly."

She started forward in her seat. "What have you—"

"We have taken him to school, where he belongs." He turned and glanced down at a file. "Mustamäe complex. Is this where you live?"

She nodded, afraid to say another word.

The admiral sat down, took out a pen, signed a paper, and tapped the small bell by the blotter. The admiral's aide entered, the admiral handing him the file. "Return the prisoner's personal effects."

"Yes, Admiral." The aide, a major, his features indistinct until he came closer, smiled down at Malle. "Follow me, please."

As he led her down the curving stone stairwell, he glanced back at Malle. "You're a lucky woman."

She dared not think of it. She dared hardly breathe, but her heart was beating so hard at the prospect of freedom, she thought it would burst through her chest.

At the front desk, the major handed her a pen. "Go on," he said. "Don't be afraid. It's a release form. Confirming that you have received all your personal effects."

The clerk pushed a Hessian bag with a cardboard label, her name scribbled on it, across the counter. Inside were her "travel in Tallinn only" permit card, shoelaces, clothes, and glasses. She looked up at the aide, still not daring to hope.

"You're free," he said. "The admiral believed you. You may change in the washroom over there."

When Malle came out, he escorted her to the door and called for a driver. "You are also to take this," he said, handing her a square package the size of a small cake box. "These papers," he added, giving her two buff-colored forms, "are your interim permits until new identity cards are issued. It is a new regulation."

He opened the door to the car, wished her good day, then returned up the stone stairs.

In the back of the drab olive army sedan, as the driver waited to pull out into the traffic, she put the package by her side and carefully folded the papers the aide had given her. Suddenly she was staring down at the release order—signed by Admiral Brodsky of the Baltic Fleet. As the car pulled away, she looked up at the window, but the reflection of the sun was such that she could not see if he was there or not. The driver cursed, beeped his horn, and assumed, because a car had been ordered for her, that she must be some kind of VIP, though she certainly didn't dress like it.

"Bad news, eh?" he said.

"What—pardon?" It was as if she were in a dream.

"They say the Americans are crossing the Weser."

She didn't know where the Weser was exactly, only that it was somewhere in Germany. Western Germany, she thought. "Yes," she agreed. "Bad news."

She had wanted to open the package immediately in the car but had restrained herself until she returned to the apartment. The can inside the cardboard box still had the blue and white duty stamp on it to show it hadn't been opened. For several minutes she merely lingered over it, then very slowly opened it, inhaling the deep, rich smell of the finely ground chocolate-flavored coffee. Detaching the plastic lid from the bottom of the can, she placed it on the top tightly so that none would be spilled. Clutching it, she took it to her bedroom and, collapsing on the bed, held it to her breast, sobbing uncontrollably.

In San Diego, following the networks' six-o'clock news, a story broke on San Diego affiliate KVTV that California congressman Hailey had been found dead in his La Jolla home. The TV story showed distraught staffers from the congressman's San Diego office saying that the cause of death was not known "at this time." Rumors that the congressman had taken his own life were vigorously denied pending an SDPD investigation.

The following morning, Mr. Jay La Roche of La Roche Pharmaceuticals, whom a reporter described as "a close friend and supporter of Congressman Hailey," was "shocked and saddened" by the tragic news, commenting that "California has lost one of her most able and compassionate representatives.''

Within a few days La Roche Pharmaceuticals announced that two scholarship funds, in the name of Congressman Hailey, would be set up, one for a male student, one for a female, at the University of California—Stanford campus.

The army driver in Tallinn had been correct. The Americans *had* crossed the Weser east of Stadthagen as part of the general counterattack all along the NATO line. Whether NATO's troops could sustain the advance was a matter of widely differing conjecture in the world capitals, but for now, Freeman, almost completely recovered from the painful paresis that had followed his back injury, undeniably had the bit in his mouth, and everywhere the Russians were in retreat.

At a crucial crossing over the Mittelell Canal at Peine, thirty miles east of Hannover, Major Norton of General Freeman's G-2 was in one of the Bradley armored personnel carriers on the pontoon bridge when the latter came under heavy fire from an eight-gun battery of Soviet self-propelled 122-millimeter howitzers. The Russian gunners, unable to retreat because they were out of fuel, had the pontoon bridge bracketed and were bringing down a deadly rain of 21.7-kilogram HE shells, taking out three of the Bradleys, killing all thirty-six men aboard in the first two salvos. Just when Norton was convinced the APC in which he was riding was the next to be hit, the Russian fire became erratic and for the next three minutes stopped altogether, permitting Norton and the rest of the U.S. Second Armored column following to cross the canal in safety.

When the Americans overran the Russian battery site, fourteen miles farther on near Braunschweig, the Russians were gone, but the self-propelled guns and piles of discarded and unused ammunition remained. Major Norton's bent for detail did not fail him, and he noted in his written report on the incident that the hitherto unexplained erratic fire of the 122-millimeters was due not to any fault with the lay of the chassis-mounted guns but appeared to be caused by deficiencies in the 122-millemeter HE rounds themselves, whose markings showed they had been manufactured somewhere in the Baltic republics. The letters ''MJ'' had been stamped on several of the duds' cartridge seals, but as yet Norton could not explain the specific designation ''MJ.''

CHAPTER FORTY-FIVE

RICHARD SPENCE, RESPLENDENT in his tuxedo at the head table, moved his arm forward on the dazzling white linen so that his sleeve would allow him a glimpse of his watch without him seeming rude. The wedding had gone splendidly, the traditional Book of Common Prayer service quite moving, and which his new son-in-law had appeared to enjoy as much as Rosemary. She had been breathtakingly beautiful in her mother's wedding gown, and he had never seen her so happy. Anne, to her credit, as Richard's barrister Uncle Geoffrey noted, had shown no outward sign of the devastating loss of their youngest. And the reception was a veritable feast.

''Surely they must be ready by now,'' Richard said to Geoffrey.

The longer Rosemary was taking to change into her going-away outfit, the more her sixth form class from St. Anselm's was going to devour.

''Well, Richard old boy, I should think this lot'll set you back a few pounds,'' said Geoffrey, looking out on the swirl of the dancers and on what he called the ''provisioning.''

''A few pounds?'' responded Richard. ''I should think it'll wipe me out. I don't know where on earth Anne got all this food and—'' Richard waited till the skirl of the bagpipes died down, secretly wishing they'd die altogether.

''Hoarding!'' Geoffrey said, raising his voice. ''They're very good at it—women.''

''Even so, we're feeding over two hundred people as well as—good Lord!'' Richard sat forward, almost spilling his champagne. "Did you see that? That boy—one of Rosemary's students, I think. He ate an *entire* cupcake at one gulp. Hate to think of what he'll cost me alone." With that, Richard sat back, sighing resignedly. "Shan't have any money left for young Georgina."

"Ah!" said Geoffrey, pausing over his sherry. "I didn't know she was casting her net."

"She isn't," replied Richard. "He is. The first officer—Zeldman."

"Good grief—a bourgeois American? Don't tell me Georgina's giving up on Mel?"

Richard was completely taken by surprise. "I didn't think she was going out with anyone called Mel."

"No, no, Richard—Marx, Engels, and that awful Lenin."

"Oh, that." Richard smiled. "Well, she has an attack every now and then. Usually when she and Rosey get together. Cats and dogs. Quite nasty at times, though they seem to care when it counts. She gave Rosey and Robert a lovely wedding present."

"Don't tell me," cut in Geoffrey. "*Das Kapital*. First edition?"

Richard raised his glass to a beefy, courtly man pushing his wife about the floor. "No," he answered Geoffrey, "but you're close. The first edition—Browning's poems. The Portuguese."

"Oh—" said Geoffrey. "Then, Richard, I'm afraid you're right."

"How d'you mean?"

"I mean, old boy, that once they start spouting that stuff—'Let me count the ways'—you'd better batten down the hatches to your bank account. It'll be wedding bells and another great cake." Geoffrey's eyes looked over to admire the remains of the splendid three-tiered creation. "I must say, that was a magnificent icing job. A Rosemary Hallowes, I expect?"

"Yes, she's very good. I believe they call it 'frosting' in America."

"Really? They are peculiar, our cousins over the water."

"Yes," said Richard softly, and fell silent.

"Sorry, Richard, I didn't mean to—"

"No, it's quite all right, Geoffrey. It's just that I'm still not over it. Time, they say—"

"Cures nothing," said Geoffrey definitively. "Merely

covers it over. It'll never go away, Richard. Why should it? He was a fine boy. Too young and too good to die.'' They both fell silent for a moment, Geoffrey sipping his sherry.

'' 'Twas ever thus, Richard.''

"Yes.''

"I know it's no help, really, but—"

"Go on.''

"Well, Georgina was telling me earlier, before the service, that Commander Brentwood's sister wrote to you about William. His nurse, apparently.''

"Yes, it was very kind of her. And very much appreciated. Meant the world to Anne.''

"There's another brother isn't there—I don't mean our young hero of—what do they call it?''

"Stadthagen.''

"Can never remember those German names—always sound like catarrh.''

"Then how about Kyle of Lochalsh?''

"Sounds absolutely revolting. Is that where they're going in Scotland?''

"It's on Rosey's list. Passing through, though, I expect. The honeymoon's to be a bed-and-breakfast tour. Western Scotland for two weeks.''

"In this weather? They'll freeze. Ah, then again, perhaps not, eh, Richard? B and B can be quite cozy, I'm told.''

"I hope so, Geoffrey. They deserve it.''

"Hear, hear. If they can grab a little happiness in this world gone mad, then the best of British—'' he paused, raising his glass ''—and Yankee luck to them! They'll need it up there. He won't understand a word of it, you know. The Scots are quite impenetrable.''

"Oh, I don't know, Geoffrey. They managed to tow his ship back to Holy Loch.''

"He'll be off again then, I expect. After the honeymoon?''

"Can't say. Very hush-hush. He never talks about it. All I know is the ship was towed up from Falmouth.''

"Should you be saying that?''

"Oh, the base at Holy Loch—that's common knowledge.''

"No, I mean 'ship'. I understand submarines are called *boats*.''

"Not anymore. 'Ships' these days, and 'sail'—no 'conning tower' anymore.''

"Ships and sail,'' mused Geoffrey. "I like that. Possibly

because it gives me the illusion, along with this rather bad sherry, that we're not in this modern world with its push-button whatsits. Must say, I'm glad I'm not in it.''

"Not yet at least," said Richard. "I'm sorry about the sherry.''

"It's not *yours*, Richard. It's mine. I gave it to Anne—far too sweet. And what on earth do you mean by 'not yet'?''

"Well, apparently there's this chap Marchenko. Quite ruthless, by all accounts. I'm sure he's not finished with us. The *Telegraph*'s reporting that if the Russians get desperate enough, they could very well push the button. Then we'll all be in it.''

"We'll all be dead, you mean.''

"No—they're talking about what you barristers, I think, would call a middle case.''

"What? Gas?''

"And biological warfare, yes.''

"By God, Richard, you're a cheery soul.''

"Just facing facts, Geoffrey.''

"But this chap Freeman's got 'em on the run. Damned tough customer, by all accounts.''

"Yes, but he can't do it alone. And now the Russians have got America on a two-front war. Then there's still this Korean business. It's not finished by any means. The *Telegraph*'s Tokyo correspondent reports that the Chinese are ready to move across the Yalu if the Americans don't stop there.''

"They're not going to stop, Richard. Why should they? They made MacArthur stop, and look what they got. They won't make that mistake twice.''

"Then the Chinese will come in and the *Telegraph*—''

"The *Telegraph*!'' said Geoffrey with a trace of irritability. "Fair enough, I suppose, but—good Lord, Richard, they're not the only source. Don't they publish those advertisements by that demented Knowlton chap? You know—the hair dryer maniac. Really. There's more than one paper, old boy.''

"Of course, but *The New York Times* says much the same thing. That no way the Russians are going to call it quits. We're not even at the Elbe.'' He paused, alarmed at a group of Anne's "Conservative Club" women purposefully approaching him and Geoffrey.

Richard smiled graciously, murmuring to Geoffrey, "It's that dreadful Mrs. Lamptini again. They're going to ask us to dance.''

"What?" said Geoffrey. "I'm off!"

"Coward!" said Richard. Suddenly the music died, followed by cheers and scattered applause. Rosemary was at the top of the stairs, radiant in a jade-green coat, white imitation fur hat, and corsage, holding her bouquet. She did not try to tease with the bouquet but tossed it gently and straight to Georgina. The ladies were drawn, by ancient rite, toward the young couple, Peter Zeldman and Georgina.

"Ah, prophecy!" said Geoffrey. "Get your checkbook ready, Richard."

Richard said nothing. Georgina had told him she didn't like the "best man," but with Georgina, he knew, you could never be sure. Only time would tell. Anne appeared, fussing about last-minute details as Robert and Rosemary headed out for the car.

"Doesn't he look wonderful?" Richard heard Mrs. Lamptini say. "Those Americans—"

As most of the guests crowded about the door to wish the couple well, the St. Anselm's boys, after having checked that their cans and various impedimenta had been firmly attached beneath the car, returned to the food, where an argument was developing about whether or not there were enemy spies in England.

"Of course there are, you twit," said one of the taller boys—a prefect. "How do you think they know where the convoys are?"

"Well, they haven't caught any, have they?" said another boy defensively.

"Don't be simple, Bingham. Those trials are held in camera so as not to upset the populace. My pater told me." The boy took a toothpick from a silver cup and looked for a cocktail sausage to stab. "Quite frankly, if I were the Russians, I'd have spies go after the captains. Of the submarines. Submarine captains aren't two a penny, you know. And if you get them, then you've effectively—"

"Oh, do put a sock in it," said one of the others. "Come on, let's see Miss Spence off."

"Mrs. Brentwood, you nit."

"All right, Mrs. Brentwood."

Richard and Anne had gone outside by the car to say their good-byes. When it came time to shake hands with Robert Brentwood, Richard was quite unable to speak, but as the men looked at each other, there was ample understanding.

Richard knew that the war would go on and that men like Robert would be returning to it soon. And that the war of the submarines would almost certainly become increasingly dangerous as more and more countries sought to redress their setbacks on land by sending their secret boats into the seas that covered over two-thirds of the planet. He was sure also that with the Russians having attacked the Aleutians, the titanic struggle would move to America's shore.

But now, for a moment, for two people very much in love, the world stood still.